To Canada's migrant workers who toil in the apple orchards and fields to keep us fed

Unburdening

BOOKS BY GARY MAY

NON-FICTION

- *Crude Genius: The Making of an International Oil Baron*, 2022
- *Hard Oiler! The Story of Early Canadians' Quest for Oil at Home and Abroad*, 1998, revised and reprinted 2021
- *Two Men and Their Monster: Rum-runner Harry Low Built a Walkerville Legend – Vern Myslichuk Raised It From the Dead*, 2015
- *Groundbreaker: How the Brilliant Inventions of Leo Ranney Transformed Water and Energy Technology*, 2013
- *A Hard Oiler Love Story*, 2013
- *Southern Exposure: How Pelee Island Winery Brought Winemaking Back to Its Birthplace*, 2012
- *The Scent of Oil: A Nicklos/Perkins Family Saga*, 2011
- *A Life Well Travelled: The Story of Gordon Sherwin*, 2010
- *Don't Tell Me It Can't Be Done: The Story of Angus Vaughan Read*, 2009

COLLABORATIONS

- *Sharing With Pride: The Story of Municipal Engineers in Ontario*, with Orland French, 2009
- *A Common Thread: A History of the Jews of Ottawa*, with Valerie Knowles, Ruth Kahane Goldberg, and Lawrence Humber, 2009

Unburdening

A Novel

GARY MAY

mosaicPRESS

Library and Archives Canada Cataloguing in Publication

Title: Unburdening : a novel / Gary May.

Names: May, Gary, 1951- author

Identifiers: Canadiana (print) 20260149446 | Canadiana (ebook) 20260149454|

ISBN 9781771617963 (softcover) | ISBN 9781771617970 (PDF) |
ISBN 9781771617987 (EPUB) | ISBN 9781771617994 (Kindle)

Subjects: LCGFT: Historical fiction. | LCGFT: Novels.

Classification: LCC PS8626.A8957 U53 2026 | DDC C813/.6—dc23

Published by Mosaic Press, Oakville, Ontario, Canada, 2026.

MOSAIC PRESS, Publishers
www.Mosaic-Press.com

Cover Design: Amy Land

Printed and bound in Canada.

ONTARIO CREATES

Funded by the Government of Canada
Financé par le gouvernement du Canada

Canada

MOSAIC PRESS
1252 Speers Road, Units 1 & 2, Oakville, Ontario, L6L 2X4 (905) 825-2130
info@mosaic-press.com • www.mosaic-press.com

1

Grace
1975

THROUGH HER BEDROOM window, Grace fixed upon a solitary plump snowflake as it hovered, then dropped through the branches of the maple tree that commanded the farmhouse's west yard. She watched as a sudden gust startled the flake out of its gentle descent and flung it ruthlessly onto the chilled windowpane, an arm's length from her face. It splattered, rivering down the chilled surface and puddling into a crevice of the frame that was in bad need of a good paint job.

Grace peered through the watery pane, through the maple's branches and out across the snow-covered field. Snow purifies. A good thing for an old sinner like me, she thought. She shivered and pulled the cowl of her oatmeal-hued fisherman's knit sweater closer around her.

What weather for early April, Grace thought with a momentary notion of disgust. The crocus had only begun to bloom in the protection of the house. And now this. A pervasive greyness enveloped the day as afternoon faded into evening. A greyness more typical of December, Grace thought, not something to be experienced in the month of showers, early blooms and other anticipated signs of spring. A month supposedly made for poets and songwriters, not for keeping old ladies inside and away from their beloved gardening chores.

An uncharacteristic scowl bruised her face. It was a face that had seen more laughter than frowns. Certainly Grace had experienced sadness. There had been a great deal of sadness in the life of Grace O'Malley, more than anyone she knew could have guessed. And now, more recently, the shame. But she had never in her four-score-less five years allowed sadness to linger and dominate, nor to sour her outlook. Her friends and family knew Grace for her steadfastly positive approach to everything she tackled and to everything fate – or was it chance – chose to hurl her way. Rarely had anyone around the village of Shannonside known Grace O'Malley as anything but happy, to be anything but aggressive in her determination to tackle life and its obstacles, challenges be damned!

Oh, probably it was this infernal weather that's got me so down, Grace thought, then recalled it was something far more insidious, more recent, than that. She sighed, choked back a weepy moment, and contemplated the gloom that imprisoned her in her drafty old house. It was a house intended to accommodate multiple generations and was woefully oversized for its current single occupant. She'd rather have been outside snipping back last year's growth in the hydrangea and the rose of Sharon that surrounded her home. Rather have spent her day pruning the deadwood from the rose bushes she'd two weeks ago released from winter's protective layer of straw, and clipping the dead shoots from last year's lavender. Those two weeks seemed a lifetime now, a period before hope had faded. Instead here she was, lodged in the upstairs bedroom of her home, peering out through the droplets that wiggled their way down the window that overlooked the apple orchards stretching out past the yard.

This blasted weather. The sticky wet snow of an early-spring storm had begun several hours ago and now clung to the towering evergreens, weighing down their branches. It stuck to the bark of the gnarled maple tree, subtly outlining its creviced bark in the waning light of day against the white-grey bleakness. The snow had wrung subtlety from the landscape, turning everything a misty white and drudge brown.

The rambling old farmhouse was turning cold. Grace had not this day put on a fire in the iron stove downstairs in the kitchen — the stove she used as her primary heat source. Nor did she light the oil burner in the parlour or switch on the electric baseboard heaters placed around the house. It had been a deliberate act of caution, rather than one of forgetfulness, for Grace O'Malley was not prone to forgetfulness despite her lifespan. Instead, she had that morning pulled on her sweater as she padded throughout the house in her lime-green sock-slippers and cozy terrycloth housecoat. She didn't want anything to go wrong this day. There must not be any fire in the stove to worry about, no electricity left on to possibly short out a wire in the ancient farmhouse.

She had spent the last few days cleaning the place to a perfect sheen. She'd polished the silver pieces in the bowed glass-front oak cabinet that commanded a corner of the dining room. She'd taken out each piece of her most cherished china, lovingly washed it and placed it back in its place in the cabinet. She had taken Murphy's Oil to clean and bring up the shine on the dining room table and chairs before moving on to the next room.

The ritual continued in the parlour. Wood was dusted and polished, fabric was vacuumed, fine china and porcelain figurines and bric-a-brac were taken from their spots and cleansed before being placed back in their rightful places.

Then it was on to each of the four bedrooms, where brass beds were left gleaming, old picture frames were removed and dusted, set back and straightened to perfection. Linen was washed, ironed and returned to each of the beds. Comforters and bedspreads were placed on the clothesline for airing, given a sturdy pummeling with an old-fashioned wooden beater and then, in a reluctant nod to modernity, sprayed with one of those store-bought pine-scented fresheners before being put back.

The worn kitchen floor linoleum was scrubbed with soap and water till it gleamed. Cupboards were emptied and dusted and scoured before dishes were put back. The porcelain sink boasted a whiteness it had not experienced in half a century.

The lone bathroom, too, was left gleaming in the wake of Grace's assault. Throughout the house, floors were cleansed and buffed, windows were scrubbed and carpets freshened, cobwebs were purged, baseboard and wainscoting were treated. Grace took a deep breath and satisfied herself that the house reeked with an air of cleanliness that would have made Martha Stewart blush with inadequacy.

Her muscles ached from the days-long workout but with a subtle smile of satisfaction at a job well done, Grace had finished her task just that morning as she marched through every room, inspected every corner, and assured herself that all was in readiness. Then she made herself a country breakfast to celebrate: coffee, bacon and eggs and fried potatoes with homemade bread. Their amalgam of aromas had brought back memories of joy. When she was finished and had downed her second cup of coffee, Grace took the dishes to the sink, washed and dried them and placed them back where they belonged. She cleaned out the stove-top percolator, then turned and declared herself ready.

When she was done, Grace walked out of the kitchen, turning momentarily to assure herself all was in place, and glanced up the narrow staircase that led to her bedroom, then began the climb. It was a climb she had made countless times since she had moved into the old house as a young bride, but one that in recent years had become increasingly laboured as joints stiffened. The stairs seemed steeper these days, the treads shallower and the risers taller.

She paused at the top of the stairs and the ache in her left knee momentarily captured her attention. She gazed at her image in the mirror that had hung there for decades. There was much to admire, if she did say so herself. The slim figure she nurtured as a young girl had not thickened noticeably after all these years. She was still lissome. Weighed no more than five pounds more than on her wedding day. Certainly her thin face was weathered by her three-quarters of a century. It was more angular now, of course. Grace had never allowed herself to put on the weight that would have let her skin fill in the little creases and lines, those badges of honour that come with age. Her grey shoulder-length hair had thinned only slightly since those younger years when its flowing auburn luster was the envy of the other young women and a source of desire amongst the fellows who longed to court her.

Pulling at some strands of her hair, she positioned them over the remnants of an old scar that still slivered down the right side of her face. For a moment, she considered the scar's origin, then glanced along the upstairs hallway to review the portraits of her husband's family members. Five generations of O'Malleys stared back at her. Five generations, starting with Old William and Lucinda, had worked this land since coming to Canada during Ireland's Great Hunger of the 1840s. Grace was the latest to live here. She was the keeper of the family heritage, the family conscience, the family memory. Was she now about to dishonour it?

Marital strife aside, she had shared her husband's dedication to the land and was ferocious in her stewardship. She had fought to protect it, just as Pete's ancestors had. Through good times and through bad, they had maintained the farm they lovingly called Ballinskellig, after the community near Cork the O'Malleys had left in Ireland.

Reaching the top of the stairs, she proceeded to her bedroom, where she settled into her worn burgundy wing-back chair. Now here she sat, watching the flakes of snow beat themselves against the panes of frigid glass. She heard the wind pick up and the cold snow swirl harder. Grace could feel a draft from around the frame and thought about how her handyman, Billy Black, had never come round last fall to re-caulk them, and paint the frames, as she had asked. Lazy swine, she thought with a momentary sense of disgust. She pulled her sweater up around her neck. Oh, the cold, she thought. When will it be spring? When will the sun finally take charge and put an end to this atmospheric foolishness?

She rose from her seat and went to the closet next to her canopied bed. She opened the closet door and pulled the chain that turned on the stark sixty-watt bulb that lit the space. Stretching to the full extent of her five-foot-eight frame, she reached up to the shelf over where her clothes hung, picked up a battered grey shoebox and took it down from its place. Grace turned and returned to the chair.

A faded rose-coloured ribbon encircled the box. Grace's fingers, slightly bent from arthritis, untied the ribbon and let it drop to the floor. She lifted the top of the box and reached in. Her hand brought out a packet of letters, she selected one at random and set the others back in the box. The letter was yellow, crinkled and flimsy from being folded and unfolded hundreds of times. Grace unfolded it one more time ever so gently so as not to tear the delicate paper. The letter and the others in the box must be protected at all cost. Their purpose was not complete.

Her emerald green eyes danced as she read the one she had selected. She smiled, even chuckled out loud a couple of times as she read the familiar words. Once her left hand slid up to some strands of hair that were tucked behind her ear and she tugged gently at them. That simple act unleashed a hint of lavender-scented perfume that was her favourite, a hint that brought memories flowing back. After finishing the letter, Grace refolded it and placed it back in the stack with the others. She rummaged along one side of the shoebox until she found a worn little envelope. She pulled the envelope out and opened it. Reaching in, Grace lifted out a set of military medals. She held their cold harshness to her cheek, then pulled the attached ribbon up under her nose and breathed in. Grace sighed. More memories.

Placing the medals back into the envelope and the envelope into the box, she ran her fingers down the other side of the box until she came up with a newspaper clipping. The clipping was unique to this menagerie, in that it was fresh and new, crisp, not flimsy from being folded and unfolded.

The pleasure the other items had brought her was missing as Grace read the clipping. Rather than a smile, its contents brought her sadness. No, it hadn't been just the weather that brought her distress and anguish. What an old fool I've been, she thought. All of these years, wasted. What was I thinking?

A single tear welled in her left eye. It sat there, unsteady, uncertain of its place for a moment, then broke away from the corner of Grace's eye and tracked down her cheek. She reached inside the sleeve of her housecoat for a thin, lavender-flowered handkerchief and dabbed at her eye and her nose. She refolded the newspaper clipping, placed it back in the box, this time at the bottom of the letters, re-tied the box with the ribbon. She got up from the chair and rather than returning the box to the closet, she set it on her bedside table, next to a book, its cover embossed in silver with the words "My Diary." A second similar book lay beneath it. She closed the closet door and came back to her chair overlooking the snowy yard and the apple orchard beyond.

Grace reached under her chair. For a moment her hands trembled as the image of her son, Jamie, came to mind. She hesitated. How could she do this to him? The pain jabbed at her heart, and yet she knew she had no choice. There was a mental shrug. He would survive. She would not.

She wrapped the fingers of her right hand around the cold metal of the shotgun she'd placed beneath the chair yesterday. It bore a sawed-off barrel, courtesy of Grace's recent hard work in the blacksmith shop her father-in-law had set up years ago across the road. She checked to ensure the gun was loaded, closed the chamber, placed the gun's double barrels inside her mouth and fired.

And with that, Grace O'Malley of Rural Route 3, Shannonside, Ontario, ceased to exist.

2

James

"Are you James O'Malley?"

The young police officer stood in the doorway of James's downtown Toronto apartment. This can't be good, James thought as he stammered out, "y-y-yes, I am."

The officer, whom it occurred to James didn't even seem old enough to be shaving, gulped audibly before continuing, "I'm sorry to tell you, sir, but I am here to inform you that your mother has passed away."

He remembers the officer said "passed away," as though it was a gentler pronouncement of death, one that would make it less painful for him to accept. For a moment James was reminded of the local Shannonside radio station's twice-weekly announcements right after the one o'clock time check from the National Observatory in Ottawa: a listing of the area obituaries. For each person the host would utter in funereal tone: "A death's occurred…"

Having left his mother in good health when he visited the previous month, and having spoken to her on the phone just days ago, James was dumbfounded by what the officer was telling him. How could such a vital, almost sprightly woman as his mother have died so suddenly? It was a question he posed to the officer because he remembers the younger man's quick retort: "Oh, she didn't just die. No, she took her own life."

That's when James's knees buckled and he found himself crumpling to the floor. The officer lunged quickly to help cushion his encounter with the hardwood, and, undoubtedly realizing how crass his words had sounded, fell over himself apologizing for speaking so thoughtlessly. He offered his arm as support as James pointed the way to a big armchair at the edge of the living room. The muscular young officer steadied James as he lowered his slender six-foot frame down into the chair. His blond hair, streaked with a bit of grey, hung shaggily overtop the collar of his golf shirt that fell untucked over the waist of his blue jeans.

James's head buzzed with the news; his stomach did a flip-flop while he tried to understand the constable's news. With the red-faced officer now stumbling over his words in a too-late bid to undo the hurt he understood he had delivered, James tried to explain that there was no way a woman such as his mother would, or could, ever commit suicide. She loathed any sign of weakness in character, James said. The officer nodded in sympathy, then stayed an inordinate length of time to be certain James was okay, and offered at least three times to call someone. James said he would be fine. He was so shocked by the news that he realized only after the officer had departed that there was no mention of how Grace had taken her life. James began to imagine his mother taking an overdose of sleeping pills, or flinging herself down the cellar stairs, or perhaps even hanging herself from a rafter in the drive shed. He shuddered.

James's first recollection as a child is of an old man in a rocker. The man's mustache hangs in alternating strands of black and white and falls over the edges of his mouth. His nose is strong, his eyes clear and dark behind round wire-rimmed glasses, glasses that make him look rather like James Joyce, or in a more modern sense, like John Lennon on the Sergeant Pepper album cover. He wears a collarless shirt, white background with pencil-thin stripes of black, three together, then a gap; three together, then another gap. Black suspenders, or braces as they used to say, attached to his brown trousers that are wide at the cuffs and show a flash of woolen long underwear above his brown socks. On his feet is a pair of green and maroon carpet slippers.

The rocker is squat and broad and rocks gently next to a pot-bellied stove in the middle of a large room. Or rather it seems large to the small boy. The rocker objects with gentle crackles as the man sways front to back, front to back. A black pipe rises from the stove and abandons the room by way of the ceiling, its exit point surrounded by a black iron grate, designed to allow some heat from the room below to escape to the upstairs.

James's recollection is bright, vivid in its detail. Despite that, he used to think that it was only a dream, one that would return frequently. It was not until he was a teenager when, sitting beneath a massive maple tree in the yard with his mother, Grace O'Malley, and maternal grandmother, Eleanor Campbell, he recounted the "dream." Mother and daughter exchanged puzzled glances.

"Grandpa?" Grace asked in a tone that betrayed her disbelief.

"I guess it must be," replied James's grandmother, only slightly less amazed. "It's Pete's dad to a T."

Inexplicably, it was that image of the old man in the rocker that came first to mind after the officer appeared at the door of James's apartment, to deliver the news that his mother had "passed away".

As a boy James had, it seems, been so affected by the image of his dad's father, Ben O'Malley, settled into his favourite rocker that sat in the kitchen of his home in town a few miles from their farmhouse, that it had left an indelible impression on his mind, even though he could not have been more than three years old at the time. His grandfather O'Malley had died just after James turned three.

The day after news of Grace's death, as James drove east on the 401 out of Toronto toward Shannonside, he conjured the jumbled image of his grandfather O'Malley, rocking sedately in his kitchen, and James's mother, Grace, proudly recounting to all who would listen that her son had so vividly described an experience that occurred no later than his third birthday.

His mother was gone, and with half a century of life under his belt, James was now the last of his branch of the O'Malley family. His baby brother, Petie, had died an infant, four years before James was born. His father, Peter, had died just months ago. James, a journalist-turned-college professor, was divorced and childless. His wife and he had split five years earlier and she was a documentary film producer, back in her native Montreal.

By dint of a recent family pact, the land at Ballinskellig would shift to a cousin, and James wondered what level of care the cousin would take to carry on the O'Malley legacy, how he would protect it.

Gripping the steering wheel to control his nerves, James drove, alone, toward the farm community of his childhood, nestled neatly into the apple country that hugged the north shore of Lake Ontario, back to deal with the loose ends of his mother's life. He had been instructed to stop at her lawyer's office in the village to learn the particulars and deal with whatever arrangements required his attention.

Shannonside grew up at the spot where the Shannon River empties into Quinte Bay, which was itself a large protuberance on a great lake's northern shore. Shannonside was little different from any number of other villages and towns that dot the wide expanse of southern Ontario. It featured a main street lined with buildings erected in the late 1800s and early 1900s, some crumbling with age, others with false fronts, stores on the main level with cheap apartments on the second, and sometimes a third level or attic, usually vacant. In nearly half of them, papered-over windows marked shops that had been abandoned. In those that remained open, retailers sold meat and groceries, pharmaceuticals, an assortment of clothing and shoes, jewelry and baked goods. There was a hardware store with a gift section, a tobacco shop that carried newspapers and periodicals, a diner and a small restaurant that indicated it was licensed to sell alcoholic beverages.

James made his way past the tiny downtown, to a row of solid old red brick Victorians, to the address for McGowan, McAllister and Walters, barristers and solicitors. He knew the building well, having grown up in Ballinskellig, and which sat just past the town's business core.

The heavy and ornate oak door squawked slightly when he opened it. He stepped inside and an older woman looked up from her desk. She gauged her visitor as about the age of fifty and noted his thick and shaggy blond hair showed signs of a slight greying. His fair complexion etched with a trace of redness, elongated nose and long, thin fingers made him the picture of his mother and the woman recognized him immediately. He had been in with his mother just a few months ago, she recalled, just after his father died. She smiled in greeting. "Jamie, welcome. I am so sorry about your mother." He nodded curtly in thanks. "Come this way," she said. "Harold's waiting."

James nodded and eked out a smile. He knew the woman had been Harold Walters' secretary for most of his career. Prim and tiny beyond belief, her hair done in the tidy bun of a bygone era, she looked to be in her seventies. She wore an immaculate dress of navy blue with little flecks of yellow. Leading him into the adjacent office, Miss Pauline Finster called in a loud, clear tone: "Mr. O'Malley is here to see you, Harold."

Harold Walters was the only one of the partners remaining. He had been Grace's solicitor for as long as James could remember and was himself well into his seventies. When the woman ushered him into Walters' office, a high-ceilinged drawing room in one of Shannonside's finest old homes, James found Harold hunched over his sprawling oak desk, head down, face almost into the papers he was apparently attempting to read with the aid of a magnifying glass. Despite the heat blasting out of an overhead vent, the portly Harold was dressed in a heavy winter tweed jacket, crisp white shirt, a flower-print tie that would not have been out of place in the 1930s slipped tight to his neck. James breathed in a combination of accumulated dust and old leather.

Harold Walters looked up from his work and smiled. "James, my boy," he called. James, a man of half a century, was not all that accustomed to being addressed by anyone as "my boy."

The voluminous room was dark, its heavy brocade drapes drawn to cut the sunlight, leaving the space lit only by three outdated floor lamps, plus the desk light that shone starkly onto the lawyer's work space. James glanced around and saw three walls filled with an assemblage of old pictures and diplomas, placed randomly against faded red velvet wallpaper. Not a single one of them hung straight. The fourth wall was lined with bookcases that overflowed with law books. Various credenzas and tables were placed around the space, each spilling over with paperwork.

Harold rose arthritically from his own seat and shuffled around the desk to greet his client. His round, fleshy face reddened from the effort. His bushy grey eyebrows bobbed when he spoke. He took James's hands in his. "James," he said, a trained solicitor's look of concern and torment commanding his expression. "I cannot tell you how sorry I am. Nor can I comprehend. Grace was such a vital woman."

"Thank you, Mr. Walters. I know. It makes absolutely no sense to me."

"No, no, of course it doesn't. We're all just so shocked. She had so many friends and people who cared deeply for her. She'd been a part of this community her entire life. But, I guess no one knows what goes on inside a person. We all have our secrets, don't we? Our torments." James remained silent and after a moment Walters continued, "sit ... sit," pointing the way to a sagging, musty wing-back chair.

"Now, as for the arrangements. You'll be pleased to know that your mother had already planned her own funeral and burial. Signed and sealed. There's really nothing for you to have to worry about. I suppose the odd thing, the thing that adds to the mystery, is that it was just last week she did it all. Contacted the funeral home, Pastor Nedermeyer, everyone. It seems her decision was a sudden one and, well, you know your mother, everything had to be just right. So, of course, she did it herself."

Harold allowed himself a gentle chuckle at this point. James nodded knowingly, and asked him what he knew about the circumstances of Grace's death. The lawyer scowled before drawing a long breath and returning to his seat.

"I'm afraid I'll have to sit down for this, my boy. You'd better sit too."

He called out to Miss Finster to bring in a couple of coffees, telling her to "toss a dollup of Canadian Club into them, too." James was going to need it, Walters knew. Within moments, the elderly woman was hurtling through the door with a silver tray containing two fine china coffee cups, a small plate of Peek Freans at the side. Without a word she set the tray down on the only empty corner of Walters' crammed desk and made a hasty retreat, shutting the huge oak door behind her. James detected the aroma of heated Canadian whisky wafting from the steaming black coffee.

"This will not be pleasant for you, James. As you know, your mother took her own life. The method ... well, the method was by way of shooting. She shot herself in the head with a sawed-off shotgun."

James gulped, then froze in sheer horror at the thought, a method of death he had not contemplated. The police officer hadn't told him that, and the image of his mother's shredded skull, blood and brains, splashed across a room, was too much. At every turn he was learning something more horrible about her death. And for the first time since that young officer had come to his door just the night before, James put his head in his hands and he cried. Walters, to his credit, sat silently, unmoving, respectfully, as James dealt with the grief. After several minutes, James self-consciously dabbed at his eyes with a tissue from a box Walters had quietly shifted to the edge of his desk, and asked him to continue.

"She was found by Billy Black. As you know, Billy did odd jobs for your mother and other people. He dropped in at her place every Monday morning. Maybe she'd planned it that way, so Billy would find her just after ..." His voice trailed off.

James smiled to himself despite the grisly image. His mother loathed Billy Black. She called him "that simple little man" and all of a sudden James was certain that she'd arranged it so that Billy would be the one to come upon her remains, rather than one of her friends or neighbours, or even James himself. She knew Billy showed up at the house every Monday morning to see if she had anything for him to do. And she knew he would hunt her out if she didn't meet him at the door. Billy was, as Grace would put it, "a nosey-Parker."

"Billy told the police the kitchen door was unlocked and there was no reply when he entered and called out. Her car was in the drive, so he knew she couldn't be far. He walked through the house and spied her when he went past her bedroom door. He says he called the police immediately."

James sighed and gave a little shudder at the same time. "And here we are, twenty-four hours later."

"You are the executor and sole beneficiary," Walters told him. "But I can tell you, your mother's will is a very straightforward one. There won't be a great sum for you to inherit, but there is a bank account, and a couple of investments that pay excellent dividends. The actual farm, as you well know, goes to your cousin Arthur through that previous arrangement from last year. As well there is a small box of mementos she left for her old friend, Alberta. Would you like us to try to contact her for you?"

Alberta, always known to him as "Aunt Al," was Grace's oldest friend and the woman his parents had designated his godmother. The two women had grown up together but their lives had taken very different paths. In the early Twenties, Aunt Al had followed her passion for art and gone off on a trip to Italy where she met Count Roberto Ribigghini. After a whirlwind courtship, Aunt Al had married him and become the Countess Ribigghini. To the best of James's knowledge, when her husband died just after the war, the countess left the family's Tuscan estate to live with a friend in Florence. The count, James seemed to recall, had been some sort of a Fascist, a friend of Mussolini, he remembered. At that thought, James unconsciously touched the right side of his face, to the remains of a scar some thirty years old.

"Yes, if you would," he told Walters. "I really have no idea how to get in touch with her. She ought to be told."

"Of course. And if there's anything else I can do … " said Walters. "Anything. Don't hesitate to call. I went to school with both your mother and dad. Grace and I were great old friends. In fact I quite fancied her back in our school days," he said, his eyes dancing with the memories. "I knew her long before I met my dear Henrietta. I would do anything for your mother. Many young men would have, but it was Peter who won her heart."

James thanked the old man and headed outside. He slipped into his two-year-old Corolla and pointed it south, down the Tower Road, to the family farm. It had been in the O'Malley family for a hundred and thirty years.

Remnants of the recent wet snow clung stubbornly to low and shady spots. Ditches were high from the runoff along the Tower Road as he neared Ballinskellig. It wasn't much of a farm anymore. Once upon a time it had been the largest apple-producing spread in the region, with smaller crops of plums, currants and blueberries a lucrative side business. At one time it had sold apples across eastern North America and even the UK. But James's father had decided not to replace some of the aging orchards when the trees started dying off. He tore many of them out and rented large acreages off as pasture and cornfields. Labour was expensive and there wasn't the same money in apples these days as there had once been.

And yet while he might have no longer presided over the thriving farm operation he had inherited, Peter O'Malley was intensely protective of the land. He saw it not only as his family duty, but as his responsibility as steward of the land that had been so good to him.

James parked the car in the long driveway, two muddy ruts through the grass leading from the road to the side of the farmhouse. Grace's ancient Dodge sat to the front of the drive near the house. The hour was still early and James couldn't bear to walk inside just yet. Instead he sauntered down the drive and across the road to the barn. His dad had cut the electricity to the barn to save money. They hadn't even had electricity down what everyone knew as the O'Malley sideroad until the late 1940s. That's when the lines were put in and it was officially named Tower Road. Indoor plumbing didn't arrive until about ten years ago, when they installed another cistern to ensure a sufficient water supply.

A jumble of timbers and hay lay piled in the centre of the barn, where the mow had collapsed the previous autumn, in the tragic incident that had killed his father. The barn was long abandoned and there had been no animals in it for years. Still, there was a familiar scent in the air, permeating from the old wood, one of animal and damp hay. Pete had kept a couple of horses to use around the place, even after everyone had a tractor. James tried to remember whether the last one, Katie, had died in 1958 or 1959. Hung around the building was a rich assortment of old farm implements and tools, making this a veritable antique store. He fingered the worn, weathered leather on a horse collar, breathed in its oiled scent and thought of Katie, his favourite.

No less so than the house, this barn represented a museum and a tribute to the lives of four generations of O'Malleys who had farmed the land. James was the fifth, but he had left a long time ago, when he went off to war. It was a storehouse of memorabilia and, for James, memories of his life. He had no descendants. There were cousins, of course, but his aunts had left years ago. The only ones who would care about any of this clutter, this detritus from a family slowly dying out, like crumbling, rotting leaves left by winter's retreating snow and ice, would be his cousin Arthur and his family. James had no use for the place and was relieved to be rid of it. With his mother gone, he wondered what would become of it all, this mad tumble of artifactory that represented the O'Malley legacy.

He must have pottered around three hours in that barn, taking it all in, making mental notes of the odd thing he might be able to salvage for himself as Arthur had urged. Remnants of the haymow remained strewn where they landed in last year's collapse.

When he emerged from the barn's gloom the sun was finishing off what was left of the snow, wisps of fog rising from the puddles of melt-water, and the sodden grass had taken on a spring-like emerald glimmer with that welcomed aroma it brought. Momentarily, the emerald hue reminded him of his mother's striking eyes. Again evading the need to eventually enter the empty house, James ambled down the road he had travelled so many times before. He thought about Harold Walters' parting remarks: that he was not to worry, the lawyer had taken it upon himself to have someone "clean up" after his mother's incomprehensible act.

As he walked, James tried to accommodate himself to what his mother had done. The occasional car passed by, but no one he recognized, and after two hours of wandering aimlessly around what rural dwellers like to call a country block, he found himself back in front of Ballinskellig's farmhouse. Picking through the swimming mass of thoughts and questions that assaulted his mind, he squinted into the sun, now low in the sky. The musky air was chilling and, underdressed for the approaching evening, he was unable to further delay entry into the house.

As he turned the key in the door, the phone in the kitchen began to ring. Hurrying to let himself in, he sprinted to the countertop where it sat and grabbed for the handset.

"Hello?"

"Jamie? It's Aunt Al."

Her voice was immediately recognizable and it gave him a moment's relief from the whirl of thoughts. Aunt Al — the Countess Alberta Ribigghini — was James's very own eccentric Auntie Mame. Wealthy, certainly by Shannonside standards, she and his mother had known one another since they were young girls, and had remained the best of friends over the years, and miles, that separated their lives.

"Aunt Al. It's so good to hear your voice. You've heard, then?"

"Yes, your mother's solicitor just rang me up. I was just preparing for bed, but oh, Jamie, it's so terrible. I don't understand. I …"

"Aunt Al," James interrupted. "Will you come? It would be good to see you. There's just no one else."

He sounded quite pathetic, he realized at once. But there really was no one else to turn to. Like his mother, Alberta had always insisted on calling him "Jamie," despite the fact he was a grown man and now, he found that comforting.

"Yes, of course. I was thinking that. Just waiting to hear you might want me. I could have my man drive me into Rome tonight and be on an early plane. I could be there by tomorrow afternoon your time."

"Oh, that would be great. I don't think I can handle this alone."

"But Jamie, how? What happened to your mother?"

James swallowed hard and told the elderly woman his mother had taken her own life. He would not give her the details over the phone; the tension and emotion of the effort brought stinging tears to his eyes. He could hear Alberta gasp on the other end of the line. "But, that cannot be. She had everything now. Finally. It was all for the future."

Unable to comprehend what Aunt Al was saying, James brushed it off and told her he would drive to the Toronto airport to meet her if she could advise from Rome what flight she was catching.

Alberta said she would do that, but she seemed even more agitated than when she had first called. James was puzzled.

"None of this makes any sense," she told her godson. "Why, I just received a letter from your mother and she assured me everything was wonderful now. She had made contact and he was coming."

James had no idea what his usually clear-headed godmother was trying to tell him. But she was so obviously in distress he felt he had to pursue it. "Aunt Al, what is it you're trying to say? I'm afraid I'm missing something here."

"Your mother," the Countess replied. "She had finally been in contact with him. He was coming home. At last. He was on his way. She had everything to live for now."

* * *

Rather than upset her with further questions, James said they'd talk about everything when she arrived. After he hung up the phone, though, he wondered: What on earth had Aunt Al meant? Everything to live for? In fact James's mother had suffered a loss just a few months before when his father, Peter O'Malley, had died in an accident in his barn, when the haymow collapsed on him. Granted, James knew that to his mother, Pete had truly died many, many years before. The two of them had lived separate lives for as long as James's memory went back. Grace usually made them both meals and sometimes they even ate together, especially if James was coming home for a visit. But for the most part they were strangers under the same roof. They kept separate bedrooms and had actually gone to the extent of drawing up a schedule for use of the home's lone bathroom so that they would never be in one another's way.

But the very fact of her husband being in the same house had provided her with a semblance of normalcy and from time to time, despite their emotional estrangement, they had seemed to share a laugh about some old incident or comforted one another against the outside world.

When James heard his mother had committed suicide, it immediately struck him that perhaps she was depressed over having to spend the rest of her life alone and yet in James's mind, she would likely fare quite well on her own. She had many friends. He had told his mother he'd visit frequently and told her she would always be welcome to come to his place in the city for the occasional chinwag. She seemed amenable to that and, in fact, quite chipper at the possibility.

In James's experience, his father was as cold and emotionless as his mother was warm and passionate. That was not to say that Peter failed to provide his son with the necessities of life; he actually provided for the family in as fine a manner as his means allowed. But insofar as emotional care was concerned, he left James bereft. It was his mother who delivered all of that.

While he pondered what Aunt Al had said, James wandered into the parlour, fingering the items that had meant so much to his mother, letting his mind wander through a kaleidoscope of memories.

Children usually grow up early on a farm, especially back in the days when James was growing up in the 1930s. They were needed for their labour on the family farm, so proper training and safety were learned at a young age. James learned to be around large farm animals and how to maintain a healthy respect for the injuries they could inflict. The horses were the gentlest creatures anyone could imagine but a careless step could easily place a child in harm's way, to be crushed between the animal's flank and the wall of its stall, for instance, or to be stepped on. These were immense animals, after all, far larger than a small child, and one misstep could be fatal, or at least lead to the crushing of young bones.

The O'Malleys owned a cow and usually there were a handful of goats around the place. Effie the cow was their source of milk and butter and James's first chore of the day, once he was old enough to carry a full bucket, was to milk her.

Effie had the disposition of an angry wasp and it took quite a while for her to become at least accepting of the boy's presence. For the longest time she would turn her giant head toward him as he settled down at the business end of things as if she were meeting him each day for the first time. She'd let out a low bellow of objection when he placed his hands on her teats and buck once, if not twice, when he began to squeeze and pull. It was James's mother who had always milked Effie before the boy took on the task and the pretty little bovine – a Holstein that had more white on her face than was normal – was determined to make the job as difficult as possible for the woman's replacement. Effie seemed determined that Grace should continue with the task at hand. James finally ended up speaking politely but authoritatively to the cow and explained he was just doing his job and he wasn't going anywhere. In later years, she seemed to reach the conclusion that co-operation offered benefits to both of them and started to be more accepting of his place in her daily routine.

Milking was one of the few farm jobs James's mother had introduced him to, and most of the duties around the farm fell to his father to teach. Pete was patient with the boy and meticulous in showing him how to handle himself around the horses, which in his early days in the late 1920s and early Depression years were Flossy, Daisy and Ralph. James was used to being around the animals almost as soon as he could walk, and even remembered being held up by his father at a very young age so that he could pat each of them on the snout and tussle the tuft of long hair that hung down their foreheads. He was probably no more than ten when he was trained on how to handle the reins and hitch the horses up to the plow or the old democrat, a flatbed wagon his father had fastened a bench seat onto so they could drive it to town. It was uncomfortable, but it did the trick. The O'Malleys did not own a car in those early years.

It was soon after that James was even standing behind the horses and plowing the fields in preparation for crops. Horses were an important part of life when James was growing up. His Grandfather Campbell owned a Model T but come winter, the vehicle was put up on blocks and out would come the horse-drawn wagon to be replaced, once it snowed, with the cutter. Farm life was hectic and James's parents were busy from first thing every morning, so it fell to Grandpa Campbell to drive the boy to and from school. The speed at which Grandpa Campbell drove the horse was little more than human walking speed, making winter travel a bone-chilling event. But James appreciated his grandfather's effort and it was during those long rides the two of them, from the time they were bundled up against winter's cold to sizzling in the summer heat, became very close.

Pete taught James all he knew about the cultivation and growing of apples, the staple of their farm that they called Ballinskellig, after their ancestors' hometown back in Ireland. It had been a talent Pete was taught by his father, as he had been taught by his father before him. It had started with James's great-grandfather William, who brought seeds with him from Ireland and commenced the family farm back in the 1840s. Much had changed in the years since, but during the Depression years one constant was the fact that the O'Malleys still grew the best apples around.

James developed a great appreciation for his father's skills. Pete could repair bridles, forge metal parts in his own blacksmith shop, fix broken machinery. He was even a decent veterinarian, able to care for the animals when they suffered an injury or illness. But just as he was efficient and dispassionate in the way he handled the animals, he was equally efficient and dispassionate with James. Hugs were nearly unheard of. Kind words were almost as rare.

In his younger years, James knew his father as a sturdy and robust man, his face tanned a deep leather shade whatever the season, because of all the time he spent out of doors. James himself was much more fair-skinned and his blue eyes were piercing in their intensity. In all of the years James was growing up, before he went away to the army in 1943, he did not recall a day his father was ever so sick as to prevent him from carrying out his daily chores, but then that was pretty much the way of the farmer. No matter how crappy they felt, they understood they must carry on. It was only after the war, after James convinced his father he ought to cave in to the popular demand for "perfect" apples and use DDT and other sprays on his crops, that James ever saw him fall sick. Then, Pete developed a horrible hacking cough that resulted in his spitting out a terrible green slime that he frequently spat into the fire in the wood stove, and his strength was ever more sapped.

On the firm demands of Grace, about 1964, Pete ceased using pesticides and insecticides, started to rent out much of his property and sold a much smaller crop of fruit to local buyers as "chemical-free." While the years of chemical use on the land prevented him from marketing his crops as "organic," they were all pleasantly surprised to see the reaction from the public. Environmentally and health-conscious customers showed up in droves from far and wide, and after that there wasn't a year the farm failed to sell out entirely.

Miraculously, Pete's health began to improve almost immediately, and the last nearly decade of his life was met by renewed youthful vigour.

There was less spitting into the wood stove and his breath came more easily. You could say Peter O'Malley was healthy until the day he died.

On the drive to Toronto airport that day to pick up Aunt Al it was strange, but while it was James's mother who had passed, he thought mostly about his father. He wished that somehow he and his father had been closer, that he had known more about him. Maybe it was James's subconscious manner of burying guilty memories of his mother, by replacing them with guilt about his father instead.

Standing in the crowd near the baggage delivery spot where Alitalia's flight from Rome was listed, James scanned the incoming passengers for the sight of Aunt Al. He hadn't seen her in three or four years and was looking forward to a big loving hug from his godmother. It had been a whirlwind forty-eight hours since that police officer's visit telling him his mother was dead. He was in need of some friendly comfort.

There she was. Even with the oversized designer sunglasses that hid a good portion of her face, James could pick her out any place. She wore an immense and of course stylish hat atop what he knew would be perfectly coiffed hair, a fur stole that failed to cover the chunky pearl necklace, dangly bracelets, a giant diamond ring and a gorgeous green dress that fit snugly over every curve. An aristocratic smile dominated her face. True to form, two handsome older gentlemen seemed to be attached to her by invisible leads, fawning over her every move. James smiled at the sight.

"Grazie. Grazie," he heard her purr to one gentleman and then to the other.

She dismissed each with a flick of the right hand, removed her sunglasses and perused the crowd for her godson. When she spotted him, she mouthed James's name, flashed him a great big smile and came bouncing toward him, precariously but expertly balancing her slim five-foot-five frame on her designer Bruno Magli shoes. "Aunt Al," James said as he gave her a big hug.

"Jamie, Jamie, you look wonderful," she said. He could detect a perfume, one that had been judiciously applied. She had learned well from her husband, the count, that old European money hated ostentatiousness.

"I'll get your bags," he said. "We've got lots of time to talk on the drive home."

"Yes, and much indeed to talk about," said the countess. "Your mother has left us with a first-rate mystery." Her face turned to concern as she looked up into his eyes. "Oh, Jamie, I am so terribly sorry. That was not intended as a light comment. I know you're hurting terribly and so, my dear godson, am I." Then she reached up and hugged him again, this time very hard and very close.

* * *

From the airport and back along the throughway that links Toronto to the rest of the world, they drove east in the Corolla, passing through the city and its suburbs, then into the Ontario countryside. Bare-branched trees waited in all their starkness for the coming of warmer weather and life-giving showers. Occasionally, along the highway's margins, were early traces of spring, omens of things to come, with dabs of colour where wildflowers bloomed. The grass was starting to turn a fledgling shade of green.

Their conversation was at first sparse, limited mainly to the banality of weather, traffic and how the city was growing. Finally they were out of the suburban maze, into what his mother always called the "beauty spots," and Aunt Al broached the subject they both were eager – yet reluctant – to approach.

"Your mother had just telephoned me last month," Aunt Al said. "I hadn't heard her so cheerful in years. She told me she had heard from Max. Just out of the blue. Totally unexpected."

"They were close, weren't they?" James said. "It took me years to understand that. I guess Mom's situation with Dad left her crying out for companionship."

Aunt Al nodded and grunted her assent to that. "She said she was now free from Pete — oh, I'm sorry, Jamie."

"No, don't worry," he said. "I fully understand they only existed under the same roof. That's all. They had grown apart years ago. I never quite understood why, but it was just a fact of life."

"Still, he was your father. I know you loved him, and your mother always knew." After a pause she continued: "She said that now Pete was gone, she felt free to … pursue other avenues. That's why she was overjoyed to hear from Max. Somehow he had learned that Pete was dead and he wanted to extend his condolences, he told her. Your mother laughed at that, then apologized for being so insensitive. But then she said there was no longer anything to keep them apart. Nothing that she knew of, anyway. She wondered if Max would come for a visit."

James gently interjected when she stopped for a pause. "I know how Max found out about Dad. I passed the message to him through his sister in Toronto."

"You? But how…? How would you know where to reach him? Your mother said he was still the same free spirit he always was. Travelling from one harvest to another, right across the continent. Just as he had done for years. She said he would never settle down, that he'd likely die picking tomatoes in Leamington, or apricots somewhere in one of those California valleys."

James explained to Aunt Al that he had never told his mother how closely he and Max kept in touch after their wartime experience. Max had asked James not to and he kept his promise. Max was a big brother to the younger man, almost a second father. He told James that he had a sister who lived in Toronto, gave him her name, address and phone number, and said James could always reach him by sending a letter to her if the need arose. Occasionally, James had used the phone number. That's how he had let Max know about Pete's death the previous fall. Now, he said, he would have to call again, to pass along the news of Grace's death.

"But why would she be so moved by a phone call from Max?" James asked Aunt Al. "I understand they were once close, but she barely saw him once a year, when he came for the apple harvest. I'm not even sure she'd seen him in recent years."

Alberta paused and gazed out the window at the passing sights. She turned back to him and bit her lip. Her brow was furrowed. "But Jamie. Surely you knew how deeply she cared for him. They had a … relationship. A relationship that had been going on for more than fifty years."

James admitted this was not a stunning revelation. He had known they enjoyed one another's company. He suspected the depth of their relationship and its importance to his mother, and yet he never knew for certain. Max was a free spirit. He travelled the continent, the open skies often his only blanket. He had no possessions in life other than what he was able to carry with him. He said he could never settle down, never work in an office or factory. He preferred to live in farmworker bunkhouses as he followed the harvests wherever they took him. In winter, he would pick crops in Florida, then head across the American South to California for early spring. He would travel up the length of California with the ripening fruits and vegetables, then back across the continent, stopping in Oklahoma or Mississippi, on up to Kentucky, Ohio, then Ontario and Quebec. Along the way in any given year there would be strawberries, oranges, grapefruit, celery, lettuce, oats, tomatoes, then peaches, pears and apples, before going to the Canadian prairie for the wheat harvest. In early winter he would head back to Florida and the cycle would begin again. The migrant worker's passage across borders was so easy in those years.

It was through these experiences with the workers that Max had developed a strong affinity, a kinship with them, and the political causes that supported them. James thought of the many conversations the two had had over the years, some of which had turned into heated debates about worker rights.

Max had arranged for years to reach the Shannonside farm, Ballinskellig, in mid-August and stay through the different varieties of apples that would ripen right through into October. Then he was off to Quebec to finish the harvest there. If there was one constant in Max's life, it was Ballinskellig. All else was fluid.

"Why did my mother never tell me that?" James called to no one in particular but, of course, Aunt Al was there to catch the query. "And why didn't Max say anything about her? It's like he had two separate relationships in our family – the friendship he had with me, and the one you say he had with my mother. He didn't want either one of us to know about how much he cared for the other? It makes no sense."

The two of them were silent for several minutes, the only sound the passing of vehicles along the motorway and the low hum of the engine. Aunt Al finally broke the hush. "Your mother didn't want to hurt you," she said. "She abided your father for your sake. She was devoted entirely to you."

James pondered this. Not another word passed between them until they turned off the highway onto the old English Road where the sign announced the town of Shannonside and he said at last: "We're nearly home," and Aunt Al replied: "Perhaps I shouldn't be here at all."

Pulling onto the Tower Road, he slowed the car so as not to slip on the tar-and-gravel surface and looked around at the familiar scenery: the old snake fence, the elm, oak and maple trees lining the road. The familiar old farmhouse came into view on the right, the weathered blacksmith shop, drive shed and barn on the left. He turned into the driveway and rolled the car to a stop behind his mother's car. Alberta waited for James to open her door. Immediately she was brought back home, watching the starlings and sparrows swoop between the trees. The still air was scented with the dampness of melting snow.

"Go on in," he told Aunt Al. "The door's unlocked, as usual. I'll get your luggage."

Inside, Alberta was taken immediately by the cleanliness of the room, both its physical perfection and the scrubbed scent that met her nostrils.

James too had noticed this upon his entrance the day before. It suggested planning but neither one of them, familiar as they were with Grace's demanding standards, found it odd. Just evidence of the way she had lived her life. Evidence too that she had meticulously planned her own demise.

James ran water into the kettle and set it on the wood stove, which he lit a fire in. His mother had only grudgingly bowed to modernity when the electric company ran lines down the road that had once been known as the O'Malley road – and had clung to her beloved wood stove like a jealous lover. There was an oil burner in the parlour that helped to heat the upstairs. In recent years, Pete had finally installed electric base heaters in the bedrooms, to remove the chill, he explained, from their "aging bones."

Aunt Al doffed her hat and stole, placed them on Grace's favourite chair. A tear came to her eye as she touched the back of the overstuffed chair, a holdover from the Twenties, its crazy-quilt upholstery now worn smooth and faded to something just above a dirty cream colour. It was Grace's favourite spot, the place where she always sat, pulled up her legs and curled up for kitchen confabs over a pot of tea. James took Aunt Al's bags to the guestroom that sat upstairs at the end of the hallway that ran from the top of the stairs. He turned the knob on the baseboard heater. His mother's room had been at the other end of the hall, near the stairs.

When he returned to the kitchen, Alberta had stuffed the tea ball with tea leaves and was waiting for the water to boil. She'd found two ornate old cups and placed them on the table.

"I'm sorry about how I spoke of your father in the car, Jamie," she said. "Your mother always admired your father, even after the love went out of their marriage. She had her eye on him back in our school days, before he even knew who she was."

James asked her how his parents had met. She smiled at the memory, and told him, "We will get to all of that. Let me collect my thoughts first."

* * *

In the morning, Aunt Al and James decided to tackle the subject at hand: Why did his mother commit suicide? What had really happened? Why had she gone from the happiness of preparing for the arrival of the man Aunt Al revealed Grace had harboured much longer-held and deeper feelings for than her son had imagined, to ending her own life? It was a mystery James was determined to uncover. And he wondered what additional secrets remained to be discovered.

James slept in the downstairs room that his father had taken when he and Grace began to live apart more than fifty years ago. These were the arrangements that they made because it was as far apart as they could possibly position themselves and still live in the same house. The room was sparsely furnished, a simple brass three-quarter bed, a nightstand, a chest of drawers, with a wardrobe in the corner. No carpet broke the starkness of the worn pine floorboards. A mechanical clock – it had not been wound in the months since his father died – sat at the bedside. Two nondescript and generic prints hung on opposite walls, one a depiction of Zeus on Mount Olympus and the other an elderly Sophocles speaking to a young woman. The walls were papered in some design that had been popular in the Twenties, its birds and flowers severely faded.

Aunt Al was upstairs in the guestroom. The space was a marked contrast to the room Pete had taken as his own. Grace's feminine touch had been at work here, with a pretty paisley bedspread on the double-width brass bed, yellow sheets and an extra woolen blanket draped across the foot. There was a pretty woolen rug at one side of the bed, a blanket box at the end of the bed, an ornate chest of drawers topped with a lace cloth and some knick-knacks. There was an electric clock that hummed politely next to them. Unlike Pete's old downstairs room, this one was equipped with a closet.

In the morning the two of them, James and Alberta, had breakfast and before they could head upstairs to enter Grace's room, the phone rang. It was Harold Walters, Grace's solicitor. "Glad I caught you at home," he said. "I telephoned Alberta's residence in Italy again today and they told me she had flown over. Has she arrived yet?" James told him she was with him just then and he said good, he had something for her, something Grace had left for her. Could he have someone run it out to the house to deliver it? James recalled the box of items the lawyer had mentioned the day before and said that was fine. Within half an hour, a cab pulled up in the driveway. It was Matt Pulford, one of the town's two cab drivers. He offered his condolences and handed James a package.

It was neatly wrapped in brown paper and string and addressed to "the Countess, Alberta Ribigghini." Aunt Al opened it and inside was something wrapped in bright yellow-and-silver paper, tied in an orange ribbon. Inside this package was an ornately carved teak box that Aunt Al recognized immediately. "It was your mother's keepsake box. She put a few pieces of jewelry and special things in it. I brought it to her from Firenze on one of my visits home. Oh, that was years ago."

Aunt Al opened the box. Inside was a pair of diamond earrings, a little silver charm in the shape of a gondola, a folded piece of silk that when opened revealed a tiny and intricate watercolour scene of a lake, a mini-book of cocktails from the Hotel Orto de Medici in Florence and a menu from the R.M.S. *Mauretania.* Beneath them was a letter written on fine paper and without a word Alberta picked it out. She unfolded it and began to read.

"I want to read this aloud to you," she told him. "It says: 'My dear Albie, I am hoping that you have come to help James during what I know will be a difficult time. Tell him I am so very sorry to put him through this, but I do not see any other way." Albie's voice caught in a tiny sob. Then clearing her throat, she continued: "My life is truly over but for the completion of the dirty deed. I have kept these items through which I share a history with you, my love, and I hope that you will be able to remember me with the same fondness I have always had for you. We have been through so much together." Albie hesitated again, then plowed on: "I am afraid, however, that I did not share everything with you, and for that I hope you can forgive me. In time it will all become clear to both you and James. My entire story lies within the confines of Ballinskellig and it is there for the two of you to discover. With all my love, Grace.'"

Aunt Al put down the letter and cried. She sobbed, the sobs soon progressing to long, hard watery inhales. The sounds of her pent-up grief filled the kitchen of the farmhouse and as she sat at the table, James stood up, walked over and stood behind her, then wrapped his arms around her. He nuzzled his face into her hair. Aunt Al clasped his hands in hers and gradually the sounds of lamentation subsided. They held in those positions for moments longer until she patted his hands and said: "I miss her so much already. Before, I knew we could speak on the phone or I could always come over to Canada to visit, but now ... now that will never happen again."

James tried to hide his own tears. His no-nonsense father had taught him that men aren't supposed to act that way but truly he wanted to just sit down and cry his heart out. Still, there was a feeling of anger beneath the grief for his mother. She was to the best of his knowledge a perfectly healthy woman, so why? Why had she taken her life? What demon had captured her?

Aunt Al looked down into the box and picked out each item in turn. She again took up the little painting on silk and told him: "This is the scene from my villa at Lago Trasimeno. Lovely, isn't it? These are all items that connect your mother and me. The menu from the ship she and I took when I convinced her to come back from Canada and join me for a visit. You were so little then, and you stayed with your Grandmother and Grandfather Campbell. I think it was 1926 or '27, and Grace was having trouble with your father. I gave her these earrings and then we visited Venezia and I bought this little charm. Oh, she protested so much but I said, 'Grace, the Count has money to burn. The money means little to him and I want you to have this.' We went to Firenze because I said I wanted to take her to see the most wonderful city in the world, and this little cocktail book is from the hotel we stayed at. Each of these items represents an adventure on that wonderful trip we had together."

James wanted to go to his mother's room and yet he held back, uncertain whether he was prepared to open the door, to walk into the space in which she had so recently taken her life. Finally he said to the Countess: "I'm going to take a look around Mom's room. Maybe she left some clue to what's behind this."

"I'll go too. You're going to need some support up there, Jamie. I'm ready now."

True to his word, Walters had arranged for the room to be cleaned up and returned to its customary tidiness. With everything scrubbed top to bottom after the shooting, James could still smell the cleaning products used. Beneath that was a faintly gentle bouquet of lavender, a favourite aroma of his mother's. It brought back memories. He looked around. Everything seemed precisely placed. The curtains were drawn so James went over and pulled them open, the light streaming in to reveal a setting that had changed little in thirty years. This was the largest of the bedrooms, one that had once been the room Grace shared with her husband. It still contained Grace's much-loved canopy bed, various tables, a highboy dresser, braided rugs and a burgundy wingback chair next to the window. The walls were studded with family photos.

James glanced at the table next to her bed and saw two books, one on top of the other, and a box. Walking over, he sat down on the side of the bed. The gentle scent of his mother's favourite lavender perfume wafted up from the bed and he momentarily choked on her memory. Aunt Al stood transfixed in the doorway. James picked up the top book and noticed it was her diary. He vaguely recalled she had kept one. But it was the box that attracted him most, a cardboard shoebox. It seemed strange that it was sitting at her bedside. She was so fastidious about keeping everything in its place, he couldn't imagine it was there for any reason but that his mother wanted him to see it. He opened it up and sitting on top of what looked like old letters was a one-page note in her familiar handwriting.

Aunt Al came over and stood beside him. "From her?" she asked. "For you?"

He nodded and began to read aloud: "My dear James. I hope that someday you can forgive me for what I have done. If there were any other way I would have chosen it. In time you will understand.

"I know we never said 'I love you' very much in our house but believe me when I say I love you so very much. And even though your father never said it I know he loved you too. He was a hard man and he had a hard life. You don't know just how hard.

"I have left for you my diaries which I started to keep when I turned thirteen. If you are patient it will reveal my life story. As well, beneath this note are letters I have kept that will explain a part of my life you knew nothing about. Again please forgive me.

"Together the diaries and letters will explain much of what has remained unexplainable to you. Things I could not share with you when I was alive. I think it will also explain why I was left with no choice.

"I wish you a long and happy life my son.

"Love, Mom."

James looked over at Aunt Al who had turned quite pale. "Oh my," was the best she could manage. "Oh…my."

Grace said she'd had a life that her son knew nothing about. He thought he'd known so much about his parents. He knew Grace was an only child, daughter of Eleanor and Will Campbell. He knew she had married his father, Peter O'Malley, the only son of Benjamin and Mame O'Malley, who had earlier had three daughters.

He knew his parents had married in September 1918. They might never have married if his father had been free to live his life the way he had wanted to: finishing school and getting a city job in Toronto. But Pete's own father, fearful that with three daughters he ran the risk of being the last to farm the O'Malley homestead, insisted he stay and take over the farm. Peter had obeyed his father's wishes, which was the practice of the era. But he did so with a great deal of unhappiness. According to James's mother, Peter had seemed better suited for city life and never had much interest in farming. That seemed odd to James, since his father had seemed to take so naturally to it.

Curious about what his mother had to say in the diaries she left for him, James set aside the box and opened the top diary to the first page where he read: "My dear parents gave me this diary today for my thirteenth birthday. I will treasure it always and include as my first entry that Mr. O'Malley paid a visit to our house just yesterday. Mrs. O'Malley has passed away. He brought his eldest daughter, Lucy, and his son, Peter. Peter seemed so ill-at-ease, fidgeting in the big chair in the parlour where he sat. My what a fine boy he is though. What wouldn't I give for him to pay attention to little old me!"

James smiled at the thought that his mother had her eye on his father at such an early age and it made him wonder that much more just what had happened between them. Maybe the diaries would offer an answer.

Aunt Al spoke up. "I will leave you to yourself for a while now, James. I'm still tired from the journey. I think I need to take a little rest. Not as young as I used to be. Why don't you keep looking through your mother's diaries?"

He said he would and they agreed to get together over lunch. In the meantime, James skimmed through his mother's neatly written entries, fascinated by the little details of her teenaged years. There was an incident with her puppy and how Peter saved it from drowning and James thought, how gallant of him. Farther on, he came to the day his dad proposed to her, "The happiest moment in my life!" she gushed. "I am beside myself with anticipation. Of course I made a complete fool of myself and shouted 'yes, yes, yes!' the moment the words were out of his mouth. It was down at the back of the farm not far from where Peter had so bravely risked his life to save Ebbie that day four years ago. I said it must be considered 'our special spot' and Peter agreed. He seemed so nervous when he asked me and I thought he'd nearly jump out of his skin when I responded. I just know we'll be so happy together, forever."

Some pages later, there was an entry about their wedding day, written in language that was unusually flowery for his mother. Pressed between two of the pages she used to describe the event was a small dried bloom of a little white flower. Grace had mentioned she wore a sprig of baby's breath pinned to her wedding gown and he assumed this must be what it was.

Still later, she wrote about how his father had joined the United Farmers of Ontario movement because he was angry at how farmers had come out of the war years virtually penniless while big business seemed to have profited from the death and destruction caused by the four years of fighting. "Peter was always a quiet man," she wrote, "but he becomes a different person when he talks about the United Farmers and all of the grievances he accuses the Ontario government of. I find it all very exciting and I love the passion he shows when he talks about the cause."

What in the name of God had happened between them? They had once been so much in love.

3

The O'Malleys of Ballinskellig

Most of what James knew about his father's family, about how they had come to farm this place deep in Ontario's apple-growing region, had come to him from his Aunt Lucy, his dad's eldest sister. Lucy was the genealogist of her generation of the O'Malley family, keeper of the family Bible, chronicler of those few stories that had been handed down through the generations. She said the stories from the past were few because their ancestors' circumstances had often been quite sad, their existence oppressive and their hardship wrenching. Lucy recalled her grandfather Sam had once said to her, "some things are best left unremembered. Those were not good times."

After their mother died, Lucy raised Peter, her younger brother who would become James's father, to the doorstep of his teenaged years. Then she moved to the city and married Burt, but paid frequent visits to Ballinskellig, the place she clearly held dear in her heart. She was James's effervescent and colourful aunt, one he came to love and consider more as a grandmother.

Despite his initial disinterest in family lore, over time Lucy's colourful tales came to captivate him. When he was very young, it was the jokes she recounted that he liked best. "Granny O'Malley told me how poor they all were when they came here from Ireland," Lucy told him one day. "She said when they got off the boat at Cobourg, Great-grandfather O'Malley was in a desperate condition. He heard there was a particular shop in town that bought rags and bones and went to investigate. 'Is it true?' Great-grandfather asked, and the shopkeeper said, 'Indeed it is, sir.' So Great-grandfather replied, 'Well then be jabbers, put me on the scale and tell me what I'm worth.'"

James giggled. "She didn't," he said.

"Oh, it's true, lad," Lucy replied. "Rags and bones. That's all they were when they arrived."

It dawned on James one day that many of Lucy's stories were real-life adventures, the ones you might more likely read about in books. But they were better than that because they were about his own family. Later, he wondered how much Lucy had embellished those stories, but he really didn't care. They were based on truth, and that is all that mattered. A little embellishment was not a bad thing.

James's father rarely talked to him about anything other than how to run the farm, so James never heard his version of family events. In fact James said he was not even sure his father was aware of most of the tales. Aunt Lucy's stories filled the youngster with pride in his ancestors' sheer determination amidst what was often unspeakable sadness and strife. She was a natural-born storyteller, and knew how to wring every drop of drama from each of them. James was fascinated by her accounts of how the O'Malleys had left Ireland to come to Ballinskellig and how they made the farm a successful business.

One day when he was ten, James asked Lucy how it had all begun. How was it that the O'Malleys decided to leave everything behind in Ireland and head for the New World?

Lucy looked the youngster straight in the eye. "I am told that it all began after someone was shot on the doorstep," she said.

* * *

Ballinskellig, Ireland: 1847

"Don't worry," the old O'Maille told his son, Liam, "no one will blame you. Padraig O'Ceallachain is a wastrel and a no-good vagabond. Everyone in Ballinskellig knows that."

Liam O'Maille's dispute with Padraig had blown up over Liam's conversion from the Catholic faith to the Protestant Church of Ireland. For that crime, Padraig had called him a *brathadoir* and a *snigh.* Liam tried to calm the situation, but Padraig would hear nothing of it. One day after a couple of pints of the *an uisce beatha*, Padraig came to the O'Maille home brandishing a pistol and making wild threats. Liam, who stood a head taller than the drunken lout, tried to take the pistol away. It went off, and the ball struck Padraig O'Ceallachain beneath the chin.

He reeled backwards and tumbled off the doorstep, falling into the dirt onto his considerable backside.

Padraig had not died, at least not then. Liam's father speculated that such an event would likely only serve to knock some sense into the *bómán's* feeble brain which, if he was not mistaken, was lodged in his backside. But the sheriff in Cork had been called nonetheless. Since in the mind of the law of the time a Protestant shooting a Catholic was less heinous a crime than if it had happened the other way around, the sheriff would not likely be in any hurry to investigate. This gave Liam some breathing space, time to escape. But he must still act quickly. He went to see his friend and employer, Lord Darby, who booked the family passage in a deck-level cabin on a ship bound for Quebec.

Cobourg, Canada West: 1847

Under a striking azure sky, Cobourg's harbour bustled. Dozens of smells filled the air of the thriving port: the farm produce being loaded onto vessels, the fish unloaded from others, the human sweat of the stevedores and the buyers and sellers who bartered with raucous passion, animal dung from the horses and oxen that drew the hauling carts. The growing town on the immense lake had become a crossroads between the fertile land and the teeming water. It was the place where the new plank road commenced and opened up the mining district around Rice Lake, and where William Weller's stagecoach passed on its route between Toronto and Quinte. Recently the town's east and west piers had been extended and a grand lighthouse stood on the east pier, beckoning to ship traffic arriving from across the vastness of Lake Ontario.

On their regular route from Kingston, the crew of a ship named *Cavalier* docked at the west pier and tossed the sailing vessel's lines to calloused waiting hands. Two of the stevedores grumbled to one another they would be in need of a good disinfecting from the latest cargo of "lousy micks and paddys" being offloaded.

The disembarking passengers to which they referred presented a sorry picture: bedraggled, their clothing little more than rags, their desolate stares reflecting the privations that had started at home and only worsened during the long journey across the roiling ocean. Their small and stooped frames spoke to the deprived circumstances that had forced them to leave their homeland and strike out to a new country, a country of which they knew nothing. Many had died on the voyage over, while some of those who survived appeared barely alive, faces emaciated and pocked with disease, limbs shriveled from malnutrition. The local traders and shoppers gave the motley bunch not a second's thought, familiar as they were with the regular stream of similarly pathetic arrivals.

Standing out from the sorry lot crowding onto the pier was one family of at least slightly grander means. The man was tall, straight-backed and robust. Prior to leaving the ship, he had donned his well-worn top hat, from under which long, dark strands of hair hung shaggily. He had somehow, despite the shipboard conditions, managed to keep his black suit neat and tidy. While the wear-points on the jacket and trousers were shiny, it was obvious to any who observed him he was a gentleman of some standing. The woman, while tired and distraught from her ordeal, stood proud and true in a ruffled dress, good Irish lace sewed decoratively at its sleeves and hem. Her round and ruddy face carried lines of worry. What did the future hold for her two young children that stood at her side? They too presented a contrast to the street urchin rabble that surrounded them, their clothing that, while worn, was clearly more than home-spun.

Liam and Luiseach O'Maille breathed in the warm summer air and thanked God for allowing them to escape Ireland and for delivering them to this little piece of Heaven. Along with their youngsters, Somhairle and Eilis, they had nearly made it to their destination. Liam hoped it would be easy-going from here. Luiseach feared it might not.

It was on this pier that jutted out into Lake Ontario and where the thriving town's commerce was centred that Liam and Luiseach O'Maille bade a final farewell to their Irish names and transformed themselves into William and Lucinda O'Malley. This they had done on the advice of friends who had already settled in the new land and when they were questioned by the authorities at Grosse Isle, the quarantine station for Quebec, they proudly identified themselves by their Anglophone names. Somhairle and Eilis would become Sam and Elizabeth, the girl soon to be more familiarly known as Bet.

They had been the lucky ones on the voyage across the Atlantic. Thanks to the kindness and generosity of Lord Darby, they had been able to slip past the law and board the ship at the port of Cork, then make the harrowing trip inside the relatively comfortable surroundings of a cabin next to the captain's, rather than in the below-deck squalor of steerage that had been the fate of most of the others on this voyage from hell. Besides farming a small plot outside Cork in the village of Ballinskellig, William had traded on his sharp mind and keen ambition into a position as a teacher for some of the children of Ireland's English ascendancy, the

Protestant class that ruled the country. His employers were drawn to William in no small part by the fact he attended their own Protestant Church of Ireland rather than the island's predominant Roman Catholic Church into which he had been born. He had made the conversion when he fell in love with his Church of Ireland sweetheart, Luiseach Nulty. Lord Darby had quietly handed William a small sum of money that guaranteed better conditions for the family's crossing.

Darby was sorry to see William and his family go, but agreed that under the circumstances it was best. That lazy sheriff would eventually make his way from Cork one of these days, Darby said, and if that good-for-nothing Padraig O'Ceallachain did end up croaking — an event Darby said would make the world an entirely better place — the sheriff could cause trouble. No matter that the shooting had been an accident brought on by the boozy oaf himself.

Besides, added Darby, there were signs of economic trouble. Peasants were being shoved off their land and placed in horrible ships to be transported out of the country that could not sustain them. Darby feared conditions would quickly deteriorate further. It was on Darby's advice they chose the Canadian colonies rather than the more brash and boisterous America. Darby believed that while both destinations were uncivilized and vile, Canada stood a better chance of transformation into a proper British society, given the opportunity and some appropriate guidance.

The O'Malleys placed every article they could take with them into three satchels and headed off across the pitching ocean. Now those possessions sat at their side on the pier at Cobourg and alongside them was a small package William guarded vigilantly. Its contents held the key to helping them make a living in their new country.

William and Lucinda's family were amongst the lucky ones. As Ireland's potato blight spread and the *Gorta Mor* – the Great Hunger in the Gaeilge language – took hold, many of their neighbours left home with nothing, gaining passage on the ships only through the financing by the landowners who just wanted to rid themselves of the hungry and disease-riddled tenants surrounding them. But their passage was in the unspeakable, rat-infested common space that lay below-decks.

As the voyage proceeded, scores of those in the ship's hold fell ill because the hunger was only part of the infestation that had struck the Irish towns and countryside. From the hunger grew the double scourge of cholera and typhus. The O'Malleys were four of the 90,000 people who fled Ireland for the Canadian colonies during the summer of 1847 and, thanks in no small part to the generosity of Lord Darby whose gift had kept them out of the ship's hold, they were among the 50,000 who made it to Kingston. Some 16,000 others died on the filth-congested ships from one disease or another while the rest chose previous points to stop. It wasn't luxury in which the O'Malleys travelled, but it was far better than the putrid conditions that existed for the bulk of the refugees who were forced into the bowels of the ship.

Now their funds were nearly gone. Standing on the pier, they were grateful for the opportunity to stretch after the cramped voyage from Kingston but wondered what lay ahead. Lucinda hung on to her son's hand and instructed him to hold tight to the hand of his sister.

"We're nearly there, my darlins," said William in as confident a voice as he could muster. "Tis been a long journey from Cork, but we're nearly home. Our new home."

Lucinda looked around in anxiety. "But now what?" she asked. "Wit' dis crowd tis best to watch out for the *gombeens*, husband." William smiled but secretly shared his wife's hesitance to trust anyone after what they'd heard on the boat they'd taken from Montreal to Kingston. A woman had told how she and her family were robbed in Montreal by a smooth-talking stranger, a *gombeen.* "Der is maggots in the colonies, just as der was in Cork," the woman had proclaimed.

"Best be movin'," said William as he put one firm foot forward and led them down the pier toward the town. While far smaller than Quebec, Montreal and Kingston where they had earlier landed, the little town's skyline was still remarkable to him, standing as it did amidst the nearly unbroken wilderness they had observed on this latest leg of their journey. The town was highlighted by a grand church steeple and a lovely bell tower on a magnificent and boastfully proportioned public building. This Cobourg might be small, but its citizenry seemed to be filled with confidence. It was the way of the New World, he thought. He looked toward the day he could share that wonderful confidence but at this moment, his hands trembled and his legs wobbled. So much could still go wrong and he knew nothing of this place. William spied a man who seemed reputable enough to safely approach, and asked for directions to William Weller's stagecoach. The man pointed down the street and the family commenced their slow progression against the human crush.

Weller's four-horse stage ran six times a week along Lake Ontario's north shore between Toronto and the Quinte Country, and William was determined to get his family on it. He desperately hoped he had saved enough from Darby's gift for the fare. There was land waiting at Shannon Bay, a place that sheltered earlier Irish immigrants, including their friends from the Old Country, John and Jenny Morrow. It had been the Morrows, known as Moireach back in Ireland, who had advised on dropping the Gaelic names and reverting to English. "You'll be in a new land," John had written in his last letter. "Best to adopt their ways as best ye can." The Morrows had promised to lend a hand to get the newcomers started.

The stationmaster told William that if the children could sit on their parents' laps, the remaining funds would "do." Leaving Cobourg for the last leg of their long journey, the grateful O'Malleys harboured high hopes.

"Imagine, a town by the name of Shannonside, right here in Canada," said William. "I'm wagering it's a grand place."

Bet and Sam snuggled up close to their parents on the coach's simple wooden plank seat. The slat back was made somewhat more comfortable with the addition of a couple of pungent bear hides and the vehicle began its jarring trek the final few miles to their new town. The horses' natural pungency was amplified by the persistent farting from one of the team.

"Esther!" the coachman admonished the creature after several noisy toots. Then doffing his soiled cap and waving it around to chase away the horse's gassy emissions, he called down to the passengers: "Sorry, folks. Esther got intah some green hay, I'm afraid."

Dust billowed through the open windows and William unrolled a screen to cover the opening closest to his wife and daughter, even as he began to list the plans he had for once they'd arrived at their final destination. He would work for John Morrow to repay that family's kindness and generosity, while all the time looking for other jobs around town. Before his career as a teacher, he was known as a fine stonemason back in Cork and Morrow had assured him there would be plenty of opportunities here. Eventually he would save sufficient funds to get his own land.

Ultimately, the stifling heat made the O'Malleys and the other passengers agree that dust and Esther's farts were preferable and William rolled the covering back up to allow a bit of air. From the windows the O'Malleys could see immense trees that came nearly to the road's edge. There were frequent cleared fields, an occasional log cabin from which they could catch the whiff of a fire, even on such a hot day. After all, a fire was necessary for the cooking. Once in a while they came to a village, its main street lined with crude wooden shacks. After passing perhaps three of these small settlements the driver shouted down: "Shannonside comin' up." A bridge crossed a slow-moving river, its deep, black waters rising out of the forested hills that formed the northern horizon. Soon, the coach pulled up outside a long, low wooden building.

"I imagine we are here," said William. He opened the door, hopped out and helped out the children, then Lucinda. There was little one would consider "grand" about this Shannonside. Along its main street, its wooden buildings were for the most part unpainted, some even without glass in their windows. For those, hastily constructed shutters lulled at the sides of the openings, ready to be slammed shut when required, such as when it rained or snowed or the mosquitoes grew too bold. Two mangy hounds scuffled in the dusty street, snarling and snapping over some pathetic and unidentifiable scrap they apparently considered food.

Leading them inside the dark terminal building, William inquired of the stationmaster as to whether he was familiar with the Morrow family. Without looking up the man replied: "Yup. Moved on 'bout a month back. The missus died so the mister took the rest of the kiddies and moved away."

William turned to Lucinda, his mouth dropping open in shock. "Oh," is all Lucinda could manage. Her eyes conveyed her despair. They had come so far and there was no turning back. What were they to do? They had pinned their hopes for this new land on getting a boost up from the Morrows. They had no other plan. William had feared something would go wrong but he had not considered the possibility that their friends would no longer be there to lend a helping hand. His heart raced and he tried to calm himself. He would not allow the family to see his panic.

As the couple stood silently, wondering what other options they had, the manager finally looked up. "Yew wouldn't be the O'Malleys by any chance?"

"Yes," replied William, his voice betraying a slight quiver. "From Cork."

"Got a letter here fer yeh," the manager said in a slow drawl. "John left it, said ta give it teh yeh if yeh shewed." He disappeared for a moment and returned with the letter, then handed it to William.

While Lucinda tried to calm the youngsters whom she appreciated had been uncharacteristically patient during the entire ordeal, William opened the letter with an unsteady hand. When he finished reading it, he looked at his wife and said: "John moved on with the family after Jenny died. Said he was headed to his brother's in the Old Northwest, wherever that is." Lucinda's heart sank further. "But listen ta this. He says he left the farm in the care of his neighbour, Isaac Black, with the instructions to keep it for us. Says we are welcome to take it over and we can make arrangements to pay him something for the land whenever we can.

"*A ghra*," William said tenderly to his wife. "We are goin' to be landowners." He smiled and patted the small package he had been guarding along the way. "And here, *a mhuirnín*, here is our future." Through tears, Lucinda smiled back at her husband. They would make it work. After all, they had no choice.

* * *

Only through the kindness and generosity of their neighbours did the O'Malleys pull through those first months in Canada. The Shannonside residents, who had been through the experience themselves, offered unending support and advice for living in their new land. Through that support, the O'Malleys had been given an invaluable opportunity and for that they were immensely grateful. No one had much, so there was never anything to be jealous of. Everyone had the same goal: survival.

Water and shelter were essential requirements. The old well next to the simple log structure that the Morrows had built after their arrival four years ago was quickly put back into order. William was warned by neighbours that any cracks in the chinking between the cabin's logs needed to be tended to before winter's cold began to set in. "Ireland's never seen such cold, I can tell you now," advised Bob Hamilton, a recent arrival from Belfast. Within a few years, that crude cabin would be amended and added onto. It would never again resemble the original, but as they made their additions they never forgot their home's welcoming origins.

On the eve of their first Christmas, Lucinda was in the throes of making the most of her meager holiday meal ingredients when she heard bells outside the cabin door. William had gone into town with the children to purchase supplies. Lucinda went to the door just as a man was helping a lady out of their cutter, which was drawn by a sleek black horse. The handsome animal was bedecked in a string of silver bells, which had attracted her attention. "Hallo," Lucinda called to her guests.

The man turned and, holding the woman's hand, returned the greeting. "Merry Christmas to you, missus," he said. "Mrs. Campbell and I wanted to welcome you to your first Christmas in the New World." The woman smiled and held carefully onto a bundle as she and the man made their way through the ankle-deep snow to the cabin door. The couple, cheeks and noses rosy from the frost, introduced themselves as John and Sadie Campbell, neighbours from just down the concession road.

"Won't you come in?" said Lucinda, her voice filled with delight by the prospect of Christmastime guests. "Come and sit by the kitchen fire to warm yourselves." It was a lonely existence in the Canadian wilds and she relished the opportunity of conversation with newfound friends. "I'm afraid my husband and children are away to town right now but I expect them back soon. Will you have a cup of tea?"

The Campbells were gracious in their acceptance and settled themselves inside around Lucinda's cooking fire. Its welcome warmth slowly seeped into their chilled bones. Mrs. Campbell handed Lucinda the package she had been carrying. "We thought you might have a challenging time your first Christmas in this new land. Please, accept these humble items as a welcome. We are truly sorry it has taken us so long to come for a visit."

Lucinda's eyes brimmed with tears as she opened the package and looked inside. She picked out a plum pudding, a ham and some potatoes and carrots. "Oh my," she said. "I cannot tell you how much this is appreciated. Having just arrived this summer, we are still scrambling to make ends meet."

"That is quite understandable," said Mrs. Campbell. "We have been through the very same experience. There was folks to help us and we are just passing on their kindness."

Just then William arrived home with the children whose excited chatter carried across the calm, cold air. Sam burst through the cabin door with Bet right at his heels. "Ma, Ma," the children shouted. "Come see what Da has brought!" A look outside revealed an evergreen tree William was now lifting from the back of the cutter. "I had to sit on Sam's lap all the way home," Bet giggled. "The tree took up all the rest of the space."

"Children, children, mind your manners," Lucinda told them. "We have guests."

William came through the door and greetings were exchanged. "What's this about a tree?" Lucinda asked her husband.

"It's a Christmas tree, my love," he replied. "I am told that Prince Albert introduced one to Windsor Castle a few years ago. It is a tradition come from Germany. You cut down an evergreen tree, bring it into the house and decorate it with anything you might have, the idea being to make the home a little more festive for the holiday. Surely you'd agree our humble cabin could do with a bit of brightening up."

"Indeed it could," she replied. "And William, look at what our new friends have brought for us. It is a veritable feast." As William's eyes grew large at the sight of the gift of food, Lucinda turned to the Campbells and said: "The two of you must stay and help us enjoy it. Please, you will be our Christmas Eve guests."

And so it was that on their first Christmas in Canada, the O'Malleys welcomed their young neighbour newlyweds, the Campbells, into their home for Christmas Eve dinner. The cabin was filled with scents from the feast of ham, potatoes and carrots. The meal was finished off with Mrs. Campbell's Christmas plum pudding, a concoction that consisted of dried versions of the many fruits that the new land nurtured, spiced and redolent with sweet and savory native herbs such as mint, yarrow and rosemary, herbs that Sadie Campbell had learned about from the Indian people nearby.

Later, after the Campbells bade the O'Malleys goodnight and the children were snug in bed, Lucinda looked at her husband. "I feared the voyage when you told me we were coming," she admitted. "I wondered what we were getting ourselves into. But this is a wonderful place, William. I'm going to love this Canada of ours. It is a truly blessed country."

* * *

The precious package William O'Malley had kept so close to him on the terrible voyage across the ocean contained, literally, the seeds of the O'Malley family's future. Apple seeds. Seeds obtained from some of the fruit from the trees William had tended on his small section of land back in County Cork. William had raised the apples just as his father, Henry, had before him. He had learned the peculiarities of the apple, that its seeds did not behave in the manner of most of the other crops. For instance, you never knew quite what variety would come up once the seed was germinated and planted.

Consistent apple varieties were obtained only from grafting the apple variety one sought onto another sapling. Saplings must be planted in pairs in order to assure they bore fruit. Two varieties of apple were required in order for pollination to take place.

William had lovingly placed his seeds in a protected cold place that first winter, during which time they began to sprout in anticipation of the warm weather to come. In spring, he prepared a small area out back of the log house, expertly adding just the right amount of animal dung to the soil to provide them with the nourishment they required. Not too much, he knew, or their roots would get burned.

While they were still saplings, William knew he needed to protect them from pests, specifically the deer that found the tender shoots much to their taste. The insects that plagued fruit trees in North America were different from those William had known in Ireland and he began to rely on his neighbours for tips on how to control them. Isaac Black was a tremendous help and recommended a good all-encompassing compound created by adding arsenic to soap and potash. William discovered it proved remarkably effective.

As they grew, William transplanted the young trees to a spot that offered good drainage, and was careful to provide each with enough space to spread and grow to its full potential height of up to thirty feet. Within seven years, the trees were producing fruit and William hoped in another year to be commencing his first full harvest. Then he would be able to put some serious money away to continue the process of repaying John Morrow. John had written that first winter to inquire as to how the O'Malleys had gotten settled and William quickly wrote back to convey his gratitude.

William looked out over his growing orchard and smiled. The trauma of leaving his family's old life behind and crossing the Atlantic was already proving to have been a worthwhile sacrifice. Once more he thought of Lord Darby and the great gift he had bestowed.

Before the apples began to bring in a profit, William used credit to obtain a cow and a couple of sheep that fed off the farm's natural grassland, and raised oats and barley. Sam was growing into a strong young man and proved to be a great help to his father. William counted on him to expand their fields to grow even more grain and apples.

With Sadie Campbell's help, Lucinda carried on with raising the root vegetables such as potatoes and beets, crops she had relied on back in Ireland. To those, she was soon adding some staples of the New World. The native people had taught the settlers about the "three sisters" – corn, squash and beans – and how they flourished in harmony. First you planted the corn over top of a buried fish or eel for fertilizer, then surrounded the corn with beans and beyond that, the squash. In no time she was adding all types of cabbages, onions and pumpkins to the garden. A neighbour gave her some raspberry canes and strawberry plants.

The O'Malleys found the ground, sandy loam for the garden near the house and clay for the apples, incredibly fertile and before long were trading part of their produce for tools, cloth and other household necessities. The sheep were a great source of wool Lucinda expertly turned into clothing.

Bet was barely able to toddle behind her mother when Lucinda first introduced the girl to the gardening chores and by the time she was ten, the child was invaluable. When autumn came, Bet helped to dry, pickle and can enough food to last the family through the frigid winters.

William and Lucinda agreed to make a full break from their Irish past. They raised their children to speak English only. They were, thankfully, in Canada now. The children got along well with the local youngsters who, besides being of Irish background, were the descendants of English and Scottish settlers.

In 1854, Sam, barely eighteen, married Catherine Simpson who was a year older, and whose family had come from Scotland. The next year, son Benjamin was born. Before they were finished, Sam and Catherine would raise seven children. The growing family was spilling out of the Ballinskellig farmhouse, so Sam convinced William they needed to expand the place. In 1860, the same year the Prince of Wales, Queen Victoria's son, came to Canada West and laid the cornerstone for the new parliament building they would construct in Ottawa, Sam called on his neighbours to donate their draft horses to hitch to the house and turn it on its foundation. His father, the expert stonemason, had carefully extended the foundation for this purpose. That made way for the addition of a new wing, which Sam turned into a kitchen and dining area large enough for the entire family, and then some. At the back entrance, Sam built an attached woodshed with a door placed in the floor that led down to a root cellar. The woodshed and cellar would be of great value as storage for overwintering vegetables and keeping them close at hand.

The turning of the house was a massive undertaking and brought onlookers and teamsters from miles around. Neighbours watched in awe as the giant horses strained against their bridles. When they were done, Sam and Catherine, helped out by William and Lucinda, hosted a party for the entire bunch. It was the biggest gathering anyone had ever seen around Shannonside.

It was at that gathering that Bet met the strapping young man whom she would commence being courted by and eventually marry. Right after the ceremony, they headed west and ended up in the Red River country near Winnipeg. Bet would never see Shannonside and Ballinskellig again.

William turned fifty that year and Lucinda was forty-eight. Both were more than happy to hand over more of the farm work to Sam and Catherine. For Sam, recollections of the Old Country were dimming as he put his strong back into the labours that kept him busy in building an ever more prosperous farm. Sam once told Catherine he felt as though he was an extension of the land and his overriding responsibility was to protect it for the future.

William loved his new land but kept thoughts of Ireland close to his heart. He retained the Ballinskellig name on his farm as a morsel of what they had left. Lucinda was the keeper of the family heritage and delighted in conveying stories to her seven grandchildren. It was the middle one, Emily, with whom the details stuck, including the story of the doorstep shooting that had commenced their emigration.

Sam did his duty and joined the local militia. He was called up to service during the Fenian Raids in the late Sixties. Old William was not too happy when he learned his son was going off to fight what William considered his countrymen, the Fenians, whose lofty goal was to capture Canada and hold it ransom for the release of Ireland from the British grasp. Sam felt differently. He held no ties to the Old Country and told his father that now they were in Canada, it was time to forget their old animosities. William told his son he had no idea what terrible hardship the English had inflicted on the people of Ireland and he could never forget. Sam considered his father a bitter old fool but held his thoughts to himself.

Sam's regiment fought at the Battle of Ridgeway in 1866 and he was wounded by a Fenian bullet to the upper arm. The injury caused him pain for the rest of his days, and hardened his views against the "hotheaded Irish." His views created a rift between father and son that lasted for the rest of William's life. Sam nearly dropped the farm's name, but when his father passed in 1878, his sister, Emily, convinced him there was still a spot for nostalgia in the O'Malley family. Sam reluctantly agreed the moniker could stay.

Just before Old William died, Benjamin, eldest of Sam and Catherine's seven children, became the first of the brood to marry and in 1877 he took Mary Jane Thompson, better known as Mame, as his bride. Ballinskellig was still very much in Sam's hands, however, and Mame never got along with her in-laws. She convinced Benjamin to build a cottage on nearby Shannon Bay, and Ben travelled back and forth daily to help his father with the farm.

Three of Sam and Catherine's other six children found marriage partners in the area and one, James, stayed in Shannonside where he and his wife, Livinia, took over the farm supplies and hardware store. O'Malley Farm & Hardware remained an institution in Shannonside for decades. The other siblings moved away.

Two of the boys headed West together to mine for gold and were never heard from again. The day before they left, sometime around 1880, the seven children of Sam and Catherine gathered in the hayloft of the barn and Ben led them in a ritual he said would cement the O'Malley clan's hold on Ballinskellig forever. Up among the rafters, Ben took out his pocket knife, carved the words "the seven wonders" into a beam and then carved his own initials beneath it. Then he handed the knife to James. "Your turn," he said. In turn, each of them added their initials.

When Catherine died in the early Eighties, Sam pleaded with Ben and Mame to "come back home." Against her better judgement Mame agreed, on the condition that they keep the cottage so they had someplace to escape to whenever the old fella got too bad. Mame knew that while Ben was well into his thirties, Sam had no intention of giving him an inch of say on running the farm. Papa's word was law.

When Sam died of a heart attack in the spring of 1898, Mame, who was six months pregnant at the time, wasn't the only one to breathe a sigh of relief. Secretly and with a heart that was heavy with guilt, Ben was relieved as well. Ballinskellig was finally his.

4

Peter
1898

BENJAMIN O'MALLEY CAME bursting through the farmhouse door, with Dr. Farr right behind. It wasn't a grand farmhouse, but it was home. Erected by William O'Malley around the nucleus of the original Morrow cabin, it had been added to, subtracted from and even turned on its foundation over the course of the past five decades to accommodate the family's changing circumstances. A bright whitewash covered its exterior walls and made it glisten in the summer sun.

Ben was a bull of a man, tall, barrel-chested, but with not an ounce of excess fat. His dark hair had commenced to streaks of grey. His chiselled features lent an air of strength and determination. "This way, doc," Ben said, leading Phineas Farr to the bedroom Ben shared with his wife, Mame.

Mame's cheeks had gone sunken and sallow. At her bedside stood and sat their three daughters, Lucy, Alice and Anna. Lucy, the eldest and named for her great grandmother Lucinda, sat in a chair and held her mother's hand, a look of deep concern on her face. Alice stood on the other side of the bed and wiped her mother's brow with a wet cloth. The two girls exchanged worried glances. Anna, the youngest, stood helpless at the end of the bed, balancing first on one foot and then the other. The girls were the spitting image of what their mother had once been, dark-haired, sultry-eyed Irish beauties.

"Alright, everyone out but for Lucy," the doctor ordered. "Lucy, your mother and I'll need your help," he told the eldest of the three girls. Lucy nodded stoically. She had helped with births before, including that of the younger of her two sisters, but was particularly nervous this time. Her mother was past the normal age for birthing and Lucy was fearful for her.

Benjamin O'Malley led the younger girls out and closed the bedroom door. They waited.

It was a good two hours before they heard the sounds of a crying baby and Benjamin sighed with relief. The doctor came out of the bedroom and met the father and his two daughters in the kitchen as Lucy stayed behind. Farr's face was grave. "The baby's fine," he said. "A big, healthy boy." Benjamin and the girls shouted their joy and hugged. He loved his daughters, but Benjamin had so wanted a boy this time. Someone to pass the farm to, he had told his wife many times. Someone to carry on the family name and to love and care for the land as he did.

"But," added Doctor Farr, "Mame. She didn't make it, I'm afraid."

Ben blanched and ran into the bedroom where Lucy was holding her mother's hands. The baby had settled down to sleep in a tiny cradle next to his mother's bed. Huge tears rolled down Lucy's cheeks as she turned to her father. "She should never have had this baby," she said. "Why, Papa? Why?"

* * *

1905

Doc Farr had labelled Peter O'Malley a "big, healthy boy," and he always was. With his dusky complexion, smoky, brooding eyes and a physique that was sturdier than the other boys his age, he was the one they turned to as their leader. It was a source of pride to the boy, and yet it was a curse too. People always thought of him as older than his years and expected him to somehow act more his size than his age. It was a fact that in some manner robbed Peter of his childhood.

In the summer after Peter's seventh birthday, he already looked as though he was ten and was often looked to for guidance and leadership by his friends, Dave Hanson and Percy Reilly, who called him "the big fella." One day the three boys found themselves walking along the Shannon Canal that linked Quinte to Shannon Bay. At one time the canal had been a busy commercial waterway, plied by coal barges and commercial vessels. By 1905, it had passed its heyday and had turned into a place more often frequented by swimmers and fishermen.

Percy was aged six and Dave was eight, and all three were certainly on the young end of those who were supposed to be testing the canal waters on their own. Peter had been warned on many occasions by his elder sister,

Lucy, to avoid the water unless he was accompanied by an adult who was able to swim.

"I know you're bigger than your friends, Peter," Lucy told him, "but you're still a boy." Despite his stamina and physique, she knew her brother was not a particularly strong swimmer.

The canal's water was a seemingly fathomless, dark blue and the friends tossed stones into it, rippling its stillness. They chased water bugs and peered into the depths for sunfish. The day's rising heat had made them sweaty. Dave Hanson, oldest of the three, stared longingly into the canal's tantalizing waters. Finally he could take it no more and announced the heat was too much for him. He was jumping in to cool off. Peter and Percy warned against this, but Dave was insistent. Anyone who didn't join him was a mama's boy, Dave declared. "I can't believe you, Peter O'Malley. Where's your sense of adventure?" Then he took off his clothes and dove from the canal's edge into the water some five feet below.

"Come on in," he shouted to his friends when his head bobbed back to the surface. "It's beautiful and cool."

The dark water grew murky from the mud Dave had disturbed and the two boys looked at one another. "We're not supposed to ever go in here," Percy said, glancing over at Peter. "My Papa says only to go in where it's level and grassy, not dive off the wall. And only if there's an adult with me."

Peter nodded. "I know. My sister says so too," he replied.

Dave ignored their protests. "Hey, fellas, watch this." Dave dove down into the water, held his breath and remained submerged for what seemed like forever before he popped back up a good twenty-five feet away. "Yer missin' out," he called to them. "This is powerful! Come on in."

The two boys looked at one another. "Come on outta there, Dave," said Peter.

"Aw, tarnation!" Dave yelled back. And with that he dove again.

As the moments passed the boys looked for him to pop up somewhere but he didn't. Worried looks passed between them when suddenly Dave rose to the top again, this time face down.

"Stop kiddin' us, Dave," said Percy. "Come on out." Dave didn't move. He floated, motionless on the surface. The boys grew agitated as their friend continued to lie there face-down in the canal.

"I've gotta do somethin'," said Peter. "He's in trouble." Peter took off his shirt and shoes, looked for the spot in the wall where steps led down to the water's edge and ran down them. He hesitated for a moment on the final step, then steeled himself and slipped into the water, swimming awkwardly out to his friend. He wished he was a better swimmer, and stronger, but he would do his best. Paddling out to his friend and grabbing onto him, Peter began to pull Dave back to the edge, where Percy had by this time run to help. Peter sputtered on the muddy canal water as he tried to push Dave close enough for Percy to get a hold on him. "Hang on to him," Peter yelled in the short breaths he was now reduced to. "I'll climb out and help."

The boys together pulled Dave's motionless body up the steps to the top and Percy ran for help. It was later determined Dave had bumped his head on what was likely a submerged rock or chunk of concrete and knocked himself out. He had ingested too much water by the time help could be summoned.

"You did all you could have done," Ben O'Malley later assured his son. "It was a fool crazy thing for him to have done. It was his own fault, not yours."

Peter wasn't so sure. He was never one to show his feelings and through the entire ordeal he had remained calm. Now that it was over, he took a calculated look at what had happened and how he had responded. Peter determined that he would learn to be a better swimmer. He would never let such a thing happen again.

Lucy could read her brother better than anyone. She could see the subtle signs that the incident had seriously upset him. She tried to console him by telling him stories she had been told by her Aunt Emily and Uncle Jimmy – Ben's sister and his brother who ran the hardware store. Jimmy had become almost as good a source of family lore as Emily. Not only did he possess a great memory for detail, he had inherited what they all called the Irish "gift of the gab." When she was a girl, Lucy loved to curl up in a big chair and listen, rapt, as Jimmy and Emily shared memories and theories about the O'Malley clan. As she honed her own storytelling skills, Lucy found Peter a willing and eager listener.

"The O'Malleys ought to be proud of their heritage," she told the boy. "Old William and Lucinda, it's hard to imagine the hardship they endured and the sacrifices they made in those early years."

It seemed just the right thing to say. As Peter thought of the tales of strife and privation his great-grandparents had endured to create Ballinskellig, it put his own sorrow into perspective. Somehow it eased his guilt over Dave's death.

His sister's tales did something else, too. Peter realized he was the man of the family despite his young age. He had a reputation to uphold. The family legacy rested heavy on his shoulders. The land he had grown up to love would some day be his to protect and pass on to his own children.

5

Grace
1913

THE CAMPBELL FAMILY had come to the Shannonside region and settled in even before the O'Malleys. It had been two of the Campbells, then-newlyweds John and Sadie, who had introduced themselves on the O'Malleys' first Christmas Eve and welcomed the newcomers so warmly. The families remained close for many years. Most of the Campbell clan had moved on by the early years of the twentieth century, however, leaving only Will Campbell, his wife Eleanor, and their daughter Grace behind. Two other children had died in infancy. The Campbells' home lay just past the old-growth stand of maple, oak and elm – one of the few that remained anywhere in the region – on the other side of the O'Malley farm.

It was in the waning days of Grace Campbell's Grade 8 school year, and her parents had just presented her with a beautiful Irish setter puppy she named Ebenezer. Grace had been partial to the name since she read Dickens's *A Christmas Carol* and been introduced to Ebenezer Scrooge, a man she felt had been entirely misunderstood. She came to love Scrooge and decided it was a name that fit her little dog. She dubbed him Ebbie for short.

Grace and her best friend, Alberta Johnson, took Ebbie for a walk through the woods. The girls, just commencing their teen years, made their way along the path that led to the Shannon River. It was the weekend that led into the final week of classes. Summer vacation was near. The day had turned sunny and warm after a cool, misty beginning and Grace removed her hand-knit woolen sweater, the one she had made herself in her home economics class. Grace and Alberta chattered excitedly about plans for the coming summer months. Finding a favourite sunny field next to the water, the girls sat down in the wild grass and played with the rambunctious puppy. He was particularly enamored with the tall blades of grass the girls pulled off and waved in his face. He yipped and scampered his appreciation for this newfound game. The girls did not notice that Peter O'Malley, two years their senior, had approached from the opposite direction, the direction in which the O'Malley farm was located. Despite the long association of their families, Grace and Peter were only passingly familiar with one another, separated as they were by two years in age and the activities of their respective genders.

"Hello, girls," Peter called out, and the two of them jumped at the sound of a confident male voice. The puppy ignored him and continued to jump and yelp at the girls. "What you got there?"

"Oh, Peter O'Malley!" replied Grace. "As if you'd care." Peter was a big, burly farm boy with a square jaw and dark, brooding eyes. There was a slight scruffiness to his dark hair where it hung over his collar. Grace had kept her eye on him for quite a while. She had watched quietly from the sidelines when he joined the other boys for a game of baseball, in which he excelled, and on cold winter days she loved to watch him strap blades to his boots and play hockey on the frozen pond into which the Shannon River emptied just before the bay. If the truth be known, Grace had a bit of a crush on him.

"This is my new puppy, Ebenezer. He's an Irish setter. Going to be a hunting dog when he grows up."

Peter laughed but it was a gentle laugh, not unkind. "He's got some pretty good growin' to do before he's ready for any huntin'. I'm afraid a good-sized jack rabbit would get the best of him right now."

"Well, of course, you silly," said Grace. "He's just a puppy. Want to hold him?"

Peter smiled and walked over to Grace. He took a moment to admire her pearly skin, her soft green eyes and her maturing figure. As he reached to gently pick Ebenezer from her grasp, their arms brushed and the slight scent of lavender reached his nostrils. It made him shiver. Peter hugged the puppy. It licked his farm-tanned face and wagged an energetic tail in greeting. "I think he likes me. But isn't that a pretty long name for such a little dog?"

"Ebbie. We call him Ebbie for short."

Peter rubbed the puppy's tummy and scratched him behind his ears. The dog was so happy anyone would have thought he was smiling. After a while, Peter handed Ebbie back to Grace and gazed into her fresh young face. "Guh-gotta go," he stammered, momentarily tongue-tied by their proximity. "Off to Uncle Jamie's hardware store for Dad. Talk to ya later. Bye girls, bye Ebbie." Peter turned and jogged along the forest trail out of their sight.

"He's a nice boy," remarked Alberta, whom Grace had nicknamed Albie. "I think he likes you too," she said to her friend in a teasing tone.

Grace blushed. "Don't think so," she replied. "A boy like Peter? He likely doesn't even know I exist."

At that moment, Ebenezer caught sight of something that attracted his canine mind and he jumped out of his mistress' arms and ran for the river, stumbling head-first into the water in his enthusiastic dash for a dragon fly. After a rainy spring, the Shannon was unusually high for June. Ebbie yipped his alarm as he slid into deeper and angry water.

"Oh, no!" screamed Grace as she heard the frightened puppy and watched its furry little head dip under the river's foamy swells. "Albie, what will we do? Help him. Help him!"

Alberta's equally piercing screams filled the air as the puppy's sounds of terror were nearly drowned out by the rushing water. Then, just as he seemed about to be dragged under and flushed down the waterway, the puppy was able to scramble atop a tree branch to which he held on for dear life. But the branch too was washing farther away from the terrified little girls. "Ebenezer! Oh, no!" cried Grace.

The girls ran up and down the riverbank, desperately thinking of anything they might do to save the little dog. Then the branch Ebenezer had climbed aboard momentarily wedged between two rocks that were slightly submerged in the foaming water no more than forty feet from shore. Grace kicked off her shoes and began to wade gingerly into the raging water, tentatively at first, but determined to do all she could.

"Get out of there!" called a male voice from behind her and Grace turned as she waded knee-deep into the surge. "Stand back!"

It was Peter O'Malley. The boy had heard the girls' desperate cries and had come rushing back through the woods to see what was wrong. Peter ripped off his shirt, doffed his boots and jumped headfirst into the water. Aiming himself slightly against the current, he dug his strong arms deep into the water and slowly made his way toward the rocks between which the puppy was desperately clinging to the branch. Reaching the rocks and choking on the water that seemed determined to fill his nose and mouth, Peter grabbed for the puppy just as the branch gave way with the force of the water and continued its trajectory downriver. For a moment he feared the animal would be snatched from his grasp and an image of his friend, Dave Hanson, floating in the canal face down, flashed before his eyes. Then somehow, willing it to be so and determined not to allow a repeat of the Dave tragedy, Peter held on and began to inch his way back to shore. Gripping the puppy in one hand he held above the water, he used his other strong arm to pump gallantly against the fearsome wash.

Partly swimming, partly scrabbling against the river's uneven bottom, Peter slowly made his way to dry land, just as the girls arrived from upriver. Running down the shore, Grace gently took Ebenezer from the sputtering boy's hand. Peter coughed and hacked to get the water out of his lungs and throat but Grace was too concerned about the puppy to pay him much heed.

"Ebbie! Oh, Ebbie, you're okay," she cried. The little dog choked and sputtered as it tried to rid its tiny body of the invasive water. It whimpered and closed its eyes. "Ebbie, no. You have to be alright." The dog made tiny grunting sounds and Peter gently took it from Grace's grasp. He looked around and spotted Grace's nearby sweater.

"Give me that sweater," he quietly ordered her, and Grace ran to get it. Peter took the woolen sweater and wrapped it around the little dog. Using his strong hands to massage its chest between the folds of the fabric, in a few seconds the pup gave two big coughs and threw up water and bile. "There," said Peter. "I think he'll be okay now."

For the first time, Grace took her mind off of Ebbie long enough to notice Peter's tanned and muscled torso. "Oh, Peter," she said, "thank you. Thank you so much. Thank goodness you're such a strong swimmer. You saved him!"

"Be more careful next time," replied Peter as he turned and, dripping and shivering from the cold river water, trotted over to where he'd tossed his boots and shirt. Drying himself as best he could with his shirt, he turned toward the girls and called: "you're lucky I was here." Peter slipped on his boots and, carrying his damp shirt, turned his back to them and headed into the woods.

"I don't know what we would have done without Peter," said Albie, shaking her head. "Ebbie would have been gone for sure."

Grace shivered at the thought. "He made himself useful," she replied with a smile.

* * *

Walking away from the rushing Shannon River and into the woods after saving the puppy's life, Peter O'Malley smiled as he swabbed down his torso with his shirt and continued through the woods toward town. At the age of fifteen, the strapping, athletic teenager was now nearly a man. Eight years ago, he had let Dave Hanson drown, or so Peter always believed. As a result of that incident, he was determined to grow stronger and become a much better swimmer. This he had achieved and thanks to his strength and swimming skills, he had been able to save Grace Campbell's puppy. He longed to have the opportunity once again to save his friend.

Peter thought he quite fancied the young lady he'd just helped. She was his damsel in distress. That wasn't a term he used to describe her when he talked about her to his best friend, Lloyd Porter, but the tone of Peter's voice made it clear to Lloyd this girl was someone very special in Peter's life. Grace would be going to his high school that coming fall and Peter looked forward to getting to know her better. Fair-skinned, green-eyed and with lovely long auburn hair that fell gently upon her shoulders, there weren't many young women as lovely as Grace Campbell in the small town of Shannonside.

"Boy, I wish I had someone that special in my life," Lloyd told his friend. Peter grinned.

No one had much money in the farming community but somehow Grace managed to dress just a bit better than the other girls. His eldest sister, Lucy, who had raised him after his mother died, always said she admired Grace Campbell's sewing and dressmaking skills. "That girl's going to make some lucky young man a great wife someday," Lucy always said. Peter's dark eyes sparkled. He figured there was absolutely no reason it couldn't be him.

By the summer of 1913, all three of Peter's sisters had moved away from Shannonside. Lucy had stayed the longest but having seen her little brother – who already towered a head above her – to his fourteenth birthday, announced she was leaving too. After all now that she was into her thirties, people had stopped calling her an old maid and began to whisper she was well past marrying age. Lucy had fooled them all, and once she moved to the city it took no time at all for her to hook up with an eligible old fellow of forty.

That evening as he mused about his rescue of Grace's puppy, Peter thought about the future. His father and Lucy had filled him with the thought that someday the O'Malley farm would be all his. It was a legacy that had begun in 1847, when his great grandparents, Liam and Luiseach – William and Lucinda – had taken over the old Morrow homestead. They had built and expanded it and their son, Sam, had carried on and rebuilt the house, while his son, Benjamin, continued after them. Now, Ben was getting on in years. Peter had arrived late in Ben's life and his next birthday would see Ben reach fifty-eight years. The backbreaking work of maintaining his two hundred acres was getting Ben down. Peter worried about his father. How much longer could he maintain the pace?

His father was the third generation to farm, the third generation to grow apples on this land. Apples formed the backbone of the O'Malleys' Ballinskellig Farm, and had done so ever since the little seeds Old William had carried in his precious package from Cork germinated, were planted in the fertile ground and grew into sturdy, fruit-laden trees. Within a decade of being planted in the spring of 1848, the trees were producing bumper crops of crabapples, Kerry pippins, scarlet croftens and Irish russets. Trained by his own father in Ireland, William had been expert in the art of raising apples back in his homeland. In Canada, more varieties were added as he germinated more seeds, began grafting them and swapping some of his own trees for a few of the local varieties that included northern spies, snows and the king of all apples, the Canadian-bred McIntosh.

Initially, his produce was sold at the farm and at the market in Shannonside, then in surrounding towns such as Belleville, Kingston and Cobourg. Before long, the O'Malley name was known in Peterborough, then Toronto, Ottawa and Montreal, to where apples were shipped in hampers. The railway even sent someone to visit William and his son, Sam, to convince them it could ship their apples still farther afield, to Hamilton, London, Windsor, even Buffalo, Rochester, Detroit, Cleveland and New York. The railway, eager to gain a foothold in the business, even provided the O'Malleys with their first barrels for the purpose and within half a dozen years the O'Malley name, stamped on baskets and barrel lids, became known for miles, in two countries, then even across the ocean in the United Kingdom.

William had established Ballinskellig so that future generations of the O'Malley clan could carry it on. The farm had thrived for more than half a century, but Ben was growing older and slowing down. It became ever more difficult for him to maintain the place, and when his foreman, Jimmy Clark, retired the past fall, things really started going downhill. It was too much for Ben to handle and Peter was still growing into the task. There was so much to learn. Besides, Peter was conflicted about the future. The O'Malley heritage was important to him. He was proud of the way three generations before him had built the farm into a thriving business, built it from the nothing they had arrived with. Still, in a way farming was not enough for him. What he really wanted was to continue his education and move to the city. Ben would hear nothing of it. Peter must stay; he must run the place when Ben was gone. It was the O'Malley destiny.

Peter sighed a deep sigh of inevitability, and continued on.

* * *

That summer, Grace took greater notice of Peter O'Malley than ever before. He would often be in town doing errands for his father, working long hours on the O'Malley farm and occasionally spending an evening with his chums in a game of baseball at the high school field. Grace often dragged Alberta along to the games. "I had no idea you had taken such an interest in baseball," Albie joked.

"Oh, just hush," Grace would say with a blush.

Sometimes Peter would drop by the grandstand after the game and make some excuse to chat with Grace. Occasionally he would offer to walk the girls home, knowing Albie's farm would be reached before Grace's. "We could always go by way of Henderson's Lane and get Grace home sooner," Albie chided. "I don't mind being dropped off second."

"That's enough from you," said Grace. Peter ignored them. He seemed partial to the longer route that gave him more time with Grace.

That fall when school reopened, Peter entered Grade 11 and confided in Grace that he would likely have to take a lot of time off to help with the farm. Times were tough, as they so often seemed to be on the farm, and his father needed him. Grace commiserated. "You should be thinking about continuing your education," she said. "You're very smart. Why, I'll bet you could even go to university if you wanted to someday."

A scowl came over Peter's deeply tanned Irish face. It was a handsome face, Grace thought, strong-jawed and sculpted, putting her in mind of a Roman statue. She didn't like to see him ruin his looks with such a scowl. "There's no money for university in our family," he replied. "Dad says he needs me on the farm. That's where my future is."

"That's too bad," she said. "Oh, there's nothing wrong with farming, but you don't need to do that. Why, you could do so much more in the city and I'll bet you could help out your father a lot more that way.

By sending him money when he needs it. Or just sell the farm. My father says it's the best one for miles around and anyone with the means would be happy to have it."

Peter said he could never see that happening. The O'Malley name was a farming name and it was his destiny to make sure it remained that way. Whether it was his fervent wish or not, however, that was the way it would have to be. The O'Malleys were at one with the land. It was their destiny, their duty.

When school resumed that year, Peter was one of the many boys his age who stayed back to work in the farm fields. There were crops that needed tending and on the O'Malley farm there was a bumper crop of apples to harvest. After a handful of poor years, now was the chance for the O'Malleys to rally. Peter would never see the inside of a schoolroom again.

Grace saw much less of Peter that year, with the young man taking on ever-increasing responsibility for the O'Malley farm. His father, Ben, was nearing sixty and was quickly slowing down, worn out by years of backbreaking work. Ben called Peter "a true blessing in my later years," and now the burden of the work fell to the son. Two of his sisters, Alice and Anna, had financed university for themselves in Kingston and Montreal and the third, Lucy, the eldest, stayed to help her father and little brother after her mother had passed.

Grace would sometimes take a stroll with one of her girlfriends — frequently Alberta — down the road that passed the O'Malley farm everyone knew as Ballinskellig. Ebbie would be running after them or sometimes ahead, sniffing enthusiastically in his search for a rabbit or woodchuck. On rare occasions, the girls would catch a glimpse of Peter out working in the fields, or hitching his horses to a plow, or in the fall, directing the picking of the apples that formed the lifeblood of the family operation. Sometimes Peter would spy them and smile and wave. One day he was taking a break under the shade of a giant oak tree and when he spotted Grace and Albie, jumped up and ran over to the fence to say hello. Grace's heart rose into her throat.

"Hi-ya," he shouted. "How's Ebbie doin'?"

"Oh, superbly," replied Grace. "He misses you, I think." She felt the fool as soon as the words were out of her mouth.

"Yeah? Well maybe I could drop by the house some night and say hello properly."

"That would be brilliant," said Grace. "Ebbie would love that."

Moments later, Peter excused himself and said he had to get back to work, but said he would definitely stop by the Campbell farm before long. As they continued their stroll Alberta said to her friend: "You know, of course, Peter wants to come over to see you, right?"

Grace blushed a shade that made her long, silky auburn hair glow in the dying sunshine. "Oh, don't be silly. He's just coming over to make sure we're treating Ebbie properly."

"Uh-huh," said her friend.

The very next evening, Peter showed up at the Campbells' back door. "Come on in, son," said Grace's father, Will Campbell. "We were just getting ready for our evening cup of tea." As they settled in the parlour, Grace's mother served her special apple crisp with a dollop of cream. Her father asked the young man his views on the prospects of war in Europe.

"If there's fighting, I'd want to go, of course," Peter told them. "I'm only fifteen, and I don't suppose it'll last long. So I likely won't get the chance."

Grace's parents glanced over at one another and smiled. Grace caught their shared moment and blushed.

* * *

1918

Grace Campbell and Peter O'Malley fell hard for one another. It was no surprise to anyone they knew that, in the last summer of the war, when finally it appeared as though peace might be just around the corner, the young couple set a date for their wedding. They were, in fact, the handsomest couple in Shannonside, pretty well everyone agreed. Grace's mother set the wedding date based upon an old rhyme she recalled from her own youth. "Marry on Monday for health, Tuesday for wealth, Wednesday the best day of all, Thursday for crosses, Friday for losses, and Saturday for no luck at all. Grace, I do believe it should be Wednesday."

The wedding was held at high noon on a September Wednesday, at the modest board and batten farmhouse of Eleanor and Will Campbell. Eleanor splurged and purchased some beautiful lace to gussy up Grace's otherwise plain wedding dress, then made the cake with the help of her sister, Isabella. It was Isabella who recalled Grace's beloved lavender and cut some sprigs from next to the side door at Ballinskellig to place among the bride's wedding bouquet. Alberta Johnson was Grace's attendant, her father gave her away and Peter's friend, Lloyd Porter, was his best man.

Lloyd had done his duty and called some of the lads over for a bachelor party, making sure Peter had one last chance to get stinking drunk on Will Campbell's home-distilled hooch. "You need to raise a few tins while you can, my boy," Lloyd told him. "You're gonna feel yer stepmother's breath soon enough."

For the wedding, a couple of the neighbour ladies made sandwiches and punch. Will kept a pitcher of his finest liquor, surreptitiously pouring it into the glasses of those who preferred a more robust beverage.

As a farm son, Peter was never expected to join the armed forces and go off to war, although he desperately wanted to. He had spent his youth learning to tend the farm which Ben was about to hand over to him. The day before the wedding, Will Campbell and Ben got together some of the neighbour men to build a dance platform in the Campbells' main barn. Ben splurged and even bought his son a new suit for the wedding ceremony. As was typical of the times, the event itself was short. After all, folks needed to get home to tend to their livestock. The day produced a brilliant blue sky; the temperature was just right. After the ceremony and a little stomping on the floorboards, the couple was driven off in Sam Black's 1913 Hud sedan to Kingston where overnight reservations had been made at the Queen's Inn Hotel. As the Hud pulled away, Lloyd led a gaggle of Peter's friends in a chorus of catcalls and ribald shouts of encouragement for the wedding night.

When they returned to Ballinskellig, Peter, Grace and her Irish setter, Ebenezer, set about making a life together, just as it seemed the war in Europe was slowly grinding to a halt. On November 11, as the last shot was fired and an armistice called, Grace and Peter sat at the kitchen table with Peter's father, Ben, and they bowed their heads in prayer, in thanks for the arrival of peace, and in thanks for a good harvest. Ebenezer kept watch on the side porch and as prayers were said, he lifted his huge head and peered at them quizzically through the screen.

The war had ended apple shipments to the UK but healthy sales in Montreal, Toronto and New York had nearly made up for the shortfall. Nonetheless despite the bumper crop, the war had brought hard times to farms across the North American continent. Profits were down as everyone hitched in their belts an extra notch, volunteered to accept less for their products, and gave their all to the effort toward victory.

Now that the war was over, though, Peter grew resentful of the wealthy business interests in the big cities that had benefited strongly from the massive expenditures of public money to pursue that victory. In his mind they had not shared in the nation's pain, they had not lost their sons and they had not contributed a dime toward the joint "national effort" that the politicians in Ottawa and in Washington had called for. They had sat back and watched their profits rise as the farmers and the vast majority of the country's labour population had agreed to take less and to contribute more.

Now that the war was over, Ontario farmers were doing more than grumble. They were putting their support behind a group called the United Farmers of Ontario, a group that was initially created as a lobby organization to convince the professional politicians that change was needed. With early signs of success, however, its creators decided to form into a political force as well. Reluctantly, Peter supported their effort. In conversation with other farmers around Shannonside and beyond, he had reached the conclusion that neither the Liberals nor the Conservatives would ever, despite their best words, lift a finger to help farmers survive in the new post-war world.

Ben O'Malley argued that the farm-based political movement consisted of a bunch of radicals who could never succeed. Peter, backed by Grace, disagreed with his father that they were all radicals and came increasingly to the conclusion that they just might succeed. Grace went a step farther and said farmers should unite with labour to rise up and demand reform. Together they could do it. Peter was beginning to believe she was right; Ben just shook his head and walked away.

6

Max
Toronto, 1918

ON FRONT STREET, across and slightly east of Toronto's bustling Grand Trunk Union Station, sits the Queen's Hotel. Once the most luxurious hostelry in the city, it was the first hotel in Canada to have elevators installed, the first to have a hot-air furnace and the first to offer running water in every guestroom. Its immaculate gardens had hosted grand parties. Sir John A. Macdonald himself had stayed at the Queen's whenever he was in town and it was rumored that the first plan to establish a united British nation on the northern half of North America was hatched in the hotel's famed Red Parlour. Its rooms were booked by the rich and the famous, including visiting royalty. Sitting at the hub of Ontario's first city of commerce – one that was coming to rival Montreal in national status – it enjoyed a privileged location, a location that one day would see the building of an even grander and more famed hotel, the Royal York.

By the end of the war, the Queen's had begun to impart an air of fading gentility. It had been eclipsed by other hostelries in the city. Yet it still enjoyed a certain status amongst the fashionable moneyed set, including the wealthy automobile baron, Henry Huddlestone.

On the upper level of the four-floor hotel, in its most luxurious suite of rooms, Huddlestone maintains his permanent home. It is filled with brocade French provincial furnishings, all curated, or even designed, by his late wife, Eleanor. Its walls are covered in ornate palm frond wallpaper. They are hung with works of fine modern art, including Winslow Homer and William Merritt Chase. Its windows are concealed behind heavy velvet draperies. The suite is one of Toronto's finest residences, a place where the Huddlestones have entertained the cream of two nations' societies, including the Masseys, the Rockefellers, and the Vanderbilts.

Huddlestone strains the bonds of the term rich. His Oshawa-built horseless carriage, the Hud, had swept the nation and was taking the American market by storm. When production was shifted to the wartime effort, profits spiralled upwards. On the first Christmas Day after the war, Huddlestone himself paid for a grand feast for all of the hotel's guests. In the hotel's refined dining room, great long tables were set with the finest linens, silverware and chinaware – the snow-white plates specially etched in gold with "Huddlestone Victory 1918" around the edges. Liveried staff filled guests' crystal glasses with the best French champagne. Sated and happy, grateful guests thanked Henry Huddlestone for his generosity as they returned to their rooms on Christmas night. The hotel's general manager stopped by to shake his hand. Huddlestone smiled, slapped backs, teased the ladies and laughed with them all, telling them it was his extreme pleasure.

Back in his suite of rooms, Huddlestone, a balding, florid man of middle age, medium height and a slight paunch, loosened his bow tie so that it dangled around his neck, and doffed his tuxedo jacket. He placed it over the back of an intricately carved walnut chair. As he sighed and sank down into the big overstuffed chair that was his favourite, his son, Maximilian, approached from his own room.

At six feet tall, the slender young man was jaunty in his crisp high-collar shirt, his long double-breasted jacket and cuffed trousers. He was the epitome of privilege. Henry looked up into the sixteen-year-old's handsome face. Clean-shaven, the young man's flowing blond locks, a finger in the eye of current style, lent him an air of rebellion. His piercing blue eyes, seemingly now on fire, put Henry in mind of his son's late mother and her Norse-Gael roots.

"And where did you disappear to this evening?" the elder man asked his son quietly.

"I couldn't take it any longer," the young man replied. "All of those people fawning and purring in your ear. It disgusts me."

Henry scowled. "Your father is a much-admired man of affairs. I cannot for the life of me comprehend why it is that you cannot share that sentiment."

"Much-admired, is it? For what? For lying and cheating the people? For becoming even wealthier from the labours of the poor of this country?

From growing ever fatter as the average man and woman toiled and fought the Hun? What is it that you ever did for this country, for its people, to become much-admired?" His disgust growing with each sentence, Maximilian Huddlestone spat out his final words.

The elder man sneered at his son. "You have benefited mightily from my work. Look at you, and look around. You live in this place because of it. You dress in those fine clothes because of it. You go to the finest schools because of it. Don't talk to me about living off the people. I gave this country the fighting machines it required to win the war. I deserve at least some praise for that, don't I?"

"Alright then. You built the machines of war, for sure. But in exchange you profited beyond all reason. Yes, I have enjoyed my share of the wealth as well, Father. But no more."

"What do you mean by that?" Henry snapped, his voice rising.

Max took a long breath and straightened his back, rising to his full height. Clenching his jaw and fixing his riveting eyes upon his father, he stepped closer to the man who was a good five inches shorter, peered down into his face and replied: "I mean I am leaving. I have had it with this place. With you. I don't need your money. My mother escaped your tyranny years ago by getting herself killed. And then you only cared about my brother. Sister and I mean nothing to you. Well, I won't stay here any longer. As if you'd give a tinker's damn." Max turned his back and strode to his room. He tore off his fine clothes and tossed them into a corner, then changed into a worn pair of blue jeans, a plaid work shirt and battered boots. He finished stuffing a duffle bag with a few belongings as his father came to the doorway and peered in.

"You won't last a week without me," Henry said in a voice that was again level and controlled, yet shaded with sorrow, although Max was too angry and occupied to detect it. "But I don't need you either. Go, if you want to. I don't care."

Max snatched up the bag and stormed out of the room, glancing at the portrait of his late mother on the wall. The violent emotion aroused by his father slipped away into waves of sadness that came at him whenever he thought of her passing. How many years had it been? Eight? Eight years since Eleanor Huddlestone had been gaily laughing and taking her little boy's hand as they stepped off the curb to cross Front Street. Eight years since the heavily soused driver of a Hud automobile had careened around the corner of York and slammed into her. She had had just a moment to react and in that moment, Eleanor Huddlestone had been able to scoop her son out of harm's way. It had been one of her husband's own cars that had been the instrument of her instant death.

Then had come the death of Max's elder brother, Winston, just two years ago. Huddlestone had been grooming Winston to take over the company and placed him on the plant floor in Oshawa where he was to learn the grittier aspects of the business.

Max had been at school, at Upper Canada College, when word came of his brother's death in a fiery explosion at the Hud Motor Car Company. His father did not even send a car to pick him up, to bring him home to join his father in mourning. Max retreated to his dorm room where he remained a week.

While she lived, his mother had protected Max and his sister, Margaret, from their father and after her death, Winston had taken the younger siblings under his wing, shielding them from their father's insidious indifference. Max had not really ever known his father because Henry Huddlestone had never paid him much attention. Everything had been done with Winston in mind. Henry Huddlestone was far too busy building an empire to concern himself with trifling matters such as the parenting of Max and Margaret.

But as his grief festered, Max was changed. In his sorrow and reflection, he had come to understand that all his father cared about was the company. He learned to hate his father and in fact blamed him for the deaths of his mother and brother. Not that there was any logic to that, but it had been, after all, one of his father's cars that struck his mother down, and an explosion in the Hud plant that took away his idolized brother.

Max put on an old woolen coat, then slammed the door to the suite as he left. Exiting the hotel, in the early hours of December 26, 1918, Max Huddlestone walked east into the silence of Front Street and made his way to the railway tracks that zig-zagged along the city's lakeshore. It was a moonless night and light snow was beginning to fall. Max walked between rows of rail cars and, standing in the darkness, he looked around and chose one he felt fit his needs. Tossing his duffle into the open black maw of a boxcar, he swung himself up and slid silently inside behind it. The darkness was so total he could not see the two men who sat silently against the car's wall to the left of the opening. His first hint that anyone else was there was when one of the men walked up and slipped a knife into him below the rib cage and violently pulled it back out. The other man grabbed Max's satchel, then rolled him to the edge of the opening and out onto the dirt and coal cinders. Max groaned, then passed out.

7

Grace and Peter
1919

THE QUINTE COUNTRYSIDE leaped to life in the early spring. Apple trees bloomed in pink and white, maples offered forth their keys, and barn cats gave birth. Lavender, Grace's favourite, sprouted outside the side door of the farmhouse. Grace and Peter O'Malley looked excitedly to a new season at Ballinskellig, their first as husband and wife. With the war over, Grace and Peter had soaring hopes for their farming future. Grace's friend, Alberta Johnson, had been visiting over the long Easter weekend and as the hours clicked down, she gathered her belongings before catching the train back to Toronto, back to finish her studies in European art history at the university. "Grace, you don't know how exhilarating it is to live and breathe the art of the Great Masters," Albie told her friend. "I look forward to the day I can go to Europe, to see their works for myself."

"Oh, Alberta Johnson, I know you. You will never leave this place. You were born to be here."

"No, Grace, you're wrong. This is my calling. Once I'm finished my studies, I will go. That is a certainty. My Italian is getting pretty darned good, too. I'm sure I'll be able to get a job in Rome or Florence. Or rather Firenze. That's the way they say it there. Fi-REN-zeh," she said with a flourish and a gay wave of her hands. "I want to work in one of the great galleries or art museums. It's my destiny."

Grace laughed but beneath the laugh was a tone of apprehension. "I don't know what I'd do without you here."

At that moment Peter and his father, Ben, walked into the kitchen, the big Irish setter, Ebenezer, trailing behind. "Whew, sure getting hot for this time of year," said Peter. "Dad, you'd better sit down and Grace'll get you a glass of water."

"Leave Grace alone, I can get it myself, my boy," insisted Ben. There was stiffness to his step, a slight grimace on his face, as he crossed the linoleum floor beneath the fir strip ceiling, to the pump room in the far corner. "I'm no invalid, you know."

The three younger people smiled. "Dad, you have got to start slowing down," Grace implored, a look of concern coming to her. Turning to her husband she said: "You know how he overdoes things so."

"Not much I can do about that," replied her husband. "You know Dad."

At that moment a thud came from the pump room and Peter and Grace raced to see what had happened. Ben O'Malley sat on the floor across from the sink, his forehead and cheeks streaming sweat, a dazed expression on his face. Ebenezer licked his face in sympathy. "What happened?" Ben asked.

Later, after Doctor Farr had been called in and checked Ben over, he left the older man's bedroom and motioned for Peter and Grace to follow him into the kitchen. "Peter, you've got to make your father take things easier. He's nearly sixty-five. He cannot keep working like this."

"Tell him that," Peter said, a tone of frustration in his voice. "I try but he won't listen. Thinks the farm will go to rack and ruin if he's not got his finger into every pie in the place."

"Next time it could be a stroke," said Doc Farr. "The summer heat's going to be hard on him."

Peter frowned, then turned to his wife. "Grace, I've got that farmers' meeting tonight in town. Can you keep an eye on him?"

"Don't worry, honey," she said. "I've got this."

Peter drove Alberta to the train station in town, gave her a hug and bid her farewell before he headed over to the Masons' Hall for the gathering. Pretty well every farmer from Cobourg to Kingston was expected. There would be a provincial election that fall and it had been decided the United Farmers clubs would run independent candidates across Ontario, hoping to elect enough members to the legislature to prevent another Conservative majority.

By the time Peter arrived at the Masons' Hall, the overflow crowd was spilling into the street. His best friend, Lloyd Porter, spotted him and waved him over. "Peter, hello," said Lloyd. "Boy, the fellows are sure mad. I've never seen the farmers around here so riled. If they had old Billy Hearst here tonight I wouldn't be surprised if someone didn't try to lynch him."

Peter whistled. He knew how unpopular the provincial government of Conservative Premier William Hearst was. It was failing them, they believed, cozying up to big business and taking farm votes for granted. If the United Farmers could elect a good rump of members, it could wrest concessions from Hearst and his gang in exchange for rural support.

"I'm looking forward to hearing this fella, Bowman," Peter told his friend. "I hear he makes a peck of sense."

Beniah Bowman, the member of the provincial legislature for Manitoulin Island and the first to be elected under the United Farmers banner, had come to speak at the meeting and was introduced to the charged-up crowd by Jed Beamer, one of their numbers from the Quinte area. By the time Bowman stood to speak, the throng of several hundred had been whipped into a frenzy by the litany of Tory government grievances Beamer read into the record. Bowman, an occasional Mennonite preacher who dabbled in fishing and lumber, had been elected earlier that year in a byelection, despite the vicious, take-no-prisoners campaign against him by the Hearst government. The crowd roared their approval, clapping and stomping their feet on the wooden floors till the old building shook like an autumn leaf. The building echoed with their fervor. With the hall filled to brimming, Peter and Lloyd made their way along the hall's exterior, to a window that had been left open to allow a cool breeze inside on the sultry night.

The friends peeked inside, watching while Beamer urged the crowd to hush. The din died down and Bowman, his dark, brooding eyes surveying his rapt audience, waited for the final murmurs and rustlings to turn to anticipatory silence.

"They don't know what they've done," Bowman said in a low voice to the hushed audience. "They don't know what it is they have unleashed." Then, his voice rising in controlled indignation, he continued: "The big-business government of Billy Hearst has ground you down for…the…last…time!" Farmers whooped and shouted their support and Bowman raised his arms to urge them to silence. He waited again. "Rural Ontario is angry. We are tired of the businessmen and the lawyers running our affairs." As the crowd again heated up and their outrage rose, Bowman's voice rolled out overtop of them: "The egg-suckers at Queen's Park have had their day!" he shouted, his right index finger prodding the air for emphasis. "It is time to bring back good government, government that is responsive to the will of the people."

When the cheers died down, Bowman listed off United Farmers demands in exchange for their support of any party, including more direct democracy with referendums and recalls, proportional representation in the legislature, support for the Ontario Temperance Act, and establishment of farm co-operatives. Peter went away energized by Bowman's words.

Back at home, his dark Irish eyes glowed while telling Grace about it. Grace smiled. "You sound as if you've made up your mind. Bring on the election."

* * *

Winnipeg

Twelve hundred miles away, a young man not yet seventeen chatted with the other young men who surrounded him in a Winnipeg street. The air was electric and the excitement rose while they shared stories of how they had arrived at this place. They had walked, come in horse-drawn wagons and motorized vehicles, and ridden the rails from east and west. They were on a mission. They were here because of a nationwide call for support, to tell big government and big business that they weren't going to take it any more. After the war, young men, many of whom had fought for Canada and Britain, returned home to discover the severe shortage of jobs. If they could find employment at all, wages were dirt poor. Inflation had made housing — if they could find it — and food unaffordable for many. And yet the businessmen who had profited from the wartime economy were not sharing the pain. It wasn't fair and something had to be done.

Yes, the pain. The young man clutched his stomach where the pain of injuries he had suffered when he was stabbed less than six months ago came back with a vengeance. He shook off the nausea that plagued him still, a telltale sign that he was not yet healed. Perhaps it was the adrenaline coursing through his body that triggered it. The adrenaline that came from knowing he was involved in a historic event.

Max Huddlestone had been lucky. After being stabbed by an unknown attacker in the boxcar of a westbound train, then tossed out of the doorway and into the gravelly dirt at the side of the tracks like so much rubbish, he lay there for hours. Blood seeped from his wound and he drifted in and out of consciousness. Luckily it had been a mild winter night, and a watchman for the railway had finally stumbled upon him, saving him from certain death. In a cold world, the man had shown his compassion. With a colleague's help, he had brought Max home, then called upon a friend, a disgraced former physician who had been drummed out of the profession after showing up drunk too many times. It was Max's lucky day that the disgraced man of medicine was that day sober and able to sew up his wounds with a darning needle and thread. In time and with the gentle care of Max's rescuer and his wife, the teenager had by-and-large healed. But his internal injuries, never properly tended to, were taking longer to self-correct.

Frustrated by his inability to find decent employment and determined to never again contact the father he had grown to hate, Max scrimped and saved the pennies he accumulated from the few odd jobs he could obtain. The kindly couple who had saved him refused to take any compensation but one night as they slept, Max left all the funds he had on their roughly finished homemade kitchen table and slipped away into the night. He left with little but the clothes on his back.

This time when Max hopped into a railway boxcar headed west, he made sure that no attackers lay in wait. He met others – young and old men alike – travelling in the same fashion. And this time, as he made his way west, hoping to find work in the Prairie wheat fields, he heard their stories of the thousands of others who were in the same predicament. He heard, too, of the plan to organize One Big Strike in Winnipeg, to bring to the country's attention the plight of those who were frustrated in their simple attempts to earn a living.

Now, as thousands of workers came together from all walks of life, from factory workers and returning army vets, to telegraph operators, store clerks and firemen, Max felt as though he was part of something very important. It would be a turning point, the moment when the authorities would have to understand that all these people wanted was to work for a decent wage.

The protesters knew they would need to contend with the concerted opposition of the privileged and the business elite. A few days before, when the workers had first walked off their jobs, a special force hired by the city and supplied by the T. Eaton Company with horses and baseball bats, had broken up a peaceful gathering and sent the participants scattering. But even after that, they had not counted on just how determined the protest movement would be. When another walkout was organized, big business and government rallied and put out the word that the strike was the work of foreign agitators, anarchists, Bolsheviks and syndicalists hell-bent on bringing down capitalism and foisting Marxism onto Canada.

Now, as Max stood with the men and waited, word spread that under government order, the authorities had arrested a handful of strike organizers. In protest, the men were all here in the streets, ready to march silently to City Hall in support of those arrested. "How can they do that?" Max asked a newly made friend, Tom Merritt. "How could they arrest those men? They weren't doing anything except standing up for their rights."

"Woodsworth says capitalism's not working," Tom replied. "He wants to try something he calls a co-operative way of managing things."

"Who's Woodsworth?" asked Max.

"J.S. Woodsworth. Runs that paper you and I was reading yesterday, the *Strike Bulletin.* He says human needs is bettern' people's property rights, whatever that means."

Max pondered what Tom had said. He thought about his father's company and how Henry Huddlestone had bragged so many times about how he'd made such a pile of money selling weapons, machinery and vehicles to the military during the war. Max thought about how he himself had tried so hard to find decent work and how there seemed to be nothing available. And when he was able to pick up something to do for a few days, how poor the wages had been. He had grown ashamed of his father. But no one he met on his journey had any idea of who Max Huddlestone was, let alone Max's connection to the man. Max had not told anyone and he never intended to. In silence, he would do his part to atone for his father's sins.

As they approached City Hall, Max heard a commotion up ahead. He craned his neck to get a better look. "What's going on?"

Tom was conferring with a man Max didn't know and in moments Tom turned to him and said: "Oleskow here says some of the fellers got hold of a streetcar and are tryin' to tip it over. Let's go see. But be careful. This time they've brought in the Mounties."

As the friends drew closer to the sounds of the commotion, Max heard the swoosh of a mounted policeman's baton pass close to the side of his head. He ducked. Shots rang out ahead and men began to yell and scatter. Others flailed harmlessly at the flanks of the Mounties' horses and two men grabbed a policeman and tried to drag him from his horse. Some of the police horses were spooked by the commotion and one reared up in alarm. More shots and a scream of pain came from Max's left. Tom fell to the ground.

Max ran to his friend's fallen figure and tried to shield him from the crush of men that closed in around them, men running, tripping and scrambling in their haste to escape the pandemonium. Max squatted and as he leaned over Tom, another man stumbled blindly forward and right overtop of them. The man fell to the ground with a bang and lay there stunned. "Help me get my friend out of here," Max shouted to two fellows who had stopped just short of joining the fallen man. Wordlessly, the two got on either side of Tom and lifted him. Max grabbed his feet and with a nod of the head, directed the way as they proceeded through the thickening and increasingly panicked crowd. They carried Tom down an alleyway, to a nearby barn, went inside and laid him on some hay.

Max's instinct had been to run, but he remembered the man who had come to his rescue back in Toronto just a few months ago. He would stay with his friend. Tom moaned with the pain of a shattered arm. "Tom, hang on, I'll find help," Max said.

He stumbled back into the alleyway and ran to the first door he found. He knocked gently and hoped someone would be willing to respond. With the chaos all about, he feared the natural reaction would be to stay hidden inside. But the gentleness of his rap seemed to work and in time a woman opened the door and peered out. Her grey hair was pulled back and the dress she wore, while worn, looked clean and well cared for. "Ma'am, I'm sorry for bothering you, but my friend needs help. He's hurt."

"Minute," she said, and shut the door. In moments she returned with a young man and said to Max: "My son was an army medic in the war. He can help."

Max saw that the young man wore army pants and boots. His face seemed drawn, his tawny eyes were sunken and held a far-away gaze. "Show me," he said.

Max led the man and his mother to the barn and they went inside where Tom had passed out from the pain. The man inspected Tom and declared, "His arm's shattered. I'll make a splint." Sending his mother to the house for some materials, the medic hunted for a few sturdy sticks in the barn and over the next few minutes fashioned a crude yet satisfactory splint for Tom's arm. The medic's mother had fetched a square of an old flannelette blanket and from this he fashioned a sling, then gently slid it onto Tom's arm. He turned to Max. "It's going to hurt him, but it'll mend proper now." The man handed Max a couple of powders in an envelope. "When the pain gets too bad for him, give him one of these," he ordered.

* * *

1920

Peter O'Malley was still ecstatic over the election results from the previous autumn. In the October 1919 vote, the Farmers had contested sixty-four of Ontario's one hundred and eleven constituencies and been victorious in forty-four. The governing Conservatives had been reduced to twenty-five, there were twenty-seven Liberals and eleven Labour members, as well as four independents. It was a far better result than they ever expected, but now what?

The United Farmers didn't even have a leader for the election. They had run as independent candidates and later had to decide how to proceed. Peter's friend and neighbouring farmer, Jed Beamer, said no one expected the movement would end up with the bulk of the seats. After all, the United Farmers had started off as nothing more than a club. Beamer said the rumour was that Ernest Drury, one of the founders of the United Farmers movement, would be asked to take command and try to work something out with the Labour members and independents. Before long, a working government had been established and the Farmers took office at Queen's Park with Drury serving as premier. Peter was certain better days were ahead for him and the others who tended Ontario's agricultural lands. He and his friend, Lloyd Porter, who worked with his own parents on their farm east of Shannonside, chatted optimistically about the future.

Grace smiled at the excitement that lit her husband's face as he talked about what could be achieved by the new government. While not particularly politically inclined herself, she enjoyed watching Peter's enthusiasm. The vicarious happiness she felt turned to her own joy, however, in the early months of 1920, when she suspected she might be expecting a child. A visit to Doctor Farr proved her suspicions correct and when she told Peter, the father-to-be was so excited he couldn't keep still.

He knew there would be hard work ahead as he took further control of Ballinskellig. With his own father finally heeding commands to take things easier, the previous growing season had been tough on Peter and he knew he must hire more help for the coming crop year. After all, with the apple business booming, it only made sense. The farm was a growing concern.

On September 4, Grace gave birth to a healthy baby boy and the proud parents decided to name him Peter, or "Petie" for short. Petie was a delight who rarely gave his parents a moment of grief. Right from the start, he pretty well slept through the night, took his feedings at regular times and as soon as his eyes could focus, peered up at everyone who stopped by to admire him in a serious expression of studying them fastidiously. It was almost as though little Petie already understood what would be expected of him. His expression was so serious, in fact, that Grace and Albie started to call him "the professor." Peter insisted his son would be raised to be a strong-backed farmer who was going to take over Ballinskellig and turn it into the grandest farm in Ontario. There would be no "professors" in his family, he said. But it was a statement that was always said with a twinkle in the eye and a tone of pride in his voice.

Winter came early that year. By the first week of December, snowdrifts filled in the rural roads and Peter had to get the old sled out of the drive shed and pack the democrat away for the winter. Buffalo robes were draped over the seats and irons were taken out of storage so they could be warmed on the wood stove and placed at the feet of passengers during trips into town and back.

Just before Christmas, Alberta Johnson's parents decided to throw a party on Christmas Eve. It had been a good crop year, the United Farmers and their allies were firmly in control at Queen's Park, and there were signs that the coming years could well mark a turning point for the farmers of Quinte and Shannon Bay.

While December had been cold, Christmas Eve was the coldest yet. The temperature hovered around zero Fahrenheit as Peter hitched horses Flossie and Ralph to the cutter and manoeuvred it around the side of the house just as Grace appeared at the door with little Petie. She had him well wrapped in several woolen blankets. As Peter sat in the front of the sled, Grace snuggled into the back seat with Petie and pulled a buffalo robe around them both to keep out the biting air. The sleigh runners squeaked sharply against the snow and a few snowflakes swirled as the horses carried their precious cargo down the O'Malley road to the Johnson homestead. In the distance they heard a lone wolf calling with its signature bark-howl.

It turned out to be a fine night of celebration and conviviality for the dozen couples that had been invited to join the Johnsons. Glasses of warm homemade soft cider were consumed and later, Will Johnson hauled out his bottle of port to share with the men and the few ladies who chose to imbibe in something stronger. Ontario had declared a prohibition on the sale of beer and hard liquor but wine, including ports and sherries, were excluded because of their widespread use for religious ceremonial purposes. And with Christmas upon them, said Johnson with a twinkle in his eye, what better reason could there possibly be to celebrate with a pinch of port.

The partying came to a close just before midnight and Alberta, home from university for the holidays, gave Petie a peck on the cheek. He was warm and sleepy and Alberta's brushing of his rosy baby's flesh awakened him momentarily. He opened his eyes, stretched his arms and gurgled contentedly. "Take good care of this little one," she told the proud parents. "He's something special."

"Oh, don't we know it," said Peter. "He's the love of our lives. I can't imagine going on without him."

Grace smiled up at her husband. She hugged her friend goodnight and urged her to come over Christmas Day. "We're not doing much this year," Grace said. "Just enjoying Petie's company."

"I'd love to join you," Alberta replied. "It sounds divine."

As they climbed into the sleigh, Peter urged Grace to come and sit up front with him. Grace demurred, saying she wondered whether the baby might not be best in the back seat where she could better wrap him up against the cold. "Oh, come on," said Peter. "Just wrap him up good and set him back there in the furs. He'll be nice and cozy."

Grace smiled and said that was probably alright. She took particular care to bundle the baby well in his blankets, then pulled the buffalo robe snugly across to further protect him from the crisp cold. Then she got up onto the front seat next to her husband and they snuggled close on the way home. In the windless silence, husband and wife gazed up together and watched the trillions of stars set the heavens ablaze. "Look," Grace said, pointing to the northern horizon where waves of colour marked the shimmering Northern Lights. They watched together until turning in unison and gazing into one another's eyes.

Peter said quietly: "Maybe it's time for another one. A little sister for Petie. Or another boy, I don't rightly care."

"So soon?" replied Grace. "You know I couldn't help out at the farm during harvest time as much as I would have cared to do this past year. Another pregnancy now … I don't know."

During the harvest, Grace's job was to set up tables under the giant maple trees in the front yard and serve a hot cooked meal at mid-day for the itinerant workers. It had been a tradition at the O'Malley farmstead for decades and once word spread, a tradition that always ensured they attracted the best workers available. Grace had been expected to manage the service but being pregnant this past year, then giving birth in the midst of harvest time, meant she had not been able to perform much of those duties. Her mother had frequently come over to help and the daughters of other farm families were hired on occasionally.

"The farm's doing fine," her husband responded. "I can maybe hire one of Alfred Taylor's girls to help out some."

"Wouldn't that be shirking my wifely duties?" Grace teased. "Could you ever forgive me?" As Pete looked straight ahead and gave the horses a flick of the reins, Grace gazed into what she could see of his face, his head well wrapped in a thick woolen scarf. As they began to move, he turned toward her and looked into her eyes, slipped his right hand into her left hand and squeezed.

"Ma'am, you do all of your wifely duties right well," he said. Grace smiled back shyly.

The ride home was one of the most exquisite moments either of them could remember. Despite the cold, neither wanted it to end. Finally, Peter pulled the sleigh up to the side of the house, Grace jumped down and slipped into the back seat. She reached into the wrappings and gently lifted the baby. "Oh, he's cold," she told her husband. "I'd better get him inside." As Grace took the baby into the house, Peter took the horses and sled back to the drive shed.

With the horses stabled for the night, Peter turned toward the house. Trudging through the snow, he made up his mind that he would tell Grace that yes, he believed they should have another baby, immediately. Have two, then stop and think about the future, he'd say. If it was another boy, the future of Ballinskellig would be assured. If it was a girl, he'd love her just as much. He looked up at the house and was surprised to see Grace had not yet lit the kerosene light in their upstairs bedroom where they kept Petie's cradle, the one Uncle Jimmy had built for him. Pete was surprised, but surprise turned to alarm as he neared the side entranceway, the one that led into the kitchen, and heard an unfamiliar sound. It sounded like a wail of anguish. Above it, Ebenezer let out an eerie howl that put Peter in mind of the wolf they'd heard earlier.

Pete opened the door and stepped inside, where Grace was standing holding the baby. She sobbed, then looked up at him with tear-stained face. "Why?" she asked. "How?"

Peter raced to his wife's side and took the baby gently from her. The child's complexion was no longer the rosy pink colour it had been earlier. Instead it was a lurid blue. His lips were purple and his eyes were tightly shut. His body was turning cold.

"He's dead, Peter," said Grace. "He must have suffocated in the buffalo robe. Peter, we did this. We did this!"

8

Apart

It is five days after Christmas. The numbing cold that pervaded the countryside over the holiday has given way to a thaw. Icicles drip and snowbanks collapse into crystalized mounds that grow soggy in the weak winter sun. Clots of sodden snow tumble from tree branches.

Outside the Ballinskellig farmhouse, horse-drawn sleds are lined up along the roadside. Inside, in the parlour, friends and relatives of Grace and Peter O'Malley gather around the tiny pine box that sits on a table in the corner. The box lacks ornamentation; its contours are square and sterile. The only simple nod of recognition to its solemn importance is the dark shade of stain that Ben O'Malley has applied. This is the box that contains the body of Petie, a little baby barely three months old whose life has been ended in one imprudent moment. The coffin's lid remains shut. Ebenezer lies on a mat beneath the table and whimpers, sensing the solemnity of the moment. The room hangs heavy in grief and regret. Grace O'Malley sits on a straight-backed chair, one brought from the dining room table to be set at the head of the little coffin. Dressed in black, a veil hiding the tears that stain her face, she occasionally looks up and acknowledges the condolences the visitors present to her as tribute.

The parlour is the best room in the simple farmhouse and as such has been chosen for the wretched deed, the funeral of a baby. Flower-patterned wallpaper adorns the walls. Heavy drapery covers the two tall windows, mirror images of one another, that look out onto the front yard. A chesterfield, tables and chairs have been removed from the room to make space for the mourners to stand, leaving only the single table with its miniature coffin and the straight-backed dining chair that offers Grace some infinitesimal degree of relief from her terrible duty. The only thing missing is the baby's father, Grace's husband. No one knows where Peter has gone.

Albie alternates between standing silently next to her friend, occasionally placing her arm around the grief-befuddled mother, and thanking mourners for coming by. She, plus the presence of Grace's parents, Eleanor and Will Campbell, and Peter's father, Ben, at least make the day bearable for her. Her husband has abandoned her. In the moments she needs him most, he is nowhere to be found.

* * *

In a city miles away, Peter O'Malley tries to shake off the haze of a drunken binge. His face is coarsened with five days of stubble. In a moment of clarity he wonders what he has done. How could he have run out on his wife? At the moment he realized their infant son was dead, he recalls handing the tiny body back to his wife and stumbling out the door. He remembers walking to town and wondering all the way how he could have been so rash, so reckless as to tell her to put the baby in the back seat by himself. He might as well have murdered the child by his own hand. He can never forgive himself so how could he ever expect his wife to? This good woman, the love of his life, is gone from him forever. He sinks back into a haze of self-recrimination, of self-loathing. The stench of shame and guilt will always hang over his life, will transcend any good he does from this moment onward. He ponders suicide, then rejects it as too good for him. His proper punishment is to suffer.

* * *

Peter returns home without comment or explanation two weeks to the day after the baby's death. When he walks through the door, Grace is in the kitchen ironing some of her clothes. She turns from her work to see him enter and without a word, turns back to her toil. Peter is dead to her. At this moment she is not even interested in an explanation. None is offered anyway. The house is home to them both and here they will both live. But separately, unencumbered by words, bereft of love.

* * *

1922

The silence, the blame and the guilt that now marked Grace and Peter's marriage extended throughout 1921 and into the next year. Grace fell into a routine of taking a weekly trip into town for supplies, Peter got away one night a week to play poker and the farm was operated in much the same way as it had always been. But over it all, a cold hush settled menacingly.

Albie was no longer around for comfort. After she finished her studies in the spring of 1921, she bade farewell to Grace, saying it was finally time for her to make that long-planned relocation to Italy. No matter how long it took her to adjust and to find a job, she said, she would take it. Grace bade her friend a teary farewell and wished her all the best. Letters passed frequently between the two.

One evening in the summer of 1922, while Peter was in town, in the back room at O'Malley's Hardware where the poker games were held, he was having a run of good luck with the cards. Large sums of money were never exchanged by the gents as none of them had enough to be able to afford to lose. It was the usual penny ante stuff, but to Peter it was the achievement of a big win that mattered, not the money. Near the end of the evening he picked up his cards and studied them. Two black aces and two black eights. He blanched. Dead man's hand. The same hand that Wild Bill Hickok is said to have drawn just before he was shot from behind in Deadwood, Dakota.

"Look what I've got." he told the others when he set his cards down. The others laughed, so Peter laughed too. No one truly believed the superstition, they told themselves.

It was the very next week when Grace took Ebenezer and hiked one evening across the fields to the Campbell home to pay a call on her parents. Emotionally, she was feeling better than she had since before the incident. She had a nice enough visit with Eleanor and Will, and they were all deeply engaged in conversation about myriad topics that studiously avoided Petie. Thunder began to rumble in the distance. It had been a hot and oppressively humid day and an evening thunderstorm was not unexpected. Ebenezer's ears pricked up at the menacing sound. He looked up expectantly at Grace and she said to him: "Come on, Ebbie, we'd better be getting home." With the threat of a storm, her mother wanted her to stay the night but Grace said no, she had to get up early in the morning to hitch a ride into town with Ruth Taylor and get groceries. She would just take the shortcut across the field again and be home in no time.

As Grace and Ebbie walked across the field that was planted in clover to rest and nourish the soil in preparation for a crop the next year, the sky darkened. Massive thunderheads billowed in from the northwest and the wind began to whip up. Grace hastened her pace, not wanting to be caught in a sudden downpour she now felt was about to hit. Ebbie barked and ran ahead, as if he was beckoning her to pick up her pace.

All Grace could recall afterwards was the feeling of spinning like a child's top. Everything around her turned white, a dazzling white that changed the storm-blackened evening into day. She later said she had the sensation of flying through the air, then there was a bright flash. She tried to move but nothing worked. Her arms and legs went numb. She had no idea whether she was standing, sitting or lying down. They told her it rained as she lay prone on the ground but Grace said she had no hint of that. All she could see was rivers of red flowing down in front of her eyes.

Ebbie nearly jumped out of his hide at the deafening crack of thunder and simultaneous lightning. He turned back and stood transfixed at the sight of his mistress lying on the ground, then ran to her, barking furiously. Grace heard none of the commotion.

Nearby, a man ran down the O'Malley road, avoiding the puddles that were forming and trying to make it back to the Ballinskellig bunkhouse before he got totally soaked through by the torrential downpour. He instinctively ducked and shuddered when the terrific crack of thunder and accompanying flash of lightning told him the storm was right on top of him. Through the heavenly din, he heard a dog barking furiously, its sharp calls interrupted with whines and howls of anguish. The man looked across the field from where the sound seemed to be coming and there, amidst the rain-flattened clover, he spied the dog, standing over a figure lying on the ground, a figure from which smoke was now rising in the rain. What on earth? he thought.

Was the storm playing tricks on him? No, he realized this was no mirage: there was a figure out there in the field, and it was not his imagination that it lay on the ground. The man ran across the field, his boots caking with mud from the suddenly sodden field. The dog continued to bark and whine as the man reached the figure and saw it was a woman. Her clothing was smoking, scorched. The dog suddenly turned quiet and looked up at him as it stood over the prone figure. The man bent down and leaned over the woman. The dog seemed to sense this man represented help and suspended its instinct to protect.

Grace stared straight ahead, unable to move her head or her eyes. In slow motion she could see through the red rivers that impeded her vision, saw that something, or someone was looming overtop of her. Like an angel, she said later. A white glow hovered like a halo around the figure's head.

The dog somehow comprehended the man's good intentions and stepped back as if to make way for him. The man put his arms beneath Grace and picked her off the ground. Despite the cool rain, her body radiated heat. Her long auburn hair was plastered to the sides of her head. Blood covered her face. Using his strong legs and back, the man slowly straightened, while the rain ceased as quickly as it had commenced. The wind immediately stopped. The man walked back to the road and gently carted his precious cargo to the O'Malley house that stood across a field from the bunkhouse where he was living during the harvest season. He made his way to the side door and kicked it with his mud-caked boot.

"Mr. O'Malley," he called out. "Mr. O'Malley."

Peter came to the door and reeled back, horrified at the sight. He did not at first recognize his wife, lying there in the stranger's hold, her clothing scorched, her face a terrible bloody mess and water dripping from the two of them, the rescued and the rescuer. Only when he looked down and saw Ebenezer, his long hair caked to his slim body, did he realize it was Grace. Peter guessed the man was one of his seasonal workers, a newcomer he'd never met. "Bring her in," he said as he opened the door for the man and stepped aside. Ebbie squeezed himself through the doorway. "This way," Peter said. "Don't worry about your boots," he added, leading the man to the downstairs bedroom that had become his own. Peter stripped off the quilt, one he was told his mother had made, and motioned to the man to put her down. "What happened?" he asked in a weak voice.

"I, I think it was lightning," said the man.

Peter said he was going to fetch Doc Farr and asked the man to stay with her until he returned. It was a risk, leaving the stranger with his injured wife, but there was no choice. After Peter left, the man hunted down some rags and came back, gently cleaning up Grace's face and arms as Ebbie watched him carefully. When the man first touched her face he quickly pulled away. While her body had been unusually warm, the skin of her face was hot and as he wiped the blood away he could see a dark red scar on the right side of her forehead.

Grace still stared straight ahead but now she was beginning to regain feeling. "My teeth," she mumbled. "They hurt."

Peter was back with Doc Farr within half an hour. As the doctor began to examine her, Grace suddenly screamed out. "It burns!" she shouted. "It's burning me alive!"

Doc Farr touched her and felt the heat. "My word," he could only say.

The man who had brought her stepped shyly back from the bed and out the doorway. Peter came out and shook his hand. "I can't thank you enough," he said. "You saved her. What's your name, sir?"

"Huddlestone," said the man. "Max Huddlestone. I arrived just yesterday. I work for you, sir."

"Well Max Huddlestone, you've got a job here anytime you like. I can never thank you enough for what you've done."

"It was nothing, sir," Max replied. "The lady was in need."

Inside the bedroom, Grace asked Doc Farr in a weak and quavering voice: "What happened to me? I can't move. And all I feel are my teeth and this terrible heat inside me."

The doctor shook his head. "Never seen anything like it," he said, "but Grace, I think you were struck by lightning."

In the coming days as Ebbie stood vigil, Grace slept often but would frequently be awakened by searing pain. Doc Farr had left a sedative that was to be administered when it became unbearable. Her legs, her back, her arms, her head, they all ached in a way she had never before experienced. She would scream out when the pain came to her in waves, then relax as it subsided as quickly as it had come. When she touched her forehead, she traced the line of the scar down the right side. She lay in bed for three days before she was able to move her legs. Doc Farr insisted she try to sit up, maybe get up from bed with the help of others and see how her legs worked. The first time, Grace collapsed and the doctor and Peter had to help her back to bed. But in two more days, she was actually able to stand unaided for a short time. The first time she looked in a mirror, she wondered at the red mark just beneath her hairline. When she touched it, her skin prickled.

Grace's parents came by the house twice a day, and Pete's father stopped each evening to visit. He had moved to a small bungalow in town soon after the couple were married, in order to give his son and daughter-in-law "your own space." Peter had heard the stories about how his grandfather Sam had tyrannized Peter's parents and assumed his own father, once the victim of such tyranny, was determined to give the children their space as they started their lives together. Other neighbours sometimes stopped in to say hello. Grace did not recognize all of them. She seemed most comfortable with her parents and they took turns helping her to eat and held her hand when the pain became excruciating. Doc Farr had left Grace a modest supply of morphine, which he advised should be used only sparingly when absolutely needed to ease the pain. Later, he came by with some cocaine drops he said would wean her off the morphine. "The wonders of modern medicine," marvelled Eleanor Campbell.

Ebbie often placed his muzzle on the bed next to her and Grace found comfort simply stroking him and holding tufts of his hair in her hand. She rarely spoke in those first days.

Pete's eldest sister, Lucy, arrived from the city to spend a few days and while Grace slept, Pete enjoyed spending evenings chatting with the woman who had raised him to his teen years. It had been lonely at the farm with the wall of silence that had built up between him and his wife. He also enjoyed the company of his sister, Anna, who brought her eldest child, Arthur, for a short visit. Arthur enjoyed listening to his mother and Aunt Lucy talk about the old days growing up on the farm and snippets of Ballinskellig's earlier inhabitants that had been passed down to them.

Before he knew it, Peter was tending to his wife just as if it was the old times, before the incident. He often served her meals and sat beside her as she ate, encouraging her to eat everything on her plate to keep up her strength. Grace was guarded but grateful for his attention.

A letter arrived from Alberta Johnson in Italy. "My dear Grace: The most wonderful thing has happened. I have fallen in love! And believe me, he's hotsy-totsy."

Grace was flabbergasted. "Well, that didn't take long," she said to her mother.

"I was attending a party with my art group at the Uffizi Gallery in Firenze, turned around and there he was. The most handsome man I've ever set eyes on! Yes, Grace, even more handsome than your Peter, if I may be so bold as to say. And guess what? He's a count! Count Roberto Ribigghini. Loaded!

"Now to be sure, there are more counts here in Italy than you would ever be able to imagine. But this one is really the berries. My girlfriend here, Dora, she's a fellow art aficionado from New England, says the count is a real egg! That means he's old rich, my dear. And he's fallen head over heels for little ole' me. Can you imagine?"

For the first time in ages, Grace actually smiled and then laughed at her friend's words. She read on and when she finished the letter said to her mother: "I guess that art program really paid off."

Eleanor laughed. "Happy to see you're feeling better, my love."

For a while, it appeared as though Grace's brush with mortality had started to break the ice between her and Peter, at least insofar as he was concerned. Grace was less certain. Lucy listened as Peter explained his own version of what had happened between him and Grace, an explanation in which he judiciously omitted to explain his own absence after the baby's death. Lucy only asked him once about it and Pete's reply was that it was a moment in time that he would forever regret. "You don't need to tell me, but you need to talk to Grace about it," Lucy had said. She encouraged him to take the opportunity to "mend fences." Pete looked far off and did not respond.

While he was gracious and solicitous to his wife's needs during her recovery, Grace remained distant and troubled. Her husband, the man she had loved, had abandoned her in her time of need. She was devastated by the baby's unexpected death and when she needed him, he had simply not been at her side. She never did find out where he had disappeared to for those two weeks. She actually tried to talk to him about it, but he brushed her words aside and changed the topic. That's it, Grace decided then. No sense in expecting he'll ever change. Yet still, she was appreciative that he was being kind to her when she needed his help. Appreciative, at least for the moment.

When Peter once again raised the matter of another child, though, Grace cut him off quickly. "I don't see that happening anytime soon," she said. Peter backed off. There would be plenty of time to discuss it later.

Grace wrote back to Alberta and congratulated her on finding love in Italy. She turned to the difficult matter of describing what happened to her, starting off by saying: "Now don't worry because I'm fine now…"

But the fact of the matter was that she wasn't exactly fine. Not at all. There were moments when blinding headaches overcame her and forced her to stop what she was doing and to lie down in a darkened room with her eyes shut. In moments like these, she imagined she heard music and over time, was able to identify what she heard as *Brahms' Lullaby*. It was the tune Grace had loved to hum to baby Petie, and to play occasionally on the piano. In her grief Grace wondered: Was Petie now speaking to her from the grave? Was he trying to comfort his mother? It seemed silly and Grace had never been one to believe in such possibilities. Still, she was increasingly possessed by the tune that played over and over in her head. And she was obsessed with the memory of Petie. Regret hovered over her like a huge black cover that threatened to smother her, just as Petie had been smothered. Why had she not simply held the baby on the sleigh ride home that night? If she had, all would have been well. Instead, she had heeded her husband's call to come sit by his side and leave the baby in the back seat. The baby's tiny hands had likely pulled the heavy buffalo blanket onto his face, and he had suffocated. It had been Grace's fatal mistake, caused by her own weakness and inability to say no to her husband.

Over time, the musical selections inside her head broadened to include more Brahms sonatas. On one particularly difficult day, Grace's head was filled to splitting with segments from the German composer's piano and violin opuses. It was driving her mad.

Grace had been infatuated by Brahms ever since she was a little girl. Back then, her mother took her to visit Mrs. Scott, a friend along the concession road who filled her spare time and made extra money by teaching piano to a few local children. Mrs. Scott would sit Grace down on the piano bench next to her and guide the child's hands across the keys to play wonderful music. Grace, like Mrs. Scott, was particularly enthralled by Brahms' piano sonatas. Will Campbell, Grace's father, had inherited his mother's piano although he never learned to play it himself and neither did her mother, Eleanor. Over time, Grace did learn to play it, under the tutelage of Mrs. Scott. When she married Pete and moved into the O'Malley house, the piano came with her.

Now those Brahms tunes came back to her. At first she feared they would not come as the comforting melodies they had once been and that instead, they would strike out at her, mocking her for being so careless with baby Petie. Over time though, as she became ever more drawn to the piano, drawn to Brahms's compositions, they became a comfort, a link to her child. They carried her through those first few horrible months and made her life bearable.

Albie wrote that she felt terrible for not being in Shannonside during her friend's time of need but Grace said not to worry, she had plenty of help. She and Ruth Taylor were becoming close friends and companions. Their conversations on their weekly trips to town and back had become periods of healing and comfort. When time allowed, Grace added, she would love to see Albie pay a visit, but there was no hurry.

* * *

1923

An uneasy truce settled over Grace and Pete's marriage, but it was little more than that. While a cordialness slipped back into the home as winter turned to spring and spring into summer, Grace still insisted they maintain their separate bedrooms. The itinerant farm workers began to straggle back as the workload picked up and Grace resumed the practice of making the main midday meal for them. The first apples began to ripen in the August sun.

One day a young man arrived at the farm looking for work. He approached Pete's foreman, Mel Brewster, and reminded him he'd been there the previous year. Brewster recognized him immediately. The man was tall and sturdy. His shockingly blue eyes seemed to burrow right into Mel's own. His blond hair was scraggly and unusually long for the era, kind of old-fashioned, Mel thought. Like some character from the Old West, like pictures he'd seen of Wild Bill Hickok. Or Buffalo Bill Cody. The man had grown a moustache since the previous year and its bristles had come in darker than his fair hair.

"Sure I remember you, son," said Brewster. "You're the one saved the missus last year. The boss said you're welcome back anytime. And so far as I'm concerned, you're one of the best workers I've got. Come on in and settle down."

Despite his fair hair, Max Huddlestone's complexion was tanned to a deep leather tone. He spent much of the year out in the sunshine, travelling from one harvest to the next, from Florida to California, from Ontario and back to the Canadian Prairies. He couldn't imagine the miles he put on by foot every year – boots were just a necessary expense of the trade – and when it came time to pack up and move to the next job, an empty boxcar was his preferred mode of transportation. Once he got close to his destination, Max would get to a main road, put out his thumb and rarely had any trouble catching a ride. It was the way of the time: strangers helping strangers. Max was at home in the out-of-doors. Unless it was raining, he preferred sleeping out in the fresh air to bunking down with the other workers. He was free and he was beholden to no one. But it was a lonely life, one bereft of any serious female company. Friendships were fleeting.

Grace had never been introduced to her rescuer and had no reason to recognize Max the first day he showed up for the noon meal. Max nodded, but said nothing to her as he passed by and took his plate of potatoes, carrots and a chunk of beef covered in gravy. There was a hunk of bread on the side. Homemade, of course. She did, however, glance up into the tall stranger's face and smiled. "New here," she said more as a statement than a question. Max smiled back and moved along.

Pete came by the bunkhouse at the end of the second day Max was there to say hello. His foreman had mentioned "that fella that saved Mrs. O'Malley" was back and had quickly settled in to his normal vigorous pace. "Wish'd I had a dozen like him," said Brewster.

Pete sized the man up and asked how he found his set-up. "I try to make things comfortable for the men," Pete said.

"Better than most," replied Max. "The farm worker would be a lot better off if every employer paid as much attention to work conditions as you did, Mr. O'Malley. In some places down in the States they send the coppers after us when all we ask for is fairness."

Pete paused to think that over, then said: "Farmers around here want to be fair. We want our men to be fair to us. We elected a Farmers' government here in Ontario and for the last four years they've been working hard to make things better for the average people. They pushed through more electric lines, made better rural roads, explained to the rest of the people why a strong farm economy is good for everyone. They set up a bank that doesn't send farmers away when they come asking for some reasonable help. They set up allowances to help widows and children. Gave women better wages in the cities. It's the way I like to do things here on the farm. I'm sorry the Farmers lost the election back in June. Hope things don't go back to the way they were, now the Conservatives are back. Hope they made their mark the little time they were there."

"I marched in the big strike out in Winnipeg," said Max. "Back in nineteen. Not sure I ought'ta be telling you that, Mr. O'Malley. You might not much appreciate it that I hooked up with those fellows. But all they were trying to do was make it better for the little guy. Not sure it helped much, though."

"I don't rightly believe in Bolshevism," said Pete. "That's the honest truth and I don't mind saying it. I wouldn't much like to hand over my farm to some fellers in Toronto so they can tell me how to run it. But I sure believe in being fair."

"Then we'll get along just fine," Max replied. The men shook hands and Pete took his leave. He mentioned to Grace the fella who'd found her was back.

The next evening, Max was putting away some equipment in the barn when Grace entered the cavernous space holding a kerosene lantern, Ebenezer trailing. She spotted someone over in a dark corner and said: "Oh. I didn't know anyone was here. I was just hunting for something I thought was out here."

"Just me, Mrs. O'Malley. Max. Don't mind me. Just putting things away for the night."

Grace immediately recognized the shaggy blond hair that set the man out from Pete's other workers and recalled her husband had mentioned it when he told her that her "rescuer" had returned. "Oh, so you're the man my husband says I'm obliged to for saving my life last year. I could have died from exposure out there in that field. I can't thank you enough."

"Not so sure it was all that dramatic," replied Max. "But you were in need so I came to your assistance." Max noticed Ebbie just then and bent down to scratch the dog's ears. Ebbie's eyes closed in pleasure and he wagged his feathery red tail. If Grace hadn't remembered this kind stranger, the dog seemed to have.

As Max walked out of the shadows and back into the evening's dimming light, a final ray from the setting sun struck his face. It glowed and Grace was immediately reminded of the angel — her word — who had appeared when she most needed him. The angel whose head was bathed in a halo of light, the one who had come to her in her moment of need. She remembered her mother's words: "Everyone encounters Jesus once in their life," Eleanor always said. "Grace, I guess that was your time."

"No, I'm quite certain," Grace said to Max. "I was in bad shape out there. You saved me. I still get flashbacks when the shooting pains return. In my legs and arms mostly. And sometimes I can't recall things. Things I should know as good as my own name." She reached up to her forehead and moved aside a lock of auburn hair. "And I've still got this."

Max came closer and stared intently at her forehead, to a spot where a nasty red scar marked where Grace had been struck by a bolt of lightning. He touched it and their hands brushed. Ebenezer growled a warning. Max pulled away and lowered his gaze.

"Sorry," he said shyly.

Grace liked the touch. It was gentle and warm. She hadn't allowed Peter to touch her since the incident, since the night little Petie died. And to be fair, she missed the sensation.

"I'd better be getting back to the bunkhouse," Max said. "Feels like it might rain tonight. You'd better get back to shelter too, Mrs. O'Malley."

"Grace," she said then. "Call me Grace."

Max laughed then. "Grace O'Malley, is it? Well isn't that the limit."

"What do you mean?" Grace asked, taken aback by the man's laughter. She didn't know whether to take offence.

"Oh, I didn't mean anything disrespectful by it, ma'am. It's just the name is familiar, from my childhood. The story goes that back in Ireland nearly four hundred years ago, Grace O'Malley was a notorious pirate. She was known for attacking the English after they did her some wrong or other. You know the English, they were always doing that to the Irish. My mother used to tell me the story when I was a little boy. I hadn't thought about it in years, until you mentioned your name. It reminded me of my mother. She was Irish. Gould, her name was. I'm told they came to Ireland with the Vikings, from the Nordic countries. Guess that's where I got my blond hair."

Grace then laughed too. "Well, I can assure you, sir, that I don't do much plundering these days. And in spite of my husband's Irish heritage, I'm actually quite partial to the English. My family's Scotch – Campbells – so I guess we ought to keep a wary eye out for the English too. Well, goodnight, then."

"Goodnight," he replied.

They parted then, with Grace and Ebenezer heading back down the road one way to the house and Max going the other way to the bunkhouse. As she neared the driveway, Grace had a powerful urge to turn around for one final glimpse. When she turned right into the drive she could stand it no more and turned her head. She caught her breath and stopped dead in her tracks. Down the road and right in front of the barn where she had left him, stood the man, his gaze still on her. In the dying light of evening, he waved and she waved in return before heading toward the house. "I didn't even ask his name," she realized.

Max's heart palpitated when she waved. It was lonely on the road and he missed the company of a woman. He savored the short moment their eyes locked. It had been so long since he'd had anything that approached the definition of a conversation with a woman, even longer since he'd experienced a woman's touch.

Grace entered the house. She had a sudden urge to listen to the piano. No, not listen to the piano exactly, but to play it. This was something she had done only rarely in the past months, since the lightning strike. Right after Petie's death, she had played the piano a great deal. Her infatuation with Brahms had deepened after that incident. She realized then that the baby's death had come to be known as The Incident. Everything was measured as happening before The Incident or after The Incident. She shuddered to think that such a terrible event had taken on such an eerie and macabre importance. She hoped it had not trivialized the baby's very existence, turned it into a circus sideshow.

Still, it was a convenient marker in her life. And now, she was compelled to go to the piano, the Campbell family piano, sit down and play. With Pete in town for some meeting or other, she was alone in the house. Grace began to touch the keys, softly. She didn't quite know what she was going to play but within moments it came to her that she was picking out the first notes of Brahms' Lullaby. The music seemed to course from her cognizance and through her fingers onto the keys. She was glad that she knew the notes off by heart because she could never have been able to read the notes in her Brahms playbook through the tears that streamed from her eyes and obliterated her vision. Drops fell onto the keys.

* * *

The Encounter

Several evenings after Grace encountered her rescuer in the barn, she cleaned up the supper dishes and took a wander down past the south pasture and along the Shannon River toward the woods. Ebenezer was nowhere to be found and she assumed he was off chasing gophers through the fields. She had not mentioned to Peter that she was going anywhere, because she didn't really want to speak to him that evening. She needed her solitude. She watched a flock of swallows diving down to the water's surface and then pulling up quickly and soaring skyward. She knew they were diving for insects but often wondered if they additionally gained some sense of exhilaration from their near misses with the water and other objects. Their control in flight was remarkable to her.

Grace found a spot near a rock that gave her a vantage point to enjoy the swallows' show and didn't hear the man approaching from behind, from the woods. She started when his deep voice called quietly: "Is this a private gathering?"

She turned and looked up into the face of her rescuer. She had thought of him multiple times since their chance encounter in the barn. She smiled. "Oh, hello. No, please join me." Max came and sat next to her.

"I realized after we met the other night," she said. "I never asked your name."

"Max. It's Max."

"Max," she smiled. "Such a strong name. Well, Max, I'm just enjoying the show," she said. "That's what I call what the swallows do. They perform first thing in the morning and in the evening, before dusk. Diving for insects. But I like to think they're doing it just for me. Putting on their show. It amuses me."

A breeze came up and carried Grace's fresh scent toward Max. It smelled slightly of lavender. "Are you a bird-lover?" he asked.

"Oh, yes. Very much. I think my favourite are the blue jays. Yes, I know they squawk terribly, but they're the most beautiful birds, don't you think? They swoop in and out of the cedar trees out back of the house. In the winter I love to watch them from my kitchen window. And cardinals, they're lovely too. But these little fellows, they hold a special place in me. I adore the way they plunge and dive for the insects. They're so brave and so graceful."

"I enjoy the different birds I see on my travels," Max said. "There's a different type of jay out West. And I love the hummingbirds out there. They have so many of them. They're the cutest things."

"You've been out West?" Grace asked, intrigued rather than just making small talk.

"Yes. I travel a lot. You see I move with the harvests. I go from Florida and out to California, then up here to Ontario and then Quebec, then out to the Prairies. After that it's time to head back down South. I work in the orange orchards, pick strawberries and celery, cherries, apples, then I get to the wheat fields. You name it … I've picked it," he laughed. "The apples are my favourite. Not too big and not too small. Just fit into your palm properly. I can develop a rhythm. You might say I'm an outdoors kind of guy. I would never survive in an inside job."

A broad smile came onto Grace's face. "No wonder you're so tanned. It's so unusual with your blond hair. It makes you look very … avant garde."

Max felt himself blush but Grace would never know, it did not show through his bronzed skin. He covered his shyness by looking down and there he spotted a grasshopper that had leapt onto Grace's leg. He brushed it aside just as she noticed it herself and went to swat at it. Their hands touched and reflexively Max closed his fingers around hers. For a second he panicked, but Grace failed to object, so he left his large, calloused hand wrapped around her delicate one. She looked into his clear blue eyes that seemed to penetrate into her. Her stomach took a gentle, happy flip.

While Grace possessed the delicacy of a city lady of means, Max wasn't tricked for a moment. He knew that before him sat a farm wife, someone who was accustomed to hard work and long hours. He could see the quiet determination in this woman's demeanor and the strength she exuded. Her small hands, wrists and arms were sinewy, familiar with toil. Her green eyes put him in mind of emeralds. They were gentle, yet resolute. He had a feeling that when Grace O'Malley put her mind to something, she was unwavering to the end.

Max leaned in closer to her. What would she do? For a heart-stopping moment she remained still as the night. Had he made a mistake? Should he draw back, just get out of here? Yet there was a confidence in him, a belief that if he leaned further and stole a kiss, this woman would not object. He sensed it with every part of his being. Besides, it had been so long and he decided it was worth the risk. He drew closer and Grace responded with an infinitesimal move toward him. He was right, and her simple subtle motion was all he needed. He gently nuzzled her and the warmth of her skin aroused his every sense. Her lavender scent intensified. His lips brushed hers. He put his big work-hardened arms around her in an embrace and pulled her close.

For a fleeting moment she thought of Peter, of the love they had shared before ... before the incident. That relationship felt desiccated now; it was a moment that had fragmented and blown away as an autumn leaf would. Gone for good now, she knew. It could never be recaptured. The loss of a child they could have — and should have — faced together. But regardless of what had happened that night in the sleigh, Peter had then abandoned her. She could never forgive him. She could never forget.

Grace had not felt a man's arms, his lips, she had not breathed in and felt the exhilaration she felt now, for a very long time. She sighed and responded to him by pressing him to her.

As two lonely people held one another in the dimming light of a warm September evening, the sound of the night insects filled the moist, motionless air. There was no rustle of a tree's leaf, no sound other than the nightlife and their own intensified breathing. It felt so good to hold onto one another, each of them thought. To share a yearning. To be wanted. To be desired and longed for again. Holding her in his arms, he gently compelled her down into the grass. Still she did not resist. When he softly pressed his body upon her, she realized how much she wanted this. How much she wanted him.

His momentary nerves fell away into a feeling of bliss. He traced her breast with his fingers and felt the hardness of her nipple through her dress. He moved his palm to her breast and squeezed gently. A tiny involuntary sound of pleasure escaped her and his body responded, a response she could now feel pressing against her groin. She was ready and he sensed it.

When he entered her, there was a shared delight, a mutual belief that this was right, it was correct. It was a new beginning for them both.

9

Jamie

At first Grace thought it was nothing much, just a new chapter in the after-effects from her terrifying experience with lightning. There had been so many already. Blinding headaches, muscle pain, forgetfulness. She even blacked out one day when she was working in the kitchen and couldn't remember how she ended up standing in the garden with Ebbie looking up at her, whimpering, his head cocked to the side. But this? This time it was different and it puzzled her.

The next day, Grace awoke to the realization that she was about to be sick to her stomach. She stumbled up from her bed, squatted down and reached for the commode that was stored away in the bedside cupboard, her head spinning from the exertion. Setting the commode on the floor in front of her, she leaned over it and retched, but nothing came up. This is a new one, she thought. A new symptom.

When her mother came over later in the morning, she found Grace sitting in her kitchen armchair, head in her hands, swaying lightly back and forth. Ebbie sat curled at her feet.

"What's the matter, dear?"

"Not feeling too well today, Mumma. Just give me a moment and I'll be alright, though."

Grace rallied and felt quite a bit better afterwards but the next morning the same thing occurred. "Grace," her mother said, "you must have a touch of the flu."

But a sickening sense of dread was already creeping over Grace and she knew, deep down, it wasn't the flu. It wasn't caused by the lightning strike either. It was something else, something that was leading her to the terrible realization it could bring her down for good if she wasn't careful.

"Mumma, I have a feeling that I'm … pregnant."

"Oh, dear, that's wonderful!" her mother said. "I didn't know you and Peter were trying again."

Grace looked at her mother. "We weren't. Peter and I haven't been together since before Petie … "

Eleanor blanched. "Then … how?"

"Come sit down, Mumma. We have to talk."

As Grace poured out the story of Max to her mother, Eleanor Campbell bit her lip so hard she began to draw blood. "Don't panic," she told her daughter. "Let us think. Grace, you have to make Peter believe the child is his. There's no other way."

Grace was taken aback by her mother's resolve. There was not a word of reprimand as she had expected. It was simply a matter of getting down to business. Grace marvelled at her mother's resilience, at her Victorian sense of no-nonsense practicality. Why, she had never even asked who the man was. Grace on the other hand had been raised in an era in which she was inclined to allow her sense of shame and regret to get the better of her. Eleanor had made it clear Grace must make her husband believe the child was his; there was no other way, she insisted.

Grace was not so sure. All day the dread of coping with what she had done seeped into her and Grace finally thought: There is another way. After the noon-hour dinner service, Grace took a walk to her favourite spot on the river, Ebbie by her side. She heard the jays and watched the squirrels scamper after one another. A deer wandered nearby, its young fawn trailing behind. She looked at the rushing water of the Shannon River and imagined how easy it could be. How easy to wade in and let the water carry her away, just as it had nearly carried away her puppy years before. It could be over so quickly. It would be her self-punishment for doing such a stupid thing. And it would teach Peter a lesson too. He had treated her so cruelly, left her to cope with the devastating death of little Petie, alone.

Grace stood on the riverbank, mesmerized by the swirling water, the sweet sounds of nature filling her ears. She reached down and ruffled Ebbie's fur, scratched him behind the ears. The dog looked up at her quizzingly, and whimpered sympathetically. That's when it came to her.

"I have life inside me," she said, looking at Ebbie. "I owe it to God, Ebbie; I owe it to that life. There is another way." In her practical no-nonsense and non-judgmental manner, Eleanor was right. Grace realized she had already deceived her husband; she could do it again.

"He deserves it," she said. "I don't care about him and I owe him nothing. But I'm carrying another life now, and I do not have the right to kill it out of a whim."

That night, Grace made Peter's favourite dinner of roast beef and Yorkshire pudding. She forced herself to chat about more pleasant days in their past and after they ate, she joined him in the parlour while he sat reading the evening newspaper, his favourite pipe next to him in the ashtray stand. Peter looked up at her, curious that his wife, who had consistently ignored him for months, was acting this way. She sat down across from him on the couch, a lumpy Victorian settee.

"Yes?" he asked. "What is it?" In his heart, he dreaded the possibility that she wanted to return to the topic of his disappearance after Petie's death, and wondered if perhaps it was time to tell her what had happened. Maybe it would be worth the pain, if they could get this thing behind them and return to their previous life.

Grace had other thoughts. "I've been thinking that perhaps we've been a bit silly. Perhaps it's time for us to think about the future, a future that brings us back together."

Skeptical yet filled with more hope than he had allowed himself to feel in months, Peter set down his newspaper. He picked up his pipe and drew on it. Smoke rose in a narrow shaft and filled the air with the tobacco's sweet aroma. Grandfather Sam O'Malley's clock ticking from the dining room was the only sound to break the silence. "How do you mean?" he asked quietly.

"Well, you and I have been at cross-purposes for quite some time. Can we at least talk? Maybe we can … try again? I've been thinking about what you said so long ago. The baby is gone, and neither one of us will ever get over that loss. But you and I are still here, Peter. Maybe we can bring back something of what we had together. Maybe we can … have another?" It was more a question than a statement, one crafted to force his hand.

Peter broke into a wide grin and nearly jumped out of his seat. "Oh, my darling, you don't know how I have longed to hear you say that. I'm so sorry I ran out on you like that. I didn't know what I was doing. I wasn't in my right mind. It was the grief, my darling. I couldn't face you after what I'd done. I made you put the baby in the backseat all by himself. I'll never forgive myself."

Grace's heart broke for her husband just then. For a moment she saw the same man she had once fallen deeply in love with. She couldn't believe he was opening up to her like this, sharing his deepest feelings. It was far more than she ever expected. But she had betrayed this good man. She had slept with someone else, a momentary fling with a handsome stranger who had come along when she was at her most vulnerable. How could she ever explain that to him? Before she knew what was happening, Peter had come to her on the couch and wrapped his big arms around her. He squeezed so hard she let out a little yelp and he apologized sheepishly.

"You don't know how I've waited for this," he said. "Let's give it a try."

That night the two of them went to Grace's room and slept together as husband and wife, as lovers, just the way they had done so eagerly and passionately before. Before Petie had died, smothered to death in the thick hair of a buffalo hide. But now Grace was wracked with guilt and fear. Fear of what would happen if her secret ever became known.

A few weeks later when Grace told Peter she was pregnant, he was overjoyed at first, but wondered how she had known so soon. "Oh, I'll have to go to Doc Farr to find out for sure," she told her husband, "but yes, I'm pretty sure. Isn't that wonderful, darling?"

To her mother she said: "You haven't told Daddy, have you? About what really happened. You never will?"

Of course not, replied Eleanor. "It would kill your father. Let's just let him be, have the happiness he's feeling at the idea of being a granddad again. He doesn't need to know the details."

Grace withheld the "details" from all others, including Ruth Taylor, and Albie who was blithely living the life of a wealthy countess in Italy. Albie and Count Roberto Ribigghini were enjoying a fairy-tale existence in his Tuscany mansion, Villa Con Spirito. In letters home to Grace, Albie had recounted how Roberto had been involved in top-secret negotiations during the latter stages of the war as Italy prepared to abandon its Central Power allies, Germany and Austria-Hungary, and switch sides to the Allied Powers. With the war now over, the count had hitched his horse to some fellow named Mussolini, a reformed socialist who was engaged in building Italy into a "nationalist" state, Albie wrote. She seemed so happy.

Grace was delighted for her friend. She wrote back the good news of her pregnancy and Albie immediately announced she would come back to Shannonside to be with her dear friend for the child's birth. This added to Grace's deep sense of guilt about the entire matter. She knew she could never admit to Albie who the child's real father was. But there was no stopping Alberta Johnson Ribigghini when faced with a mission. She would come home now to help her friend.

Albie arrived in early June 1924 and the child, a boy, was born a week later. Peter counted the weeks and was perplexed at how quickly the baby had come. "Oh, he's just a bit premature," said Grace, "but I have a feeling he'll grow quickly." Peter held the baby in his arms, remarked on the unusual size for such a premature delivery and wondered. When he raised the topic with Doc Farr, the physician replied: "What do you mean, premature? This is a healthy full-term child. Perfect in every way. No need to worry about anything, my boy."

And Peter wondered some more. Could Doc Farr be wrong? What other explanation could there be?

* * *

They called the baby James William and appointed Albie his godmother, just as she had been for Petie. She stayed on for the baptismal. Peter was overjoyed with his son. He imagined the boy growing up to take over Ballinskellig one day, to carry on the family name and to continue to raise the apples the farm had become famous for. He would make sure the boy took to the land in the manner of the generations of O'Malleys that came before. He imagined sharing his vast knowledge of farming with his son one day and was so preoccupied by the thought that his foreman, Mel Brewster, grew alarmed at how frequently Pete avoided business that summer. Brewster did his best to pick up the slack. Pete was so fixated on the baby that he paid little thought to Grace's increasing distance from him. They had made a baby together and that's all Pete seemed to care about.

Albie stayed on to help and watched with increasing alarm as Grace fell into a dark place. Albie wondered what had caused it and spoke to Doctor Farr about it. The doctor explained to her that sometimes after a birth, mothers fell into the "baby blues," and that in time he was confident Grace would "snap out of it."

Grace knew there were no baby blues. The darkness that haunted her was from the fact she was guilt-ridden at what she had done. She had had an affair with a common farmhand, deceived her husband and now would have to live with the consequences. It sickened her. And yet as the summer progressed, she found herself eagerly anticipating Max's return for the apple harvest. Her mood picked up, much to Albie's relief. Pleased with her friend's newfound vigour and good spirits, Albie returned home in early August. Grace prepared for Max's arrival. She could hardly wait to tell him about the baby.

Unaware of the baby, Max did return. Just outside Toronto, he hitched a ride with a trucker and as the vehicle took him eastward toward Ballinskellig, thoughts of seeing Grace again filled him with an exhilaration he had never before felt. He wanted to hold her again, to breathe her in, to feel her hair, to trace her every curve with his fingers and to touch every part of her. And maybe this year, he thought, he might convince her to come away with him. If she did, he would abandon his nomadic ways and settle down someplace. Perhaps get his own spread and start to farm. And start their own family.

Max recognized the crossroads just outside Shannonside right away and thanked the driver who had brought him these past eighty miles. As he stood on the dusty country corner and looked down the road that led to Ballinskellig, he doffed his worn felt fedora, used it to whack dust from his pants, and threw his duffle bag over his shoulder. The late summer days were cooling now but the mid-day sun still held plenty of warmth, even as it dipped lower in the sky with the approaching autumn. Max paused to scratch his scraggly beard and placed the fedora back on his blond hair, darkened from being constantly outdoors. He tipped its brim lower to shield his eyes from the glare of the sun and headed south.

Mel Brewster was glad to see the familiar tanned face and welcomed him back. "We can use you right smartly, son," he said. "Ready to get crackin'?"

The next day at the noonday meal, Grace was too occupied with plating the food and handing it to the men to notice Max approaching down the line of farmhands. Ebenezer, old, grey and half-blind, lay at her feet. She offered a plate to the next man in line and realized a hesitation, a slight delay in the mechanical response she was expecting. Ebbie rose unsteadily on his front legs and gave a welcoming yip to the man he recognized. Grace looked up and found herself staring into Max's beautiful blue eyes. "Thank you, ma'am," he said, finally accepting the plate and slowly moving on.

Later, as she collected the dirty plates and packed up, Max passed her on his way back to the orchard and said in a quiet voice: "Down by the river, after supper." Without looking up, Grace nodded almost imperceptibly, but Max caught it.

Finishing her own supper cleanup that evening, she hesitated when a low rumble of thunder signalled a far-off storm. Grace had been leery of storms ever since it happened. She never wanted to experience anything like it again. But the lure of seeing Max again was too strong and about seven-thirty she called to Peter: "Watch the baby for me, honey? I'm going out for some air. Keep Ebbie here, will you? He's having trouble keeping up these days." Pete grunted acknowledgement.

Max was already there when she arrived. She hadn't noticed him at first, then let her gaze rest on some aspen trees at the edge of the forest. He had his back to her, hands in his pockets, his broad shoulders and straight spine made him recognizable from afar.

As she approached, he turned and smiled. He absorbed her presence for a moment, enjoying everything about this lovely woman. "You came," he said. "I wasn't sure."

"We need to talk," she said in a businesslike tone. At first not grasping the urgency in her voice, Max moved to embrace her but Grace pulled back. "No, Max. We need to talk."

"What is it?"

"Max, we have a child. A boy."

Max stepped back from her, his mood interrupted by this startling news. "Peter, what … ?"

"I don't think Peter knows exactly, but I think he suspects. He's asked me a couple times about the baby being premature. When I learned I was pregnant, I went to him, said I wanted to give it another try, and we slept together. It meant nothing to me. I had no choice but to make him think the baby was his. But there's a nearly seven-week gap. Peter's not stupid. It'll keep gnawing at him. We need to be careful or he'll figure things out."

"My darling," he said. "This makes things easier now. Don't you see? Come away with me. We'll start over, together. The three of us. What's the boy's name?"

"No," she said. "My life is here. I can't do that. Peter is my husband, whatever happens. The baby? His name's James William." She thought for a moment. "But Max, I don't know your name. Max what?"

The man stammered and looked down at his dusty boots. "Huddlestone," he answered quietly. Grace repeated the name: "Huddlestone. Like the man who makes the cars?"

Max nodded. "No relation," he said.

Then Max moved to hold her and this time Grace didn't resist. He pulled her tight to him and smelled her sweet hair. Grace sank into him, nearly mesmerized by his strength.

Max asked: "Where can we meet? We're out in the open here." Grace had already thought of a plan. She told him about a hut, the maple syrup cabin at the far end of the farm, on a pond in the forest they called

Morrow's Pond. Except for the spring sugaring-off, when sap was collected to make maple syrup, no one ever goes there, she assured him. She would bring coverings for the simple bed it contained. They could arrange secret rendezvous as long as he stayed. They could at least enjoy one another's company for as long as possible. And this time, she added, they needed to exercise care. "I want no more little ones," she insisted. "I'm not sleeping with Peter again."

Max nodded and said he'd take care of things. Then he added: "Bring the baby, will you? I'd like to meet him."

That was the moment in which Grace eased off and relaxed. "That's exactly what I'd hoped you'd say," she told him with a smile. Yes, she would bring Jamie so he could meet his father. This she did at their next meeting at the cabin. She held the tiny being out toward him. Max reached his own arms out awkwardly, as though he was waiting for Grace to place the child in them. Grace smiled. "He's not a load of firewood," she remarked gently. "Here, take him." Max then tentatively took the boy from her and snuggled him to his own face, inhaled the satisfying, powdered scent of his son and made nonsensical sounds that delighted the child and made him coo and giggle. Grace watched as they met, father and son. In her eyes, Jamie's fair hair and creamy skin helped make him the spitting image of Max. He lacked the black Irish features that marked the O'Malleys and she feared Peter would some day see it too.

Max had never contemplated being a father and now that he was, he realized that he very much enjoyed the sensation. He had never held any baby before, and knowing this child was his own flesh and blood instilled in him an awe that he never dreamed he could experience. As he looked into the face of the tiny stranger, he somehow felt he'd known the child forever. His heart burst with love, with pride, with trepidation for what the future held. How was he ever going to do this?

Over the course of the two or three months of Max's stay at Ballinskellig, Grace and Max met often in the safety of the isolated little pond-side cabin in the woods. The days turned colder, come the end of October, and Max wanted to light a fire in the stove. Grace warned against it. They must be totally discreet, she said. No one must smell the smoke or get any hint of their liaisons. Max nodded.

One day, Grace brought Jamie with her as she served the noon-hour meal. Her mother normally looked after the child back at the house while Grace served the men, but on this occasion she had taken the day off with a bad cold. All the men adored the little boy and some wanted to pick him up. "I've got a couple of these back at home," said one of them one day. "I really miss 'em." On that occasion, Max made a point of keeping his distance, not wanting to give Pete any cause to wonder, not wanting anyone to question their resemblance. It pained him not to go to the child and hold him.

One evening in early November, Max told her he would be heading out the next day. It was time again to move on. "You still won't come with me?" he asked. "You and Jamie?"

"No," she replied.

"Do you want me to come back next year?"

Grace looked into his face. "More than anything, my darling," she said tearfully. "I couldn't bear it if I thought I'd never see you again."

And so it was agreed that their liaisons would become annual affairs, reunions cast around the annual harvest, right around apple time. For nine or ten months, Max would travel the continent in search of farm work but once August came, it would be time to head back to Shannonside, back to Ballinskellig, back into the arms of Grace O'Malley. Back to see his child again. If anyone had ever known anything about it, they would have told the both of them they were daft. But apart from Grace's mother, no one else knew.

At first, Pete simply wondered about how such a big, healthy boy could be born in such a short time, so big and healthy that he had even fooled Doc Farr into thinking he was full-term. Pete loved the boy beyond words and was saddened as Grace slowly drifted farther away from him. They went back to maintaining separate bedrooms and sometimes days would go by without the pair ever exchanging a word. Pete considered his options. Maybe they should talk about his absence after Petie's death; maybe that would end the tension and allow them to come together again as husband and wife. But he blanched with shame. There had been a day when he was prepared to talk about that time, but the moment had passed. He knew now he could never admit to her where he had gone and what he had done.

Ebbie passed peacefully away early that winter and Grace had Pete lay him to rest in a grave down by the river, under the setter's favourite maple tree. Luckily the ground was not yet frozen. The faithful dog had spent many happy days in the shade of that tree, watching the birds, nuzzling up to Grace and, in his younger years, chasing the squirrels, the chipmunks and gophers. Grace stood and cradled Jamie in her arms as her husband tamped down the last of the soil. Grace said she didn't want another dog because there could never be a suitable replacement. Pete recalled how it hadn't been far from that very spot where Ebbie the puppy had brought them together for the first time. As a eulogy for a dog, Grace thought to herself, it rang with eloquence, and she momentarily wished things had turned out differently for her and Peter. But they hadn't.

* * *

Awakening

It was in the early fall of 1926 when the light finally went on in Pete's brain, when it finally occurred to him. He stood by as Grace was serving the men dinner, watching his workers come up one by one. Most of them would exchange pleasantries with her and she would smile or laugh at one of their funny stories. Often she would join in the banter, especially with some of the men she'd known for years.

On this particular day, Pete watched Max approach his wife who stood across the serving table from him. The hunk of bread she had placed on the side of the plate slid off and fell onto the red-and-white checked oilcloth that covered the rough wooden table. Max and Grace reached for it at the same time and their hands met. There was a brief moment that they looked into one another's faces, one instant when their hands didn't just touch, their fingers actually entwined in a purposeful act rather than by chance. Yes, it was just a fleeting moment.

But in that second, Pete knew. His heart pounded and anger burst inside him. At long last he had his answer. No, the baby wasn't his. He thought back to assure himself that Max had indeed been at Ballinskellig the autumn before Jamie's birth. Yes, of course, he had. It had been the year after Grace was struck by the bolt of lightning. She must have lured Pete to bed that time as a pretense, a cover for her pregnancy. No wonder the baby had seemed to be born full-term, yet several weeks early. Grace already knew she was pregnant when they had slept together that night, he realized. She had tricked him. She had made him out as a fool and he had fallen for her wicked deception.

He looked carefully at Max and for the first time recognized similarities in the facial features between his hired man and the child Pete called his son. He thought about all of those times Grace went out for "a breath of air." Where was she going? Were these her liaisons? He would follow her and find out.

That evening, when Grace slipped out the kitchen door and walked across the field at the back of the house, Peter did follow her. Keeping his distance, he nearly lost her a couple of times but eventually he caught on to where she was going. The cabin. The sugarhouse. And sure enough, from the other direction came Max. This was their meeting place, the spot they came to laugh at him, to make a chump, a sucker of him. This was the place they met to make love.

His anger threatened to overcome him but then a sense of calm settled in. What difference did it make now? Peter and Grace were living apart, in separate rooms. While officially they remained married, they had ceased to be husband and wife. This really didn't matter anymore. So Jamie wasn't his son, so what? He would do his part to raise the boy and someday Jamie would take over the farm, if he wanted to. If not, he would deal with it. There were other family members, his sisters' children, who would be interested. All that mattered now was that Pete loved the boy and none of this was Jamie's fault.

Peter had reached an important place in his life. He realized that he would not have a son to farm Ballinskellig, but he loved the boy anyway. He and Grace had ruined their relationship but it wasn't because of anything Jamie had done.

As Grace and Max slipped inside the sugarhouse, Peter turned his back on them and walked away.

10

Firenza 1927

Ben O'Malley enjoyed retirement living in his own home in Shannonside, a small cottage-style bungalow just off the main street. Friends frequently came calling and he loved putting a kettle to boil on the pot-bellied stove that heated the place, and sharing a cup of tea. His childhood buddy, Amos McCormack, would pop over most days and sometimes the two of them would step out to Nel's Diner for a coffee and a grilled cheese sandwich. In their own minds the two of them always "had a gas" when they got together, reminiscing about the grand old times they had shared, about how as young men they were always "on the make" together in search of pretty young colleens. They'd shared everything over the years, about how each had "done the bold thing" for the first time, how they had asked their favourite girls to marry them, and when the first little tyke was on the way. They had shared it all.

Granted, the two of them were spending more time these days attending funerals for other old friends. It was kind of sad, yet both adored the Irish tradition of the wake, a celebration of the friend's life, equal parts ceilidh and mourning. It was much preferred to the dreary old Methodist funerals, they agreed. They couldn't stand to sit there in church as the "Bible-thumpers" railed on. Now the Irish, Catholic and Protestant alike, they sure knew how to send a fella off right. How to pipe him properly into the next life.

"Let's have a jar," Ben said to Amos one day. "We don't do that enough these days."

Amos gave him a grin and there was a twinkle in the eye. "Don't mind if I do. Just the one, then."

Ben cackled at the standing joke he shared with his friend. "Just the one" often turned into several snorts before they were done. He started to rise from his rocker and stumbled with the effort. These damned legs, he thought to himself. They just won't do what I want them to anymore.

"Mind yerself," Amos said as he noted his friend's difficulties. "I'll get it."

Ben sidled back to his chair and Amos walked to the cupboard over the sink, then reached up to where he knew his friend kept The Good Stuff, a bottle of Jamieson's Finest Irish whiskey. "I see yer getting' down," he said. "We'll hafta pick up another one of these days." Amos chose two shot glasses from next to the bottle and brought them all back to the table by the pot-bellied stove, next to Ben's trusty rocker. "Had ye heard about Harry Maybee's lad, Ben? I was just over to the barber shop and they told me ..."

Amos stopped short just as he was setting the bottle and glasses down on the table. He looked up at Ben's face and saw it immediately. Ben had passed. He had gone with the most angelic expression on his face, Amos thought. An expression of pure bliss. His eyes were shut the same way they were when he was thinking hard about something. But Amos knew the difference this time. Ben wasn't thinking about anything now.

Ben's dear friend opened the bottle of Jamieson's Finest and poured an oversized shot into each of the glasses. He moved one closer to Ben, lifted his own glass to his lips and said: "May ye be in Heaven an hour a'fore the Devil knows yer dead, old friend."

Grace and Peter actually held hands as they walked into St. Michael's Anglican Church the day of the funeral. It wasn't an awkward holding of hands as one might have imagined in the circumstances, but rather a sign of a true sharing of sadness and lost love. Grace had adored Old Ben.

The funeral was a splendid affair. Ben's girls, Lucy, Alice and Anna, all came, of course, with their various husbands and several of their children. Ben's sisters, Emily and Ellen, as well as brother Miller, came home for the affair. Brother James and his wife, Livinia, shut the hardware store for the day. All told, there were at least fifty family members for the occasion. Together with friends, the grey stone church groaned to overflowing with at least a hundred and fifty in attendance. Ben's own grandfather, William O'Malley, had himself worked on its construction half a century ago.

The pastor, Canon Evans, did Ben proud, tracing how the O'Malley family had come to Canada and how William had commenced the family tradition of raising apples. Canon Evans took mourners through the high spots of Ben's existence on Earth. "Now he's there with Mame again," the pastor told the mourners. "We like to think they're having a grand old time."

After the service, Canon Evans invited as many as could make it back to the Masonic Hall for a "gathering."

At the wake, Grace reflected on how she and her mother, Eleanor, had just visited Ben a few days earlier. She was glad now they had brought Jamie along. The little boy was wide-eyed as he entered the "town home" of his grandfather and gaped as he looked around the small house. The walls were papered in bright Victorian brocade patterns and there were photos of family members hung everywhere. While he was just past three years, Jamie comported himself as a "real little man," his grandfather had remarked with bursting pride. "I feel as if I should be offering him a whisky," Ben had said. The adults all laughed and Jamie, sensing he was the centre of attention but not understanding why, laughed along with them. Little could any of them know that day what an impression the occasion would make on the child, that he would recall it so vividly years later.

Lucy and her husband remained a few days while her sisters headed back home with their families. To be sure, Lucy was primarily drawn by little Jamie to stay on awhile. Having no children of her own, she thought of him as much as a son as a nephew. "You're a fine O'Malley," she told the little boy who gazed up at her and smiled. "I can see you farming here just like your dad and all the O'Malleys who came before him."

She didn't notice the scowl Peter cast their way and was oblivious to the manner in which he slipped out of the room.

The summer Ben died, Grace had been feeling more upbeat than she had in a long time. She looked ahead to the autumn, to the harvest, and to the promised return of Max. She couldn't wait for Max to see how Jamie had grown. She couldn't wait to run to Max, to have him hold her in his arms, to experience his adoring kisses again. To feel his hands explore every inch of her body and to slip with him into the humble bed in the cabin in the woods next to Morrow Pond they had come to share. It was humble, but it was theirs.

Just after the funeral, Grace received a letter from Albie, wondering whether Grace and Jamie would be up for her to pay a visit. Albie had something she wanted to talk to Grace about. Grace fretted. She hadn't told her friend about Max's annual visits and didn't want anything getting in the way. What should she say? Finally, she settled on telling Albie that with the harvest just commencing, it really wasn't a good time, but that once it was over, she would be delighted to have her friend visit. Could her news wait until late November?

In Tuscany, on the shores of Lago Trasimeno in Villa Con Spirito, Alberta Ribigghini read Grace's reply with a touch of disappointment. She had a great idea she wanted to share with her friend as soon as she could. She could hardly wait. But Albie acceded to Grace's wishes. She would wait and book her passage in November. Maybe she would have the opportunity to experience some of that Ontario snow she was actually starting to miss.

Max returned as promised that fall but stayed a shorter time that year. He arrived late and departed earlier than Grace had expected. He said he had promised a friend he'd help with the corn crops down in Quebec. Grace wondered whether she'd see him again. Their moments together were fewer than in earlier years but equally tender, and Grace again had to affirm to Max that she would not go away with him.

After the harvest, Albie paid her visit home to Shannonside. Her heart leapt at the sight of her godson and how he was growing. The women sat in the kitchen next to the stove until all hours of the night that first day she was there, trading news and observations on one another's lives. Grace listened breathlessly as Albie described her life in Italy with the count. "He's a wonderful man, Grace. He has changed my life. He encourages me to study art history to my heart's content and he's very knowledgeable himself. We talk and talk about it and he takes me to the most wonderful places. And oh, Firenze! What a splendid city."

There was no talk of children and so Grace finally asked: Did Albie and Roberto want to have a family? Albie waved her hands in front of her face and Grace could see her eyes were moist. No, said Albie, they had discussed the topic at length and agreed there would be no children. "Roberto's life is his work, I'm afraid. He says he wants me all to himself whenever he can get me. But he's always so busy."

So on the one hand Albie was living her dream. On the other, she felt cheated. Albie envied Grace her wonderful little Jamie, to be sure, but life with Peter had not turned out the way she had been expecting. Each had a part of the good life; neither had it all.

Albie did not know that Grace's heart belonged to Max, that she could never be with him for any more than their fleeting moments during the harvest. Grace grew quiet.

After a short silence, Albie looked at her friend and said: "Grace, I have a proposition. I hope you'll consider it seriously." Grace stared back blankly. "I want you to come back with me. To pay a visit to Italy. Now, don't reject it right away. Think about it. Roberto is dying to meet you and he says he'd like to take us both to Firenze, to visit the Uffizi, the Duomo Cathedral, see the Statue of David, walk along the Arno and over the Ponte Vecchio. Oh, you should see the silver metalsmiths and jewellers there! Grace, please come. It would be so wonderful for us both. To see you experience what I have experienced there, it would do my heart a world of good."

Grace was struck into silence. She thought about all of the reasons she couldn't join Albie. There was so much to do here. And Jamie. What on earth would she do with Jamie? As if she read her friend's thoughts Albie said: "Your parents would look after Jamie. They'd love it. And it's winter, it's the slow season here. Grace, there's nothing to keep you from saying yes."

Grace realized Albie was right. It sounded divine. She had never travelled anyplace beyond Toronto. Why shouldn't she? And so she said to Albie: "I'll speak to my parents but Albie, this sounds like the most wonderful thing anyone has ever done for me. So yes, yes Albie. I would love to do it!"

Not a word was said about Pete's part in any of it.

* * *

As she hung doubled over the railing of the Cunard liner and retched her insides out, Grace felt Albie's gentle hand holding back her hair. "I'm so sorry, my darling," said Albie. "You really ought to have taken one of those tablets I offered you. The North Atlantic does tend to get rough this time of year." Grace groaned and tossed up the paltry remains of her breakfast.

Tearfully, over the course of the voyage Grace told Albie part of the story of her relationship with Max. But not everything. Not about Jamie. Albie was happy for her friend, especially considering how during the course of her visit to Ballinskellig she had observed for herself the coldness that had fallen between Grace and Peter.

"Do you think it's terrible of me?" Grace asked. "Having an … an affair?"

Alberta laughed. "My dear Grace. It's so European of you! Why half the men of Italy and France have ladies on the side. Not my Roberto, of course, but most of his friends do. Grace, you've just turned the tables. You've struck a blow for women. Now we too can have affairs. When circumstances warrant, I think it's wonderful." Albie laughed and Grace winced.

The women landed at the Port of Hamburg and boarded the train to Rome, where Alberta had arranged to meet up with Roberto. "*Mio caro*," he shouted when he spotted Albie. "*Mi sei mancato!*"

"*O, sole della mia vita,*" she crooned back to her beloved Roberto. "Roberto, my love, I want you to meet ..."

"Grace!" Roberto broke in then, pronouncing her name as two syllables and placing an Italian's emphasis on the "e." "I am so extremely pleased to meet your acquaintance. Our home is your home. Welcome to Italia, my dear."

Grace was so touched, and so struck by the marriage her friend had and she didn't, that she totally broke down and cried. Roberto reeled back. "*Mio caro*," he said, turning to his wife. "What is it I have said wrong?"

"Nothing, my dear. You have said it wonderfully. Give Grace time. She has much to overcome. So much."

They piled into Roberto's luxuriously sprawling Fiat motorcar and turned northeast toward Lago Trasimeno. As they turned up the driveway that led to the count's waterside villa, Grace gasped. "Here? This is where you live? Why, it's magnificent."

Roberto had built Villa Con Spirito right after the war, in the art nouveau style that was sweeping the countryside amongst Italy's wealthy class. Set in a blissfully quiet setting, it was surrounded by trees and manicured gardens. Stained glass panels highlighted each of the multitude of windows that allowed light to stream into the interior. Beautiful hardwood floors in a chevron pattern, according to the count's excited commentary, recalled "bygone days of sophistication and luxury." There was a marble staircase, the railing constructed of ironwork that had been handcrafted by artisans right onsite. An elevator linked the villa's four floors. A soaring window allowed unencumbered views of the magnificent lake.

Alberta added proudly: "And each of the eight bedrooms has its own private bathroom.And the tilework. Oh, my dear, the tilework!"

Grace and Albie rested for a few days after their ocean crossing and spent afternoons exploring the trails that crossed the huge estate. Grace picked out her favourite spot, a lakeside lookout on which a gazebo had been built to offer protection from the summer sun and rain. As they sat there one day, Albie said: "How do you think it would be if we went into Firenze tomorrow?"

Roberto sent his driver to take the ladies into the city, explaining he could not join them because he had been called into Rome for business with Mussolini. "Il Duce insists on introducing me to a new friend of his. Some dreary little man from Austria who's interested in discussing politics, he says. I must go. Enjoy your trip, ladies. Mine will be a horror." The women laughed.

The next day as their car approached the hotel, Grace marvelled at what she was witnessing. They drove deeper into the city and Albie pointed out some of the sights they would be coming back to later. "But first we must go to our hotel," she insisted. "The Hotel Orto de Medici."

The women checked in and after unpacking, Albie insisted they proceed to the hotel's garden. "Look around, Grace, my dear. It was right here, in this garden, where Lorenzo de' Medici met Michelangelo Buonarroti in 1489. Right here, this is where history was made. The result of that meeting was the wonderful art, the sculptures and the architecture that surrounds us."

In the coming days, Albie showed her friend the sights and sounds of the magnificent city the Medicis had built. Grace was overwhelmed. "I had no idea, Albie. Now I know why you studied art. This is all so stunning."

The women strolled the streets and peeked into little shops. Albie chatted with familiarity to each of the merchants. At Galleria dell' Accademia, Grace blushed at David in all his nakedness and when the two of them giggled, they attracted the stern look of disapproval from a guard. They sat out in an open-air café next to the Duomo and while enjoying a gelato and espresso they marvelled at the detailing of the magnificent cathedral. They took the Via del Proconsolo to the Via dell'Anguillara and over to the Piazza Santa Croce. It was a mild December day and they celebrated their burst of energy with a bowl of fettuccini bathed in sage butter, served al fresco. Sated and slightly tipsy from two glasses of chianti, the women demurred about their return to the hotel. "I think a taxi would be in order," said Albie. Grace didn't object.

The following day, Albie told Grace she was taking her to one of her favourite places, to Café Casoni. When they arrived, Albie waved to a man across the room. The man walked over to greet her and Albie said: "Grace, I'd like for you to meet Count Camillo Negroni, a dear friend of Roberto's and, I'm delighted to say, mine too."

"Senora," said Negroni. With one hand he swept off his stylish fedora, then he bowed and kissed her hand. "So wonderful to meet you." Grace estimated the dapper gentleman to be in his mid-fifties. He insisted on buying the ladies dinner but first, he said, he had a surprise for Senora Ribigghini's "*amica Canadese*". "My very own cocktail," he announced with a flourish. "Compari bitters and vermouth, topped with gin, and garnished with orange. Voila! The Negroni. My special *aperitivo*."

Grace took a demure sip and declared: "It's delicious. Count Negroni, you are spoiling me rotten."

"Oh my," said the count with a sly frown. "Is that bad?"

The women laughed. "I believe I'll have another," said Albie. "I require further spoiling."

Count Negroni was the perfect gentleman. After dinner, he insisted on taking the women back to the Orto de Medici in his personal car. As he dropped them off, he said to them: "*Fino a quando ci incontreremo di nuovo, signores.*"

"Oh, count," replied Albie, "*buonasera.*"

Slightly tipsy, Grace giggled as they walked into the hotel lobby. "That was the most wonderful evening of my life," she told Albie. "My dear friend, you are just what I needed."

When they returned to the villa, Roberto met them at the door. "Let us go to Venezia," he said. "I have some business there and I'm certain Grace would love it. We will depart tomorrow." There was no dissuading him and Grace finally conceded, although she insisted, "at least give me a day to recover from Florence, Roberto."

She nearly swooned over the gondoliers and St. Mark's Square. As Roberto attended to business, the women walked along a quiet back street. Albie insisted they slip into a tiny little shop, saying there was something she wanted to show her. Inside, Albie presented her friend with a pair of diamond earrings. "I can't accept this," Grace said. "It's too much." Albie insisted. "The cost is nothing for the Count, my dear. Believe me. I truly want you to have them." Grace teared up as she said thank you.

Two weeks later as the two of them parted at Cevitavecchia, the port of Rome, Alberta hugged her old friend and said they must do this again sometime soon. Perhaps next time Albie would pay a visit to Shannonside and they could take the train to Montreal, she said. "I haven't been there in years. We will have to visit the Musée des Beaux-Arts." Grace said she had never been there and looked forward to seeing it in the company of an art expert.

On the return crossing, Grace remembered to take her tablets for seasickness and the voyage went much more smoothly. In Halifax, she caught the train. When she got off the train in Shannonside, Grace looked around for a cab but it so happened that the Taylors were there to pick up Mrs. Taylor's aunt who had come in from Cornwall. "We'd be happy to drop you off home, my dear," said Mrs. Taylor and Mr. Taylor smiled in confirmation.

"Welcome home, Grace," Peter said as she walked in the door. I've just put the boy to bed."

"The boy? Is it now? Can't you even bear to speak his name?" Grace snapped at her husband.

"I didn't mean anything by it," he said. "Your folks dropped him off a while ago. He was sleepy and is looking forward to seeing his mother again. Why don't you go in and say hello."

"Then I'm going to bed," was all she could manage.

Grace climbed the stairs and stepped lightly into Jamie's bedroom. The little boy brightened at the sight of his mother. The two of them hugged. "I'll tell you all about my trip tomorrow, sweetheart," she said. "I have something for you, though." Jamie's eyes widened as he tore open the gift she handed him and he screamed in delight when he saw the stuffed bear. He snuggled the bear next to him as she kissed him and said goodnight.

After he watched his wife go up to Jamie's room, Pete waited a moment before going to a corner of the kitchen where a lantern sat, lifted its glass and lit the kerosene-soaked wick. He carried it across the road to the drive shed, went inside and strode straight for a spot in the wall behind the old democrat. He opened a latch and shone the light into a cavity where a jug sat. He lifted the jug out, set down the lantern and popped open the cork on the jug, then raised it to his lips and took a long, slow swallow. The liquid burned on its way down but Pete immediately felt better.

Still, he damned himself for a moment in time he wished he could recapture and do it all differently. The moment in which it had all gone wrong. The moment he had ruined both their lives.

11

Life's Lessons
1932

"Now as I explained, the apple is a peculiar beast," Pete said to the wide-eyed boy. "You might think that if you want to grow a snow apple, you just plant some seeds that came from a snow apple. But that's not the way Nature works. If I planted some snow apple seeds, you could be pretty certain you would not get a snow apple tree at all. You would get something different entirely. That's why we graft our apple trees. And to do that, you need your bud and you need your root stock."

The boy's eyes followed every move as Pete took the small handsaw and sliced the sapling's trunk off cleanly. Then he took out his knife and gently held the sharp edge of its blade against the open cut. A thin knife mark appeared in the soft wood. Starting in that mark, Pete worked the knife blade down into the soft, buttery-coloured wood about three inches. He twisted the knife blade gently to open up the cut.

"This is called a cleft graft," Pete told Jamie. "Now watch this carefully."

He picked up one of the bud sticks he had collected from this year's growth in one of the snow apple trees. It was early in the season and the sticks had not yet burst into new leaves. He used his knife to whittle the stick's end into a wedge shape. Then, using the knife blade to slightly open the cut on the root stock tree, he gently slipped the sharpened end of the bud stick down into the cut. He took a second sprout and repeated the procedure, then a third.

"I've damaged the tree by opening up the soft inner wood," Pete explained to his son. "So now we have to protect it from insects and disease." He dipped his knife blade into a bucket of wax he had earlier softened for the purpose and he buttered the wax around the tree's opened wound, much as he would have done with a slice of bread.

He was patient with the boy, making sure he kept his hands out of Jamie's line of vision. He wanted to make sure the pupil got everything he could from his lesson. "See the tension against the sprouts," Pete told Jamie. "That is the beauty of this sort of graft. It holds the sprouts in place. But just to be sure, I'll take some twine and wind it around the outside of the branch to be truly certain the bud sticks remain in place."

Jamie giggled. "It looks like a scarecrow," he said.

Pete stood back to inspect his handiwork and smiled. "Why, I guess it does at that," he said. "You've got a good eye there, Jamie." He gave the boy a playful slap on the shoulder and Jamie broke into a wide grin, a grin that softened Pete's heart to putty. He looked into the boy's eager, inquisitive eyes, smiled and then sawed off two more branches from the root stock tree and repeated the grafting process.

"Now before you know it, when this tree begins to grow and bursts out into leaf, we will have the beginnings of a brand new snow apple tree. And later in the season after the young leaves are out, I'm going to show you how to do a T-graft. It's something different altogether. We do a bit of the one, and we do a bit of the other. It's good to vary the work. Sometimes one method works better than the other."

It was the spring of the year Jamie would turn eight. His father wanted the boy to appreciate the lineage of the apple farm he would some day inherit, to comprehend what it was they were preserving and why. Pete told Jamie he remembered back to when his own father, Jamie's grandfather Ben, had taught him the same lessons a quarter-century ago. Ben had impressed upon the young Peter how it was the same lesson he had been taught, as had his father before him. It was a lesson learned in Ireland and brought to the New World by the first O'Malley, the one who, according to his Aunt Lucy, had been called Liam O'Maille.

When she first told the boy the Irish name, Jamie pronounced it softly, pondering on it, letting it run through his brain, soak into his consciousness. Now he would forever remember it and treasure it as a part of who he was. "What would I be called?" he asked his aunt. "In Irish."

Lucy pondered the question. "Seamus," she replied. "You would be Seamus O'Maille, Jamie."

The boy smiled. "Seamus," he replied, and giggled. "It tickles when I say it."

Jamie was fascinated by the family tale, and mesmerized by his apple-growing lessons, just as he was learning about handling and caring for the animals that were so crucial to the continued success of Ballinskellig. Treat the animals well, Pete had impressed upon the boy, and they will repay you with their loyalty and their hard work. Treat the trees and the crops well, too. Together they form the community that will feed and clothe the family. The eager pupil absorbed his lessons and learned them well. The boy was beginning to love the land the way Pete did. He loved the fields of clover in summer, the swaying heads of the ripened hay in fall, and spring's bounty of apple blossoms, each so delicate and tissue-thin you could see the sun through it. And he loved it when winter came, when silence reigned across the snowy landscape.

What Pete didn't tell the boy was that the past nearly three years had been increasingly hard, not just at Ballinskellig, but across the region, the country and the continent. After the bountiful years of the twenties, everything seemed to come to a halt after the Big Crash of 1929. Everything went wrong, and no one could offer a satisfactory explanation as to why. Nor did anyone know a way out. Harsh weather led to bad crop years. There were layoffs in the cities because no one seemed to be buying anything more than they absolutely required to survive. And many weren't even surviving. There had been hunger and starvation, suicides, men and women wandering the countryside searching for work. Work that didn't exist.

Apple exports to the States had ended. Prices dropped. In 1930, three times the normal number of men showed up for work and Pete had nothing for them. Most of them hung their heads and walked away, dejected, defeated. Pete felt terrible but there was nothing he could do. For the most part these men were complacent in their rejection. They knew it wasn't Pete's fault. Everyone was in the same predicament.

One of the men who came in search of employment had had enough of it all by the time he appeared at Pete's door one day, however. When Pete told him there was no work to be had, the man's face contorted with rage, his eyes bulging in anger. He took a swing at Pete and luckily Mel Brewster, Pete's foreman, had been there to help out. It took the force of both men to slow the fellow down, and two good slugs - one to the jaw and one to the stomach - by Brewster to subdue him. Something then went off in the man's mind and he realized what he had done. The man rubbed his jaw. "I'm sorry, sir. I guess I just went loco there for a minute. I haven't eaten anything in days."

Grace had come to see what the commotion was about and heard the plaintive remarks. "Wait one minute," she told him. She went to the pantry and collected a dish of leftovers, brought it to the door and handed it to the man. "This is the least we can do for you, sir," she said.

The man thanked her and Grace asked: "Where are you from, sir?" as a way of carrying on polite conversation as the man gobbled down the food.

The man looked at her with red-rimmed eyes. "Come from nowhere. Goin' nowhere," he replied. He thanked her again, set the plate down, turned and walked away.

Grace turned and noticed Jamie had come to stand next to her. He watched, wide-eyed and speechless, as the man departed. "As long as we're in a position to help someone less fortunate, it's our duty to do so," she told her son. "It's what God wants. Always remember that, Jamie."

The boy gazed into his mother's soft eyes. He nodded subtly. "I'll remember," he said.

The next day, Brewster was in town when he heard a body had been found washed up on the shore of Shannon Bay. He told Pete he just had a feeling, so he went over to the funeral home where the body had been taken. "Sure enough," he told his boss, "it was the same fella. Threw himself into the water, it seems."

That year when Max appeared at Ballinskellig, he half-expected to be told there was no work. That had been the regular story right across the continent and he had really had to scramble to find any sort of work at all. Wages had been paltry. But Pete left word with Mel that when Max showed up, he was to make sure to hire him. "We owe him for Grace," Pete explained.

There was another reason, though, one he would never speak of to a single soul. Pete believed he owed it to both Grace and the boy. He had betrayed his wife when he walked out at the time of the baby's death. He had driven her into the arms of a stranger. When Pete looked into Jamie's face, he didn't see himself reflected back. The O'Malleys were all dark complexioned, dark eyed and dark haired, what they called the black Irish. You could see it in the faces of the O'Malleys right back to Old William, the one who had left the old country to make a new life for himself and his family. Lucy said the dark features were because they were descended from the men of the Spanish Armada of the 1500s. Jamie was sandy-haired and blue-eyed, his features much finer and more delicate than those of his father.

Despite knowing that Jamie was not his flesh and blood, was not a true O'Malley, Pete would teach Jamie all he could about the farm, because someday, if all went well, everything would be his. At the same time, though, Pete knew he could never provide Jamie with the emotional support of a true father; it simply wasn't in him to do it. He knew there was something lacking and on that score, the best he could offer was access to the boy's biological father. The man whose seed had created him. Pete didn't hate the man, he felt only sorrow for what he himself had done, and for what, under different circumstances, might have been.

Peter and Grace developed an understanding when Max was around. Pete looked the other way when Grace left at night for her engagements with Max. Pete knew where she was going, and she knew that he knew. Neither cared. Pete was comforted by the fact that Grace would make sure the boy had plenty of visit time with Max. That would be important. That would only be fair. It was Pete's penance for what he had done.

The relationship between Max and Jamie grew ever closer. Max began calling the boy Sonny Jim. Jamie found this puzzling at first, but then hilarious. Max explained to him it was a name taken from a breakfast cereal he had known when he himself was a boy.

As the friendship between the two advanced, subconsciously Jamie fluctuated between thinking of the older man as a big brother and as a father. Either way, Max was in the boy's life no more than three months out of the year. Grace could see the confusion in her son and it broke her heart.

Still, the two of them, father and son, accomplished an awful lot in those months. Even after a day of backbreaking work, Max always somehow seemed able to call upon some inner strength to do things with the boy, and to listen patiently to him and to teach him. One year, the two of them built a diving raft for Morrow's Pond and then went skinny-dipping to cool off after hot days. Jamie hadn't been much of a swimmer till that year, but began to grow stronger and ever more confident in the water. Max told Jamie stories of his travels, expunging much of the hurt and cruelty he experienced and witnessed on the road. It stood to reason that Jamie would create an image of Max's travels that took on a decidedly adventurous edge.

Over time, the two of them developed an enduring bond, with Jamie sharing with the man some of his deepest thoughts. They had conversations

Jamie never seemed to have with Pete. Pete taught the boy about the farm; Max, even in the short time he shared with Jamie, taught him about life. Jamie loved to talk to Max about baseball, not only about his own love of playing the game, but of the statistics he studied diligently in the newspaper when it came. Babe Ruth, Hank Greenberg, Arky Vaughan and Frank Gehringer were his favourites. Jamie said he'd love to see the Yankees play the Tigers someday. But mainly he'd just like to travel.

"Will you take me with you some day?" Jamie asked Max one evening as they sat around a campfire they had built outside the sugarhouse. Grace wasn't with them that day, as she said she had extra work to do in preparation for the next day's meal. "I mean when you leave here. Maybe I could go with you, when I get a bit older."

Max thought hard about his response. He decided to reply in a manner that would make Jamie think about what he had at Ballinskellig. "Why would you want to leave here? You've got it pretty good right here."

"Well, you head out on the road and get to see all kinds of places. All I ever see is this darned farm."

"Sonny Jim, the wide world isn't too nice a place these days. It's hard to find a job. I'm lucky your pop hires me on. I'll be moving on to Quebec after this and I just don't know what I'll find when I get there. It's hard times."

Jamie's face brightened. "Well there you go, then. Quebec. I've learned French. Between my school lessons and talking to the Quebec fellas who come for work, I'm gettin' pretty darn good. I could help you up there."

Max shook his head. "Do you know how many folks are going hungry these days? Here on the farm, you at least have all the food you need. It might not be the best because your pop's got to sell the very best to earn a living for you and your mom. But there's always something to eat. Your pop is providing for you and your mom very well. That counts for a lot. Plenty of people are going hungry in the cities."

Jamie thought about that. "But, aw nuts, you learn so much out there. You get to ride the rods. You see all kinds of places. You've told me about them. That's the kind of life I want. You've seen Niagara Falls, Toronto. You've been out to the Prairies. And California even. I've never been anyplace but Kingston."

"Someday you'll appreciate it more here, Jamie. I promise, you'll be grateful for what you have. And as for travel, you've got a lifetime to do that."

Jamie's eyes brightened. "Europe!" he shouted. "I'm gonna see Europe. You just wait."

Max was himself grateful – grateful to Pete for giving him employment at a time when work was so difficult to find, although over the years the two of them had ceased speaking to one another. Not since when Max had arrived at the farmhouse door with the injured Grace in his arms, or the next year when they had talked about working conditions and politics. In those days the farmers and the workers had worked in common cause against the wealthy big employers who had grown ever fatter from wartime production. The Twenties had seen the two classes grow apart as work was plentiful and farm production was healthy. Now, in the Dirty Thirties, workers and small businessmen such as the farm owners were again tossed together, desperately grabbing for any scrap they could find.

Amidst the cruelty of the era, the scarcity of wealth and the privation that was shared between worker and employer – at least the small ones – there had grown another sharing, another sense that everyone was everyone else's brother. The men, and more than a few women, who left their families behind to seek out work wherever they could find it created a network of sharing. While no one had much, those who had something were willing to share. Volunteers and church groups set up soup kitchens. Hobo "jungles" were created where travellers could gather, swap their stories and find companionship.

It brought out the best in some people. Those who had a bit more to pass on to those who didn't. In Shannonside, there was the grocer who tossed a bone and a couple of onions in with the groceries, saying it was "something for the dog," and knowing the family had no dog but that it would come in handy for making soup. There was the lady whose father had made his fortune as a Belleville lumber baron, going down to meet the hobos in the rail yard with a package of paper, envelopes and stamps, telling the hungry and long-faced young men just passing through to "write to your mother." And then there was the elderly woman in the odds-n-sods shop downtown who knew the most needy children and would secretly pass them a piece of candy when they came in with their mothers.

Peter O'Malley had his own modest way of giving back, of sharing his relative prosperity. There was never much left over at the O'Malley place but Pete knew he'd always have a slew of apples that weren't good enough to sell so he'd save them up and crush them into cider. At the end of harvest he'd gather the other farm owners to build a big wooden platform in the field outside the barn. When the platform was finished, he'd invite all the neighbouring families over for a proper barn dance. Sammy Martin would bring his fiddle and Katie McGregor would come with her squeeze box. Everyone would bring whatever they could to eat, and Pete would provide the biggest and most anticipated treat of the night, that fall's freshly squeezed golden cider. It was heaven.

In Calgary that year, J.S. Woodsworth had created a new political party, the Co-Operative Commonwealth Federation or the CCF, bringing together farmers and labourers under a socialist philosophy. It was the socialist stigma that turned many farmers against the party, and the party's goal to bring an end to capitalism. Pete was one of the doubters. He had told Max he believed in fairness to the workers, but socialism was another matter. Pete believed that socialism was next to communism.

Autumn also marked the annual game hunt. Pete would join a few of the neighbouring farmers and sometimes they would stay around the area marshes and hunt for ducks and geese. In his younger years, Ebenezer's Irish setter's instincts would be called upon. He'd go along for the fun and fetch the birds dropped in the shallow marshy water. Ebbie got to the point where he relished the affair and went crazy yelping and jumping and wagging his tail whenever Pete brought out his hunting rifle. It broke Pete's and Grace's hearts the last autumn of the dog's life, when he looked up at the rifle, gave his old tail a couple of thumps on the floor and promptly fell asleep. Ebbie knew full well his hunting days were behind him. "Just let me sleep," he seemed to be saying.

Sometimes Pete and the boys would go farther afield and head north into the woods for moose and deer hunting. A year never passed that Pete didn't bring home enough wild game to carry the family well into the winter. In the years of the Great Depression, the importance of those trips was magnified a hundred times.

* * *

1935

"So you was in Regina for the big strike, was ya, Max?"

"I was," Max told the man. "But it wasn't as bad as they say. The cops were determined to make something out of it but there wasn't much to it at all."

"I heard one of the coppers was killed, though," the man said. "That's something. What really happened out there?"

Max settled back and lit his pipe. It was a cool evening in August, the kind of evening that signalled autumn was in the air. Max Huddlestone had come inside the bunkhouse that evening because his bones were hurting from sleeping on the cool damp ground, his normally favoured location. One of the men had started up a conversation about wages and about how they'd dropped so badly since back in the Twenties. As he looked around, five eager sets of eyes looked to him for their nightly entertainment, a touch of sport after a hard day in the fields and orchards. Max thought back to the earlier days at Ballinskellig, to the booming days of the Twenties when there'd sometimes be fifteen or twenty workers this time of year. This year he was one of six, and wages were a fraction of what they'd once been. Like the other farmers, Pete O'Malley had scaled back because the prices just weren't there to justify the size of operation he had once run.

"I'd come up to Saskatchewan because I'd heard there might be work there and there was nothing down in Kentucky where I was," Max told his zealous audience, men starved for entertainment, for someone to tell them a story. "Well, I can tell you there was nothing there either. But some fellas were coming in on the trains from the West Coast and word passed around that everyone was to congregate at Market Square in Regina, to just let the authorities know how they felt.

"The cops came in on horses and they had their regular billy sticks, but they had guns too. And that didn't set too well with the trekkers. They were mad. All they wanted to do was send the fellas up in Ottawa a message, that they wanted work, not handouts, not vouchers. They didn't want to be on the dole. Well, there were scuffles and some of the men picked up rocks and sticks and well, they looked pretty pathetic against coppers with guns. The papers said there were four thousand of them but I don't think that's right. Not nearly that many. One copper got dragged off his horse and in the ruckus, well, he got himself killed."

The men listened in awe of Max's words. Was it the Communists? one wanted to know. Who started it all?

"Desperation," Max replied. "It's desperation that started it. You look at those men's faces and you can see it. Young fellas, some not shavin' yet, just tuckered out at not being able to find work, not able to support themselves. Some young fellas told me they left home so their mammas and papas didn't have to feed another mouth, thought they could find work and then couldn't. Desperation, that's the hand that was on the trigger."

"Someone's gotta do somethin'," said a man named Saul. "This ain't right. Back in the Twenties I made sometimes three dollar a day workin'.

Now if I can find work at all, well here at the O'Malley place, we make seventy-five cents now."

A murmur went up among Saul's colleagues and Max interrupted: "At least there's work here. I can tell you, I've been coming here for more than ten years and Mr. O'Malley, he's a fair man. You think it's cheap to give us that noonday meal we get? No sir, it's not. That's worth a lot. And this bunkhouse. It's clean, isn't it? How many places give you that? And how many, if they have one at all, are filled with rats and fleas? I'd say it's pretty good here."

"Still," said Saul, "what this country needs is a leader. And the workers, they need a leader too. The Communists, they're a joke. They don't know their ass from their mama's smile. Up in Ottawa, that's where we need a leader. Like Roosevelt down in War-shington. Least he's tryin' new things. Here, they just stumble on."

"They're all crooks in this country," added another. "Mitch Hepburn, Bennett. Crooks. All of 'em."

Max spoke up. "I'm not defending those men, but they just don't know what to do. No one knows. Sure, Roosevelt sounds good, but has he made it any better down there in the States? I don't think he has. Sure he's made some new government jobs, but that won't do it. There's something deeper happening, and no one knows what it is."

There was silence for a few moments before Saul chimed in: "War. That's what it's gonna take to end this mess. War."

There was another silence before one of the men picked up his harmonica and started on a quiet, mournful tune each one of them recognized.

* * *

One day James met Max as the older man was heading to the bunkhouse. "I wanna show you somethin'," the boy said. Max hesitated and James said: "Well, come on."

Max nodded. "Lead the way, then."

James walked toward the barn and picked up a lantern just inside the doorway. He lit it with a match that was stored next to the lantern and walked to the ladder that led to the loft. Up he went, and at the top he turned around and looked down at Max who stood there, puzzled. "Come on," he said.

Max shrugged and climbed the ladder. The boy walked over to one of the timbered walls and waited for Max. James shone the lantern onto a beam and Max stared intently at the carved letters. "'The seven wonders?' What's that?"

"They're my grampa and his brothers and sisters. See, B.O., that's Ben O'Malley. That's grampa. Each of the kids carved their initials in this beam. My Aunt Lucy says it was the day two of them headed out to the gold fields out West. They wanted to do something to remember one another. Pretty nice, eh?"

Max nodded. "Sure wish I had a legacy like that," he said. "You're a lucky man, Sonny Jim."

Jamie grinned. "I am, aren't I?"

As the decade slid by and folks began to wonder if privation was the new normal of their world, Grace watched how Jamie and Max's relationship grew, how their sharing had evolved into parent and child. They swapped stories and jokes. It did Grace's heart good to watch them laugh together. It made her love the man that much more. Her own relationship with Max evolved. She had embarked on a physical journey, based on her crushing loneliness but as the years added up, something stronger evolved. They seemed in tune, spiritually and cerebrally. There was a comfort, a solace his presence brought to her. What had begun as a compassionate love was quietly transitioning into one of companionship as well. Grace no longer had either with Pete.

But what of the brevity of her time with this mysterious man? While they could only be together for a couple of months each year, Grace began to recognize that fact simply added to the pleasure. Sure, the longing for him hurt, but maybe that was part of what she enjoyed. For those in more conventional coupleships, she noticed that the novelty, the excitement faded. Those circumstances never arose when Max returned to her.

As for Max, he desperately wanted to cement their family bond but Grace made it clear that could not happen. Not yet, at least. He would bide his time and indulge his wanderlust.

* * *

1939

Grace looked forward to her letters from Albie, who always filled in her friend in great detail about Roberto's activities, his business interests and his political connections. Over the years, there was some disturbing news from Italy. Grace shivered when she read that Roberto's friend, Il Duce, was being dubbed "the new Caesar," and how he was pressing Italy's interests in Africa where it was feared they would find themselves in conflict with the British and the French. Albie was upbeat but between the lines, Grace wondered if her old friend was getting a bit nervous herself about the direction things were taking. Italy was growing ever closer to Germany and Japan and drifting away from France and Britain. Grace worried about her friend.

At home, she was pleased, though, how Max always found the time to spend with Jamie. He watched proudly as the boy matured year to year. One day, Jamie informed Max that he now wished to be called James. And please, he added, no more Sonny Jim. "Okay, I promise," said Max. The boy was now a young man and well into high school. He told Max his father wanted him to think about how he could devote more time to the farm that fall, but that Pete was adamant James must not quit his schooling. He needed his education, Pete told him, recalling how his own father had forced him to drop out so he could work full-time on the farm. Pete was determined that would never happen to James. He must finish his schooling, because an educated farmer was a better farmer, Pete said.

In a very real sense, James enjoyed the company of two fathers. Pete was the stolid, patient teacher who impressed in the boy the lessons of the farm. Max taught him humour and passion.

Grace and Max maintained their Pete-sanctioned liaisons. It was a totally open secret and even some of the newer men had heard about it. Few ever spoke up about it, though, not since one of them had made a smart-assed remark to Max one year about "boilin' the cabbage" with the boss's missus. Max decked the man, then belted him another one when he finally staggered to his feet. That was the end of that.

Max had decided to withhold further requests to Grace that she come away with him, at least for the time. She had made herself quite clear and besides, with the privation of the 1930s and Max never knowing whether he'd be getting another job, he figured she and Jamie were better off staying right where they were. And if the truth be known, Max was a roving man. He liked it that way and had no intention of settling down any time soon. Maybe some day. His offer to Grace to do just that had been rash, made in the heat of passion.

Each season when he reached the point that he knew it was time to move on from Ballinskellig, Max would promise Grace he'd see her the next year. It was always Max who raised the matter and Grace looked forward to his announcement. But in the latter days of October 1939 when Grace could sense he was getting ready to move on, she noticed he said nothing about a return engagement. Finally she could stand it no further and raised the matter herself.

"So then I'll be seeing you next year," she said.

Max hesitated, looked down at the ground, scuffed his feet in the dust and then took her hands and led her over to the worn sofa in the sugarhouse. "I have something I need to say."

Grace's heart skipped a couple of beats. "What is it?"

"It's the war," he said. "We've been fighting the Krauts since September. I'm going over."

Grace's face registered her shock. "Why? You don't have to do this."

"But I do, Grace. I wasn't old enough for the first war and I always regretted it."

He nearly continued on, nearly explained that the real reason he felt compelled to fight was the sense of intense guilt that overcame him because of his father's profiteering from that war. A man he still hated. He couldn't do that, of course. He could never admit that he was the son of Henry Huddlestone, one of the richest men in Canada. He had always denied any connection to the man, to anyone who'd asked about his last name. Even to Grace. Max was ashamed of his father, and that shame had driven him to run from him for two decades.

"You're a good man, Max," Grace told him. "If it's what you need to do, then I know there's nothing I can say to stop you. But please, promise me you'll be careful. And if when it's over you can come back, I promise you, I'll be here."

"I'll be back," Max vowed.

* * *

That autumn, the year James turned fifteen, Pete convinced Grace to let the boy come along for the hunt. Like most farm boys, Jamie had been familiar with guns since an early age. He'd been handed his first rifle at the age of six and was shooting at gophers ever since. But Grace was reluctant to let him join the autumn hunt and had held out for Jamie's fifteenth birthday before finally giving Pete the go-ahead. "It's part of becoming a man around these parts," Pete told her. "Lloyd Porter's boy, Eric, he's coming along. He's the same age as Jamie and the boys have always been good friends."

Grace relented. "Watch out for him," she warned Pete. "He's all we've got." Pete looked her in the eye, but said nothing.

James was overjoyed as he hopped into the back of Deke McCormack's farm truck for the drive north to the Madawaska Highlands. Eric Porter was by his side and the two friends chattered excitedly all the way. Their conversation wasn't all about hunting, though. There was plenty of talk about girls, about their futures, and about the war in Europe.

"Do you think the war will last long enough for us to join up?" Eric asked his friend.

"Sure hope so," James replied. "I wanna get a chance to show those Krauts what-for. Eric, you and me would make a great team over there. I can hardly wait."

The hunting trip was particularly successful that season and when they returned, the men's families had enough moose meat to last them all for much of the long winter months.

"Jamie brought the beast down," Pete declared proudly to Grace on their return. "He's quite the fearless hunter." Pete realized he had been about to add: "Takes after his old man." Instead, he turned and joined James who was starting to haul the meat into the cellar cold room.

12

Operation Freya

MAX THANKED MR. Eddy for driving him to Peterborough as the Model T Ford pulled up outside the army recruitment office. The two men shook hands, the older one wished Max well and said his country would thank him for his service. "Be safe," were Bob Eddy's last words.

Max had run into Mr. Eddy after he left Ballinskellig and headed into Shannonside for a beer at Pop's Tavern, a beer aimed at steadying his nerves and giving him the fortitude he'd need to go through with his plan. He wasn't a kid anymore, but a man of nearly thirty-seven. It was the young pups the army was looking for to join up and he wasn't even sure what their reaction would be when he showed his face at the recruitment centre. Maybe they wouldn't even accept him, Max thought. They preferred young men who had not gained the wisdom of age that would make them think twice about volunteering for war, the ones who had not heard the horror stories from the first war. Max had heard them, yet the guilt he felt over his father's profiteering from that war was an even more powerful force. It was a guilt that had only intensified in the two decades since, as he learned more about the lives of the average people he had come to know and work with.

He was just finishing his beer and thinking about heading out to the highway to hitch a ride to Peterborough when Bob Eddy happened past the table where Max was sitting alone.

"Max, is that you?" Eddy asked. "It's not like you, taking time out for a brew during the working day." Eddy laughed heartily at his own joke.

"I'm finished up with the harvest, Mr. Eddy," he said. "Heading out to join the army."

After a short chat, Eddy said if Max was going to join the military and give it to Hitler, then the least he could do was drive him up to Peterborough to do the honours. Max thanked him and said he'd gratefully accept. On the ride up, the two men talked incessantly, about the harvest, about Hitler and about the passing landscape.

Now, as he stood outside the recruitment centre, Max was beginning to have second thoughts. Yes, he had heard the many horror stories from some of the veterans of the Great War, and wondered what might be in store for him now. Yet he had made up his mind. He owed it to the country to repay it in some small way for the damage his father had done.

Inside the recruitment centre, Max gave his name and stumbled over his age. "Thirty," he lied when the clerk, a man of his own age, asked, then looked doubtfully at him. "Sure ya are, and I'm Cary Grant," the clerk said. "But I don't give a shit. It's your funeral."

Max found basic training the most excruciating experience of his life. Training with men fifteen or more years his junior, he ached constantly. His muscles screamed out in pain and when he tried to sleep, his legs cramped up and refused to give him the rest he desperately needed. But he had no choice. He had made his decision and there was no turning back.

Besides the gruelling physical regimen that left him in the best condition of his life, the army training taught Max new skills: marksmanship and how to clean his gun, disassemble it and put it back together lightning-fast; how to kill a man by running him through with the bayonet of his rifle. The men soon looked up to him as their top marksman; "old man eagle-eye," they said good-naturedly. While he found the physical training exhausting, Max enjoyed the more cerebral aspects of his instruction and was soon promoted to corporal. "We need fellows like you with brains, Huddlestone," said his CO. "Men who can think on the fly and keep their composure. Some of the younger fellas are hotheads. You're a real cool one. Oh, and another thing I nearly forgot: you'll be leaving your lads and joining the South Saskatchewan Regiment. They're a fine group. They need you." Max couldn't care less which outfit he joined up with, as long as he got overseas. As long as he had the chance to make amends for his father.

He had never been on any sort of ship before he boarded the vessel that took his regiment to England that day in 1940. The ship rolled and rocked and Max, like many of the other men, spent much of his time hanging over the rail and wishing he were dead. The mighty Atlantic tossed the ship mercilessly, the water's green shade seeming to mimic and mock the green that most of the men had turned. When they arrived in Southampton, Max was never so glad to touch dry land. One of the South Saskatchewan's comedians, a farm boy by the name of Hap Hope, actually jumped from the final step and got down on all fours to kiss the ground. "Get up, soldier," a sergeant who lacked Hope's sense of humour barked. "I'll have your arse in a sling if you try any funny business like that again."

Most of the men were eager to leap right into the fighting. After months of physical training, they were fit and raring to go. Older and wiser than most, Max was beginning to think differently. Perhaps a longer term of acclimatization might be a good idea. But at that moment he had no idea just how much acclimatization they would be getting. The physical training continued unabated. But as Canadian troops filed into army camps across the island of Great Britain with precious little to keep them mentally occupied, the men became bored and restless. There were only so many games of baseball, cribbage, rummy and darts a man could play before he was ready to scream in frustration.

As the months wore on, the lack of military action was driving the men to distraction. It was a level of tedium they had never before known. They were told they were here to assist in the home defence of the king's realm. It was a bitter joke: In reality, they knew that with Hitler having captured nearly all of Europe, there was no toehold, no place for them to fight. At least the air force and navy men had something to do; the Canadian army was frustrated to be hunkered down on the small island that sat as the last great bastion of democracy on that side of the ocean. Max joked resentfully that Britain was the best damned fortified piece of real estate in the world.

The new year of 1942 came and still there were no signs of combat in their future. The idle time gave Max opportunity to mull things over: the estrangement from his father that arose out of the guilt he felt over Huddlestone Industries' massive wartime profits; his loneliness and the way he missed Grace and Jamie; and wondering what direction his life might take if and when he ever returned from the war. While many of the younger fellows quickly hooked up with British girls, Max resisted any emotional ties and thought only of Grace.

Over time, the Canadians realized their training exercises were being subtly changed. Then news came that they would soon see action and their spirits rose. At last they would be doing what they were here to do. The men of the South Saskatchewan knew they were ready. They were eager to prove themselves in combat.

Outside the camp, huge stockpiles of equipment began to show up along England's southern coastline. Something big was about to come down. Problem was, thought Max, the Germans were privy to the same knowledge, thanks to their regular reconnaissance flights. When finally word came that there was to be an exploratory operation onto the Continent, Max wondered: How secret was this operation going to be?

One day a man dressed in a British army uniform came by Max's barracks and told him to come along. "Where to?" Max asked. The man looked at him and said: "You'll soon see."

The man led Max to a giant black sedan with no military markings on its sides, opened the back door and slid inside. He turned to Max. "Well, come on," he said. Max followed and shut the door. The car's driver, dressed in military fatigues, started the ignition and sped off. They drove out of the camp and down the road several miles, to a long driveway that led to an isolated building surrounded by woods. Max followed the man as he got out of the car and walked deliberately to the door. The man knocked sharply, opened the door and without a word, motioned for Max to go inside. The man didn't follow but rather shut the door behind Max. In the single simple room there were two men, one who sat scribbling something at a desk and the other, a British major, Max could see, was perched on the edge of the desk. Max stood at attention and saluted when he saw the major who quickly replied: "At ease, corporal. We're all just friends here. Nothing formal."

The man who had been writing at the desk looked up. Max immediately noticed his youth, clearly at least a decade younger than Max himself. The man said: "Hello, corporal. I hope the Canadians are treating you well at camp?" His cockney accent betrayed him as East End London.

"Can't complain," Max replied. "Food's good."

"Brilliant," the man replied. "Now let me introduce myself. Name is Nissenthall. Flight sergeant Jack Nissenthall. I'm RAF and I'm quite good at understanding how radar works, or so they tell me. And this gentleman here with me is Major Leslie Thorncroft." Max nodded to the major.

"You're older than the other men in your platoon and an excellent marksman," Nissenthall said. "And I'm told quite a bit quicker thinking than most. We're looking for some special men, men who can shift on the fly, so to speak. Men for an exclusive sort of mission."

When Max remained silent, puzzled by what the man might be hinting at, Nissenthall continued: "You are about to hear details of an operation, an attack on the coastline of France."

"That's not really much of a surprise," Max said. "The rumours have been flying for quite some time. I'm sure the Jerries know as well as us."

Nissenthall looked him square in the eye. "Well there's a bit more to it than that, corporal. A trifle more, you could say. The British government has assigned me to lead an exclusive operation within that operation, if you will. I will need a handful of intelligent men, dead-eye accurate marksmen, to assist me, to join my team. We will be attempting to take something from the Jerries, something they definitely do not wish us to have. Now as I am sure a man of your intelligence can ascertain, there will be a spot of danger involved. I myself do not have much experience in these matters and so I'll need a band of fighting men, marksmen such as yourself, who can help get me through it all. You are the oldest of the group, corporal, but we are confident your physical condition is second to none."

As Max listened, dumbfounded, Nissenthall went on to explain the background of his assignment, how earlier that same year British paratroopers had conducted a raid on St. Bruneval in Northern France. They came away with key parts to a cutting-edge German radar device, one of a series that, working in tandem, was used to direct anti-aircraft fire and control night fighters that intercepted Allied bombers as they approached their inland targets.

"As a result of their excellent work, we were able to develop, shall we say, countermeasures," said Nissenthall. He went on to explain that he himself had held down a technical job of sorts with the RAF and had been called in to special service because of his talents.

Nissenthall glanced over at the major. "Perhaps you would like to take over from here, sir." Thorncroft nodded and cleared his throat.

"British intelligence has for some time detected signals from a device that sits atop a cliff outside the French village of Dieppe. It's coming from one of the Nazis' Freya early warning system locations. Freya, you might be aware, is named for the Norse goddess of love. A rather ironic use of the name, wouldn't you say?"

Nissenthall chuckled and Thorncroft continued.

"It has come down to us from the highest levels of Britain's intelligence service that we have been charged with the task of relieving the Krauts of this particular piece of equipment located at the Freya station atop a three-hundred-foot cliff and bring it to Britain for inspection. That is the mission. And that is where you come in, corporal. The Canadians have been after us to get in on the action for quite some time. And so they will. You have been chosen to be part of a ten-man team of sharpshooters to accompany the flight sergeant here, make your way to Freya and remove the listening device. Then return with it. Simple, what?"

Max whistled. "So let me get this straight. Eleven men are to cross the English Channel and approach a Nazi military installation that sits on top of a three-hundred-foot cliff that is fortified to the teeth and guarded by an early warning system, steal the workings of this thing and then return back across the Channel with them. All without getting our hair parted by the Nazis. Have I got that right?"

"Precisely," said Thorncroft, his voice flat. "But not to worry. The part we haven't told you yet is that there will be cover. This operation will all be conducted as part of a massive military campaign involving six thousand Canadian, British and American personnel, led by minesweepers, under cover from British and American fighter pilots and led by a phalanx of destroyers and gunboats. You will have plenty of support."

"Well, then," replied Max. "By all means, let's get started."

* * *

As Thorncroft and Nissenthall continued to brief him, Max learned that other riflemen from Canadian 2nd Division's South Saskatchewan Regiment, Company A, had already been selected for the mission and that one of those chosen had suffered a burst appendix that, due to complications, would take some time to heal. An emergency replacement was required. Max had been on the original long list, missing it only because he was the eldest. When a replacement was called for, his name came up first. The following day, he would meet his fellow team members and begin training, which was to take place on the Isle of Wight. Eighteen hours later, as he stood on the beach and looked up at the island's soaring bluffs, Max's stomach turned.

Max had been moved from his regular barracks to live with Nissenthall and the nine other men of the special mission Freya. Over the coming days, they developed a bond, a high degree of respect and fondness for one another. Most importantly, they came to implicitly trust one another. The men spent their days together training and planning for their exercise. One day as the men joked about their intelligence operation, one of them labelled Nissenthall the chief "spook," and the name stuck - Spook he would forever be.

Soon after their training was completed, the men were called together before being sent back to barracks. Major Thorncroft walked in the door. He silently cast his eyes over the group who sensed the importance of what was to come.

"Men, you are about to undertake a very important task, one that is known only to a small group. I have one more matter I must share with you before you depart." He took a few moments to look into the faces of the men before continuing. "Radio Direction Finder Nissenthall is a highly important asset to British intelligence. Over time he has learned a great number of our secrets. He must not under any circumstances fall into the hands of the enemy. You are part of his personal bodyguard. You are there to protect him and ensure he gets through and completes his mission. If at any time RDF Nissenthall is in danger of being captured by the enemy, your task will be to ensure this does not happen."

Thorncroft paused to give the men time to let those words sink in before he continued. "If it appears capture is about to occur and there is no other course of action possible, you are to kill him. I repeat, you are to kill RDF Nissenthall."

* * *

The cover operation for the assault on Freya was called Jubilee and was planned for July. At the last minute it was delayed because of poor weather. In August, the Canadians again received the word they would be heading out, only to experience a second delay when fog rolled in over the English Channel. Finally, the next day, on the night of August 18, with conditions perfect, the operation was launched. With extraordinary precision, thousands of men, mostly Canadians, were loaded onto landing barges at the English port of Newhaven. Finally, they were headed across the channel, to Nazi-occupied Normandy. They were told they would be landing on one of several beaches near a little French town named Dieppe.

The stated intent of the operation was to destroy German artillery positions, an airfield and a radar post. Success would rattle the Nazis, make them understand the Allies were intent on retaking Western Europe and give the occupied populace a sense of hope. It was to be a test run for the eventual all-out assault on the Continent. Behind these lofty goals was an important ulterior motive known only to a select few: capture the inner workings of a highly sophisticated radar system that, once understood and manipulated by the Allies, would greatly increase the odds of victory.

Max was one of that number who truly understood this final clandestine intent. He and the other special group of A Company sharpshooters were expected to make it happen.

Most of the five thousand Canadian soldiers involved in Jubilee rejoiced that finally they would see action. This is what they had trained for. This is what they had waited so long to accomplish. Max worried that with two delays, the enemy had had plenty of time to prepare for their arrival. With so much time having passed, how many opportunities had there been for a misspoken word at the wrong time to alert the Germans? he wondered. After all, it was an open secret the Nazis had spies among the English population, ready to jump on any hint the expected invasion was set to commence, and where it was to occur. Still, Max held his thoughts to himself. No sense alarming the younger guys, he reasoned.

A sense of quiet calm fell over the men as they were quickly and efficiently boarded onto the flotilla of landing craft. The flotilla was preceded by British and American fighter craft and accompanied by eight destroyers and motor gunboats. Earlier, word had passed around that Major General John Hamilton Roberts was to command the 2nd Canadian Infantry Division from aboard the HMS *Calpe*. Minesweepers would be clearing a path for them. The men were confident in their commanders. Max began to settle his nerves. Maybe it would be okay after all.

There had been plenty of talk about the mighty German defensive wall that had been constructed along the French coast. Now the Allies were about to learn how effective it truly was.

Outfitted in battle dress overtop an inflatable vest nicknamed a Mae West, Max's special unit, led by Flight Sergeant "Spook" Nissenthall, was to come ashore at the western end of the invasion area, west of Dieppe near the smaller village of Pourville which sat next to the River Scie. They were part of the South Saskatchewan Regiment who were joined by the Queen's Own Cameron Highlanders from Winnipeg. Minutes before they reached shore, Max and the other men checked their weapons. Nissenthall passed around a jar of rum. Nerve medicine, he called it. Each man took a sip and passed it along.

From his barge, Max watched the first Canadian troops from the South Saskatchewans begin to land on the French coast at ten minutes to five in the morning of August 19. The German barrage began immediately. Max's suspicion was right: they had been well alerted to likely enemy activity somewhere along the coast in the vicinity of Dieppe and had fortified the clifftops that flanked the village.

Max's landing craft reached shallow water and the bow dropped on the barge. Max held his Lee-Enfield rifle high over his head, jumped into a few inches of water and followed the mass of humanity that poured out onto the beach. The sound of gunfire was already deafening.

What a hell of a place, he thought. Bodies began dropping in the face of German firepower. Even in the pre-dawn light he could see the water was turning dark and Max knew it was from the blood of his colleagues who had already been wounded or killed. Silhouetted against the early light of the coming dawn, Max could see the German pillboxes, the concrete bunkers from which the enemy laid down their immense firepower.

Somehow the men of Operation Freya got off the stony beach and made it to the sea wall without casualty. There, they discovered the navy had let them off in the wrong spot. They were on the opposite side of the river from Freya. No time to worry, they must improvise. They used the scaling ladders they had brought to get over the eight-foot seawall. But they had been spotted by the Germans who manned the pillboxes and enemy fire began to drop the Canadians. Finally, one of the A Company men lobbed a grenade into the nearest pillbox's slit and ended that particular threat.

Max and the others scrambled across a bridge that traversed the river and ran up a grassy hill. His actions were automatic, born of training and initiated by necessity. As he planted one foot before the other and scrambled up the slope, Max was overcome with a sense of sheer exhilaration. Sweating, lightheaded, he momentarily thought he had never felt so alive, so filled with elation.

The pillbox fire had inflicted terrible casualties already. Of A Company's original one hundred men, just twenty-four remained, including seven of the special operation's original ten marksmen, three of whom were slightly wounded. Max and Nissenthall were unhurt. The remaining troops made their way up from back of the cliff where the radar installation was located and in the rising light of day they spotted their objective.

Nissenthall eyed the radar antenna. Their goal was so close, but standing in the way was a deadly combination of barbed wire, riflemen holed up in slit trenches and machine-gun nests. Nissenthall took moments to observe the radar, glanced at Max and smiled. Max wondered, now what?

Nissenthall took Max and a second bodyguard into nearby Pourville, where the battalion had set up its headquarters. Faced with heavy German fire, Nissenthall told his two companions: "We've got to get back to A Company."

From the decimated A Company, a mortar team was arranged to help Nissenthall's team return to Pourville for another attempt on Freya. Under enemy firepower, the Canadians were forced to fall back. Now it was time for Nissenthall to implement a plan they had contemplated during training: If he severed the telephone cables that ran from Freya to the command post, the Germans would have to rely on radio communication to relay the attackers' air movements. Those communications could be monitored, and the British would obtain valuable insight into Freya's operation.

Max volunteered for the task, but Nissenthall insisted on going himself. Max watched Nissenthall crawl across the ground to the poles between which the cables were strung. He gasped as the man wedged his body between the poles and slowly advanced his way fifteen feet up to where the cables were strung. With wire clippers, Spook snipped the cables. Max wondered: "At what point are we to kill this son-of-a-bitch? Surely he'll be captured." Max subconsciously grabbed onto his Lee-Enfield more tightly, but held his fire.

Miraculously returning unscathed, Nissenthall said to the pair: "If we are ever going to capture Freya, we're going to have to force our way into the radar station. We need a tank."

Nissenthall, Max and the other man made their way back to Pourville again, where Nissenthall approached the Cameron Highlanders commander. "I need some of your men to come with me," he said. The commander nodded. He had not been told details of this man's mission, but he understood it was important. He formed a small contingent and they made their way down an asphalt road toward another village.

Max and the others were at first relieved to hear the rumble of approaching tanks. Relief turned to horror as they realized the tanks were not theirs. The enemy spotted them and began to fire. They scattered.

Making his way back to Pourville with Nissenthall, Max looked around at the savagely diminished contingent of Canadians. He knew they had done all they could, but feared it had not been enough. As if reading his mind, Nissenthall said: "Let's get out of here."

Max was dejected. He knew they were supposed to break in to the Freya installation and they had fallen short of their goal. Still, Nissenthall seemed upbeat as the pair made their way down to the beach. Their hearts leaped as they saw an approaching escort destroyer lay down a smoke screen to shield the landing craft heading in for the rescue. A blast from the destroyer's four-inch guns sent a chunk of the massive cliff disintegrating beneath the Germans. The enemy guns fell silent in fear of attracting a similar response from the destroyer and a cheer rose up from the Canadians who were huddled along the beach.

"Come on," Nissenthall ordered and Max looked around for his partner. The man had disappeared. Nissenthall grabbed Max. "I said come on!" Max followed his lead and tore off his helmet and gear. He dropped his Lee-Enfield. They would have to swim for it and the gear was an encumbrance. As the two men dove into the water, Max's vest kept him too buoyant, too vulnerable to enemy fire. He removed the vest. Now he must depend upon his ability to swim underwater for as long as he could. He dove down into the dark water and realized he had never been so terrified.

His lungs nearly burst. He dare not swallow salt water but he could hold his breath no longer. Forced to surface, he again heard enemy fire crackling through the air. Acrid grey and white smoke, interspersed by charges of red and orange, filled the air and left him choking. There were Nissenthall and several Canadians, swimming for their lives toward a landing craft. Their flotation vests allowed an occasional moment of rest. Ahead, he saw a man flailing in the water, kept up only by his vest. The soldier was coughing and choking on the frigid salt water. He was nearly done. Max grabbed onto the man's vest, rested for a moment, turned the man on his back and pulled him toward the craft.

Exhausted by the effort of trying to propel himself forward with one arm and holding the soldier with his other hand, Max shut his eyes and moved forward, his slow progress mechanical, instinctive. Now nearly spent, Max reached out one more time and felt the cold metal hull of the rescue craft. Relief surged through him as unseen hands lifted him on board. He fell into a fully spent unconsciousness.

In his stupor, he was vaguely aware of the sound of two German fighters screaming out of the sky toward the landing craft, guns blazing. The craft was hit and began taking on water as it limped out to sea toward the destroyer. Max's mind drifted to a hypnotic state. He knew he hit the water as the landing craft began to sink, and his next recollection was being pulled up a rope ladder to the destroyer. He passed out.

* * *

Days later, as he sat in a Newhaven pub, Max's hands still trembled. While news reports made the best of it, the survivors were saying that the

Dieppe raid had been a colossal disaster. It couldn't possibly be described as anything else, Max thought. Of the six thousand men who had set out from the English coast that day, thirty-six hundred had been killed, wounded or captured and presumably sent to German PoW camps. Max marvelled how he had escaped with barely a scratch.

"Huddlestone," Max heard someone call. "Is that you, man?"

Max glanced up from the beer he was quietly sipping alone and looked into the beaming face of Jack Nissenthall. Max managed a weak smile and said: "Sergeant, you made it. I wasn't sure."

Spook Nissenthall sat down beside him and ordered a pint. "You bet I did, mate." Then quietly he added: "Look, Max, you and I are the lucky ones. Of the eleven of us, no one else made it back."

A silence fell between the two and finally Nissenthall spoke up quietly. "You know, I can't really talk about it, but you deserve to know, Max, it was worth it."

Max looked at him. "Thirty-six hundred casualties? Worth it?" he asked incredulously.

"I know, mate, I know. But what we learned about … about the enemy's communication, that will prove invaluable. I'm already working on followup. HQ is delighted, and they're really pleased with you. I believe they'll be paying you another visit soon, to explain just how pleased."

Max grimaced. "Can't wait," he replied.

Spook Nissenthall looked at the older man. "You handled yourself very well, corporal. You were an invaluable part of the team. But there's one thing I need to know." Just then the barmaid brought over his beer and Nissenthall paused, looking down at it, then up into Max's face. "Tell me, Max, would you really have done it, if it was necessary? Would you really have pulled the trigger and killed me?" Max stared back blankly. "Fuck, yes," he replied. "Those were my orders."

* * *

With the horrors he had witnessed at Dieppe still echoing in his memory, Max Huddlestone wasn't sure he was in any hurry to get back into action. Young men mowed down by enemy guns, their bodies splayed out atop barbed wire barriers, face-down on the beach or floating in the surf. Despite the terror he had felt during the assault on Freya, he had walked through his duties automatically and efficiently because there had been no time to dwell on it during the four hours or so he had been on occupied territory. Now, when he thought back, the memories were nightmarishly clear and he cowered from what he had seen. And finally, he thought about how he had gone into battle with his Lee-Enfield rifle and about how, under the correct circumstances, his sworn duty was to kill Jack Nissenthall, one of his fellow combatants. While he would have done it had it become necessary, he knew he would never have been able to live with himself afterwards.

After that day in the pub, Max saw Jack one more time, the day Jack and another man paid a visit to Max's camp that autumn. He understood immediately it was not a social visit, and quickly realized it was one intended to feel him out for further duties of a special nature. "You conducted yourself at Dieppe with nerves of steel," said the other man, who remained unidentified except as "from Intelligence." "Some of us are looking for men of your calibre, corporal. You could make yourself very valuable to your country."

Max shivered at the notion. He had heard stories of special-op military personnel who were deployed to help undermine the enemy and work with those in the occupied zones who were working for the resistance network, and he wanted nothing to do with it. He knew these people ran the constant risk of having to kill, and that wasn't in his nature. Spook Niessenthall was a particular sort of man who seemed to thrive on the danger of his work. Max couldn't see himself pursuing anything of the sort.

He had, however, thought of another way in which he could be useful. Max thought back to the horrific moments when the men of Operation Jubilee were being cut down by enemy fire. Some of them were in shock, some were writhing in pain from their injuries. Max was in awe of the handful of medics who came to offer them help on the field of battle and knew there was always a need for more. He thought back many years, to that day in Winnipeg, when a veteran from the Great War had come to the aid of Max's injured friend, Tom Merritt. That man had served as a medic in the war, someone who helped and comforted the wounded. Max was particularly taken by the notion that most of the medics went into battle unarmed, their job to save lives rather than to take lives.

The Intelligence official - he was dressed in civilian clothing rather than a military uniform - who accompanied Jack Nissenthall that day was visibly disappointed by Max's response but said the military could always use more medics, and encouraged him to pursue that path, if that's what he wanted.

Max did just that and the authorities jumped at his offer. Before he knew it, he found himself being trained. Outfitted with a helmet and armband, a kit strapped to his belt and armed only with stainless steel scissors and gauze, Max became one of those men who proudly formed the military's first line of battlefield medicine. Their job was to stabilize the wounded and prepare them for evacuation to a field hospital or medical centre. Max learned how to try to stop the bleeding, apply dressings, sprinkle sulfa powder for antiseptic and administer morphine. He was told that medics needed to make life-and-death decisions, that sometimes they needed to decide a soldier was beyond help and that in such event they needed to simply move on to the next one.

He was under no illusion that it was a safer job than that of the fighting man. He was just as susceptible to bullets, shrapnel and shells as any other soldier. But he did not have to carry a gun – although some chose to do so – and for that he was grateful. He remembered reaching out to the young soldier who struggled in the surf off the coast of France and wondered if he had made it back alive. At least Max had tried. He thought about how Grace had called him her "angel," the mysterious stranger who had seemingly come from nowhere to protect and save her after she had been struck by lightning. "Without you, I would not be alive," Grace had said. It was a phrase he held dear, one he was determined to keep as his mantra.

* * *

Grace read newspaper reports of the Dieppe raid. Under headlines such as "Canadian troops lead great commando raid" and "RCAF plays fine part in Dieppe show," she read war correspondents' accounts. "I watched Canadian troops fight the blazing, bloody battle," wrote one correspondent, a man named Griffin Stoneman.

Little was said of the devastating Canadian losses, of the fact that more than nine hundred were killed, twenty five hundred injured and nearly two thousand taken prisoner. Fewer than half of the Canadians who left England that day made it back.

But it didn't take long for the rumours to start, and Grace wondered whether Max had been a part of that raid. And if he had been, whether he had ever made it out. She feared she might never know – and wondered if she really wanted to.

13

Jamie's War
1943

JAMES HAD BECOME a valuable asset to his father at Ballinskellig. While just nineteen years of age, those short years had been filled with on-the-job lessons about the animals and the crops that maintained it, the weather that sustained it and about what factors made the difference between a good year and a bad one. He had learned how to adeptly supervise the men, and more recently the women, who arrived annually to help with the harvest. Despite his young age, James handled himself with confidence and was treated by all the workers with a level of respect, even deference, that impressed Pete. Farm foreman Mel Brewster was advancing in years and starting to slow down. It was James who had picked up the slack.

James fully understood how much his father had come to depend on him and that knowledge filled him with self-assurance and self-respect. Pete had reached the point where he just automatically shared important decisions with the younger man. It had become second-nature that James was his sounding board and Pete found himself listening to his son's solid advice. Pete knew that when the time came, James would be capable of taking the reins from his hands. He had come to rely on James to keep up with the latest trends, the changing markets and newest methods to handle the pests that bedevilled the farmer, pests that some were starting to battle with synthetic pesticides. For the past three years, James had accompanied Pete on his annual trips into town to talk to the banker about getting the necessary loans to maintain the operation and in that short time had picked up all the nuances necessary to assure the lender. Pete was fully confident James could, if necessary, handle financial matters himself and understood how to maintain the farm's account books.

There was another kind of book James had turned to in his occasional free moments. He had a zeal for learning, something Pete had recognized years ago and which led to his insistence that the boy continue his high school lessons. On one of his trips to the Shannonside library, James had come across a couple of books about the history of apple growing and had entertained his father with his newfound knowledge. James told his father how the apple had been cultivated since the days of the Persians and the early Greeks. They had learned to manipulate the fruit through cross-pollination and before them, the Chinese had been grafting apples and other fruits for thousands of years. James's eagerness for learning filled Pete with admiration. The world was changing, and farmers could benefit from a good education.

The fact that James realized how valuable he had become to his father made things that much more difficult. He knew that when he told his parents what his plans were, they would be devastated, yet he knew it was a conversation they must have. After dinner one evening near the end of the harvest season, he told Grace and Pete he wanted to have a talk. Neither one of them had any idea what was coming.

As they settled in to comfortable chairs in the parlour, James offered to get his parents a glass of port. They accepted and he poured a glass of Pete's cider for himself. James took a sip and cleared his throat.

"Pop, Mum, you both know how much I appreciate all that you've done for me and all you've taught me. I hope that in the coming years I can do you both proud." Grace and Pete glanced at one another, Pete with a puzzled look on his face and Grace with a blank stare.

"You've been a perfect son, Jamie," Grace replied. "Your father and I both feel that way."

Pete nodded. "You've already done us proud, James," his father added. "Why, if you had to, you could run this whole place yourself right now. I have no doubt on that."

James looked at them and took a deep breath. "I'll just get to the point. There's no easy way. I've decided to join the army. It's something I feel I've got to do."

"What?" "But Jamie!" his parents said in unison. Pete added: "You don't need to do anything of the sort. Farming is a noble and essential part of the war effort. You don't need to do anything to prove yourself. People need food. The military needs food."

"Yes, I know that, Pop. But it's not enough for me. I need to go. I want to get over there and help. Look, once this is over, I promise, I'll come back and get back to farming. But in the meantime, I need to volunteer my services. Mel's got plenty of good years yet and I know he can help you all you need."

"But the worker shortage. You've seen it yourself. And it'll only get worse if the government imposes conscription. I need you here."

"We had half a dozen women working here this year, Pop. As more men go into the military, there'll be more yet. Everyone's pitching in. That's what I want to do too. I want to pitch in and help, just overseas, that's all."

His mother spoke up. "Jamie, I don't want you to go. All the stories about the war. I don't want you over there." Tears came to her eyes. It was especially wrenching when she thought that now she would have two of her men in battle. Of the other one, she couldn't say a word.

"Mum, I know, I know. But you just have to understand. Do you remember the day that man showed up and how hungry he was? You went and got him something to eat. And you told me that day that if we are in a position to help someone, we were obliged. Mum, this is my obligation. It's something deep inside me. I just know it's my calling. I don't know how to explain it. I don't want you to think I'm escaping anything here on Ballinskellig, it's not like that at all. But I've got to go."

Pete stood up and stomped out of the room. "Do what you've got to do then, dammit. Do what you've got to do."

Grace stood too and came over to her son. She put her arms around him and sobbed. "Have you told Sally?"

James had met Sally Parnell a couple of years ago when her family moved to Shannonside to take over the old general store. A year younger than James, Sally was vibrant, spirited and, as might be expected from her orange-red hair, fiery-tempered. She was as quick to smile and blast a wisecrack as she was to give Jamie proper hell.

On their first date, James had treated Sally to a film, *The Philadelphia Story*, starring Katharine Hepburn and Cary Grant. Hepburn reminded him of Sally. When Hepburn told Grant, "Oh, Dexter, I'm such an unholy mess of a girl," Sally adopted the line as her own. It cracked James up every time she repeated it with an innocent bat of her eyelashes.

Sally was fun-loving, a kind-hearted girl who loved to joke. In high school, she had been on the track team, edited the school yearbook, joined the debating society and won scholastic ribbons for her proficiency in mathematics and English literature. In home economics, she cooked and baked with equal finesse.

James had grown into a strong young man and with his shock of blond hair and blue eyes, Sally had labelled him Thor, her Viking-man.

As far as James was concerned, the two were a couple and he expected they would some day marry and raise a family at Ballinskellig. The one time he brought that up with Sally, however, she scowled and told him: "Slow down, sport. I'm not ready to be talking like that. Jamie, I want to go to college and learn more about life. I don't want to think about settling down here in Shannonside." James was struck speechless. When his mother would raise the subject of his future with Sally, he would steer the subject away.

Grace had immediately loved Sally and had often hoped that she and Jamie might some day settle down, even if her son was reluctant to speak of such matters. Now she found herself asking him: "Have you told Sally?"

"No, Mum. I planned to tell her tomorrow."

James went to see Sally the next day. "Why, Mr. O'Malley," she cooed, "I had no idea you were planning a visit today. Please excuse my appearance. Had I known you were comin', I'd have baked some scones, put on a pot of tea and made myself more presentable."

James smiled at Sally's Jane Austin-like performance. She was a big fan of English Victorian romances. He opened his arms to greet her as she came to him and wrapped her own arms around him. He snuggled his face into her flaming hair and breathed in her scent. He shivered with the little frissons her closeness gave him.

"Your appearance is just fine, Lady Parnell," he replied coyly. "It's all I can do to keep my hands to myself."

"Why Mr. O'Malley," she replied. "I declare you will make me blush."

James loved their suggestive banter but he had business to attend to and decided to get right to the point. Pulling back and looking into her face, he said: "Sally, Eric and I have been talking about our futures. Eric says he's going to join up with the army and I've decided to join him. Sally, we're heading out next week to the Kingston induction centre."

The young woman looked stricken. "What? Jamie, you've never mentioned this before. How could you make this decision without talking to me first?"

James was surprised. "I was not aware that in your mind there was really anything for the two of us to speak of. You've made it clear you're not ready to talk about us."

Sally stammered. "Well, maybe not in so many words, but I always hoped that after my schooling, after college, we could still think about being together. I do wish you'd confided in me before making up your mind."

"It's just something I've got to do," Jamie told her. "It's my obligation. This could work out well for us. I'll come back after the war, Sally, and you'll be finished college by then. If we feel it's the right thing to do, we could talk about marriage. But I've got to do this first. Please understand."

Sally's eyes filled with tears. "Oh, you men! You can hardly wait to go over there and start shooting things up. I don't believe you, Jamie. I simply don't."

James assured her he'd write every week and said he hoped she'd do the same. Sally knew there were plenty of young men taking the same course of action and if she had to admit it to herself, she would say that Jamie's news was not all that shocking. She had always wondered whether growing crops was going to keep Jamie occupied and satisfied while those many other young men were heading off to war.

"Well, at least you're going to have to take me to the dance in town tonight, mister," she said. "We've got some talking to do."

That evening, James stopped outside the Parnells' general store in the family democrat, pulled by old Bess. Sally opened the door to the Parnell apartment located overtop the store and stood in the doorway wearing a plain blue pleated dress and costume pearls. She apologized for the simplicity of her outfit and said if she'd had more time to think about it, she probably could have come up with something better. "You're not giving me much time to adjust to this," she chided him. "I'm such an unholy mess of a girl." Jamie, who had donned his only sports jacket, laughed at her use of the film reference, and said she looked perfect to him.

On the dance floor, they clung to one another and swayed to the recordings of Guy Lombardo, Sammy Kay and Benny Goodman. The young couple agreed they would write one another regularly and look ahead to the day when Jamie returned. "The time will fly past," he assured her.

During a break, they sipped on a couple of colas. James reached into his pocket and pulled out a simple silver band. "It's not much, but I'm hoping you'll agree to accept it as a symbol of our engagement."

Looking down at the ring, Sally said: "No, Jamie. I can't accept this. It's not that I don't want to, but oh, call me superstitious. I don't want to tie you to me in that way. I want you to go over there and concentrate on keeping yourself safe. When you come back, we can talk. That's the way you put it before and I agree, that's the approach we ought to take."

James was surprised by her response and disappointed, but said that was okay with him. Later, when they parted at the door of her parents' apartment, Sally said she'd drop over to help him pack for Kingston.

When she did come over, Sally was all business. There was none of the normal joking and banter between them. Not a tear was shed as they bade their final farewells and Sally said not to worry about her, just make sure he stayed safe.

Later, James went over to say goodbye to his grandparents, Eleanor and Will Campbell. "Jamie, we're so glad you came," said Eleanor. "We're going to miss you so much," she said tearfully.

Will Campbell said he wanted to take his grandson for a little walk before he left. Will grabbed two apples and a knife and led the two of them out to the road. The older man pointed left and the two walked slowly down the dusty country lane. He put one apple in the giant pocket of his overalls, took his knife and began peeling the other. As a boy, Jamie had been mesmerized how his grandfather could remove the peel from an apple in one continuous piece. This time when he'd done one apple, Will dropped the peel along the roadway, handed the fruit to his grandson and started on the other for himself.

Between bites of apple, Will said to James: "I understand, son. I know why you're doing this. Don't worry about your folks. They'll be fine."

"I hope so, Grampa. They were pretty upset." After a few moments he asked: "Grampa, you served in the militia, right?"

"That's right, son. My militia outfit dates back in these parts to the War of 1812. They fought the Fenians back in the sixties. Your Great-grandfather Sam O'Malley served back then. Me, I served in the Boer War. Too old for the Great War, though. Never got over to fight in Europe."

Will wiped tears from his eyes and said: "Jamie, lad, there's a chance I won't be here to see you when you get back. I haven't told your mother, but Gramma Nora knows, bless her heart. And I figure under the circumstances I ought ta tell you. Before you go, I mean. You see, Doc Farr says I've got the cancer. No tellin' how long I've got."

James was shocked. "But that can't be. You look so healthy, Grampa. You've always been so healthy."

"Nevertheless. It's something your gramma and I got to face. No matter. I've had a good old life. No regrets."

James took the old man's hand and squeezed it. "Well, I wish you luck, Grampa. You wish me luck too."

Will smiled. "Sure do."

Eric Porter and his dad came over to the house to pick James up for the trip to the Kingston induction centre. Grace hugged her son and said she'd never forgive him if he let anything happen to himself. James smiled and turned to Pete.

Peter was stern-faced, stoic in his countenance. Jamie might not be his biological son but that no longer mattered. Peter had loved Jamie from the beginning and that had never changed. And yet they were not a demonstrative family and hugging was unheard-of.

"I get it, son. I really do. If this is something you've got to do, then you go with my blessing and my prayers. Just hurry home, okay?"

James then moved forward and hugged the man who had raised him and taught him about every aspect of farm life. Peter at first looked shocked but returned the embrace. "Thanks, Dad," James said. "For everything."

With one more kiss for Eric and then James, Grace dabbed her eyes. "Goodbye," she said. "I love you both."

The last thing James did before leaving the house was take the silver band he had offered Sally, and tuck it down inside a corner of his duffle.

* * *

The Hastings and Prince Edward Regiment, nicknamed the Hasty Ps, had landed at Sicily in 1943 and later entered the Italian peninsula at Reggio on the southwest coast of the boot. As they joined in the effort to push the Germans northward, the regiment passed through Motta Montecorvino, Campobasso and Torella. Then had come the battle of Ortona when the Canadians, despite their lack of experience in street fighting, were called upon to do just that. They learned quickly and handled themselves masterfully.

But the toll had been great and the regiment needed recruits badly. James went through fast-tracked basic training at Kingston and in the early months of 1944 he was told he'd be going overseas to join the Hasty Ps on the Italian peninsula. Eric was to join another outfit in France. The boys' last night together was spent in a Kingston watering hole.

"Get back here safe and sound," were Eric's final words to his friend, and James replied: "Meet ya back here for a beer. Farewell, pal."

Ill-prepared for what lay in store for him, James joined his regiment, part of the 1st Brigade, at Monte Cassino. The men who had been with the regiment for some months regaled the more recent recruits with stories of the house-to-house fighting and the German army's stubborn resistance as they were pushed northward. James listened in awe. While the older men looked forward to savoring victory upon their arrival in Rome, James secretly wished he had been with them during the earlier days when the fighting had been more intense. He lamented that he had missed what he considered "the real thing."

There was still life in the retreating Germans. As the Canadians proceeded, the stench of death was everywhere. It occurred to James that rotting corpses smelled worse than the time as a boy he fell into a vat of spoiled fruit and he gagged and shuddered at the thought. As the Canadians approached Lago Trasimeno from the southwest, James's thoughts turned to his Aunt Albie. He wasn't certain just where Villa Con Spirito was located but he recalled his mother talking about her visit there, and of walking along the lake's western shores. It couldn't be far.

One day James's company stopped for a break on a height of land. James breathed in and caught a sharp, unpleasant burning smell. In the distance through the dust and fire of battle he spied a glimpse of the immense *lago*. "Trasimeno," one of the men said. James saw the burning buildings and wondered just where Albie might be. Was she safe?

It was a question he posed in his next letter home to Sally as he described the scene to her. "Your descriptions are so vivid, Jamie," Sally wrote back. "I almost feel I'm right there with you." At the start, the couple kept their pledge to write regularly to one another although over time, their weekly schedule fell into twice monthly, then monthly and later still every couple of months.

Missing the action in Italy wasn't the only sadness in James's life that winter. Just after Christmas he received a letter from his mother, telling him his Grandfather Campbell had died. James remembered that last walk down the road the two of them had taken. He was glad they'd had that time together.

In the spring of 1945 with victory nearly in the Allies' grasp, the Hasty Ps were shipped out to help with the final drive farther north, through northern France, Belgium and the Netherlands. Many of his colleagues lamented this news: having been such a significant force in winning the war in Italy, they would now be deprived of the glory of final victory. In the meantime, they had also missed out on the D-Day invasion of Normandy. The men were bitter that they were already being mockingly dubbed the D-Day Dodgers. James secretly rejoiced: farther north, he believed, he would have his chance to prove himself.

As he walked up the gangplank to the American landing craft in Leghorn Harbour, James gazed back at the Italian mountains where his fellows had handled themselves with valour and skill. He hoped that soon he too would have that same opportunity.

They landed at Marseilles and boarded trucks for the trip north. They passed through parts of France that seemed little touched by war but as they continued northward and neared the coast, the picture changed dramatically. Five years ago this country had collapsed against the Nazi onslaught and now the countryside and villages stood in ruins, the scent of broken and burned plaster filling the air. Jamie used his French to talk to the people along the way and learned the depth of their hardship.

After France, the Canadians from the Italian campaign joined their countrymen as well as the British and Americans in the push through the Benelux countries and as April progressed, James learned the fighting was expected to grow in intensity. He relished the thought. There was much grumbling when the members of the Eighth Army were forced to forsake their distinctive and much-loved Crusader Cross in favour of the First Canadian Army flash. But they were excited by their mission: to help sever the main body of the German army.

James and the Hasty Ps were to head into Germany's Reichswald Forest, then cross the Dutch border to Het Loo, the Dutch royal family's palace. The royal family themselves had been long since evacuated to live in Ottawa for the war's duration. A Dutch princess had even been born there, in a hospital room declared Dutch territory for the occasion. The liberation of the palace would be a high-profile coup for the Canadians. Their excitement grew.

As they entered Germany, James noticed how different the land was from the Italian countryside. They passed by one destroyed farmhouse after another, manoeuvred around bomb craters and past the recent crosses that marked soldiers' graves. Then, as they neared a village, James's wish to encounter the enemy came all too true. The Nazi fighting machine had been heavily damaged but there was still plenty of life left in it. The enemy could still come together to fight the invasion of their homeland with fury. Knowing defeat was inevitable and fearing the consequences, they fought on like cornered wildcats.

James and another private, Kurt Harper, were on the left flank of the wedge of their company that was moving forward when a German mortar whistled in to their right and decimated the rest of the outfit. Momentarily deafened by the blast, James staggered farther left into a copse of trees and believed Harper was right beside him. In the confusion, the men became separated from the remnants of their unit. James realized he had been hit, likely by shrapnel. He was bleeding profusely, the right side of his face sticky to the touch, the vision in his right eye blurred by his blood. Yet he felt no pain.

Orange flames and billows of choking smoke rose behind him and James realized his only escape was to continue through the woods. He staggered, falling, crashing into the underbrush. Time moved in slow motion. His head buzzed, his vision went cloudy and it swirled as, for the first time, an intense pain set in. His breathing was laboured, with even short breaths seeming to fill his chest with sharp spikes. James was alone and he was badly hurt.

The battle debris and burnt sulfurous smoke had turned day to dusk, and a light but steady drizzle fell. The moist air turned the smells into something dank, moldering. No longer having any idea of the time of day, James tottered and wobbled like a drunken man, trying to move forward, away from where the enemy had engaged his company. He came to the edge of the wooded area and looked ahead where a small village lay. He stumbled forward, realizing that somewhere along the line he had lost his weapon, but had picked up a branch he was using as a crutch. James tried hard to focus through his haze and saw what he thought was a man walking toward him. German or Canadian? Enemy or confrere? James didn't know and he was beyond caring. He couldn't get out of this predicament alone. Without help, he would perish.

The man spoke to him in a language James was unfamiliar with. It was the last thing he recalled before falling into the man's arms. Dirk Van de Berg tried to cushion the young man's fall and gently laid him on the ground. He recognized the Canadian uniform. The uniform of the brave men who were helping liberate his Dutch homeland from the Nazis. The elderly farmer raced home to alert his wife, then sent their grandson to the nearby Allied field headquarters for help.

* * *

"Medic," barked the Canadian army colonel. "Go with this boy. He's found an injured soldier in his village. Take a Jeep."

Max Huddlestone motioned to the boy of no more than eight to jump into the vehicle. Max pointed forward and said to the boy: "which way?" The child pointed right and off they drove. In fifteen minutes the Jeep pulled up to the neat little stone structure the Van de Berg family called home. Dirk Van de Berg ran out to greet them. "This way," he said in English, and Max followed him inside.

The young Canadian lay on a cot in the main room of the tiny home. Blood had soaked his uniform. A hastily applied bandage around his head was equally soaked. Blood dripped onto the stone floor. Max wondered if this patient was one of those beyond saving but without hesitation he rushed forward and bent over the unconscious figure. When confronted with his first wounded patient, the olfactory assault had threatened to overpower him but in time, Max had learned to push the smells aside and attend to his job. He noticed that shrapnel had pierced the right side of the young soldier's face, shredded his shirt and pant leg. Max cut away what was left of the clothing that surrounded the injuries and surveyed the damage. Clearly there were broken bones as well as untold internal damage. Max was glad his patient was unconscious. The man's next few hours would be painful.

After applying morphine, sulfa powder to fight infection and bandages to stanch the bleeding, Max asked if the Van de Bergs might be able to help him carry the soldier to the Jeep. He needed to get the man back to camp, back to the field hospital as quickly as he could where doctors could tend to him properly. Dirk and Margreit Van de Berg jumped into action and the three of them got the soldier to the Jeep. They gently arranged his crumpled and broken body across the back seat. Margreit took a blanket from her grandson and handed it to Max, who tucked it around the injured soldier. The man groaned. That was the first moment that Max had taken the time to look closely into the face of the soldier whose life was in his hands. Even through the blood he recognized his patient and there was a flutter in his stomach.

"Sonny Jim," he said softly.

The youthful soldier stirred at the familiar name and looked up at his angel of mercy. Through his pain, through the haze of the morphine Max had administered, James managed a semblance of a smile of recognition. "I asked you not to call me that," was all he managed, before slipping back into unconsciousness.

For a split second, Max was transported back to the cabin on the pond, to the day he had first taken the baby into his arms. It had been two decades ago, and yet it seemed just a moment in time.

* * *

James O'Malley was strong. But besides the shrapnel injuries, the blast from the big German guns had concussed his lungs. One was collapsed and the other was partially collapsed. He spent much of the next few weeks slipping in and out of consciousness as his body slowly healed. Having been given initial medical attention at a field hospital, James was sent to England on a hospital ship and ended up recuperating at Lady Astor's estate, Cliveden, in Buckinghamshire. Cliveden had served as a hospital during the First World War and was a natural to serve that same purpose when once again it was needed.

The American-born Nancy Witcher Langhorn, who had moved to England and married Lord Waldorf Astor, spent much of the war years at her London home but often came to her Cliveden estate to visit the patients. She was passing by James's bed one day as he awoke from a sound sleep. "Hello, young man," she said when she noticed he was awake. "How are you feeling? What would you like?" "A beer, ma'am," James said without hesitation. "I'd love a beer."

Lady Astor smiled and turned to her assistant. "Get this young man a beer," she ordered. In a few minutes she came back and served it to him herself. A beautiful, black Guinness.

James thanked her and asked: "The war. How's it going?"

"Splendidly," she replied in her mid-Atlantic accent. "Hitler's dead. And the Japs, well, they'll be surrendering any day now, I should think. You've done it, young man. You and your kind. You're heroes."

James took a sip of the stout beer they called Irish gold. He'd first experienced it when he arrived in England but it had never tasted as good as it did now.

James smiled then and an image came into his head at that moment. An image of an angel. He remembered the blood-soaked cot in a little cottage in Holland, remembered being carried to the back seat of a military vehicle where he had looked up and was certain he had heard someone call him Sonny Jim. Silly, though. It couldn't have been. Only one person called him by that name and he had no idea where that man might now be.

In the following weeks James grew stronger. The scars, including the one that tracked down the right side of his face, began to fade a bit. There was a horrible indentation in his right leg where a large piece of shrapnel had pierced it, a handful of ugly scars on his right side, but he was healing. A nurse dropped by daily to get him out of bed and walking around the corridors. He was beginning to feel good again.

While there had been frequent letters from his mother that always included a greeting from his pop, James had not received one from Sally for quite some time. Then one day one arrived. He recognized her handwriting immediately. "Dear James," she wrote, "Your mother tells me you're recovering well from your injuries. I was so glad to hear that. All is well here in Shannonside. Everyone's talking about the war soon coming to an end so I'll bet you can hardly wait to get back to the farm. It will be wonderful to see you. Take care of yourself, James. Sally." James was taken aback by the perfunctory tone of the letter and wondered what might be up. He guessed he would soon find out. He chose not to reply.

Rumours circulated that with the Atlantic Ocean now safe from Nazi U-boats, Canadian and American troops would soon be sent home to be discharged, to be welcomed back into civilian society. One day he asked for paper and a pencil and wrote home to his parents. They would have been told of his injuries and he knew they'd love to hear in his own words that he was okay and on the mend.

The next day one of the nurses came by, a chirpy young girl who looked barely out of high school, her Scottish accent charming the daylights out of him. James looked forward to her frequent pass-bys. "There's someone here to see you, laddie," she said to him.

James looked behind her. He longed for a familiar face but apart from the occasional army buddy, he was resigned to the likelihood there would be no further faces from his former life until he arrived home. This visitor was dressed in the uniform of the Canadian army, and it was a face James knew from back home. It was a face he was never so happy to see.

"Hello, James," said Max. "How are you?"

"Max!" James nearly shouted. "Where did you come from? How did you know I was here? Pull up a chair." As Max took a seat, James noticed the "medic" patch on his arm.

"What? You mean you don't remember our long chat that day outside that little Dutch cottage?" Max joked gently as he sat down. "Jamie, that hurts."

"You mean that really was you? I thought I was hallucinating when I heard you call me Sonny Jim. What on earth?"

Max laughed and James could see his eyes were wet. "Yes, it was me, old boy." Touching his medic's patch, he added: "The army seems to have trusted me to be a field medic. I don't know how, or who led me to you, but it was me alright. You were such a mess I almost didn't recognize you. That Dutch fellow saved your life. He and his grandson and wife.

The boy came to get me, said a Canadian was badly injured and needed help quickly. It was only when we were putting you in the back of the Jeep and I was taking you to the field hospital that I took a closer look and, my God, it was you. I couldn't believe it."

"Wait until I tell my folks," James said then. "I just wrote to them yesterday so now I'll have to waste another stamp, I suppose. They're going to be so shocked."

"That they will," replied Max. "Tell them I'm alright too, will you? I'll be back working at Ballinskellig before they know it. But Jamie, what are you going to do when you get home?"

"Go back to the farm, I suppose. What else? I told my folks I'd be back."

Max leaned forward in his chair. "You're a smart fellow, Jamie. Why don't you try something else? Go to school. University. There'll be plenty of government help to veterans after the war. You could really make something of yourself, son." Max blanched when he realized the word he'd just used. "You don't need to spend your life at Ballinskellig."

14

Jamie's Self-Discovery

SAILING HOME TO Canada on a troop ship in the autumn of 1945, James thought long and hard about Max's advice. Even his short time in the military had made him realize there was so much more out there than returning to run the family farm. And yet it was what his father expected of him. His mother? That he wasn't so sure of. They'd never ever discussed an alternative future for him. Yet he realized how unhappy his mother was, sharing Ballinskellig with Pop.

James had been little more than skin and bones when he was transferred to Lady Astor's hospital but some Guinness - they said it was a good supply of iron - and solid food were starting to fill him out a bit. He had recovered from the pleurisy that developed from his lung injuries. His injured leg was still hobbling him but even that was improving. The deep scar on his leg, however, would never totally disappear. The voyage was an unusually smooth one and James had no trouble keeping the food down.

During the trip, he got to talking with a journalist, a war correspondent named Griff Stoneman who had served in the trenches in Western Europe and had found himself joining the fighting men at Dieppe. When Stoneman asked him about his experiences, James begged off. "Not yet," he said.

The journalist said okay, he'd talk about some of his own experiences there. It only served to make James realize how much he wanted to try something else. The man told James that a new university in Ottawa had just started up and one of its specialties was going to be the study of journalism. "It's time we writers got serious about our business," the man told James. "Time to start studying who we are, how we got here and what it is we're all about. Treat it like a profession. I know I'm thirty-five, but I'm thinking of going back to school myself." James said he'd give it some thought.

There were long hours of idleness onboard the ship and James sought out some reading material from among the books and magazines he found strewn around the place. One of the men had picked up a new book called *The Unknown Country*, by a Canadian journalist named Bruce Hutchison. James devoured it and even read it a second time. The book delved into the Canadian spirit and for the first time made James, who was always partial to history at school, appreciate just how and why Canada was unique. On his second read, he treated it as an exercise in truly studying its contents.

The ship landed in Halifax and James took the train to Montreal where he spent a few days. He was dressed in his military uniform and found himself surrounded by more men and women in uniform. Instead of heading directly home to Shannonside, James decided to take a side trip to Ottawa. Even though he'd grown up not far away from the capital city, James had never ever visited there. He'd sacrificed a lot to protect his country's interests the past couple of years and he thought that it was about time he go to the nation's capital to see what it was he was protecting, a place that had featured prominently in Hutchison's Canadian narrative.

In Ottawa, James got off the train and walked out onto the street. To his left was the Rideau Canal and directly across the street was the railway hotel, the Chateau Laurier. James directed his gaze to the left of the hotel and up to the Gothic buildings that stood atop a hill. He'd never been there but he knew immediately, that was Parliament Hill, the centre of Canada's government. His leg was stiffening and he needed to limber it up. James slung his rucksack over his shoulder, turned west, crossed the canal and walked to the war memorial. There he stopped and thought about the Canadians who had given their lives for their country. Then he turned and walked to Elgin Street and past the Langevin Block. When he reached Metcalfe Street he stopped and directed his gaze across Wellington, directly toward the Centre Block of Parliament Hill. He crossed the street and walked through the gates onto Parliament Hill. He strolled to the Centre Block and asked an older man in the front lobby if he could go inside.

The man looked at the red scar on James's face and wondered about his other wounds. He didn't ask. "There will be a tour starting in half an hour," said the man. "Why don't you just step outside and enjoy this beautiful day, soldier. Come back then. And welcome home."

James thanked the man, walked outside and luxuriated in the peace and tranquility of the sunny early-autumn afternoon. The giant elm trees that lined Wellington Street were turning a golden yellow that shimmered and glistened in the sunshine. A few minutes later he walked back inside and found a small group waiting for a guided tour. The guide commenced the tour by leading the group down the Hall of Honour toward the House of Commons. Forty-five minutes later, the tour ended at the entranceway to the Peace Tower.

While his leg ached, James walked around Parliament Hill and marvelled at the fabulous views from behind the Library of Parliament. In the distance he saw the Gatineau Hills, turned a continuous blanket of red, yellow and orange in the brilliance of the sunny autumn day. He looked up and down the rushing Ottawa River and thought about how this waterway had allowed the voyageurs and the fur-traders to do their jobs. It was the gateway to the interior of the continent. Now this simple lumber town was the place where the great decisions of a nation were being made. James knew at that moment he wanted more than Ballinskellig. The farm life was not going to satisfy him. He walked back to the front of the building just as a man and woman were exiting a cab. James hailed the cab. He had not walked so far at once since being injured and his muscles ached.

"Can you take me to Carleton University?" he asked the cabbie.

"Sure thing, soldier. Come on in. Free ride to the vet."

The newly founded university was currently housed in a series of low-rise buildings along Bronson Avenue. When the cab driver let him off at what he said was the main administrative building, James offered to pay but true to his word, the cabbie wouldn't take his money. James insisted on giving him a good tip anyway, turned and walked inside the building.

"Who do I talk to about how to sign up here?" he asked the first person he encountered.

* * *

Once he'd conducted the business at hand, James took another cab back downtown to the railway station, got a train to Toronto and went immediately to where he had been directed to obtain his discharge papers. He was finished with the military. It was time to move on.

It rankled him to read on his release papers: "Discharged under routine order by reason of unable to meet the required military physical standards." It seemed so blunt and so unjust, he thought. He was "unable to meet the required military physical standards" because of the injuries he'd sustained in Holland fighting for his country. There was nothing more and nothing less involved. He tried to put those thoughts out of his head. It's just bureaucratese, he told himself. No point in taking offence. Time to head home. It'll be good to see Mum and Pop.

When he got off the train in Shannonside, the first thing he did was head over to Mike's Pool Hall. Walking in to the dimly lit entranceway, he proceeded to the hall where the tables were arrayed and looked around. Several sets of eyes landed on him and several of the older fellows came over to offer a hearty welcome home. Another young man in military uniform approached and held out his hand. It was his left hand because he had no right arm. There was a black patch over the spot where his right eye ought to be.

"Jamie, welcome back," said Eric Porter. "You seem to have all your pieces. As you can see, I'm missing some."

James set down his bag and hugged his old school friend. "Eric," he said then. "I'm sorry. How are you?"

"Pretty good, considering," said Eric. "Obviously I won't be able to take over the family farm so my future's been changed for me. But the school board says they'll give me a teaching job if I go to Kingston this fall and get my certificate, so that's what I'm gonna do. Everything will be fine."

"That's great, Eric. You'll make a cracker of a teacher. Hey, I was thinking of walking over to the general store and see if Sally's there," James told his friend, a big grin coming to his face. Eric was stricken silent, then placed his hand on his friend's shoulder.

"About that," said Eric. "Jamie, Sally left town a couple months ago. Took off with some fella from Toronto. I don't think she's coming back."

"Oh," said James. His smile melted slowly away. "Oh well, I've been away a while. Can't expect her to wait forever, can I?" James immediately changed the subject and Eric Porter knew his old school buddy was hurting but was determined not to show it. Eric went along with the ruse and tried to stay upbeat while the topics switched from one to the other. By some mutual and unstated consent, the two of them avoided the topic of their wartime experiences.

As the men chatted, a mighty bellow came from the entranceway. "Where's James O'Malley?"

James turned and saw Bob Eddy's large frame come through the door. "Jamie," he said as he shook James's hand enthusiastically. "You're looking good, lad. Can I give you a ride home? Your folks will be mighty eager to see you."

"That would be great, Mr. Eddy. Don't mind if I do."

* * *

Miles away, at the top of a set of time-worn stone steps leading from an old church, the former Miss Sally Parnell held a bouquet of flowers to the bodice of her ivory-coloured wedding gown. At her side stood her new husband. She wondered for a moment what might have been, wondered what might have happened if she'd stayed in the hope James would come back home. Did she really love James? She'd been momentarily angered by his decision to join the army without any consultation, with apparently no thought of their future together. And yet he had then offered her an engagement ring as his parting gesture. That certainly counted for something, must have been an indicator he'd been thinking of them in the long-term.

But she had made her choice. Perhaps it was a choice made as much in residual anger as in reason, in retribution rather than in thoughts of the heart. Still, she thought of him often.

"Darling," the young husband said to Sally. "Come along. We need to get to the reception."

Without turning, Sally said to him: "Oh, Jamie, just a moment. I want to enjoy the view."

Lyle Ingliss, startled by her slip of the tongue, chose to ignore that she had called him by the name of her old boyfriend. He wondered how he might measure up. He wondered how long it might take him to prove himself worthy of taking Jamie's spot.

* * *

Grace rose from picking beans in the garden, lifted her kneeling board and walked back to the house. It was getting on toward time to start supper. As usual, her thoughts turned to her son and she wondered where he was that evening. Surely he'd be home soon. She and Pete had received a letter from him the other day, the one he wrote from the ship and mailed when he arrived in Halifax, but he hadn't mentioned a specific date for his arrival. All he said was that he planned to take his time and see a bit of the country along the way. Grace figured if anyone deserved such a luxury, it was a returning veteran who'd sacrificed his health for his country. Jamie had said one other thing in the letter: He had run into Max Huddlestone and he was well. Grace's heart fluttered at that simple sentence while Peter's stomach dropped.

Grace and Pete had shared one of their rare tender moments when the letter had come from the war department advising them James had been injured during combat in Holland. Pete had put his arms around her and Grace sobbed uncontrollably. But at least he was alive, Pete told his wife. That was something. In time he would heal. James's own words, written from his hospital bed in England, had later been a tremendous relief to them both. They laughed with joy when he told of staying at Lady Astor's estate and how she'd personally served him a Guinness. "The boy's recovering in style," Pete had joked with pride and relief. Grace had the heartiest laugh she'd enjoyed since before Jamie had left. Even Pete chuckled at his little witticism. Then the letter from the ship came and it was upbeat. It spoke of how eager Jamie was to see them both.

Grace had often gone into Jamie's room during the years he was away. Sometimes she would launder his sheets. Sometimes she would pick up items he'd left on the dresser or on a set of shelves in the corner. A handful of toys from his boyhood. A hockey puck. A baseball glove. She would put the item to her nose to breathe in his scent. For a while, she wondered whether she would ever see him again. Now, they knew he was on his way home. She had begun coming in to wind the mechanical alarm clock that sat next to his bed.

Now, as she sat in the kitchen to string and clean the beans, Grace heard a car's tires crunch over the gravel as it came up the drive and wondered who'd be paying a visit so close to suppertime. She heard two car doors close and then boots on the side porch. The screen door squeaked on its unoiled hinges and a tall, very slender man walked through the doorway. Back-lighting made it hard to make out his features.

"Hello, Mum," the figure said, and Grace's heart jumped at the familiar voice.

"Jamie!" she screamed as she dropped the dish of beans and ran to the doorway. She hugged him and then loosened her grip when she felt him wince, although he didn't say a word. "Jamie, did you just arrive? How did you get here?" She looked up in to his face and swallowed hard when she saw the nasty red scar down the right side. It was Grace's turn to wince at the sight but she held firm to her composure.

Bob Eddy popped his head through the door and said, "hello, Grace. Look who I found wandering the streets. I'll just head home and leave you folks alone. You've got lots to talk about. See you later."

"Thank you, Bob. Yes, see you later. Say hello to Emilie," Grace said as he walked back to the car. She took Jamie's hand and led him to her own favourite chair. She turned toward him and said: "Let me look at you. You're so thin. My word, you're skinny. Don't they feed you in the army?" James laughed and fought to hold back tears. "You should have seen me before they fattened me up," he was able to barely choke out.

A few minutes later, the screen door creaked open again and in walked Pete. "James!" he shouted. "Oh my God, James." Before James could struggle to his feet, Pete ran over and leaned down into the chair to hug his son. James knew emotion was difficult for this man and marvelled at the greeting.

Then Grace chimed in. "I'm going to make you the best darned supper you've ever had. Pete, go get that pork roast from the cold cellar. And Pete, go over and bring Mumma. She'll never forgive me if I don't have her here for the celebration." Pete delivered the roast to his wife and then left for his mother-in-law's.

It was the most joyous meal any of them could recall, their joy tempered only by the absence of Grandpa Will. The topic of Sally's sudden departure from town remained unspoken, until James announced halfway through the blueberry pie dessert: "I heard about Sally, folks. Don't worry about me. I'll be fine." The others tried to smile but James noticed Grandma Campbell had to dab at her eyes. Pete replied simply: "Sure you will, son. We know that."

Grace and Eleanor vowed to put the fat back onto Jamie's meager bones. Pete concurred, reasoning, he said, that he'd never be able to get any work out of Jamie as long as he was so skinny. James stared at him, wondering how he was going to share his news. How was he going to tell his father that he wouldn't be doing much more farm work on Ballinskellig?

Finally he said: "I've never been one to beat around the bush, Pop. You know that. So I'm just going to say it. I've spoken to the folks at Carleton University about going to school there. I could start as early as January if that works out."

Pete glanced over at Grace. His mouth moved, but no words came to his lips. His tanned complexion blanched. "Well I never," he finally said. "I can't believe what I'm hearing. You promised. You said you'd come back and take over. You promised me. I was counting on you."

"Pete," Grace chimed in. "Not now. Not this way. Let's just enjoy the moment. Our job right now is to get Jamie back to full health. And Christmas is coming. Let's not spoil it."

Without further words, Pete got up from the table and quietly walked out the door. Grace watched him go, and thought about all of the other times Pete had just walked out the door.

The O'Malleys had no telephone but Grace's mother did and the following day Grace went over to call James's aunts and share the good news. Jamie was home again. Aunt Lucy was down in a flash, peppering him with questions. She for one was delighted her nephew was going to university. "Don't worry about your father," she whispered to her nephew. "He'll get over it."

But James wasn't so sure. He explained to Lucy and his mother that while he wasn't certain what he wanted to do once he left university, he had become interested in the world of journalism. He told them about his conversations on the ship with the war correspondent and about the Bruce Hutchison book he'd read. He called the book his awakening to who he was, to what his country was all about, and to what he wanted to do with his life. Grace savoured every moment of her time with her son and told him she was entirely supportive of any plan he came up with. She always knew he was cut out for higher education and she was so proud of what he was doing.

One evening after dinner, James walked through the back pasture and made his way to the river. It was a perfect night, a night of autumn's scents and sounds. Some of the trees still stubbornly held on to their leaves in their annual tug-of-war with autumn's building chill. James reached into his pants pocket and pulled out a small silver ring. He inspected it, put it to his mouth and let his lips brush its cool surface. Then he flung it far out into the water. Sally was gone now. He had no further need for it.

* * *

Over the next days, James reconnected with Grace and Pete. He never told his mother details of his encounter with Max at the hospital in England. Only that they had met and Max was well. Grace wondered if she would ever set eyes on him again.

He helped Pete work out a plan for the farm's next growing season and harvest. He'd be there to help when he could, he said, and he planned to pay a visit to the National Experimental Farm in Ottawa to learn the latest theories and routine for pest management. At first, Pete was cool in his treatment of James. For a moment in time when James had returned that day from war, Pete had been almost like a different man, almost like a caring father. Now he was back to the cold hardness that had defined their relationship for most of James's life. It was back to employer and employee, not father and son.

When Pete stormed out of the house the day James returned, he had been stung by the boy's words. He needed an explanation. What had happened? Why was the son he had raised to take over the farm turning his back on the land Pete loved? Over the following days, though, Pete admitted that he himself had at one time wondered whether the farm was really what he wanted. He had been drawn back to maintain the farm by the lure of the land and a sense of duty to the family legacy. But had it truly been what he wanted for himself?

A few days later, Pete and James were working together in the barn when Pete stopped, set down what he was doing and turned to his son. "I've been thinking about your decision, Jamie. I want you to know, it's alright with me." James tried to interject but Pete waved him off. "No, let me finish. I've been practicing what to say so let me say it. Jamie, when I was a lad I had big thoughts about finishing high school and going off to college. Getting a job in the city. It was your mom who encouraged me and it got me to thinking that maybe there was something else out there for me. Something that didn't involve just taking over from my father and carrying on in the same way.

"But my father, he was determined I was gonna take over Ballinskellig. To his way of thinking, there was no other way. He had sacrificed everything for his father and now I had to do the same for him. It was a sad day when I left school, knowing I was never going to see the inside of a classroom again. It was like I'd just lost my best friend, it hurt so bad. Jamie, I don't want to be like my father was to me. You're a man. Hell, you've just come back from serving your country in a war that had to be fought, and there's no higher calling than that. You deserve to do what it is you want to. What it is you feel in your bones you want to do. That's all."

James didn't know quite what to say for a moment. Finally he told Pete: "Thank you for that. I'll do you proud, Pop."

Just before Christmas, James went in to Kingston with his school-days friend, Eric Porter, to spend some of his military pay on proper clothes for university. Eric was himself planning to attend Queen's University in the new year to get his teaching certificate. "Two college men," Jamie said to his old pal. "Can you believe it?"

The boys actually spent quite a bit of time together that fall but spoke only in generalities of their experiences in the service. By a still-unstated understanding, neither seemed prepared to relive the horrors they'd experienced. It would be years before Eric was prepared to share with James some of the details of his war injuries.

All of Pete's sisters and their families arrived for Christmas, the first time in years anyone could recall that happening. The husbands all wanted to know about the war. Pete, quickly recognizing James's unease, ordered them to pipe down. James was eternally grateful. He was getting the idea that Aunt Lucy was right, his dad seemed to be getting over his disappointment. But for the first time it began to occur to him to wonder what would become of Ballinskellig.

Some of the cousins dropped in during the holidays, including Arthur, Anna's boy, who had served in the Canadian Navy. Arthur too understood the reluctance to speak of the war. "Maybe someday," Arthur said to his younger cousin. "It's still too soon."

When the time came just after New Year's Day for James to head to Ottawa, Grace, Pete and Eleanor accompanied him to the train station to say farewell. Inside the coach car, James took a seat next to a station-side window and waved to his family as the train pulled out.

In the months that followed, James eased his way into his new school life and tried to put behind him the terrible experiences he had had mere months before. There were nighttime terrors for sure, images that screeched into his head and made him awaken in a cold sweat. Slowly, he began to find comfort in the sharing of his thoughts and, without a lot of detail, a few of the less terrible memories, with other veterans he met at university. On breaks from his studies, he usually went home to Ballinskellig and did what he could to help out with the farm work. While his body grew increasingly stronger, James's injured leg still bothered him and ached by the end of each day. He said nothing. Pete noticed him rubbing his aching leg one day and told him: "Take it easy, son. You're not all healed yet."

Grace heard Jamie tell Pete one day about the days during which his outfit made their way up the Italian peninsula and how they had come upon Lago Trasimeno. Grace had not heard from Alberta during the entire wartime period and wondered about her old friend. Where might she be? And was she safe?

15

The Return

That August, in 1946, there were two people eagerly anticipating the return of the man each considered their guardian angel. Grace and James both looked forward to Max's arrival for the harvest but he never came. Both were disappointed but of course they never spoke of it to one another. James had not mentioned to his parents the specifics of the injuries he'd suffered in Holland, nor how it had been Max who saved his life. It hadn't been the right time to talk of such things. All James had said was that Max was well. Max said that he would return to Ballinskellig. But if he didn't, James wondered if he'd ever see him again.

Just as James knew he would, Pete fared quite well without him labouring in the fields. At James's urging, Pete began utilizing the marvelous new insecticide called DDT and regularly sprayed his apple crop with it. The orchards seemed to thrive on the chemical and brought forth nearly perfect specimens of fruit. No one paid much heed when Pete almost immediately began hacking and coughing after each application of the DDT-laced spray. It seemed a small price to pay for better apples. It was important to keep the farm productive, he felt, even if he wasn't sure what would happen to it when he was gone.

In August 1947, Grace had given up on ever seeing or hearing from Max again. Then on a cool, misty afternoon, Pete was taking a break from his chores and chatting with Aart Vos, the man he'd hired to replace Mel Brewster after he retired that year. Aart had arrived from Holland with his young family and had impressed Pete with his credentials. Before the war he had run a dairy farm with his father but with most of what they had worked for destroyed by the Nazis, he decided to build a new life in Canada.

Pete noticed a man walking down the laneway toward him. The recognition was immediate. "Hello, Mr. O'Malley," said Max Huddlestone. How are you?"

Pete stared blankly at Max. Surely now it was time just to cut the man out of their lives entirely. Finally he said: "I don't think we've got work for you here this year. Best to move on."

"Okay. Fine. I'll head on out then," said Max. He turned to go.

From down the road James, home for a few days from Ottawa, had spotted Max talking to his father and began to run toward them. He stumbled into an awkward run, still hobbled by the damage done to his leg. When he saw Max turn and begin to head away, James feared he'd miss his chance. He shouted: "Max! Max! Stop!"

Max stopped and turned back. Pete glared at his son. "I've got no work here. Not now. Not again."

"Pop, I have to tell you something. I couldn't before. It was too painful. But now I've got to tell you. Max saved my life, Pop. He's the reason I'm here today."

Pete gaped at his son and groaned. Would he never be rid of this loathsome man?

James then told the whole story to Pete. Aart Vos listened intently. "The Canadians saved my country, Mr. O'Malley. Any Canadian soldier, well, he's a friend of mine."

Pete raised his hands in exasperation. "Alright. Give this fella a job then. Why should I care? Maybe I outta give him the whole damned farm while I'm at it."

Vos was puzzled. Jamie cringed in embarrassment. Max said in a low voice: "Just a job, sir. That's all I ask."

That evening, James finally told his mother the full story of his encounter with Max and of how Max had saved his life. She turned white as a ghost, even if Jamie did omit some of the worst of the details. It was a privilege he did not grant Pete the next day when he recounted the story again. He wasn't sure why, but James wanted his father to know everything, every specific he could recall. It had just all come rolling out of him and it actually felt good to tell someone. After James went to bed, Pete stayed up with Grace and they shared a cup of tea. Grace grew uncomfortable at the silence that fell between them, uncertain whether she ought to say anything. Finally her husband spoke up.

"So your sweety's back now. I suppose it'll be just the way it was before with you two."

"Maybe not," she said. "Now you two have something in common. You've both abandoned me. I'm not sure I want anything to do with either one of you."

Pete's eyes flashed in anger but he held his tongue. "Will I ever have paid for my sins? No, I suppose not. Grace, it was my baby who died that night too. And I don't suppose either one of us is really at fault. It just happened, that's all."

"How many times do I have to tell you? It's not the baby's death I hold against you, Pete. It's when you walked out on me, left me alone to deal with my sorrow. I'll never understand, Pete. Why?"

"I guess I'll never know either," he responded. "I have no explanation. Look, I do love Jamie. He's been a wonderful son, even if he's not my biological son. I was prepared to see him take over the farm and run it as an O'Malley but now that's not going to happen. I don't know what's going to happen, but I'm fearful that you and I are the end of the line, Grace. When we're gone, will there still be a Ballinskellig? I don't know. This place means a lot to me. I'm the fourth generation to farm the land, to grow the apples that my great-grandfather brought over from Ireland. Liam. Liam O'Maille. And his wife Luiseach. They built this place. It meant so much to them and then they passed it on to their son, and he to his son, and again to me. Now here I am, the last of the line. It breaks my heart, Grace. I feel like I've let them all down.

"Listen, Grace, Jamie's back and he's safe. I suppose that's all that matters. I'll be forever grateful to Max Huddlestone for making that happen. And I don't care if you believe it or not, but I'm grateful for him saving your life too. I've already decided that he can come back here for work for as long as I can offer it. That's my decision. My feelings mean nothing. I owe it to him. And if you still love him, then go to him. Go away with him. Do whatever you want. The only thing you mean to me, Grace, is that you're Jamie's mother and for better or for worse, I love that boy. I always will. None of what's happened is his fault. He's a good man."

In the dim light of the kerosene lamps that illuminated the parlour, Grace looked at her husband and noted the deepening lines in his face, the weathered and defeated expression. She thought of their last moment of happiness, the Christmas Eve ride back from the Johnsons', baby Petie in the back seat, the stars and the Northern Lights illuminating the frigid sky. The feeling had been wonderful. The future was theirs.

She wondered how they had come to this point but one thing she was certain of, they would never return to being husband and wife. As for Max, she just didn't know. For sure she had another important link to him. Now she knew that he had saved her son from death, just as he had saved her. What was it about this Max Huddlestone, about his life-and-death link to both of them? She was not a religious woman, but somehow Max had become a guardian angel to them both.

"We've done all we can for Ballinskellig, Pete," Grace said. "Maybe it's time for both of us to just let it go."

Pete got up and stormed out of the room, crossed the road to the barn and grabbed a big shot of the booze he had stored there. He had some serious thinking to do.

* * *

Grace entered that harvest season intending to pay as little attention to Max as she possibly could. The first time she passed him a plate of food, she said nothing and looked down. Max said simply, "thank you, ma'am." With the sound of those words, her heart melted and she glanced up at him. Their eyes met. Grace thought of Pete's words: "Go away with him. Do whatever you want." Perhaps. And yet the feeling gnawed at her: "It's not right. What would Jamie think? And besides, this is my farm too. Why should I leave it?"

An almost imperceptible nod from Grace was all Max needed. It had been their old signal, the mutual agreement for the two of them to meet at the sugarhouse that evening. It was a signal that hadn't been used since before Max left for the war. When they met that evening, Max said nothing, instead grabbing her in his arms and smothering her in kisses. Grace's body tingled. She had so missed him, ached for him, so missed his loving. "Why didn't you come last year?"

"I'm sorry. I didn't know what to think. Wondered if maybe we were best to just drop one another and go our separate ways. But I couldn't, Grace. I have been angry at myself ever since for not coming back. Grace, let's start over. Together. Come away with me. We'll tell Jamie about us. I mean the whole story. We can start to be a family. Please. Grace, I love you more than anything in this world."

Grace's eyes filled with tears. "I've thought about that so many times, my love. I so want to. And yet, Max, I'm afraid that I'm a product of my time, of my upbringing. It's not done. It's not the way. And never, ever would I want to hurt my son. He is my everything. No, Max, I can't go away with you. Please, I hope you can understand. If it means losing you, then that's the way it will have to be. I can't think of any other way. If it's alright with you, I would be satisfied with being with you this one time each year, each harvest time. But I cannot leave this place. Please understand me. As long as Pete's alive, my place is here."

Something then snapped in him. Max realized he would never have the only thing that he truly wanted. His eyes grew misty and he held her tightly in his arms. He gently kissed her hair, picked her up and took her to the bed. Wordlessly, he caressed her, removed the dress she was wearing and leaned down to kiss her breasts. He took off his own clothes and slipped in under the covers. His erection brushed against her and she shivered in anticipation.

Grace loved everything about Max, right down to the gentle fashion in which he made love to her. Every tender, warm stroke sent a thrill through her body, through her very being. He warmed her from within. Tonight, however, she needed something else, something more. Tonight they might be saying goodbye and she needed to feel she was being punished for the musty, passé conventions that held her in their grip. She hated herself for the attitude she held that was driving them apart, and yet she realized it was a feeling she could not shake. She gripped his shoulders and dug her nails into his flesh. "Harder, Max. Harder."

He looked down into her eyes, quizzically. Then he smiled. Max thrust himself deep inside her, plunging faster, faster. She grabbed his buttocks and pulled him toward her. She brought her mouth to his ear, placed her teeth against the flesh of his lobe and bit down. He gave out a small yelp, one more of astonishment than of pain, she thought. Max's warm smile turned to something she had never seen before. A smirk? A sneer? He reached over and gripped both of her hands in one of his, then used the other to snatch up the belt from her dress. He wrapped the belt around her wrists, lifted her hands above her head and back toward the head rail. He looked into her eyes for validation. Grace's initial look of surprise turned into a smile.

Max slipped deeper, deeper inside her. For this night their usual vanilla lovemaking had evolved and they both revelled in it. Grace drifted into a new dimension and from somewhere in the distance she heard a piercing scream. Then she realized it wasn't in the distance, that the scream had come from her own mouth, from deep down within her. Was this what lovemaking could be about? she wondered. Max gave out a full-throated moan of pleasure and she realized he too had reached a new level of ecstasy.

If this was the end of the line for them, each of them thought, they would at least have something worth remembering.

* * *

When it came time for the workers to move on at the end of the apple harvest, Grace stared out the window at the red and golden leaves. She wondered whether she would ever see Max again, and if she really wanted to. But then she realized that was silly. Of course she wanted to see him again, and then some.

When Max left Ballinskellig that autumn, he wondered whether he would ever return, and if Grace even wanted him to. Maybe it was time to create his own life someplace new, someplace where he could finally put Grace O'Malley out of his mind. Maybe he was just fooling himself that his annual liaisons with her were enough. There was also the matter of Jamie. Jamie was his biological son. Grace and Pete had raised him and turned him into the fine upstanding individual he was. Pete had trained him to take over the farm but now, Jamie had made it perfectly clear that was not the life he wished for himself.

Max did not wish to say a final farewell to Grace, and he certainly had no desire to cut Jamie out of his life. And yet he was lonely and longed for a more complete relationship. For a family. He wondered what lay ahead. His father, Henry Huddlestone, had died the previous year. Years earlier, Henry had sold his automotive company, turned his attention to real estate and distilling and had created a massive empire.

After a very young Max stormed out of his father's hotel suite that day so many years before, Henry had dropped Max from his will. Only in the latter days of Henry's life had Max's sister, Margaret, been able to convince their father to put Max back in the will. But Henry's price had been that Margaret must remain in charge, the public face of the corporation she had been such an important part of creating. It had been Margaret who stood by their father's side over the years, Margaret who possessed the sharp financial mind that left her father breathless with pride and forced him to overcome his instinct to dismiss out of hand the prospects of a female chief operating officer.

Yet Max possessed a brilliant mind of his own, and an instinct for what the public, and the workers, wanted. Unbeknownst to his father, Max had already offered his sister sage advice before Henry's death. After his death, Max became the *éminence grise* behind his sister and she soon realized he brought to the corporation a brilliance that was pushing it into uncharted and lucrative territory. It was a territory that separated Huddlestone Enterprises from most of the competition. Max had convinced his sister to treat staff with compassion and respect, and not just as a means to make greater profits. Huddlestone paid its employees better than the others and offered more benefits. Max had learned well from his years as a labourer and now that he was in a position to help his workers, he was determined to do so.

What might Grace and Jamie say if Max told them he was a silent partner in a multimillion-dollar empire? He had been so close to telling her that he had slipped out of his life as a roving farm worker and into the head offices of Huddlestone Enterprises. He had come so close, but feared the consequences.

16

Albie

That fall, word finally came from the Countess Alberta Ribighinni. An airmail letter addressed from Firenze. Grace was overjoyed to hear from her. It had been years since last she'd been in touch – nothing since the war that had left much of Europe in ruin. "Dear Grace: it has been so long and so much has happened since last I have been able to contact you. I hope you and the family are well. We have been through so much here I barely know where to begin."

Grace's heart skipped, at first with joy at finally hearing from her friend, but then with trepidation over what had become of her. The war had changed everything. Grace went to her favourite chair and sank into its familiar cushions. It was a long letter. This was going to take a while.

Albie went on to say that the Count, Roberto, had passed away two weeks ago. He had grown "sick at heart" during the latter couple of war years as he realized all that he and II Duce had strived to achieve for Italy was going up in flames. Roberto had blamed "that disgusting little Austrian, Hitler" for the entire fiasco and said Mussolini's error had been in failing to go his separate path. Roberto had always despised Hitler, she said, and had urged Mussolini to avoid him. Mussolini's death at the hands of his own people was, for Roberto, the final straw. The villa had been badly damaged in the war when the hated Nazi soldiers set fire to it before their retreat north. Just one wing was left intact. Roberto confined himself to his own suite of rooms there and rarely came out, cutting Albie out of his life entirely. Albie was heart-broken that she had lost the love of her life, even before his actual death.

When the end finally did come, Albie said, "it was a blessing to us all. But most certainly to my beloved Roberto." Now she was taking her time and picking up the pieces of her own life. The Count had left her a very wealthy woman, having much earlier secreted most of his wealth to Switzerland. There was no fear for her future. Albie had left the estate and had accepted an invitation to share the beautiful quarters of a friend, the Countess Spezia, at her ancestral villa in Firenze. It was from that address that Albie was writing now. "I am just around the corner from that lovely piazza you and I spent such a wonderful time in, just in front of the Basilica of Santa Croce.

"Thankfully, much of the beauty of Firenze remains intact," she continued. "I am told by a friend of Roberto's that the Fuhrer himself saved the Ponte Vecchio and many of the city's priceless treasures, so impressed was he by its beauty during a visit here in 1940. All of the other bridges were destroyed, however. I do believe that it was my dear Roberto who played an important part in the preservation of this stunning city, since it was he who, at Il Duce's urging, arranged for Hitler to view Firenze's most magnificent treasures.

"There are shortages and the poor roam the streets. It is not always safe for us to be out and we spend much time shut in at the villa. We are thinking of leaving the city and finding a place in Switzerland until life returns to normal here. Geneva would be nice for a short time, I imagine."

Grace's heart ached. She felt she might well have lost Max forever. But her old friend needed her now. She knew immediately what she needed to do. "Dear Albie," she wrote back. "It's time for us to get away. Meet me in New York, my dear. We need to plan a girls' week away from it all. I won't take no for an answer."

* * *

Grace and Albie hugged for a good minute and a half when they met at the Park Plaza Hotel. Grace had arrived in New York earlier in the day by rail, while the Countess said nothing would do but that she would take one of those new cross-Atlantic flights that stopped at Gander and continued on to LaGuardia. And now that she was here, Albie said she was taking care of everything, all the bills. "The Count would have wanted nothing less," she insisted. Grace roared with laughter.

Their week in the Big Apple was a whirlwind experience of fine dining, Broadway plays, galleries and concerts, highlighted, Grace later told her mother, by the lighting of the Christmas tree at Rockefeller Center. Grace was in awe as the two of them took a cab up Madison Avenue to

59th Street on their way back to the Park Plaza after the tree lighting. She had never seen so many lights as those that lit their way.

"Driver," Albie said to the cabbie. "Before you drop us off, please take a spin around the park, will you? Oh no, wait. Take us to one of those carriage ride places. Grace, let's do the park in style. The Count insists."

Grace laughed heartily, delighted to see that despite all she had been through, Albie hadn't changed much through all those years. At the park's edge, they hopped out of the cab and walked over to one of the carriage stands. "I'll bet it's cold," Albie said. "Have you got a blanket for us?"

"Yes, ma'am," replied the driver. "Hop in and I'll get you each one."

The friends chattered excitedly as they toured the sprawling park. The driver slowed down and pointed out certain sights, including the Tavern on the Green, and took them to the iconic spot from which to admire the magnificent Park Plaza Hotel where they were staying. "This is magical," Grace declared as the driver helped them down across the street from their hotel. "It's something I'll never forget, Albie. Thanks so much."

17

The Power and the Glory

GRACE THOUGHT OF Manhattan's multitude of lights a few weeks later when back in Ontario, the provincial power company announced in the early days of 1948 that it would be building towers through the rural parts of Quinte to bring hydro-electricity to isolated areas that had not previously been served. Towers were to come down the road that passed Ballinskellig and the laneway everyone had always just called the O'Malley sideroad would now be given an official designation: Tower Road. Farmers were given the option of hooking in to the power grid and advised that if they did, the farmhouses, many of which were over a century old, would have to be retrofitted for the purpose.

James and Pete had a long conversation about the matter, as to how electrical power could benefit the farm operation and whether it was worth the expense. Pete had seemed to accept James would not be taking over the farm, but continued to value the younger man's advice. Pete said regardless of what happened to Ballinskellig, putting in full electrical service would be a good investment. Grace introduced herself into the discussion, reasoning that if the house was to be affected by this new set of circumstances, her voice needed to be heard. It was agreed among the three of them that yes, Ballinskellig would join the new age of hydro, and loans were arranged to cover the outlay of funds required. Excited chatter spread up and down the concession roads as farm families mulled over their introduction to the age of electricity. At Grace's insistence, they put in a telephone too. That way, she said, they could keep in closer touch with James. She argued that Pete had purchased a second-hand car just after the war, a 1932 Willys Overland roadster, and said electricity would be their final step into the modern era.

James would be finishing up his Carleton studies in the next few months and had begun looking around at prospective employers. In the past year he had spent time as part of his studies apprenticing as a reporter at an Ottawa newspaper and then at The Canadian Press news agency. He became friends with the CP managing editor and they spent many evenings after work discussing the future of their business, as well as where James might fit in. The editor was Griff Stoneman, the war correspondent James had met up with on the ship coming home from Europe.

"So, are you going to see us about a job when school's finished?" Stoneman asked. "We're hiring, you know."

"I'm trying to figure that out," James said. "I'd like to. I'm just not sure which track to take. I'd like to end up overseas as a foreign correspondent. You saw all the action, Griff, in the war. There's not likely to be an opportunity like that anytime soon, though. So maybe I'd like to end up in London or Paris someday. My French is pretty decent. I guess for that to happen I'll have to pay my dues here in the Ottawa office first. Or maybe at a daily newspaper. What do you think?"

Griff took a long drag on his Meerschaum pipe before he spoke. "Any experience is good. Don't suppose it makes much difference where you go, although we'd be pleased to keep you at CP. Why don't you give us a try. If you don't like it you can always move on. There's going to be plenty of opportunities for smart and educated journalists in the next few years. Me, I barely finished Grade 10. But now we're looking for fellows and gals with some knowledge of the world from a more academic perspective. People who can bring some depth and background knowledge to our reporting. You'd fit the bill."

James took Griff's advice and got himself hired on as a CP reporter, at first covering routine committee meetings on Parliament Hill and then press conferences the politicians called. That's how he became acquainted with Mike Pearson, the external affairs minister in Prime Minister Louis St. Laurent's government. Pearson was himself a veteran of the Great War and later lectured in history at the University of Toronto. He joined the foreign service and was counselor at the high commission in London during the Thirties. After serving as ambassador to Washington, he was chosen to head the Canadian delegation to the United Nations. The pair of them — divided by more than a quarter-century in age but bound together by their wartime experiences and a love for baseball — quickly hit it off. Pearson clearly liked the lad and started calling him Jim.

During their frequent background conversations, the older man helped James gain insight into some of the world's trouble spots.

"Jim, why don't you talk to your boss about coming along with the Canadian delegation to Washington when we set up the North Atlantic Treaty Organization," Pearson suggested one day. "This is going to be an important part of the new world order. The future's going to be based on international organizations and agencies solving our disputes within the rules of international law, rather than resorting to war. It is unconscionable for us to have another war like the one we just came through."

James made the approach and Griff went to bat for him. The plan was set and in April 1949 James was off to Washington D.C. with Pearson's team. He watched and listened as Pearson told the founding meeting: "This treaty is not a pact for war, but a pledge for peace and progress."

Pearson later explained to James his thinking about NATO, that it was more than a military alliance, that in its greater form it represented the establishment of stronger political and economic ties. "If this works," Pearson told him, "NATO will prevent future wars rather than simply act as an alliance to fight them." Pearson looked at James and asked: "Jim, can we go off the record for a moment here? I'd like to explain my thinking more."

Reluctantly, James set down his pencil and paper. "I'd rather we just talk for attribution, sir, but just for a moment then."

Pearson rose from his chair, came around to stand behind James, then turned and looked out the window of the embassy office. James swiveled in his chair and found himself staring at Pearson's back. Pearson stood arms folded. "We just got through two terrible wars and frankly, I don't know how Canada would fare in a third one. The cost, in dollars and in human loss, has been devastating. Maybe the Americans could afford to fight again, but we can't. Two wars have left the British reeling. They'll never recover. The United States is the next great super-power but even they recognize they have their limitations. The Soviets are on the way up and frankly they scare the hell out of me. I don't know what to expect from them. Jim, we have got to find ways to talk to one another and to prevent anything like Hitler and the Nazis from ever happening again. That's why I believe international organizations such as NATO and the UN, backed up by the Marshall Plan, represent our best hope. It's in Canada's best interest to make them work. That's why we're here, Jim. That's why we're here."

James's editors were pleased with the reports he filed on the NATO trip. They said he did a great job not just reporting on what had happened, but on explaining the background, on why, in other words, his readers ought to give a damn. That's the way Griff Stoneman put it to him: "As journalists we need to show our readers why they should give a damn. You could go far, O'Malley. Keep up the hard work. This is important stuff."

* * *

Grace had waited anxiously to see whether Max would return for the harvest of 1948. He did not. "That's it," she said to herself. "You've sent him away for the last time, Grace."

The next August, her heart skipped with joy when he did come. Since they parted two seasons ago, she had reached the conclusion that if she was ever going to lead a life in which love again played a part, it was going to have to be with Max, if he would ever have her under her demanding conditions. Swallowing her pride, she chose her moment carefully and two weeks after his arrival, she approached him. "Would you meet me down at the sugarhouse? Tonight?" Max nodded.

"Look," she said to him that evening. "I'm lonely beyond belief. My husband and I will never again have a relationship. We live separately under the same roof. We do nothing together. We rarely talk. Without Jamie, we'd be total strangers. I need a relationship, something to hang onto. Can you and I have that? Even if it's just during harvest time?"

Max stared at her blankly. In the past, he had tried to convince her to go away with him, to bring Jamie into their lives. She had given him a definitive no and after she virtually ignored him two years before, he truly believed that would be the end of their affair. He went away that time vowing to establish a new life without her and this he had done. As a silent co-manager of Huddlestone Enterprises, he was making his way in life without Grace O'Malley. And he was making a difference in the world.

But he missed her and frankly, he longed to leave the city and return, at least occasionally, to the life of a rambling and carefree farmworker. He realized he still loved Grace, and probably always would. That is why he had gone to his sister that summer and told her he was taking a break. He was going back out on the road for a few weeks.

Now as he stood face-to-face with Grace he only momentarily pondered her question: "Can we still have a relationship?"

"Yes, of course we can," he said. "Why do you think I came back? Last year I stayed away and it was the most painful thing I've ever done. Now I'm back. Grace, I love you. You say you will never go away with me and I accept that. But if we can have this together, for ten weeks of the year, then that satisfies me. I'll be alright with that."

Grace raced to Max's arms and fell into them. No further words were needed.

And so it became their apple time passion, their harvest fling. They lapsed into not caring who knew about it. Pete had given his consent and with his gratitude to Max for being the angel who had saved the young man he loved, and the woman who had given birth to that young man, he allowed their relationship to continue unencumbered. His only stipulation was that he would never speak another word to Max and that Max was to avoid him as best he could. But there would always be a job waiting for him. He was, after all, Pete's best worker.

Grace and Max had established a sort of pact that, regardless of what was to come, they would always have one another. At least during the annual harvest. Max would take an annual sabbatical from his office duties and go out on the road. Grace would be none the wiser about the life he maintained away from her. She seemed okay with that, although she wondered, as Max aged, just how he was able to maintain his life on the road.

Before he left that year, Max told Grace he wanted to cement their pact, and reached into his duffle bag, pulling out a smaller cloth bag. He handed it to Grace. She looked into his eyes and he said, "well, go ahead and open it." Reaching inside, she felt both hard metal and a coarse cloth. It was an odd mix of textures and she looked puzzled. "You have to look at it, sweetheart," he said.

She pulled out a number of items that had entangled in their cramped space. When she inspected them, she realized they were his military service medals. "Max, no," she said. "You've earned these. You need to keep them."

"No. They represent a moment in time that is long past. It's hard for me to carry them around. I want you to have them, to remember me by when I'm gone."

Grace nodded. She noticed one stood out, a medal showing the silhouette of King George VI, hanging from a small strip of cloth, two red stripes and one blue. She could not know this was called the Distinguished Conduct Medal, nor that it had been given for Max's special assignment at Dieppe.

"What's this one for?" she asked him.

Max regarded it coldly. "Nothing really," he told her. "Nothing… really."

* * *

In late 1950, James was sent to Korea to cover the war they preferred to call a "conflict", and remained until the UN-backed force pulled out three years later. He was just back in Ottawa when a knock came to the door of his modest Glebe apartment, a walkup on Bank Street overlooking a creekside greenspace. When he opened the door, James found himself staring into the face of Max Huddlestone. "Sonny Jim," Max exclaimed. The men embraced and James ushered him in.

Over beers, James told Max about his exciting life in Korea, about his close calls and the life of a foreign correspondent in Seoul. "I can only hope Mom never finds out," he said.

Max laughed. "Yeah, there are certain things a mother should never know." Then they caught a cab and headed across the river to Hull to take in a handful of the bars.

Talk turned to politics, a subject James had never been that interested in, until his reporting began to change that. Max expressed his support for the labour movement and James mentioned the case of Igor Gouzenko, the clerk at the Soviet embassy in Ottawa who had, after the war, handed over the names of Canadians who collaborated with the Soviet Union. It was an event that, probably more than any other, had kicked off the Cold War.

"Jamie, don't get caught up in the hysteria," said Max. "Fighting for labour rights is not synonymous with betraying your country. The CCF are not communists."

"Hey, I know that, Max. I believe workers have a right to decent wages and working conditions. That's something my dad always hammered into me. Human rights and personal freedoms. I believe strongly in that. But the CCF? Sure, I know they're not communists, but nationalization of industry? That's something I can never accept. I see that as the antithesis of personal freedom."

"If industry's going to avoid nationalization," said Max, "it has to prove it's got labour's interests in mind, right along with profits."

The men swallowed one final beer before staggering onto the sidewalk and hailing a cab.

Before he left Ottawa, Max handed James a name, address and a telephone number. "This is my sister in Toronto. Her name's Margaret and she can always reach me, if the need ever arises."

"Why can't you tell me where you are?" James asked him. "And besides, isn't it time you settled down, Max? Hey, you're no spring chicken anymore."

Max swatted playfully at James. "Smart-mouthed kid."

So Max had made light of a situation that James frankly did not understand. He still didn't know where Max went every year and he realized that in reality, he was no further ahead in understanding this mysterious man who had once come to him as a lifesaver. He supposed he might never understand. Nor did he understand quite what Max's relationship was with Grace. Max had said they were friends; Grace would never speak of him to her son.

Soon afterwards, James was hired away from The Canadian Press by a large newspaper chain that maintained its own news service. The managing editor wanted him to rotate through a progression of foreign correspondent positions and in the coming years James moved from Washington, to London, then to Rome and Paris. He was stationed in London in 1956 when political crisis in Egypt threatened to split the United States-UK alliance. James wanted to go to Egypt to cover the story but his Ottawa boss had other ideas. "The fighting is part of the story," James's boss told him. "But it's not the whole story. You've done a great job explaining the behind-the-scenes stuff. That's where you're most valuable to us. Go see Pearson and find out what he thinks. I want you to report the stories that will become history. We'll send someone else to cover the bullets."

James was the first to report Canada would make diplomatic overtures to bring its allies, the United States and Britain, back together through the establishment of a United Nations emergency peacekeeping force. It was evidence that Pearson's plan to create the apparatus for multinational diplomacy could succeed, James wrote. It heralded a new era when middle powers such as Canada could play a significant role in world affairs. Canada could never again afford to take on the crucial role it had undertaken in the war, but it could share the load, and it could influence. That was something normally preserved for the world's superpowers and there were bound to be benefits to the country. Even as a smaller nation, Canada could make a difference on the world stage.

Grace put down the morning newspaper that arrived in the late afternoon, six days a week, from Ottawa. She had been reading her son's story about Canada as a middle power and about how Mike Pearson had been awarded the Nobel Peace Prize for his plan for peace in the Middle East. She never fully understood what it was Jamie did for a living, nor how he obtained his information. Nor, for that matter, did Max or Pete. But they were proud of him nevertheless.

As for Pete, sure he worried about what would become of Ballinskellig, but James had done the family proud. Ballinskellig was resilient. It would work itself out.

18

Sherry 1960

SHERRY TREMBLAY COULD barely contain her excitement. It was like she was a schoolgirl again and her mother was taking her to the circus for the first time. But she was an adult now, a filmmaker, and this was probably going to be the biggest day in her career. Since coming to France nearly a year ago, Sherry had been working on a documentary that followed the journey Canadian troops had taken on the ill-fated Dieppe raid of 1943, a military manoeuvre that had cost thousands of young Canadian men their lives or their freedom. Now, here in Paris, she was about to sit down with a Canadian journalist to talk about her work. The article he would produce could bring her to the attention of Canadians. Perhaps even make or break her career.

Across the city from the Paris loft Sherry had called home for the better part of a year, James O'Malley took a final glance at the press handout photo of the up-and-coming independent filmmaker he was about to interview. This story was quite different from the normal political and breaking-news events he covered, and he wondered whether everyone in the entertainment business was as beautiful as this young Canadian woman. If so, he wished he'd been assigned more such stories. She had stunning brown eyes, a fashionable beehive hair style that set off her tawny complexion, and chiseled features that suggested some native blood in her background. That wasn't unusual for a French-Canadian, he knew, as more than a few of the early French settlers who had created Quebec back in the seventeenth and eighteenth centuries had married into the native population. As James left his office and got into the cab that would take him to the filmmaker's address, he reflected on his time as a foreign correspondent and how while the whole thing had been exciting and rewarding, it hadn't really left him with much chance to find a suitable life partner.

There had been no one serious in his life since Sally Parnell, and for this he was a bit sad. Sad, too, that he and Sally had never spoken about what had happened. He assumed his absence had been too much for her to bear and that the young man she chose had simply been the right one, in the right place at the right time.

James arrived at the address he'd been given by his editor, found the woman's loft apartment and knocked on the door. When she answered, James gulped. Sherry Tremblay's photo had done her little justice. This woman was stunning. Before him stood a more sultry Rita Hayworth, the actress the press had dubbed the "love goddess". He stammered his own name in introduction and felt like a fool but she didn't seem to notice. She smiled a broad smile and welcomed him inside. She offered him an espresso and led him to the little bistro table that sat in front of French doors and opened onto a distant, yet breathtaking view of the Eiffel Tower. They sat at the two chairs and began with some small talk.

"How old are you, Miss Tremblay?"

"Twenty-seven," she told him. "I was born in Montreal in 1933." She spoke in a soft, warm Montreal accent, a kind of collaboration of English and French speech.

"What brought you to film?"

Sherry took no time at all to respond. "It was my father, really. He served in the army and was part of the raid on Dieppe. The subject of this assignment that has brought me to France is really itself the instigation for my interest in film. I grew up listening to his accounts of what it was like to step off the landing craft onto the beach, of running like all hell across the beach before they got their heads blown off, and of trying to make their way up those cliffs. It was all so insane to me, and I think it was right then, when I thought about all those poor men deliberately running straight into the clutches of such horrible danger, that it came to me. I wanted to tell their stories. I needed to tell the world how insane the entire event really was. In a manner of speaking, this film will give both myself and my father closure to that day, to that event."

"But it's taken you a while to get to this point, hasn't it? I mean, of course you're still very young, but you've been making films for six years now, haven't you? How did you get to this point?"

Sherry nodded, took a breath and sped quickly forward. "It has been a long road to work my way to the point at which I can initiate the sort of project that really appeals to me. It took me some time to find the right people who were willing to back me, who shared my vision when I explained it to them. I thought on a couple of occasions that I had found the right partners, only to have something happen at the last moment. Canadians have some incredible stories to tell, but we're a small country and there isn't a lot of money available to undertake this sort of project. You know, I think there's more interest among the Québecois than there is in the English-speaking population. You Anglos, you're too infatuated with American culture. But I didn't want to just do a French-language film. I was determined to bring this story to all Canadians, not just to Quebec. That's what's taken me so long."

James and Sherry talked for the next two hours non-stop and as she proceeded to explain her work, Sherry's enthusiasm and eloquence not only fascinated him, but made him realize he wanted to know more about this fabulous young woman. More about her, not her work. But he didn't even yet know if she had anyone important in her life already. If not, he was falling into the realization that he wanted to be that person.

"So before we wrap up, can I ask you some more personal questions?"

Sherry smiled and then laughed. It was a friendly laugh. "Like what, Mr. O'Malley?"

"You're not married, are you? Is there someone in your life? Someone you can share all of these fascinating experiences with?"

"I'm afraid not," she sighed. "Oh, sometimes I wish there was, but the life of a documentary filmmaker is pretty crazy and it can be a lonely existence. I don't really have much time for that sort of thing."

Great answer, James thought. File that one away for after the article comes out. "Your accent is … interesting. Sometimes I detect a bit of Québecois, and sometimes a touch of Westmount."

"Is that a question? Well, I grew up speaking both English and French in the home. My father is francophone, from Quebec City. My mother was indeed raised in west Montreal, but NDG, not Westmount.

"NDG? That's what, Notre Dame de Grace?"

"Exactly. Actually when we were growing up and we moved a few blocks away to Westmount, we said it stood for No Damned Good."

They both laughed then, before he said: "I wish I'd known you were working on this a few months ago. I have a friend back in Canada who fought at Dieppe and made it back. Fairly unscathed, I gather. One of the few."

Sherry's interest was piqued. "Oh? Perhaps I could meet him when I get back home. Could you put me in touch with him?"

"I can try. He's pretty elusive. And very evasive about those times. I've tried to talk to him about it before and he's never been very forthcoming. So yes, I'll do my best to put you in touch and see what you can get out of him." James laughed then. "Maybe someone who's not so close can finagle a couple of words from him."

True to his word, James went back to the office and immediately reached out to Max through the phone number he'd been given for his sister in Toronto and she promised to try to reach him. He sat down at his typewriter and scanned the notes he'd taken during their interview. Then he phoned the contact Sherry had given him at the National Film Board, the government agency that was financing the film. There were others still to call, some of the men interviewed for the film, for example. The following day he began writing the article. The phone rang.

"O'Malley," he said when he picked up the receiver.

"James, it's Max. How are you, Sonny Jim?"

James smiled at the sound of the familiar voice. "So you got my message. I'm doing fine, Max. Where are you?"

"In Toronto visiting my sister. I'll be staying with her for a couple of weeks. Getting a bit old for all of that fieldwork. Slowing down some. So, what's this about a film?"

James filled Max in about Sherry's work and when he was finished there was a silence at the other end. Finally Max spoke.

"James, you know I've never said much about my war experiences. I don't like to think much about them. Especially Dieppe. It was pretty terrible. It's just like how you feel about Holland."

James understood. He recalled only fleeting moments of the time he was wounded and those moments were painful. Added to that were the images of his colleagues being blown up, slaughtered by German firepower. Yes, he knew all too well what Max was saying. But then Max added something James had never heard before.

"There was another facet to the operation, Jamie. One I simply am not allowed to speak of. Maybe someday, but I took an oath. It's not something I can talk to your friend about at all."

That was a puzzle. An oath, Max had said. That suggested something secretive. Something clandestine. James's journalist's instincts kicked in and he knew he had to know more. Yet he needed to be wary. His source in this case was a dear friend and the man who had literally saved his life in a muddy field in Holland. He would have to tread softly. For the moment, then, he said simply: "So you'd rather I not pass on your phone number to this film lady, I gather?"

"I'm afraid not, Sonny Jim. I can't add anything to her story."

"Alright, then. Will you be at Ballinskellig this year?"

"Oh, absolutely I will. I wouldn't miss the apple harvest for anything. I hope we can visit then."

* * *

James passed on the news to Sherry and told her simply that the wounds were too deep, too painful for his friend to speak of. She understood. It was a story she had heard time and time again. She did not press the matter. After all, the film was coming together well. She couldn't imagine what of value James's friend could add to it at this point.

When James's article was published and carried by newspapers across Canada and into the United States, he called Sherry up to let her know. "Yes," she replied. "I've already heard. My editor at the NFB called. He's delighted. Says the publicity's going to be great."

She said she was about to return to Montreal for the editing phase of the project and hoped the film would be delivered for distribution in about a year. "Film-making is a very slow process," she told him.

James wondered if this might be the time to make his move. What if she said no? Well, at least try, he told himself. Sure he was nine years older than this young woman, but what the hell?

"Listen, I was thinking. Before you leave for home, maybe we could get together for a celebratory dinner someplace. Maybe down on the Champs Elysées. My favourite spot in all of Paris is there. I'd love to take you." He held his breath and the short seconds of silence seemed an eternity.

Finally came the reply: "Sure. That would be really nice."

It was a beautiful July evening when they met at Fouquet's. James told his guest he sometimes came just to watch the people pass by and those who stopped for late-night fare. He had spotted Audrey Hepburn and her husband, Mel Ferrer, not long ago, he said. And now, he thought with a thrill, here I am sitting with Rita Hayworth's even more arresting twin.

When Paris is at its worst, it's still a very romantic place. When it's at its best, as it was that evening, it can be stunning. James and Sherry talked for hours. She was fascinated by the experiences he had had as a journalist and intrigued by what little he had shared about the war. She made a point of not pressing too hard. She had been through all of that before with others. She told James about growing up in Montreal and about some of her other film projects. She'd led a fascinating life for such a young person, he thought. She'd worked up on Baffin Island with the Eskimos, off the coast of Newfoundland with the fishermen and on the floor of the Bay Street stock exchange.

Over time, each revealed small bits of their own hopes and desires. James began to wonder whether Sherry really had any place in her life for companionship, committed as she was to a career in film. He understood all about having a total commitment to one's career. Sherry had met fascinating people along the way but at no time did she ever indicate any interest in a personal life, in maybe meeting the right person. While the two of them were getting along really well, he wondered whether he might some day mean something special to her, as he felt she could to him, or whether he was just one more acquaintance, one more check mark in her book of life.

Finally, after a rare lull in the conversation, Sherry said: "James, I'm leaving tomorrow for Montreal. Do you ever get back to Canada?"

James dared to allow himself a smidgen of hope. "Yes," he said. "My contract calls for two three-week visits a year. I'll be heading home before Christmas and again next summer. I fly into Montreal and take the train home to see my folks."

Sherry smiled. "Good. I'd like to see you again. It's been fascinating meeting you. Next time dinner's on me."

James's heart shot through his chest. "I'd love that," he said.

* * *

It was two weeks before Christmas when James's plane landed in Montreal. He arranged to stay in the city a couple of days before taking the train to Shannonside and had wired ahead to Sherry to let her know. She said she was taking him to her favourite spot, a little bistro on Rue Montagne. The snow was falling in big wet flurries when they stepped out of their cab in front of Aux Anciens Montréalaises, set in a lovely stone building along one of the city's coolest streets. James opened the door and stepped aside to let Sherry enter first and was startled to hear someone call her name inside. She began speaking excitedly to the man, whom James somehow seemed to recognize but couldn't quite place.

After a few moments of chatter, Sherry turned to him and said: "James, I'm sorry. How rude of me. This is my good friend, the writer, Eli Bachman. Eli, this is a new friend, James O'Malley. He's just arrived from Paris. James, Eli is living in London these days. But he says his heart will always belong to his hometown, Montreal."

"Good to meet you, James," said Bachman. "This is one charming young lady you have here, I hope you know. And she's going to go far. I can assure you of that."

"Yes, I know," James replied. "It's an honour to meet you. I've just read your book, *The Education of Levi Goldmann.*"

"What took you so long?" Bachman snapped in mock outrage delivered in a deadpan tone. "It came out last year."

All three laughed before Bachman excused himself. "I'm off to a Habs game," he said. "I never miss the Habs when I'm home in Montreal. James, if you're ever in London, give me a ring." James promised.

Dinner went as swimmingly as had their first date in Paris and as they walked out onto the street James wished desperately to keep the evening going. From a nearby club, the gentle strains of a violin solo wafted through the crisp air. Sherry put her hand in his and gently turned him toward her. "Dance?" she asked with a smile.

James's face burst into a big grin as he took her in his arms and while passersby looked on, bemused, the newly minted couple performed a waltz right there on the sidewalk. When the unseen violinist ended his performance, James and Sherry stopped and gazed into one another's eyes. The onlookers applauded and one couple shouted, "bravo! Encore!"

James never wanted to leave. He had just about made up his mind to simply come out and ask her if she thought they should make these events a regular occurrence when Sherry beat him to the punch. "Would you like to come back to my place?" she asked. "It's not far."

James was elated.

Two days later when he arrived at Ballinskellig, James announced to his parents: "I've met someone. We're getting married."

* * *

On the day of the Bay of Pigs invasion of April 1961, James and Sherry were married in Montreal. James was distracted; Sherry was not amused. The following day as the couple were supposed to be preparing for a honeymoon in New York, James was on the phone to Pearson, who was then the Canadian Opposition leader in Parliament and who told him: "Jamie, I have a feeling the CIA is involved. But aren't you supposed to be going on your honeymoon? For God's sake, man, get on with it. We'll talk when you're back."

Not a good start to the marriage. The whole thing blew up the next day after they checked in to their Manhattan hotel and James switched on the TV set to see what Walter Cronkite was saying. Sherry scowled. "Do you intend to watch that damned thing or pay attention to me? Hello, wife here," she said with a snap of her fingers. "Over here, James."

"Honey, my job is to keep up with world events. This is big and I need to know about it."

Sherry frowned. "Jamie, this is our honeymoon. Your job is to pay attention to your new wife." James sat down in a chair and listened to Cronkite. Sherry sighed, grabbed her coat and walked out the door.

Hours later when she returned, Sherry and James had makeup sex. "I'm sorry, honey. I don't know what came over me," he told her. "I promise to put the job aside and we're going to have a great time in New York."

Sherry wondered.

It had been agreed that when they returned to Montreal, James and Sherry would maintain a home in her downtown flat and pay as many cross-Atlantic visits to one another as they could for as long as James was stationed in Paris. He promised to ask his employer for a transfer and if they could not accommodate him, then he would simply look for a job back in Montreal. Sherry was busy finishing up work on her Dieppe documentary and assumed James was keeping his part of the bargain. Several months passed, and there was no further word from James about a transfer. One day she ran into James's editor, Griff Stoneman, who had left The Canadian Press to run the Montreal operation of the news service that employed James.

"Griff, how are you? How's that transfer coming for James?"

Griff look puzzled. "Sorry. Transfer?"

"The transfer back to Montreal. The one James asked for a few months ago. Will it be happening soon?" But the moment the words were out of her mouth a sickening feeling came to her.

"Oh, that. Yeah, sure. I'll have to get back to James soon and have a chat with him," Griff replied before excusing himself and rushing away.

"Jamie, you son-of-a-bitch," Sherry said under her breath.

The next morning she rose early and phoned James in Paris, timing her call for when she knew he would just be arriving at the office. "I ran into Griff Stoneman yesterday," she told him.

"Oh, really? How … how is he?"

"He didn't seem to know anything about that transfer, Jamie. What's going on?"

James hesitated. "Okay, I've got to tell you something. The timing's been all wrong over here. They can't let me go back right now. There's a big conference coming up in Geneva they want me to cover."

"Jamie, did you ever have any intention of asking for a transfer? And remember, you said if they couldn't accommodate you, you'd come back to Montreal and get another job. You said the *Daily News* would be happy to have you. What happened?"

"Listen, honey. We have to talk. Can you come to Paris? It's time we had a good talk."

Having explained to her editor she needed to spend a few days in France to recheck some matters that had come up in connection with the film, Sherry was on a plane to Paris in two days. James met her at Orly Airport. He hugged her and could sense the stiffness in her. They headed to his apartment with barely a word exchanged.

"I should have told you, I know," he said. "I didn't ask for the transfer. Yet. But I'm going to. I'll do it next week. I'll talk to my editor here in Paris and make sure the message gets back to Griff the same day. And I promise, if they can't accommodate me in the next while, I'll go talk to the *Daily News*. I'm definitely coming to Montreal."

She looked at him, tears welling in her eyes. "James, I love you. I don't want to lose you. But this relationship is going nowhere. Now you've lied to me. Why didn't you level with me? If you don't want to come to Montreal, just tell me. Is your career as a foreign correspondent more important to you than I am? Is that it?"

"No, not at all. I'll be back in Montreal by the end of the year, one way or the other."

They fell into one another's arms and spent the next twenty-four hours in bed. They both had to agree, the experience was divine.

James took Sherry to their old favourite on the Champs Elysées, they toured the galleries and wandered the streets of Montparnasse. Along the way, they stopped at a streetside café and ordered a glass of wine. They cuddled and touched one another with the same old passion that had brought them together and made them fervently believe a cross-oceanic marriage could work. As they snuggled in a corner of the café, a voice broke the silence. "Hey, you two, get a room, won't you?"

They looked up, startled. Sherry immediately recognized Eli Bachman, strolling along the street with a woman she didn't recognize. "This is my friend, Hannah Posner," he told them. "Hannah, this is James and Sherry O'Malley."

"I thought you were living in London," said Sherry.

"Just over for a visit to my favourite city in the world," he said. "Except for Montreal, of course."

The two couples agreed to meet for dinner that evening. When they were settled in, Bachman said: "So, where are you two living these days?"

"We've been discussing that very topic," said James. "I guess it's time for me to be heading to Montreal so I can spend more quality time with my lovely wife. I'll miss Paris, though. It's been a great place to live and work."

Hannah and Eli exchanged glances and a smile. Bachman turned to James. "Montreal's not too shabby either, James. Hannah and I have been beginning to wonder if it's not time to get out of London and head home. London's getting too tame. I want to get back writing for newspapers again and I think there will be plenty going on in Quebec in the next few years, plenty for an astute journalist such as yourself to get his teeth into. With what's happening there, it would give me enough to pontificate on for years. This fellow Lesage, he's really bringing Quebec into the modern age. Union Nationale is history. The Liberals are going to turn things upside down and Montreal is about to be one of the world's great cities. I think I'm going to want to be there to see it and write about it. You should too, James."

"Tell me more," James said. "Just what do you think is going to happen in Quebec?"

By the time Bachman had shared his views on Montreal and Quebec politics, and on the face of things to come, James was convinced. It was a wakeup call of sorts, one that brought back memories of the work Bruce Hutchison had done years earlier, work that had initially piqued James's interest in journalism. And now politics. He gazed into the face of his beautiful wife. Yes, Montreal would do them both good.

19

Changing Times

Max and Grace continued their annual liaisons at the old sugar shack. Grace had fitted the place out over the years with more comfortable furnishings and had long ago ceased worrying about anyone detecting smoke from a fire in the stove. In fact last year she'd even put in a new stove and was making sure there was plenty of firewood. The little cabin in the woods was looking ever more cozy. Over the years, rumours had spread throughout the community about Grace's "man" and she had come to care less and less about what people thought. It didn't ever seem to have any effect on her friendships with neighbours, men or women. Everyone had just come to accept that Grace and Pete lived under one roof but not together, and that Grace and "her man" shared a true and enduring love. That's just the way it was. Still, when it came time to sharing intimate secrets, the only friend Grace would confide in was Alberta.

The topic of James often came up during the times Grace and Max spent together and one year Max asked her what would be so bad about finally telling him the truth. That's where Grace drew the line. She said she would never, while she was alive, ever acknowledge to Jamie that he was not Pete's son. The O'Malleys formed the framework for his life and she would never do anything to break the bond that had been created. Jamie had come to learn a great deal about the O'Malley family story and was passionate in his pride for all they had achieved at Ballinskellig and in the community the family had called their home for more than a century. It was who he was, and Grace would never do anything to jeopardize that.

Grace sometimes wondered what Pete's sisters knew, or suspected about Jamie. After all, Pete very much resembled the O'Malleys as was clearly on display in the old photographs that lined the wall up the stairs at Ballinskellig. Grace was fairer skinned but certainly not as blond and fine-featured as her son was, and she wondered whether Jamie himself ever questioned his own background. When Grace looked into Jamie's eyes she could just barely make out Max but not as clearly as when he was a boy. Luckily, she felt, the resemblance was now only fleeting. She didn't think it would be obvious to others.

There was something else she wondered about, too. Max was getting on in years. Wasn't it time he eased up on his work as a farm hand? Perhaps he should be looking for a less strenuous job, maybe closer to Ballinskellig. When she raised the subject with him, he made a joke of it. "Are you calling me old? I'll have you know I've still got a few miles in me, Grace. Don't try to slow me down."

Grace, fearful of rocking the very comfortable boat she found herself in, just let the matter go. But she wondered nonetheless.

She and Max were very proud of their son and she was so terribly happy that he had finally found a woman with whom he could share his life. She worried about their trans-Atlantic relationship, though, and wished Jamie would make good on his pledge to find a suitable position in Montreal where they could finally live together in uninterrupted bliss. She feared that Jamie might never settle down, that the wanderlust he had displayed as a child would never allow him to be happy in one place. One day when she was waxing particularly nostalgic, she told Max about the hours Jamie would spend as a little boy poring over the pages of the atlas his grandfather Campbell had bought for him. It was a vintage 1930s atlas and the boundaries of all the countries had changed so much with the disruption of the Second World War and the increasing independence movement that was sweeping former colonies. Jamie had worn the pages thin with the turning and the tracing of the lines he had done. Jamie loved maps and always said he wanted to go everywhere when he grew up.

Max had that time nearly revealed that he and James had talked about that very thing on more than one occasion. He could not, he believed, share with Grace the many times the two of them had spent together in Jamie's adulthood, getting to know one another far better than Grace ever suspected. If Grace remained adamant that the three of them remain apart, Max was adamant that he would maintain his own strong wall between the relationships he had built with the two of them, mother and son. It was a strange triangular relationship the three of them – father, mother and son – shared, James standing as the pivot. Max had also come to fear that by revealing the whole story to one or the other of them, the entire web of his own story would be revealed and that everything would be destroyed. He had always been fanatical about his privacy, his secrecy. On the rare occasions he actually wondered whether it might just be best to reveal everything, Grace's words came back to him as a caution: She did not under any circumstances want Jamie to know he was Max's son. He would honour her wishes and also maintain his own secret identity.

James was back in Montreal before Christmas 1961 where he was hired by the *Daily News*. Grace could not be happier. His job would be to report on what was being called Quebec's Quiet Revolution, and the political, cultural and social storm that was sweeping the province since the election of Jean Lesage's Liberals. The idea to make such a proposal to the newspaper had come out of his conversation back in Paris with Eli Bachman, who had become an international sensation in the wake of his novel, *The Education of Levi Goldmann*. The news service James worked for since he left The Canadian Press was owned by the same company that owned the *News*, and his boss had been reluctant to let him go. But after hours of discussions, it was decided James was a perfect fit for the newspaper job and could produce material that would put the entire chain at the forefront of reportage on what many were beginning to believe could become the most important story in Canada.

Sherry's film, *Dieppe: Prelude To Normandy*, came out and a gala event was held at the Queen Elizabeth Hotel for the launch. She was in her glory and James couldn't have been prouder. Important film people and documentarians from across Canada and even the States came to recognize what the *New York Times* called "a seminal work on a little-understood chapter in Canada's wartime history." An instructor from Concordia Film School, Emory Caplan, introduced himself to Sherry and asked whether she had ever considered teaching her craft. "If this film is any indication," he told her, "you have so much to share." Sherry said she'd think about it.

James and Sherry purchased a home in Le Plateau-Mont-Royal near Lafontaine Park, a beautiful greystone terrace with a colourful mansard roof and iron stairs that led up from the street. Sherry's parents were their first dinner guests and soon afterwards they invited Grace and Pete. Pete begged off, saying he was just too busy preparing for spring crops. Grace took the three-hour train trip from Shannonside to Montreal's Gare Centrale where James picked her up in his newly purchased car, the first he'd ever owned. A couple of weeks later, Max was asked to pay a visit. When he came, Sherry made a wonderful coq au vin served with the perfect French white burgundy and after dinner the men retired to James's study for rye and gingers. James built a fire in the stone fireplace and they sat back in their comfortable chairs.

Max asked James about this Quiet Revolution he'd been reading about and James said he believed it was going to be the biggest story in Canada over the next few years. Quebecers were finally rebelling against the Church and its virtual monopoly over every aspect of life, from health care, to education, social services and family life. It had been a system that served Premier Maurice Duplessis and his Union Nationale well and kept them in power. But now, modern Quebecers looked around at the rest of the western world and said "enough". They wanted the same things other people had.

What made it "quiet?" Max asked. James explained that for the most part, the Church was okay with the modernization, with the loosening of its hammer-hold. Certainly, it insisted on maintaining control over education and family life, but it seemed able to accommodate itself to the reforms Lesage was implementing with incredible speed. That's what made the whole thing quiet, he said. One of the two chief targets of the revolution – the Church – was actually complicit in it.

Still, James wondered whether the route forward would remain so peaceful. There were hotheads in the movement, those who wanted to move more quickly and create a francophone state within the Canadian state. James wondered where that might lead if their numbers increased and if they took the reins of power.

"You've happened upon a very exciting topic, James," Max observed. "This could keep you busy for years."

"Exciting for sure," James responded. "But I'm not so sure the whole thing's going to take as long as some people believe."

There was something else on James's mind, Max could tell. The younger man looked at him and asked: "You and Mom have known each other for a long time, haven't you?"

"Yes, we have. I consider your mother a very good friend. And I'm grateful to your father for having me back every year. Back in the Thirties when it was hard to find work, your Pop was always there for me. He was a loyal employer and I've always been a loyal worker."

"Sometimes I think it's too bad you and Mom hadn't met before. She and Pop have been strangers to one another for my entire life. But you, you and she have an obvious chemistry. You're the one she should have met, not Pop."

Max stammered and blushed. He needed to tread lightly here. He wondered, what did James know that he wasn't saying? Or what might he suspect? "Your mother is a wonderful woman and she loves you more than anything else on earth. She would never do anything to hurt you. When she takes a certain direction you might not always understand, it's because she has your feelings and well-being in mind."

"I wish that sometimes she would do what's right for her," James said. "Max, you're right for her. It's so obvious. Look, I know you love one another. And I suspect that you have been, well, intimate." Max began to say something but James waved him off. "No, let me finish. If you are, that's fine with me. Mom deserves you and you deserve her. You both deserve to be happy. I just wish she would stop feeling so guilty about me. That's all."

Just then Sherry entered the room. "Would you gentlemen like coffee? And Jamie, pour me one of those drinks, will you?"

* * *

1963

"No, Max, I won't. Our relationship is completely separate from my relationship with my son. They're two different rooms in my life. I want it to remain that way."

Grace was as stubborn as ever. Grace knew best. Grace always knew best. Max sighed. He had done his duty. He had recounted the conversation he'd had with James and added his own nuances to what he believed James knew, and thought he knew. He believed James had actually wanted him to speak to Grace, to help to bring the three of them closer. He wondered if this was now the time to tell James about who his real father was.

It made no difference. Grace insisted on maintaining their three-sided relationship. Max knew it would never change. In a way, he was relieved because it gave him license to maintain his own cloak of secrecy, an excuse to never share with her the whole truth about his identity and the life he lived away from her. Let Grace continue to believe what she wanted. She had just given him the go-ahead to maintain his clandestine identity. It was easier that way. He wondered whether perhaps he had been prepared to come out into the open about the rest of his life, if Grace had given him a different answer. But now there was no need.

Strange, he thought, that Grace never questioned him too closely about what he was doing these days. Had it never occurred to her that in 1963, as he approached the age of sixty, he was not likely going to continue his peripatetic lifestyle in the manner of before? On one of the rare occasions she expressed her concern for the hard life on the road he was still supposedly living, he'd made light of it and she quickly dropped the topic.

In fact he was no longer a young man, and he couldn't imagine maintaining a life of traversing the continent with the carefree fervor of his earlier years, following the harvests from Florida, to California, to Ontario and the Prairies. Living under the stars. Content to have a fleeting relationship for two months of the year. How could Grace truly imagine that was what he was still doing? For a moment he felt a tinge of guilt over keeping so much from her. And yet he had given her the opportunity to change all of that. Time and time again before the war she had turned him down. Soon after the war she had again rejected his suggestion that they go away together and start a new life. Now, through mutual agreement, that subject was no longer broached. She would never leave Ballinskellig which was, after all, the home and the business she had also worked hard to build, would never abandon Peter, never disappoint James and never jeopardize his future.

Pete too was getting on in years. One evening over one of those rare suppers they shared together in the kitchen of the old farmhouse at Ballinskellig, Grace became alarmed as he coughed uncontrollably. Finally he was able to get it under control and Grace said: "You need to go see the doctor. And I know he's going to tell you to stop using those damned sprays on the apples. That's what's doing this to you. Get away from them."

"I can't stop. It would be the end of the farm if I did."

"That is pure nonsense. You never used those chemical sprays until after the war. You could go back to the old ways. Who knows, maybe if we advertised our fruit as chemical-free, people might appreciate it. So what if there are a few blemishes or if the yields aren't quite as large? You need to protect your health, Pete. This is our farm and it needs you. It needs us both."

It was the same story Pete had heard from James for years: Stop using chemical pesticides. Ironically it had been James himself who had introduced his father to the so-called modern era of fruit production, which entailed the extensive use of chemical sprays to eliminate pest damage and increase crop yields. Now, as he watched his father's health deteriorate, James said he'd get in touch with his old friends at the National Experimental Farm in Ottawa and seek their advice on what alternative methods they advised these days. As Pete fell into another coughing fit, James's words came back to him. After his coughing had settled down, Pete said to Grace: "Alright."

Once he stopped using the chemicals, the transformation in his health was miraculous and by the next apple season Pete was nearly back to his old self. A trip to the doctor showed his lungs had recovered three-quarters of their former elasticity and capacity. The doctor said there was every reason to believe further improvement would follow as his body rid itself of the spray chemicals. Pete felt better, he had more energy. Meanwhile word had quickly spread that Ballinskellig was producing chemical-free apples and people began showing up unannounced, wanting to know if they could try some of them out. Sales were up to heights Pete hadn't seen in years. There were barely enough apples left at the end to justify his annual cider production.

"See? I told you so," said Grace. She and Pete had fallen into a comfortable understanding. They lived under the same roof, she made his meals and they were at least civil to one another. But Grace looked forward to her two months every year with Max. She loved the feel of his arms around her, his scent, the intimacy and their wonderful conversations. They talked often about Jamie, shared recollections of their days together over the years and tried as best as they could to pretend their relationship was a normal one. In recent years, they even threw caution to the wind and took the second-hand car Grace had purchased, a Volkswagen Beetle, driving places together, not around Shannonside, but to places farther afield such as Kingston and Ottawa, and small towns along the way. One place she would never see fit to accompany him was Montreal, where she was adamant they could never be seen together. They would never visit Jamie and Sherry together. She seemed pleased, though, that Max finally told her he had visited, met Sherry and found her a lovely woman.

Once every few years, Alberta came to Ballinskellig for a visit. Albie and Grace's first reunion after the war, after the Count had died, had taken them to New York. At first evasive about her husband's wartime experiences, Albie had finally opened up to some extent, but continued to keep certain details close to the vest. About the war Albie would say only that it had been a rough time, there had been shortages and that near the end their villa was seized by the Germans and when they retreated north, they set fire to it. Then Roberto suffered a massive heart attack and died, leaving his widow a very wealthy woman. Alberta had travelled to Roberto's bank in Geneva, made arrangements to take over his account and walked away content in the knowledge she would have more money than she could ever spend.

Albie came to Ballinskellig for a visit in the mid-Sixties and she and Grace went to Montreal to see Jamie and Sherry. It had been years since Albie had seen her godson. Jamie asked her about the exact location of her Italian villa and said he thought his army outfit had been stationed nearby as they pushed the Germans north. He recounted the day that he stood on a height of land overlooking Lago Trasimeno and watched a huge mansion burning in the distance. Albie said nothing and Jamie dropped the subject.

James got to know the Montreal journalistic community well and particularly loved comparing notes with the francophone journalists. It was through them that he met a recently elected Quebec politician by the name of Pierre Laporte. Before James arrived in Montreal, Laporte had been a crusading writer for the French-language newspaper *Le Devoir* where he had written extensively about the corruption of the former Union Nationale government of Maurice Duplessis. After he entered politics, Laporte maintained close connections to the newspaper world. He and James enjoyed long conversations about Quebec history and politics. It became an important part of James's education and of his understanding of the Québecois society. He honed his French-language skills listening to, and debating with Laporte. Over time, James began to think of Laporte as a strong contender to replace Jean Lesage when the time came for him to retire, but Laporte himself said he didn't think he'd have much of a chance against a fellow cabinet minister named Robert Bourassa.

There was another journalist serving in Lesage's government, a television reporter named René Lévesque. James never much liked Lévesque and neither did Laporte. "I don't trust him," is the way Laporte put it. Toward the end of the Sixties, Lévesque proved Laporte correct. Having lost in an attempt to persuade the Liberals to opt for a policy of Quebec sovereignty, Lévesque left the party and began campaigning for independence.

The year 1967 was to be an exciting one, a proud moment for all Canadians as the country celebrated the centennial of nationhood. But in Quebec, the francophone nationalists who were coming to be dubbed separatists were determined to ruin the celebration. When French President Charles de Gaulle paid a visit, James told his editor he wanted to be there. He stood in the crowd as the French general proclaimed "vive le Québec libre" from the balcony of Montreal city hall, parroting the separatists' slogan.

Lester Pearson, who was Canada's prime minister at the time, called de Gaulle's words "unacceptable" and the general immediately left for home without continuing on to Ottawa as his itinerary had stated. The next day Pearson called James.

"Well, Jim, what did you think of the general's speech?"

"I believe you were correct, sir, in the way you handled it. You made it quite clear de Gaulle's behavior was unacceptable but you were your old diplomatic self. No one could fault you in any manner. What do you think will happen now?"

Pearson did not hesitate. "I have a feeling that the separatists will grow in strength. I'm thinking it's time a new leader took control of the national Liberal party. I'm satisfied that I've accomplished much of what I wanted. We have national health care. We have legislation on bilingualism and biculturalism. We finally have our own flag and a national pension plan. I'm pleased with what we've done but it's been exhausting. It's time for someone else. Someone younger and someone from Quebec, I believe, who can stand up to these separatists and defend Canada."

"It sounds like an exciting time," James replied. "They've been after me to move into the newspaper's editorship, but I'm thinking I'm not quite ready to hang up my reporter's hat quite yet."

"Good man," replied Pearson. "Hang onto that thought. You can be more valuable to your employer, and your country, as a writer."

As he contemplated those words, James came to realize the reason for Pearson's call. He wanted "Jim" to write a speculative story, to lay out the prime minister's plan. Pearson might be ready to step down, but he had very definite opinions about the party's – and the country's – future. While he would undoubtedly remain officially neutral in the coming campaign for the party leadership, Pearson believed it was time for a new direction, one that placed Quebec front and centre.

James called the prime minister back to confirm some details and said he planned to write a background piece anticipating Pearson's retirement and the prospects for a new leader. Pearson said he would look forward to reading it. That's all James needed to know. He wrote on the likely transition that was about to come to the federal Liberal party, about Pearson's achievements and the new generation of Quebec intellectuals, including Marchand, Pépin and a new man named Trudeau, who stood ready to replace the leader and fight the pending battle with the separatists.

The next year, James covered the meteoric rise of Pierre Trudeau. On a visit home to Ballinskellig, his parents were eager to hear what he thought of the new prime minister whom, it was said, was about to call an election. "I think the separatists will be testing his mettle over the next couple of years," James said. "I'm reserving judgement."

At Ballinskellig, Grace prepared for Max's annual visit with her usual enthusiasm. She adored her time with him and actually approached Peter about giving him more "free time." Peter laughed bitterly. "He's here to work, dammit. I've turned a blind eye to your ridiculous infidelity, but I'll be damned if I'm going to keep him on my payroll so you can fuck him on my time. What else do you want? More money for you to fix up your little love nest down by the pond?" Grace's eyes blazed but she turned quickly and walked away. She didn't want her husband to see that those fiery eyes had suddenly turned into rivers of stinging tears.

"Max," she said one night at the cabin. "I want us to be together more. Maybe you're right. Maybe I should just leave Ballinskellig. We could move in together someplace. Spend our remaining years together. Everything I've done has been for Jamie but he's a grown man. I don't need to keep up this pretense forever, do I?"

Shocked at her sudden change of mind, Max's breathing shortened and his heart pounded. He had to think quickly. "I don't want you to do anything you'll regret, my love. You've been so determined to maintain your life here. Your whole life has been devoted to James. What's changed? Why now?"

Grace's mood deflated. "Yes, I suppose you're right. It was just a moment I was going through. Really, nothing's changed, except for the fact we're not getting any younger. Max, I love you. I wish we'd met earlier, wish we'd been able to spend our lives together. Wish, I suppose, that I'd left Pete years ago. But this is my home too. Oh, I don't know. The world has changed so much, these things don't seem to matter to most people any more. The sexual revolution, they say. But I guess that somewhere inside I really do care what other people say. It's a hard feeling to shake. I'll go so far, but no farther. No, you're right, my dear. You know me so well, don't you? Thank you."

A small sigh escaped Max's mouth. His breathing returned to normal. "I promise, we'll spend more time together. Here at the cabin. I don't need to be travelling for the harvests as much as I used to. I am getting on in years; a little long in the tooth, I guess they say. We'll be together more, my darling. I promise."

Grace thought about the time she confided in her mother that the baby inside her was Max's, not her husband's. Her mother's first response had been "how can we hide it? How can we make Pete believe the child is his?" What an old-fashioned thing to do, she thought. How Victorian of her Victorian-era mother. Not shock that it had happened, but an immediate move into action to fix the problem. To maintain a semblance of public decorum. She realized she was no different. Her mother had died a few years ago and Grace was certain she never once breathed a word about Jamie's real father. Grace would follow her lead.

After Max left that fall, Grace wrote a long letter to Albie. She poured out her heart and shared more than she had ever done before. She explained her arrangement with Max but stopped short of telling her that James was his son, about how she had pretended all these years. She would maintain her current situation, living with Pete, having an "amorous liaison" with Max. She momentarily laughed at the term she had chosen. "An amorous liaison, Albie. Imagine. I hope this is the right thing to do. Life is so short, isn't it? I deserve my happiness as much as anyone. Please, Albie, tell me I'm doing the right thing."

The Countess wrote back: "Oh, Grace, my heart goes out to you. What do I think? I think you should leave Pete and be with Max. If my many years here in Italy taught me anything, it's that we need to follow our hearts. All else will fall into place. I miss the Count horribly, Grace. I will never regret our wonderful years together, through better and through worse. I do not for a moment have remorse over my decision to come here. But only you, my dear friend, know what's best for you. I cannot make up your mind for you."

Now Grace was more confused that ever. How had it come to be that she had been ready to go away with Max, only to be talked out of it? By Max himself. She was so mixed up. She just wished she could be a woman of the modern times and not worry about these things. To just follow her heart, as her friend had advised.

* * *

It was a chilly, rainy day in September 1970 when James received a phone call from his friend, Laporte. "Come have lunch with me," Laporte said. "It's been weeks since we've had a good hard conversation." As they ate, the two men discussed the rise of the separatist cause. Laporte was now labour minister in the Quebec government of Robert Bourassa who had bested him and Lévesque for the party leadership earlier in the year. Laporte said he sympathized with the separatists from the perspective of a Quebecer who had watched the Anglophones control the levers of government and economic power for far too long. He was a proud Canadian but at the same time a proud Quebecer. Yet he feared what certain small cells of radicals were capable of. They had been behind bank robberies and bombings and tossed around threats of further disruptions to come. A few days after their lunch, British diplomat James Cross was kidnapped. Five days after that, Laporte was home tossing a football with a nephew when members of one of those radical cells he had spoken of drove up to his home in suburban Montreal and kidnapped him at gunpoint.

Cabinet ministers and their families in Ottawa and Quebec City were given armed security detail and the army stood guard on Parliament Hill and at the Quebec National Assembly. James thought about the peaceful scene that had greeted him on his first visit to Parliament Hill after the war. Looking back, it now seemed like such an innocent time. It was a new world now. He headed to Ottawa and Parliament Hill where he joined a throng of reporters awaiting the prime minister's remarks. A television reporter named Tim Ralfe asked Trudeau about the armed presence that encircled this bastion of Canadian democracy.

"Well, there are a lot of bleeding hearts around who just don't like to see people with helmets and guns. All I can say is, go on and bleed. But it's more important to keep law and order in this society than to be worried about weak-kneed people who don't like the looks of ..."

Ralfe interrupted: "At any cost? How far would you go with that? How far would you extend that?"

In steely-eyed response Trudeau said: "Well, just watch me."

James shivered. In the coming days he did watch. He watched the federal cabinet declare a state of armed insurrection and the imposition of the War Measures Act, resulting in the arrest of dozens of people who were "suspected" of separatist ties. He watched army tanks rumble through the streets of Montreal and Ottawa and James feared for the country he loved, for the freedom they had come to take for granted. Everything happened so quickly. Laporte was murdered and his body was found in the trunk of a car. The terrorist cell that had kidnapped James Cross demanded safe passage to Cuba in exchange for his return alive. Human rights advocates blasted Trudeau for what they called his authoritarian bent, saying he was sacrificing Canadians' hard-won rights for short-term expediency. Several hundred Canadians were rounded up and held without charge. James knew some of them.

"I'm ready to tell you what I think of Trudeau," James told his parents on his next visit. "He faced one of the greatest challenges any prime minister has ever faced in this country's history. And he failed." He and Pete then got into a heated argument, Pete claiming the prime minister did the right thing. "He had no choice," Pete said. "He had to keep order."

"Yes, he did have a choice," replied James. "This is what I joined the military for, Pop. This is why I fought the war and this is why thousands of young Canadians lost their lives. I'm angry, Pop. Trudeau failed the test. He should have trusted us and trusted the system. It would have worked."

James was saddened, angry and alarmed by what was happening around him. He wondered whether it was enough for him to report on such events. He began to contemplate whether there might be another place for him to make a difference and pondered where his future lay. He could not know at that moment that Sherry was about to make his decision easier.

It was right around Christmas and James planned to surprise his wife by coming home from Ottawa two days earlier than previously planned. He walked into the house and found her and Emory Caplan, that guy she knew from the Concordia Film School. The two of them, half-dressed, were enjoying a glass of wine in the kitchen. Anger seared James's mind and his first thought was to run over and pound Caplan into the hardwood floor. Instead, he turned on his heel and walked out the door.

"James," Sherry called after him. "James, please."

Two days later when he returned, James told his wife: "I've watched my parents all my life and I cannot bear to repeat their mistakes. Sherry, I love you and I guess I always will. But I can't forgive this."

"James, I love you, too," she said. "But your entire life is tied up in your work. I love my work too, but I need more. I need a husband to share my life with, someone I can count on. Emory provides me with so much you won't provide, James. He fills that emptiness you leave inside of me. Yes, my sweet, I love you and I probably always will. I'll be there when you need me, but I cannot live my life the way it's been. If we have to part, then let's part now, as friends."

James told her they were finished and he moved out. But he had to get out of Montreal as well, away from her. He called his friend, Eli Bachman, who was back in the city and working for the *Montreal Post.* They discussed James' situation and his sense of betrayal, both by Sherry, and by Trudeau's actions.

"Trudeau trampled on our right to freedom of expression," James told Eli. "I fought to uphold that right."

"You might see it that way," Bachman said, "but most Canadians don't. You're disillusioned, James, but I don't know whether it's a disillusionment with the prime minister, or with your job. Maybe it's time to look for more. Look, you've accumulated a great deal of expertise as a journalist. Maybe it's time you found a way to share that expertise, maybe with young people just coming into the business. It's something I've often thought of myself."

They talked about a teaching position and James called Carleton University to find out whether they might have a job in the journalism department. They told him his timing was bad, but maybe in a few months. James didn't have a few months, so he approached Ryerson Polytechnical Institute in Toronto. He was called in for an interview at the journalism school and laid out his credentials, sketched out details of a position for himself and asked: "Would you have employment for me here?" They jumped at the opportunity to hire someone with James's experience and reputation. In the spring, he took up his new job as a journalism instructor and lecturer on the history of rights and freedoms in Canada. He would turn his sights on the next generation of journalists and instruct them in the art of holding their politicians accountable.

Just before he picked up the phone to call Grace and Peter about his plans, he thought about whether his marriage might have turned out differently if he'd done this before, if he'd taken a step away from the job that had come to consume his life.

Grace bit her lip to hold back the tears when her son gave her the news of his marriage breakup. "Honey, are you sure? Would it be worth another try?"

"Mom, are you serious?" he asked. "What about you two?"

Grace could think of nothing to say. She placed the phone back on its cradle. She cried.

After settling in to his new Toronto apartment, James called Max's sister. "Please tell Max I'm working in the city now. Here's my number."

Max never called.

20

Peter
1974

THE DAY PETE took the train to Kingston, he told Grace he was visiting a man about selling some of his pesticide-free apples in that city. In fact it was a lawyer he had gone to see. A lawyer who advised about wills and inheritances. Pete had thought a lot about what he was about to do but still, as he walked into the man's office, he was uncertain. By the time he left the lawyer's office and headed back to the train, Pete had convinced himself he'd done the right thing.

That was nearly two years ago. Over the past few months, Pete's eyesight had been getting progressively worse. He reluctantly went to the optometrist for glasses which he hated wearing. He'd even cut back on his regular poker games in town because he found it embarrassing to admit he really couldn't see the cards very well. On a cold early December evening in 1974, however, Grace convinced him to go play cards. She was desperate to get him out of the house because he was driving her crazy. It was one of those times when she couldn't stand the sight of him.

That night he drew a Dead Man's Hand but this time he didn't show it to the other players; nor did he make light of it. He remembered what happened last time he'd drawn such a hand, but it was different now. He won big this night, or as big as the penny ante stakes would allow. He went home with $1.50. The jubilation he felt made him totally forget about the ominous hand he'd been dealt. Forgot, that is, until a few days later when he heard a cracking sound above his head in the hay barn. He looked up and the card hand flashed through his mind. The last thing he ever recalled was watching as the haymow collapsed and tons of hay came hurtling down on him.

Grace was not alarmed when Pete failed to show for dinner that evening. She figured he was in the middle of something and wanted to finish up. She put his dinner aside, thinking she'd warm it up when he was ready but by nine, she grew concerned, grabbed a flashlight and walked over to the darkened barn. She flicked on the flashlight and when she saw the tangle of wooden beams and hay, she reeled back, clasping her hand over her mouth in horror. She ran to the house and telephoned the fire department.

The coroner's conclusion was that Pete had been knocked down and rendered unconscious by the cascading hay, then smothered beneath its immense weight. Apparently none of the collapsing timbers had struck him even a glancing blow. He had smothered to death. When Grace heard the conclusion, her mind went immediately to the memory of baby Petie. He too had smothered because Grace had pulled the buffalo hide overtop him to keep the cold out. How stupid she had been that night so many years ago to have heeded Pete's entreaty that she come and join him in the front seat of the sleigh.

While they were older than Pete, all three of his sisters were still alive, although only the youngest, Anna, was well enough to make the trip to the funeral. Alice was spending her last days in a small country town nursing home fifty miles away, while in Toronto Lucy, who had raised Pete as a mother after Mame had died, was mentally alert but physically unable to go far from her home. When Grace called to tell him about the accident, James said he would head over to Lucy's house and give her the news. Grace called Anna and the two decided there was no point in upsetting Alice with the news. She likely wouldn't understand anyway, they agreed.

Lucy and James had always been close but even more so in the past four years since he had taken up a position at Ryerson. He made a point of visiting at least once a week and their conversations were something he always looked forward to. Lucy was a perky ninety-five now and adored talking politics with the nephew she considered more of a son, especially since she had never had any children of her own. She lived alone now, her husband having passed a decade ago. She was so proud of Jamie and never missed a chance to brag about him whenever one of her caregivers came by to help. While she always took her time at it, she still insisted for the most part on preparing her own meals and despite her age, Jamie never feared a mental lapse would cause her to leave the stove on or that she'd forget to lock the door.

James and Lucy had had more than one knock-down debate over Trudeau's declaration of the War Measures Act, Lucy adamant that it had been a necessary evil, while James argued that if the government could find an excuse to take away people's rights once, it could always do so again. If rights were inviolable, he said, then they ought to be in every case. That's what democracy was all about and you had to take it, warts and all. Lucy believed the government "knew best" at the time of what had been called the October Crisis, and was merely imposing a temporary restriction in order to keep the people safe and secure. Their debates had often been heated and on one occasion, they agreed they had better call a halt before things got out of hand and someone said something they would regret. They ended the tussle with a cup of herbal tea. "It's calming," Lucy had said.

When James arrived at Lucy's door to tell her about Pete, his aunt knew immediately something bad had happened. Through the smile he always greeted her with, there were tears in his eyes.

"Jamie? What?"

"It's Pop. There's been an accident."

The two of them went to her couch and held one another's hands as they sat quietly. Death was a big part of Lucy's world, with her own husband and all of her friends having passed away before her. She wasn't calloused about death, but rather resigned to it, although the fact the victim was her little brother, the one she had raised, made it harder than the others. It was Lucy who broke the silence. "I first set eyes on him the moment he came into this world. I regret what I said to your grandfather that day. I told him he and Mumma should never have had the baby. Oh, gosh, Jamie, I so wish I had not lost my temper and that I had never said that. A child should never be regretted. And your father, he brought such joy to all our lives. He taught you so much."

"What do you think happened between Mom and Pop?" he asked her.

Lucy stared off into space and then glanced over to an old family photo that had been taken when Pete was still a little boy. She was sad that their mother was not in that photo and that in fact there could never be any picture of all of them together. James wondered whether she had even heard his question.

"I'm afraid it was the death of your brother, Petie. At first they blamed one another, but then your father went away. Or rather he ran away because he couldn't accept what had happened. By that time, he had come to blame himself for the baby's death and couldn't face up to it."

"How did Petie die, exactly? How was it anyone's fault?"

Lucy recounted the story of the sleigh ride, the buffalo robe and how Pete had urged Grace to leave the baby wrapped in the robe and come sit up front with him. And of how Grace had found the baby, suffocated. James had never before heard the story and he started at the word suffocate. Just as his father himself had died, James realized. He wondered at the coincidence, at the symmetry.

"What do you mean, my father ran away? Where did he go?"

Lucy looked up at her nephew, her rheumy eyes now filling with fresh tears. "Your father never spoke of it. But I heard." She paused, uncertain whether she ought to proceed and whether it really mattered now. "An old friend here in the city told me he came here, to one of Toronto's shabby districts. He fell in with some bad types, gamblers and certain women. Wherever the red light district was in those days. He was there about two weeks. He was just about over the edge when he met my friend's husband who was a preacher at a Baptist church. Not certain how that happened but my friend said her husband often came down to talk to the people there, offer them support."

James was shocked by what he was hearing. Never had he even a hint of anything like this happening. Why, he had not even known how his older brother had died. No one ever spoke of it.

"I guess your father latched on to what the minister had to say. He wasn't that far gone, I suppose. Began to feel the tug of home, remembered he loved your mother. But he felt so ashamed. He told the minister he couldn't go back and the minister said Jesus would forgive him if he truly renounced his sins. Yes, I know this all sounds so odd because none of us in the O'Malley family is what you might call religious. But I think it helped that this man was not of the same faith, and that he took a different tack, told your father things he'd never thought of before. It was enough, I suppose. Enough to make him realize what he really wanted. He wanted to go home, to your mother."

"And later they had me," James added. "So it seemed they had made up their differences. So why? What happened afterwards? Why did they spend fifty years estranged from one another? Here they were living under the same roof and saying barely a word to one another. What happened?"

Lucy looked at him. "I don't know, son. I really don't know."

* * *

Pete's funeral was held at the same old Anglican church that his great-grandfather William had helped build. True to her word that she would forever be there for him, Sherry came down from Montreal and sat on one side of Grace while James sat on the other. Grace was totally dry-eyed until the priest mentioned Jamie as the pride of Pete's life. Sherry handed her a tissue and James put his arm around her shoulder.

Grace drifted into a different place then. She imagined herself kissing Peter that first time and thought about how in love they had been. There was the image of her puppy, Ebenezer, and of Peter coming heroically to his rescue. There were images of Peter, strong and handsome, working in the fields as Grace came by with her friend, Alberta. There were snippets of young-woman conversations between the two of them as Grace confided in Albie her deepest thoughts, thoughts of how she imagined herself and Peter spending the rest of their lives together. How foolish the two of them had been, she thought, to allow one incident to come between them, to pry them apart. If only Peter had spoken to her about why he'd run away that time after Petie's death, about what he had done and where he had gone. His refusal to let her into his life, to talk to her about his true feelings, that is what had ruined their marriage and sent her running to the handsome stranger, Max. Now after so many years, she could almost forgive Peter for leaving her alone to cope with the baby's death, but no, she could never, ever forgive his silence, his secrecy, his concealment of what had happened. They were two stubborn people, and stubbornness had ended their relationship.

After the service, everyone headed to the Masonic hall for sandwiches and coffee. Arthur Vankamp, Pete's nephew, wandered over to chat with his Aunt Grace and cousin James. "Uncle Pete and I had some great conversations over the years," he told them. "I've always loved visiting the farm."

"Your uncle always spoke fondly of you, Arthur," Grace said. "I know he was well aware of how much Ballinskellig means to you. Don't be a stranger, okay? Please feel free to come by anytime."

Arthur thanked her, said he would do that, and wandered away.

A couple of days later, Grace sat at her desk and penned a letter to Alberta to let her know of Pete's death. It was a calculated, detached sort of letter, one devoid of the inner thoughts that she often shared with her oldest friend. She just wanted to get it over with. Albie telephoned as soon as she received the letter, a rare occurrence. The two of them spoke for only a few minutes, as Albie explained that she would not be able to get away before Christmas. She was sorry. Grace said not to be, it was not an important enough event for Albie to disrupt her schedule. They would be together another time, perhaps in the spring.

Back in Toronto, James again wondered what had become of Max. The last time he attempted to reach Max through his sister, Margaret, was back when James had announced his arrival in Toronto. Max had not returned the call. James wondered why the man who had saved his life in Holland had so totally dropped out of his life now. James missed Max. He wondered if he'd ever see him again.

* * *

The last will and testament of Peter O'Malley was a puzzle to Harold Walters. He read it front to back and then over again. Rare was the occasion when a husband did not leave the bulk of his estate to his wife. In fact under normal circumstances, the transfer of a person's holdings to their spouse was pretty well automatic. This was one of those rare occasions, and Harold shook his head in dismay.

Harold knew as well as anyone in Shannonside that Pete and Grace had not gotten along for years. He was familiar with Grace's frequent outings with "her friend," the mysterious Max, who had worked the harvest at Ballinskellig for decades. Still, he found it shocking to read Pete's will and embarrassing to have to tell Grace and Jamie what it said. He telephoned Grace and asked her to make an appointment for her and her son so they could all "read the will together."

"Grace," Harold said somberly, "Peter had a new will drawn up a couple of years ago – one the contents of which I was not aware of. Some lawyer in Kingston did it for him. I had a copy, of course, dropped off by Pete himself, but I never had any reason to look at it until now. I must prepare you for what it says. Grace, Pete didn't leave the farm to you."

Since Ballinskellig had been passed down through Pete's family, and since it was common practice for property to be placed in the name of the husband with no co-ownership arrangement on the deed, it had never occurred to Grace to question why her name was omitted from that document. Now she realized what an oversight it had been to not question Pete's intentions. But surely he'd simply left it to Jamie, she said to Harold.

"I am afraid it's not that simple, Grace," Harold said. "Please, I need the two of you to come in as soon as possible."

An appointment was made for the next day so James took a day off work and came down from the city. He picked up his mother and drove her into town. When they arrived at the law office, Miss Finster ushered them into Harold's office. "Coffee for the three of you, Harold?" she asked. The elderly barrister nodded and in a minute she returned with three cups of the brew and a plate of cookies.

Harold looked up at them seated across from him at his huge desk.

"This is indeed an unusual circumstance," he told them. "But Pete has stipulated that the farm is to go to his nephew, Arthur Vankamp, his youngest sister Anna's boy." Arthur was Anna's eldest son, and in turn he was the father of four, two sons and two daughters. Over the years, he had often visited the O'Malley farm and brought along all or some of his children with him. Pete and Arthur remained close right up to the time of Pete's death.

Grace gasped. James said: "That can't be possible. Is it even legal?"

"I am afraid it is, son," Harold Walters replied. "Pete stipulated that all Arthur needed to do to inherit the entire farm was to pay you a sum of money that was equal to one-third of its assessed value. Of course this could be done with no difficulty through a mortgage arrangement. Your mother is to get nothing.

"We can contest the will and argue that your mother has a significant expectation that having formed a partnership with your father for the past fifty-plus years, the farm is at least partly hers. How do you think your cousin will react to this news?"

"I have no idea. I hardly even know Arthur. I know Pop liked him and his family but this is a total shock."

Grace sat silent. She took out a tissue and dabbed at her eyes. "This is my fault. I drove Pete to hate me this much. But Jamie shouldn't suffer. Harold, we have to fight this if it's the only way."

"I will have to call Arthur in to speak to him and show him the will, but might I suggest that one or both of you contact him beforehand and let him know what to expect. Feel him out. See whether an arrangement can be reached. That would be much preferred to a lawsuit."

* * *

Back in 1927, around the time of his sixteenth birthday during his summer school vacation, Arthur Vankamp paid a visit to Uncle Peter's farm. Arthur's mother, Anna, was Pete's sister, eleven years his senior. Arthur had joined his mother and father on trips to the farm before, but this time he was on his own. He was in the fifth day of a weeklong vacation with his Uncle Pete and had learned plenty about farm life. As usual, Pete made them both a big country breakfast, having explained on his nephew's first day there that the days were long and the work hard, and Arthur would need his nourishment.

Aunt Grace was over in Europe, in Italy, visiting her friend, the countess-something-or-other. Arthur's little cousin, Jamie, was staying at his grandparents' place.

Pete looked up from his bacon and eggs and stared at his nephew. "You ever think of being a farmer, Arthur?" he said.

"Me? Sure, Uncle Pete. It's been swell these past few days, learning about the animals and the crops. And those apples. Maybe I could come back when they're ripe and help with the harvest?"

Pete smiled. "A true O'Malley, he is. Apples run in our blood, son."

Arthur thought about that visit years later, when he got off the telephone from a call he'd received from his cousin James. Uncle Pete had passed away recently and Arthur and his siblings had come down from Brockville with their mother Anna to the funeral. Now James had called to say there was something in his will that pertained to Arthur. He couldn't imagine what, but he was touched that his favourite uncle had remembered to mention him at least. James wanted to get together, just Arthur, his Aunt Grace and himself, to talk about it.

As the three of them sat in the kitchen of Ballinskellig, James got right to the point. "Dad left the farm to you, Arthur. You're to be the new owner of this whole place. All you need to do is pay me one-third of its assessed value and I go away. We can go see the bank about a mortgage and you'll have the money you need to pay me off."

Arthur was flabbergasted. "But that's not fair. Aunt Grace, the farm should go to you. And you, Jamie. I'm just a nephew. Why? Mom and her sisters left this place years ago and Grandpa Ben's wishes were that his only son, Uncle Pete, would inherit Ballinskellig and carry on the family tradition. Why would Uncle Pete do this?"

Grace knew why, but kept her thoughts to herself. She thought about how Max had urged her to come away with him and how she had turned him down. For Jamie's sake, she couldn't bear the inevitable scandal. But that wasn't the only reason. Ballinskellig was her farm too, or at least she'd thought it was. She wasn't about to abandon it and risk her own inheritance as well as that of her son. Now neither one of them had it.

It was James who spoke first. "I told Dad a long time ago I didn't want this place. I suggested he sell it but he wouldn't hear of that. Said it had been in the O'Malley family for five generations and he wasn't about to be the one to put an end to that. Arthur, my only concern is my mother. I have no objections to you taking the farm over and we won't contest the will, provided you allow Mom to stay here for as long as she wishes, free of charge. You're welcome to do what you want after that. When you arrange the mortgage and pay me what my father stipulated, I'll hand the money over to my mother. Do we have a deal?"

"Why, of course, Jamie. Aunt Grace, you stay here at the house as long as you like. Look, I'm too old to be taking up farming now, but frankly, a couple of my kids have been talking about this place a great deal lately and I think maybe Philip would like to come and farm it. He's got a small parcel of property outside Brockville he raises hay on, but says it's full of rocks and no good for much else. He'd need some time to straighten out his affairs, but if that's alright by you, then let's draw up the paperwork and get things going. Let me talk to them."

Grace wondered how Pete had come up with the one-third figure for Jamie. One-third of its value would go to him. To the boy he had raised as his own. Did Pete believe that Jamie was one-third his? She wondered. But all of that was irrelevant now. Grace was a practical woman and knew there was no time for sentimentality. This was a business transaction. She smiled and said to her nephew: "Thank you, Arthur. If that arrangement is alright with Jamie, then I guess it's alright with me. It's a compromise."

Grace then turned to her son. "But Jamie, are you certain you don't want any part of Ballinskellig?" James said no, although he would like to claim a few items of sentimental value. Arthur said that was fine with him. "Anything at all," he said.

Later, after Arthur had left and as Grace and James sat down to dinner the night before he was due to head back to Toronto, she looked at her son and said: "I am so sorry, for everything. Your father and I should have worked this all out years ago. Jamie, please understand I truly regret dragging you into this awful situation. I didn't want to hurt you."

"Don't worry, Mum. I played my own part in all of this. After all, he wanted me to take over the farm and I said I wanted another career instead. I think that was the last straw for him. I guess this is his way of getting back at us for the hurt we both caused him. Not sure I can really blame him. He knew I didn't want the place and figured I'd likely sell it. This way he still gets his preference. He gets to keep the farm in the O'Malley family. Really, that's all he ever wanted, wasn't it?"

Grace looked down. She had never in her life felt as guilty as she did in that moment. Guilty about the secret she had kept from her son his entire life. How could she tell him now? What would he think of her? And what did she think of herself?

21

Max
1974–75

IT HAD BEEN more than four years since James had moved to Toronto to take a job at Ryerson Polytech, and four years since he had telephoned Max's sister to pass on the news that he was now in the city. Max had never returned the message and James had not tried to reach him again. He reasoned that if Max had wanted to contact him, he had the means to do so. Now, however, James felt he owed it to the man to let him know that Pete had died. He picked up the phone and dialed the number Max had given him years ago.

"Hello?" said the woman's voice on the other end of the line.

"Hi, this is James O'Malley calling. Max's old friend. I have a message I would like to pass on to your brother."

"Oh, hello, Mr. O'Malley. It's been a while since we last spoke. I think you'd just moved to Toronto. My brother was pleased to get that message back then."

James was puzzled. If he was so pleased, why hadn't he ever returned the call? To Margaret he said: "But Max never called back."

Now it was Margaret's turn to be puzzled. "He didn't? He said he would. I don't understand. I was certain he wanted to stay in touch. Oh, you know Max. He's pretty odd at times. Alright then, what would you like me to tell him?"

"Please let him know that my father has passed away. An accident in the barn. My mother is well. Can you tell him that for me?"

"Oh, of course. I'm sorry to hear about your father. Please give your mother our condolences. I will let Max know the next time I speak to him. Thank you. Goodbye."

"Goodb…ye," James began as the call was cut off. It was clear she couldn't wait to get him off the phone. He wondered: Why had Max never called back?

That had been in early December. The following March, when the phone rang at Ballinskellig and Grace answered, a familiar voice came on the line. "Grace, hi. How are you?" While they had never before spoken on the phone, she recognized Max's voice immediately and her spirits soared.

"I'm well, darling. Where are you?"

"I'm in Toronto at my sister's place. I heard about Peter. Thought I'd call and see how things were going. I'm sorry it's taken me so long. You understand."

"Oh, Max, Max. You can come now." There was excitement and elation in her voice. Now she could be with him. "There's no reason to pretend anymore. Max, if we wish, we can be together now. Finally. What do you think?"

There was a short silence on the line before Max responded. "Yes, of course we can," he said in a calm, monotone voice. Then, "Grace, before anything is decided, I'd like to come down and have a chat. About us. About the future." It was a businesslike tone, somewhat surprising, she thought, given they were, after all, long-time lovers.

"Yes, my darling. Please come. Any time. Just tell me when. Oh, Max, yes I'm sorry that Pete has died, but think of how this changes everything. Oh, sweetheart, please come down."

"Alright. I have some things to do here in the city but I can come the end of the week. I'll look at the weather forecast and decide for sure but it will likely be on the weekend. I'll call you Friday. Just as long as it's not icy. I'll be driving down. When I decide for sure, I'll call again and let you know. Goodbye, Grace. I love you, darling."

"Oh, I love you too, Max. More than anything. Please hurry. But be careful."

Grace's joy was only slightly cooled by the somewhat distant quality in Max's voice. He had not seemed to share her exultation at being able to finally be together. Yet she contemplated the circumstances. In all the years they had known one another they had never spoken on the phone. People sound different on the telephone. Some exhibit a dispassionate approach with that artificial link they hold in their hands. She did not want to read too much into the way he had responded. In fact he had said he was coming and they could talk. That was all that mattered.

Grace was elated. Finally, they could truly be together. No more playing it coy. Now was the time: she would tell her son about her longstanding relationship, although she still couldn't fathom telling him Max was his true father. She would have to think about that. Maybe that was a detail that would come another time. In another way. First things first. She began to prepare the house. Max would be staying here, right in the old farmhouse. No pretending they were just friends. No secret rendezvous at the sugarhouse. Why, maybe they would even get married.

Max called back on Good Friday, March 28. He would drive down Monday, he said. Outside the old farmhouse, a steady mix of sleet and rain fell and the wind howled. Max said it was straight rain in Toronto but with the temperature near the freezing mark, some of the roads were treacherous. He didn't want to chance it. It looked better by Monday, Easter Monday. Grace was elated. After waiting all of this time, a couple more days would do no harm. Best to wait and be careful. Her heart ached with joy. She imagined holding him and kissing him, telling him how much she loved him.

But she could not get out of her mind that it had been well over two months since Jamie said he'd telephoned Max's sister to pass on word of Pete's death. Odd it had taken Max so long to phone back, but she assumed he had been on the road again. Yet why, at Max's age, would he still insist on travelling so much? Why in heaven's name would he still be working the crops? And how could he have such stamina, such strength?

In Toronto, Max put the phone back in its cradle and turned to his sister, Margaret. "I'm leaving Abby," he told her. "There's no point pretending anymore. We've had twenty-seven years of marriage and I just have nothing left for her. I told her last evening about Grace and she said she wasn't surprised. She had become suspicious of my annual fall business trips, she said. She knew there was someone, someplace. She knew this day would come, eventually. She actually wished me luck. Can you imagine? She actually wished me luck."

Margaret said: "Just leave her the house, Max. That's all she cares about now. And a relationship with the children, of course. But they're all grown up. She's expecting a big settlement and if she gets it, she'll be happy. She wants her share of the Huddlestone fortune. It's been clear for some time she couldn't care less about you anymore."

Max scowled. "Sure, I'm paying her off. But I get Grace. Finally. For years it was the kids that kept Abby and me together but there's no need to pretend anymore. They're grown, moved out for work and university, and living their own lives."

"I'm happy for you, Max," she said. "It's been so long coming. This has been hard on me too, keeping your lives separate and secret." She hesitated a moment before asking: "But tell me. Why didn't you call James back last year when he called about Peter's death?"

Picking up a half-empty drink glass, he inspected it and then drained the remaining contents. After he swallowed, he said to her: "I didn't know what I was going to say to him. I wanted Grace and me to be together years ago and she wouldn't have it. I thought it was her final word back after the war and I finally just gave up. Realized nothing would ever change. I wanted a family. That's when I came back here and decided to marry Abby.

"After James called, I started to think and finally I realized the kids were grown and out of the house and there was no reason for Abby and me to pretend any longer. It took me a while to work my way through all of that but finally, I decided to call Grace. I'm going to tell her everything. It might end our relationship but I can't live this lie any longer. She has to know about Abby and the kids. There's no other way this can work."

* * *

At Ballinskellig, Grace went to her writing desk and penned a long letter to Alberta to let her know the good news. "At last, Albie. At last the two of us can be together. Everything is wonderful now. Can you imagine?" She posted the letter in town the next morning. A big wide grin was pasted on her face and everyone who saw Grace O'Malley in town that day knew something wonderful must have happened. She stopped in to the liquor store and purchased a bottle of Italian wine. There was going to be a grand celebration.

Easter Monday dawned sunny and mild. Grace was relieved, overjoyed. Today her Max would arrive. Today they would begin the next phase of their lives. They would finally be together. The minutes ticked by, then the hours. No sign of Max. Grace wondered what was keeping him. She had planned an elaborate welcome dinner and held off putting the roast of beef in the oven. No sense spoiling the meat. The potatoes sat in a pot on the stove, ready to be cooked. The green beans were waiting next to them. The table was set in the dining room with a good lace tablecloth and real napkins. Candles had been put out. Wine glasses that hadn't been used in years were washed and ready to go.

At six, she switched on the radio to the local news and walked to the front window, peering out. The days were getting pleasantly longer now and there was still plenty of light in the western sky. The top news story came on. Something about a multi-vehicle crash on the eastbound lanes of the 401 near Pickering. Grace started. When had it happened? Sometime just before noon. Max could well have been on the highway at that time. She began to wonder…

The evening hours ticked by with still no sign of Max and Grace's wonder turned to fear and then panic. Exhausted and fraught, she fell asleep on the sofa and awoke at six the next morning when the deliveryman came with the Toronto paper and slammed the screen door shut. She had a stiff neck from her fitful sleep on the lumpy sofa. She got up, rubbed her sore neck and padded to the door to get the paper. She unfolded it and stared at the photo of the highway crash on the front page. Five dead, the story said. Many more injured. A tagline at the bottom of the page said the names of the victims were on page 2. She turned the page and read: "Max Huddlestone, 71, of Toronto."

There was an obit next to it. "Max Huddlestone was the husband of Abby Huddlestone and father of Rebecca (John Moore) and Stephen (Greta), all of Toronto and area. Huddlestone and his sister, Margaret Huddlestone Morrison, also of Toronto, were the heirs to the Huddlestone fortune left by Henry Huddlestone, founder of the Oshawa-based Huddlestone Motor Car Company which for many years manufactured the Hud automobile. During the First World War, Huddlestone Co. was one of the largest suppliers of Canadian military equipment. When the elder Huddlestone sold the company to the Detroit-based international giant Automotive Partners (AP) in 1920, he plowed his millions into real estate and whiskey production and solidified his position as one of Canada's wealthiest entrepreneurs.

"Max Huddlestone was known for his sometimes eccentric behavior. At a young age he became estranged from his father and embarked upon a peripatetic life. A labour activist after the First World War, he is said to have 'ridden the rails' during the Great Depression, taking employment as an itinerant farmhand in places that spanned the continent and stretched to its four corners. He served in the Canadian Army during the Second World War and took part in the Battle of Dieppe in which many Canadians were killed, injured or captured by the enemy. Later he became a medic and served in Northwestern Europe.

"When his father died in 1946, Huddlestone returned home to help his sister manage the family fortune. In 1948 he married the former Abby

Durand and they had two children. Despite his wealth, Huddlestone was known for his reclusive lifestyle. While he gave generously to charity, Huddlestone never allowed himself to be featured in news reports or photographed at public events. In recent years he turned over management of his business interests to his children. The Huddlestone companies are known for their industry-leading wages and benefits packages. It has been speculated it was Max Huddlestone who sparked this business approach."

There was more but Grace had seen enough. She put the paper down and the room spun around her. She felt sick to her stomach and ran to the bathroom where she threw up in the toilet. She splashed cold water on her face and grabbed a cloth, wet it and held it to her forehead. Then she made her way slowly to the kitchen and plopped down in her armchair. Silent tears began pouring from her eyes. She couldn't believe the betrayal. She couldn't believe he could have lied to her for so many years.

Her immediate thought was to call Jamie, to tell him everything. But no, she couldn't. How could she involve him? How could Jamie ever forgive her for her years of deception? There was only one way out. Grace thought back to the year 1923, when she learned she was pregnant with Jamie. She had momentarily contemplated taking her life then and in hindsight was so terribly glad she had not. If she had, she would have killed her precious Jamie as well. Now, however, there was nothing left to live for.

It was bad enough that Max, the true love of her life, was gone, but the betrayal she had suffered made it too much for her to bear. Now she knew Max had lived a secret life and raised a family. She was angry and hurt beyond comprehension. Never had she contemplated she was having an affair with a married man and father.

A knock came to the kitchen door and Grace went to answer it. It was Billy Black, that empty-headed little weasel who normally came by on Mondays to see if she had any odd jobs for him. But it was Tuesday. "Sorry, Miz O'Malley. I'm a day late this week. With yesterday bein' the Easter Monday holiday I took the day off. Anythin' I can help ye with?"

Grace knew her face would betray her grief to any reasonable human being and hoped that Billy, being no sharper than a wooden mallet, would fail to see it. She wiped her eyes, collected her wits and scowled. As if he needs to take a holiday, she thought. Every day's a holiday for this layabout.

"No, thank you Billy. Nothing today. But next Monday for sure. I'll definitely need you then. Don't be late, eh?"

"Surely I won't," Billy said. "Next Monday's a date." He turned and walked back to his bicycle and pedalled away, apparently no wiser for their encounter.

Grace had decided. She would take the week to get her affairs in order. That ought to be enough. But she had plenty to do. The pastor, her lawyer, cleaning the place to spotlessness. All needed to be ready.

On Saturday night she telephoned James. "Hi, honey. How are things?" She seemed cheerful and James was pleased to hear her voice.

"Mom. All's fine here. Just watching the hockey game. Having a beer. What's up in Shannonside?"

"Oh, nothing much. I just wanted to hear your voice. It's kind of lonely here tonight."

She contemplated telling her son at that moment that Max had died because apparently James had not seen the name in the newspaper. Clearly he would have called if he had known. Since he didn't know, Grace felt it best to leave him in the dark for a little while longer. All would be revealed … in time.

"Tell me about your plans for the next week," she said. "Is it busy?"

James didn't give a thought to her question beyond momentarily thinking that her normal practice was to ask about the past few days rather than those upcoming. "My students are gearing up for their last few weeks before final papers and then exams. Monday morning I've got a lecture at nine and then office hours, then my seminar class in the afternoon. We're going to talk about Trudeau's response to the FLQ crisis. I've got a really sharp class this semester. They really keep me on my toes." He went on to highlight the rest of the week's work.

Grace felt guilty about what her plans would be taking her son away from, but it couldn't be helped. They chatted about all sorts of nonsense before finally she said: "I'd better go now, son. Don't want to occupy your entire evening."

"Hey, no problem, Mom. I love our talks. Take care. I love you. See you soon."

"I love you too, Jamie. Goodbye."

It was the last conversation they would ever share. Grace picked up her diary and pen. She needed to make one final entry.

22

James 1975

In all the years James was growing up at Ballinskellig, and into adulthood, no one ever mentioned the circumstances of his infant brother's death. He still would not have known what happened if his Aunt Lucy had not told him many years later, on the day he went to deliver the news that Peter had died. He understood that the details had been too painful for either one of his parents to ever speak of. But still, he found it curious. He had only ever been told that he'd had an older brother who died as an infant. There had never been a word more.

In the week that his mother made plans for her own death, she meticulously thought out what it was James ought to know, needed to know about himself and his parents. The pieces he needed to put together the full picture lay in the diaries and the box of letters she had left for him to read. Apparently creating a jigsaw puzzle for him to complete made it somehow more palatable for her, easier to cope with. He cringed at the pain he knew his mother had borne in order for her to carry out such a macabre plan.

Now as he sifted through his mother's belongings, James read the diaries she had left for him. He devoured her prose, turning the pages as if they were a classic novel. There had been a gap of several weeks between entries during the late summer of 1922 and James was shocked when later on he reached his mother's reference to an event about which he was totally in the dark, one of many such events, it now seemed to him. She never mentioned that before he was born she had been struck by lightning and nearly died, and that her rescuer, her guardian angel, had been Max. That was how they first met. James never knew that. The scar on his mother's forehead she referenced in her diary account struck a familiar chord. She always combed her long hair down to hide it, but occasionally he would catch a glimpse of the faint pinkish line that remained. The first time he noticed it, James asked what it was and she said it was nothing, just an accident from years ago. He imagined her falling off her bicycle or stumbling in the barn. As he read on and learned about the excruciating pain that racked her body after the lightning strike, and the times when her memory failed, James realized that the incident's cruel legacy had been far more than she ever let on. He couldn't recall his mother ever complaining about anything, while clearly she had had reason to.

It occurred to him that both he and his mother had Max Huddlestone to thank for coming to their rescue when they had needed him most. Each owed their life to him. What an incredible coincidence. Some say there is no such thing as a coincidence, that everything happens for a reason. Some believe our lives are predetermined, that those who cross our paths are intended to do so, and that they all play a part in our destiny. James thought back to a conversation he and his mother had once had about Max. She called Max her son's personal guardian angel. They had both laughed that time, and he remembered that when he looked up a moment later, he could swear he'd caught a small tear in the corner of his mother's eye. He wondered about that.

As he read on through the diary, James was surprised to see an entry about how his mother had encountered Max in the barn one evening the year following the lightning incident, and was further surprised to find additional entries that mentioned him over the coming weeks. Even back then, she seemed quite smitten by him. What James was encountering for the first time was evidence of what Aunt Al had alluded to: His mother's relationship with Max had been far deeper than he had imagined.

He assumed that he had finally come upon the true reason for his parents' decades-long estrangement.

When he took a break for lunch and went downstairs, Aunt Al was already preparing their meal. "I read my mother's account of Petie's death," James told her. "Aunt Lucy told me last fall how it happened but the diary, that was in Mom's own words. It was so vivid and so tragic."

Alberta turned from the stove where she was warming some soup and looked at him. "Oh, that was just so sad," she said. "It shattered your parents. I kept telling them it was no one's fault, but they never forgave themselves, or, I suspect, one another. I remember it happened Christmas Eve after a party at my parents' house. Before they left that night, your mother and father invited me over for Christmas the next day. I went and of course I knew nothing of what had happened just the night before. When I arrived, oh my, it was awful. Your father had left and your mother was here, all alone. She was still cradling little Petie's body in her arms as she rocked back and forth in that old rocking chair over there. Of course there was no phone here then and so no one else knew. Not even her own mother. Imagine that."

James cringed at the image of his mother, rocking the dead baby, holding him sweetly in her arms. She would have been broken-hearted, filled with grief and self-recrimination. And she would have been alone, abandoned by the man she had loved so deeply.

Aunt Al said she vowed she would stay with Grace to help get her through the worst of it, regardless of how it affected her own art studies in Toronto. Grace was inconsolable. Cried for hours that day, then went totally silent. Just stared off into the distance. No one ever knew where Peter had gone. He left his grieving wife to deal with the baby's body but of course she couldn't. It fell to Alberta to send word to the doctor, make the arrangements. There was a funeral, of course, but still no one knew where Peter was. The baby was laid out in a tiny coffin that was placed in the parlour, Aunt Al said. Grace sat in the corner and just stared, comatose. Everyone came but of course they didn't know what to say.

James thought to himself: I know where he went. Thanks to Aunt Lucy, I know exactly where my father went. He said nothing, but his anger at his father welled up inside him. How could the man have been so selfish, so thoughtless the way he left it all to his wife to contend with? Of course he, too, was grieving, but that was no excuse for shirking his responsibility. His father's reaction was something James could not fathom. It suggested a weakness in his father that James had never seen.

Albie continued that James's Grandma and Grandpa Campbell were a huge help. They stayed with his mother and let Albie go home once in a while, but she always returned to stand by her closest friend. Months earlier, Pete's father Benjamin had moved out of the house and into his own place in Shannonside, to give the couple their space. He didn't know anything had happened until Christmas morning. But as soon as he was told, Ben went out searching for his son and was gone for twenty-four hours before returning to report he couldn't think of anywhere else he might be. Ben O'Malley and Will Campbell looked after the livestock for two full weeks before Peter finally walked back in the door. No explanation of where he had gone. Benjamin just glared at his son and according to

Aunt Al who was there at the time, said to him: "Come out of it, Peter. You've got a wife to comfort and a farm to run."

Albie remembered Peter nodded and went to work. Just like that. But he never offered a moment of comfort to Grace, nor a word of explanation.

"Eventually your mother insisted that I return to art school in Toronto and I picked up as best I could. That spring when I was finished with my studies, your mother told me it was time I get on with my own life, that I should not stay around to fuss over her any longer. She said I had done more than enough for her. I told her then that I had decided this was the time to go to Europe. I said I was going to Florence on a trip of self-discovery, hopefully learn more of the language and find a job. Once your mother gave me the all-clear sign, I believe I was gone inside a week. Your mother had given me her permission, her blessing. So in my mind it was alright to go.

"But the truth, Jamie, was that what happened to your mother and dad was the push I needed to put my plan into action. I realized through their loss and their grief that I could not spare the time thinking about my own future. I needed to get on with my life, even if it meant taking such a big chance. I had no time to waste. The death of Petie made me understand how fragile our very existence truly is, and how we must make the most of every moment and opportunity."

James listened intently to his godmother and realized what a gamble she had taken back then, leaving her old life behind and going out into the great, wide world. She was about to realize her dream and for her, it had all turned out well. Sure, there was sadness and loss, but who could say their life was without that?

Alberta continued her story of that long-ago time: "That summer, when the workers began to drift back to work the farm, your mother returned to her duties of cooking the noon-hour meal. One of the Taylor girls, Ruth, came by every day to help out. She and your mother became close friends and I was so happy for her. Your mother needed that. Often your grandmother was here too."

James said he was struck by the fact that there were few entries from that summer in his mother's diary, except to indicate that she and Peter never communicated. A glacial silence fell upon them. They each performed their jobs, but they rarely spoke. Once a week Ruth came by in her father's 1912 Model T pickup truck and took Grace into town for supplies. She said it was her only break from the gloom of Ballinskellig. Peter went off once a week to play poker.

James pondered Aunt Al's account and thought about how it fit with the words he'd read in his mother's diary. He was astounded at how his parents could so quickly become totally estranged. How could the love they shared, the love she had professed so eloquently and with such heartfelt passion in her diary, be snuffed out so totally? Had it been so fragile that it was kept together only by the strength of a tiny infant? Was his father so fixated on maintaining the family farm that nothing else mattered, and that when he no longer had an heir, his world crumbled?

James went on to tell his godmother he'd read the diary account of his mother being struck by lightning and how Max had come to her rescue. Grace had been coy about her relationship with Max but the diary revealed all - or nearly all. And for the first time he asked himself which had come first - the total break-off between his parents, or his mother's encounter with Max? His mind raced with possibilities, possibilities he found it difficult to contemplate since they all related to his mother's behavior. Albie said she never fully understood Grace's relationship with Max but that in her opinion, it developed because of Grace and Peter's estrangement.

"I firmly believe she fell for Max because she was so lonely. Your mother wrote me a letter not long ago, after your father died, and everything about Max spilled out," Alberta told her godson. "Oh, I suspected something for quite some time, but now I knew. And then I just received another letter from her, just before the call came from her solicitor about her death and I left home to come over here. She said everything was now fine and Max would be coming to Ballinskellig. She was so happy. I wonder what happened? It certainly didn't sound as though she might be ... su-suicidal." Albie tripped over the dreaded word. James had to physically turn away from its sting.

James wondered the same thing. It added further to the confusion that filled his head. After lunch, he told Aunt Al he was going to return to his mother's bedroom to read more from her diary. Aunt Al asked if he wanted her to join him and James said sure, that would be a comfort. He turned back a couple of pages to pick up the thread of his mother's story. As he read through the diary he would occasionally stop and read a passage out loud but for the most part, he read silently as Aunt Al sat and looked around the room, sometimes getting up from her seat and inspecting her friend's possessions, gently touching pieces of Grace's clothing and picking up every bit of bric-a-brac. Albie said little, and occasionally pulled out her hankie to wipe away a tear.

After a while, she rose from her chair by the window and walked over to where her godson was sitting on his mother's bed. While Albie herself was grieving for her lost friend, she was more concerned about Jamie. He seemed lost, forlorn as he read through his mother's diary and Alberta imagined his pain. She sat down on the bed and put her arm around him.

Her gaze settled on the shoebox tied with a purple ribbon and asked: "What's in there?"

"That's where Mom's note to me was. I set it aside to read the diaries. Don't know what else is in the box. Let's see."

He opened it and saw the scramble of letters. He picked up the one on the top, unfolded it and noted it was dated January 1956. "My dearest," it began. When he realized it was a love letter he raced to the bottom and read the signature: "Max." James rifled through the stack of letters and found they dated as far back as the 1920s and each was signed by Max.

His heart pounded. "So, here it is then," he said. "Here is the evidence that they were in love, even all the way back then. My mother and Max."

"Yes," said Albie. "But she kept his letters? That's a surprise."

They were written from all the places Max visited to take work in the fields. California, Florida, Oklahoma, Saskatchewan, Alberta, Quebec, Kentucky. They spanned the decades. There were references to Max being on his way to Ballinskellig or in some cases to his having just left Ballinskellig and missing her already. There were details of the intimacy that had bound them together and James occasionally stopped to catch his breath from the discomfort caused by his understanding now that it was his mother this man was writing about.

There was no longer any doubt. James's mother and Max had had an affair, one that had lasted for decades.

He read on and came frequently upon references to himself, how Max had so enjoyed spending time with him, and the opportunity to teach him. "He's become such a great swimmer," Max said once. Another time he wrote: "Sonny Jim has a natural rhythm with the baseball bat. I believe he's star material."

One letter written in 1939 made James stop and ponder. "I have to accept the possibility that I might never return from the war," Max had written then. "I might never see you and Jamie again. But this is something I must do. I owe it to my country and to myself."

There was a large gap in the letters before the next one, written in 1947 from Quebec. "It was so wonderful to see you again this fall," he wrote, "to feel your touch on my skin, to breathe in your wonderful scent.

I so wish we could be together always, forever. While my heart is breaking, I will honour your wishes. You have sent me away, my darling, my love. I will treasure the memory of you and our wonderful times together."

"Listen to this," he said to Albie, then read the words to her. "Let me see that diary again."

James opened the book to a part he had not yet read, to the autumn of 1947, and skimmed through it. He read aloud:

"My beloved Max has asked me to go away with him, but I cannot. I guess my old-fashioned upbringing has gotten the better of me. Peter is my husband, for better or for worse, forever. Even if I could get over that hurdle, even if I could forget my Edwardian upbringing, there is the matter of our son. I can never do anything to disappoint Jamie, never embarrass him, never bring him into this affair. None of this was ever his fault."

"Our son," James repeated. "Our son?" He turned to Albie. She stared at him, a quizzical look in her eyes.

James then turned back through the diary to another portion he had not read, this time to the latter part of 1923. "Here it is," he said to Albie. "Listen to this."

James steeled himself for what was to come. "Today Doc Farr confirmed my suspicion. I am pregnant. What have I done? How will I ever be able to tell Peter?"

Farther on she mentioned a conversation with her mother. "Mumma wants me to convince Peter the baby is his. How could I trick him so? This isn't his fault. I walked down to the river and looked at the rushing water and realized how easy it would be. How quick. The water would cleanse it all away. But I cannot. The life inside me is innocent of all of this. My decision now is not only for myself, it is a decision that would be made on behalf of that life and I cannot snuff it out. I will have to talk to Peter."

Still later she wrote: "The deed is done. Peter will now be convinced the baby …" James gasped … "the baby is his."

"Aunt Al," James said. "Max was my father."

Alberta's jaw literally dropped. "Oh, Jamie. Oh my!"

James realized that with Max constantly on the road, his mother had no way of writing back to him. The thought made him sad. She had lived such a lonely existence, waiting from harvest to harvest for him to return so they could sneak a few weeks of intimacy. In all those years, there had been no one to share her thoughts with but her friend, Alberta, who lived far away, in Italy. Her other good friend, Ruth Taylor, had died from cancer a decade ago. Grace's diary was her only outlet for her thoughts and emotions. James understood why she had kept the letters: it was her only consolation during their long times apart. He thought about Max's words: "I will honour your wishes." Max had been prepared to make their arrangement more permanent. He had asked Grace to go away with him. Grace had said no. And still he returned with the harvest.

The hours passed and James had gone through maybe half the letters that were in the box. As he reached for another he noticed something else that lay beneath them. It was a newspaper clipping. His mother had dated it and the date was just around Easter. He picked it up and started to read.

As he read the words his mother had so recently seen herself, James gasped. A lump came to the pit of his stomach. How could this be? Max was dead? He had heard about the terrible crash on the highway but did not read details. He'd had no idea Max was one of the victims. Further, Max had had a family in Toronto, the article said. A wife and two children. He was no longer an itinerant farm worker at all, but the heir to a wealthy businessman's fortune, and for many years the manager of an immense investment portfolio. How could this be? How could Max have tricked his mother and himself? Now James understood why she had taken her own life. She could not bear to read of her own betrayal in the pages of a newspaper, to say nothing of the death of the man she'd loved for years. A man married with children.

To assure himself, James leafed through the later years of his mother's diaries. He could find no evidence of her ever knowing Max had a family in Toronto, nor that he was actually the heir to a fortune. James thought about Albie's words: His mother had told her in a letter they would soon be together. Everything was alright. She would never have written those words if she had known of Max's family.

James then imagined his mother coming across the news of her betrayal mere days after she believed that Max would be racing to her side, unencumbered no more by her own marriage.

James had to read more of the diary his mother had left for him. She did leave it for him, after all. This was her way of telling him who he really was, and why she had taken her own life. As he scanned the diary he encountered one piece of evidence after another about his true identity: James was Max's son. He wasn't an O'Malley at all.

He skipped other passages and flipped to the last page. It was dated the day of their last phone conversation.

"What a fool I have been!" Grace wrote. "My life has been a lie. Max tricked me. I suppose though I deserved that. After all, I tricked Pete. I lied to my own son and my best friend. What else should I expect? Now everyone will know. I cannot live with all that I have done, with the shame, the regret, and now the humiliation. The life of this silly old fool is ended."

* * *

The funeral was a small affair. James suspected some of Grace's friends and acquaintances were kept away by the realization her death had been by suicide. Sherry had come down from Montreal but left quickly afterwards. In the following days, Alberta helped James to clear out his mother's things. James took a few keepsakes and handed the farm over to his cousin Arthur. He truly had no wish to ever see Ballinskellig again. A few days later, on a drizzly weekend morning in Toronto, he allowed himself the luxury of sleeping in and it was only the sharp sound of the phone's ring that startled him out of the deep sleep of exhaustion and sorrow.

It was Sherry.

"James, I'm just calling to see how you're coping. I hope you're getting back on your feet. Is there anything I can do?"

"Thanks, Sherry. I appreciate your thoughts. It's been a difficult few days."

"We didn't have the chance to speak at the funeral. Would you like to get together? For lunch maybe? I'd like to come to Toronto and pay a little visit. Just to say hi and see how you're doing."

"Sure, that would be nice."

The following Saturday, Sherry walked in to a steakhouse on Elm Street and spotted James almost immediately. They hugged and James held out a chair for her. When they were settled, Sherry placed her hand tenderly on James's wrist. "How are you doing? Really? I can't imagine how difficult this has all been for you."

"No, you can't," he replied. "Sherry, I've been uncovering the craziest story you could ever imagine. And it's the story of my life."

"Well hang on there, Tonto. I think I've got something that's going to add another chapter to that story." She reached into her oversized bag and pulled out a book. "I brought this for you. It's something you'll be interested in."

"*Green Beach*? What's it about?"

"It's a wartime story. A novel. But it's based on interviews the author did with real-life veterans of the Dieppe Raid. It's about what has been until now a secret side to the invasion, a story that was kept under wraps for twenty-five years. Classified information. James, remember you told me back when I was working on my Dieppe documentary you had a friend who was in the Dieppe Raid? You said he would never talk about it. He came once to visit us in Montreal. What was your friend's name? Max Huddlestone?"

"Yes, how did you remember that?"

"I remembered being very impressed by him. I really liked him. And how could I forget the name of the man who saved your life after you were injured in Holland? Saved the life of the man I loved." She paused at that moment and looked down. "The man I still love." She cleared her throat and James reached over and cupped her hand in his.

Sherry continued: "And then I read this book. There's a character in it named Rex Stoneman – same last name as your old boss. And it struck a chord. Huddlestone … Stoneman? Kind of similar, right?"

"I suppose. And Rex is sort of close to Max, I guess. What are you getting at?"

"In the book, this character Stoneman was a sharpshooter, a member of a ten-man security force who went in to protect a guy, a radar technician, whose assignment it was to capture the secrets of a German communications system. Apparently, and this book is supposed to be based on actual fact, apparently there was a secret operation that was cloaked in the guise of a test raid on the coast of France. For years the military authorities have been blamed for botching the raid on Dieppe, for sending thousands of Canadians to their senseless deaths. That was the nugget of my documentary, that their deaths had been such a waste. Well this book suggests there was more to it than that. It suggests the raid was a cover for the true mission."

James paused to let Sherry's story sink in. "Max was in fact a crack marksman," he said. "He mentioned one time he'd been part of the South Saskatchewan regiment and that he was … "

"That's it!" Sherry jumped in. "The South Saskatchewans. That was the regiment from which the special detachment was chosen. James, your friend was part of that top-secret team."

James looked her straight in the eye. "He was more than my friend. He was my father."

"What?"

"Yes, you heard that correctly, Sherry. Max Huddlestone was my real father. He had an affair with my mother. I just learned about it since her death, and his. Sherry, I was the product of their … liaison."

As Sherry paused to let these new facts settle into her brain, James settled back in his chair and said: "There's more, Sherry. How much time do you have? I'd like to fill you in on what I've uncovered the last week or so."

Sherry said she had all the time in the world, and she was all ears. Over the next ninety minutes James recounted for her the highlights of what he'd learned from his mother's suicide, her diaries, the letters from Max she had kept over the years and evidence of Max's secret life. Finally he paused and then said: "I think that's about it."

"Oh, Jamie, I can't imagine how you must feel right now. It's as though you've lived your entire life thinking you were someone else."

"I was," he said. "They all lied to me. They were all in on it, Mom, Max and Dad. Not one of them ever came clean. I'm numb, Sherry. I feel anger and sorrow and … and every other emotion you can think of. I just don't know why no one ever told me."

"But your mother did tell you, eventually. That's why she left you all that information. She wanted you to know. She just could never bring herself to tell you face-to-face."

"I know, I know. She was protecting me. But at the end of the day it hurts that much more because it's taken so long for me to discover the truth, and then only after all three of them are dead. Can you imagine how confused that leaves me? I know I should be so angry at all of them, but what's the use? What could be gained by that? So I'm even deprived of the satisfaction that might have come from being angry."

"There's never any satisfaction from anger, Jamie. Only more hurt. You'd only be hurting yourself if you couldn't let it go. You've got to move on, to remember all of the good that each of those people brought to your life."

James looked into Sherry's eyes and held her hands in his. "You're a wise woman, my love. Hey, wanna come back to my place?"

23

Reconciliation 1980

It is one of those exquisite August mornings that heralds a perfect day. The air is clear and fresh-scented from an overnight shower. The birds are singing, the flower gardens and lawns are touched with light droplets that glimmer in the growing sunshine. James and Sherry savour their morning coffee on the front verandah of their East York bungalow and watch the early dog-walkers and joggers pass.

James glances at his watch. "Guess we'd better get moving," he says to his wife. She nods and collects the coffee mugs while James ducks inside the house to collect their picnic supplies. He returns loaded down with a cooler filled with hamburger patties, a salad and beer, an extra bag with buns and unopened containers of relish, mustard and catsup. A new bottle of sunscreen is tucked into the bottom. Sherry follows, wearing a floppy sun hat, sunglasses, a skimpy little flowered halter-top and pink slacks, sandals flip-flopping on her feet. The sharp facial features and high cheekbones have become slightly rounded with the maturity of age. Behind those sunglasses, though, her brown eyes have not lost any of their flash.

James is dressed in a faded T-shirt emblazoned with a big sun-and-sand logo – a shirt he bought last winter in Cancun – a pair of red and white checked shorts and flip-flops. His midsection has softened, his hair has begun to slightly thin. After setting down the items he's carrying behind the car, a shiny new Pontiac sedan, he goes to the garage and picks up a couple of folding lawn chairs and adds them to the miscellany of picnic gadgetry and supplies sitting behind the car. Sherry carries the single suitcase they have placed their overnight items and clothing into. They manoeuvre the entire load into the Pontiac's cavernous trunk and settle in for the drive to Shannonside. It is James's first visit back to the place where he grew up since his mother's death, the place where four generations of O'Malleys lived, raised apples and died. Now there are fifth and sixth generations, Arthur O'Malley Vankamp and his son Philip. With Philip comes a seventh generation: teenagers Graydon and Angela.

With the knowledge that Max Huddlestone was his biological father, James has inherited a second family, albeit a smaller one. When the shock wore off, James called Max's sister, Margaret, and the two struck up a friendship. While he would always feel betrayed that neither his mother nor Max had ever told him who he really was, James was comforted in the knowledge he had gained an aunt.

James has also regained a wife. He and Sherry Tremblay will soon celebrate five years of reconciliation. During their reunion that day at the Toronto steakhouse, they agreed to give married life another go and Sherry said she'd come to Toronto. She said there was a job awaiting her doing television commercials. "It's a hell of a lot more lucrative than documentaries," she reasoned. But James said no. He knew it would be a sacrifice she was willing to make for him, setting aside her artistic career in favour of one that paid better, one that would bring them together in the same city. She had put on a brave front and he told her he was very grateful, but he could not bear to see her move on from the career in documentary film she adored. She must hold out until she found something more suited to her immense talents, he insisted.

That position took her little time to find and now Sherry was back in her element. At the moment she was working on a film about itinerant farm workers from Mexico and the West Indies. As usual, she had taken to it with passion and verve and James adored her even more. As for himself, James was fully ensconced in his teaching career at Ryerson and was sometimes called upon for interviews when the news media sought comment on some issue of political or journalistic ethics. He had developed a reputation for delivering intelligent opinion with precision, eloquence and clarity.

Within a month of their reconciliation, they bought a neat little bungalow north of O'Connor that backed onto the Coxwell Ravine. Each day they took the bus to the subway train that took them downtown to their places of employment. Sometimes they arranged to meet for lunch halfway between their respective offices.

In Shannonside, James's cousin Arthur and his wife, Amy, moved in to Ballinskellig with Philip and his wife, Bonnie, about the same time and began the process of making the old farmhouse acceptable to a family in the final quarter of the twentieth century. Bonnie had just about had a conniption the first time she saw the old farmhouse and insisted on all the modern conveniences being installed before she agreed to move into it. That has been a long and drawn-out process and a month ago, Arthur telephoned James to say they were having a big family barbecue to celebrate the fact it was finally completed.

Now family members were arriving from all over the place to make their pilgrimage to the O'Malley homestead and take a peek. James is at first reluctant to accept the invitation. He is not, after all, an O'Malley by birth. Over time, however, he reasons that it was Peter O'Malley who raised him and who, in many ways, made him the man he is. He has accommodated himself to that reality and, after giving the invitation a great deal of thought, and after a long conversation with Sherry, he decided to go. With the rambling old farmhouse filled these days with three generations of O'Malley-Vankamps, he took the leap and reserved a room at the nearby Water's Edge Motel.

James notices the new sign on the highway indicating the old township and its villages have been amalgamated into something called Quinte. There is no mention of Shannonside until he spies a small sign once they turn onto the Old English Road. As he nears his birthplace, James grabs the steering wheel hard to steady his nerves. He has avoided this place for five years. His heart races. Ballinskellig represents the horrible death of his mother, his birth father's betrayal of her, and his own knowledge that the family he thought for more than half a century was his, was really not. He is returning out of duty, out of a sense of obligation to the O'Malleys and to all they have done for him. Sherry senses his discomfort and puts her hand on his. "Are you really okay with this? Being here, I mean."

"Yes," he replies. "None of them knows Max was my father. As far as they're concerned, I'm a true blue O'Malley. It's fine." He momentarily takes his eyes off the road, turns to her and says: "Thanks for asking."

He has made it a point of showing more care and love, more thankfulness, since they got back together. This time James was determined not to lose, and not to drive away the only woman he had loved since he'd gone off to the army. Sherry responded with her own outpouring of affection and their marriage was far healthier the second time around.

James parks the Pontiac across the road from the house, in front of the barn. Slipping out of the vehicle he pauses, instantly jolted back to his childhood by the aromas of the warm summer day. The sharpness of ripening apples that always put him in mind of the colour red. Subtle floral blooms and distant pastures. Maturing tomatoes, melons and the array of other vegetables and herbs growing in the kitchen garden at the west side of the house. Fields of hay beckoning to be harvested.

A young fellow in his mid-teens, lanky and dark-haired, comes up to them and calls out: "You'd be my grampa's cousins, Jamie and Sherry, right? I'm Graydon, Philip's son. Welcome home."

Sherry is immediately charmed by the teenager's manner and smiles broadly. "Thank you, Graydon. We haven't been here in years. We're looking forward to seeing what you've done to the old place." James comes around the car and shakes hands with the young man. "Yes, thanks," he says perfunctorily.

Graydon has already put out his hands to help carry picnic things, and James goes to the trunk to pull out the various items they'd brought.

As he hauls stuff toward the house, Graydon calls to an approaching woman: "Mom. This is Sherry and Jamie. Grampa Arthur's cousins from Toronto."

Bonnie Vankamp is a somewhat squat woman dressed in a flowing paisley-print dress that harkens back to the hippie days of the Sixties. "Jamie," she says. "Welcome. It's been years since I've seen you. At your mother's funeral. And Sherry. I don't know if you remember but we met briefly at the funeral. Let me wish you a belated welcome to the family." Bonnie hugs them both warmly before stepping back with a slightly sheepish look on her face. Her eyes are moist. "Oh, don't mind me. I'm just kind of emotional. Having the family back here, back to where they came from. It's very important to Arthur and Philip. And to me. Especially since Grandma Anna died last year. Your father's sister. She was the last of her generation."

When James says nothing, Sherry speaks up. "Thank you, Bonnie. We're delighted to be here."

Graydon returns and just then he leans in to James and whispers: "Come to the barn with me, Jamie. There's something I want to show you."

James's heart is racing and he tells himself to calm down. This was once his home. He might have felt betrayed by more recent events here, but there were good times, too. Happy times. He has made the decision to embrace the O'Malleys as his own, and he will do so now.

James motions to Graydon to lead on and as they stroll across the freshly manicured grass under the great maple trees that have witnessed more than a century, it dawns on James what Graydon has in mind.

He thinks back to his own youth, to the discovery he'd made in the barn's upper hayloft. "I have a feeling I know what's coming," he grins. The warm memories come pouring back.

As they are about to enter the barn, James looks down at the patch of lavender that grows next to the opening. He bends down and twists off a sprig. "My mother's favourite," he tells the boy as the disturbed plant gives off its strong musty scent.

Graydon smiles, then leads the way into the cool darkness and right to the ladder that leads to the loft. James notices the ladder has been replaced since his days, as has the floor of the loft. It needed to be replaced and braced after the accident that had killed Peter and now looks new and sturdy. The teen scampers effortlessly up the ladder, walks over to the wall across from the entranceway that is used to load hay into the building and swings its door wide open. The light streams in and falls upon the wall across from it, flooding the supporting beam with its brilliance. James takes longer to navigate the ladder's rungs, swing his leg over the top and steady himself on the loft floor. He envies Graydon's youthful agility. As he looks over to where Graydon has gone, James recognizes the spot immediately. Graydon points to the letters carved into the ancient wood and James thinks yes, it's just as I remembered it.

James walks over and reverently fingers the carved letters. It was just like yesterday, it seems, when he had discovered them himself, but in fact it has been, what, half a century ago.

"The seven wonders," James reads aloud. "The seven children of Sam and Catherine. The seven of them carved their initials in this beam the day two of the boys headed out West to pan for gold. The family never heard from them again.

"You know it was their father, Sam, who really built this place," James continues. "William and Lucinda were the first here, of course, but Sam expanded the house to make room for all of his children. The seven wonders. My Aunt Lucy told me Sam was hell-bent against keeping the name Ballinskellig but his father, Old William, he insisted, and Sam's sister Emilie agreed with her father. It was the last vestige of their Irishness, she said. Sam, he was Canadian to the core, and damned proud of it."

Graydon nods. "And I'm proud of this place. Ballinskellig. It's been in the family a long time, hasn't it? And I plan to keep it that way."

Somehow James has warmed to the conversation. Perhaps it's this young man's natural charm, perhaps something has tweaked inside him. Despite what he has discovered of his past, James now warms to the

O'Malley story. "Did you ever hear how the journey began, Graydon? How it was that the O'Malleys left Ireland?"

The boy shrugs. "Guess it was on account of the famine, right? The potato famine. They were starving, I suppose."

"No, I don't think so. They say there was a shooting. Someone was shot on the doorstep. That's the way the story went. One of the few stories ever passed down through the generations. Liam O'Malley shot someone, some good-for-nothing lout, apparently. It was self-defence. But he had to skedaddle before the sheriff caught him. That's the way I heard it."

"Cool!" says Graydon. "I never heard that before. Wow! We're related to a real, honest-to-goodness outlaw. The family scandal. I can't believe it."

"Well, you know how things get exaggerated. But according to Aunt Lucy, my dad's oldest sister who died three years ago, that's what happened. And some English lord who employed Liam to school his children, gave the family the money to make the trip over. Yes, I guess you could say that's a pretty cool story."

Graydon looks at his cousin. "I hear you've got some cool stories to tell too. Stories about the war."

James looks at him and his heart thumps hard in his chest. It occurs to him that he is now in the position of being the keeper of the stories, just as his father's ancestors had been. He had once been critical of those ancestors for failing to share more of their stories, for failing to fill in the blanks. Now it is his turn and he understands how much it hurt to speak of them. The easy route would be to simply refuse to get into those painful details, to protect himself from the hurt of remembering. But he will not make that mistake. He will do his duty and share with the boy the information he seeks. It is his responsibility to the younger generation.

"Come over here and sit down," James tells Graydon. "This is going to take a while. But remember, you asked for it."

The sun has been momentarily hidden behind a cloud and at that moment the cloud drifts on. The shifting sunlight illuminates a portion of the barn wall that had previously been in darkness and James glances over at something unfamiliar, something else that had been scratched into the old beam: "Sonny Jim, Grace & Max."

"What's that?" Graydon asks. "Who's Sonny Jim? Who's Max?"

"Well, I'll be," James says. He ponders for a moment. With the boy's eager eyes upon him, James feels enveloped by a sudden calmness. Is it something about this barn? About this place? Finally, James feels at peace with the man he really is, part O'Malley, part Huddlestone. He has steeled himself to talk about the war, but this is a new wrinkle in the family story. He is ready, finally, to talk about it, and the lucky recipient of his newfound openness is this young man, Graydon.

A smile comes to his face. He turns to the teenager: "Graydon, I guess there's going to be an addendum to my story. This is going to take longer than I thought."

ACKNOWLEDGEMENT

THE EXPERIENCES OF my father's family and the stories passed down to me helped to inform my writing. While this is a work of fiction and the characters sprang from my imagination, I want to thank the late Francis May, Howard and Marjorie May, their daughters Georgina, Rosalind (Loffredo) and Margaret May, and Evelyn Lute for the family stories that inspired me to write this book.

I wish to thank my wife, Linda, whose sharp editing skills, inquisitive mind, and demanding standards pushed me to reach just a little bit beyond.

My friend and author Joan Barfoot read an early draft of the book and provided insightful observations in those early days.

Later, my friend Donna Llewellin Carlson of Waterdown, Ontario, gave me a reader's perspective that helped to fine-tune details.

ACKNOWLEDGMENTS

GARY MAY IS a retired newspaper editor and writer and the author of several acclaimed works of non-fiction. A longtime journalist, he spent more than thirty years as a reporter and editor with major Canadian newspapers, including the *Hamilton Spectator*, the *London Free Press*, and the *Ottawa Citizen*. His research into the early Canadian oil industry has earned awards and recognition in Canada, the United States, and Europe, and he was recently honoured with a Lifetime Achievement Award from Canada's Petroleum History Society for his book *Crude Genius: The Making of an International Oil Baron | William H. McGarvey* (Mosaic Press, 2022).

Unburdening is his first novel. Born in Grimsby in Ontario's Niagara region, he now lives in Windsor, Ontario, with his wife.